The Girl on the Titanic

A Novel of the Titanic

Eileen Enwright Hodgetts

PRELUDE

North Atlantic, April 14, 1912

West-bound steamers report bergs, growlers and field ice in 42° N, from 49° to 51° W, April 12th.

Greek steamer Athenia reports passing icebergs and large quantities of field ice today in latitude 41° 51′ N, longitude 49°*Titanic*

From Mesaba to *Titanic* . In latitude 42° N to 41° 25′, longitude 49° W to longitude 50° 30′ W, saw much heavy pack ice and great number large icebergs, also field ice, weather good.

The moon is dark but the stars, shining with unnatural brilliance, illuminate an island of ice, three miles wide and five miles long, drifting with the Labrador Current on the ink dark ocean. The ice floe and its accompanying icebergs have traveled far south of their normal route and now the unforgiving ice has drifted into the shipping lanes. Blue-white in the starlight, it lies across the path of the many ships that carry the rich and the poor between Europe and North America.

The *RMS Titanic*, on her maiden voyage, is three days out from Cherbourg. Her passengers are warm and safe and wrapped in luxury. Only her two lookouts, high up in the crow's nest, brave the frigid air of the cold strange night. Her captain has ordered the lighting of four more boilers and her speed is a satisfactory twenty-two knots.

The *Titanic* is not alone on the ocean. She is surrounded by ships of all sizes, some carrying passengers, some carrying cargo, and some on dark business of their own and unwilling to reveal their presence. The ships who had the good fortune to pass the ice field in daylight are now steaming away, eastbound to Liverpool, Southampton and Cherbourg, or westbound to Halifax, Boston and New York.

Those who were not so fortunate have heeded the Marconi messages and are stopped and surrounded by ice that growls and grinds but does little damage. Those who have no business to be on the ice either by day or by night, remain silent but observant.

Most of the *Titanic's* passengers are sleeping soundly. They are not aware of what is about to happen, although for some it will be the fulfillment of prophecy.

Edith Evans in first-class had been told by a fortune-teller that she should "beware of water." Henry Wilde had written to his sister to say "I still don't like this ship. I have a queer feeling about it." Edith Rosenbaum cannot overcome her feeling of depression and premonition of trouble.

Up in the crow's nest, Frederick Fleet narrows his gaze. The sea is so unnaturally calm that he cannot discern waves breaking against the ice but he sees something - a shadow on the water - a dark mass. An iceberg!

PART ONE – DISASTER

Dr. Washington Dodge.
First class *Titanic* passenger.
"Having been told that there was no danger, and believing such to be the fact from the general conduct of the passengers and such officers as I saw, I insisted that my family remain in bed and await developments."

CHAPTER ONE

Sophie Paxton,
Sunday, April 14, 1912

The *Titanic* forged steadily westward pushing aside scattered ice floes that shone white in the starlight. Although the moon was dark, the starlight was brilliant and the night was clear.

The ship's progress created an icy wind that swirled around the first-class promenade deck and Sophie saw that her cousin, Maxine, was clutching at the collar of her fur coat and making a sour, disapproving face.

"Really, Maxine," Sophie said. "You don't have to wait out here with me. I will be perfectly fine by myself."

"Nonsense," Maxine said. "You are a nineteen-year-old unmarried woman with no experience of the world. It is my responsibility to chaperone you now that I am married."

Sophie almost laughed at the emphasis Maxine placed on the word "married." She understood Maxine's desire to celebrate - at twenty-six, Maxine had only just avoided becoming an old maid – but the groom she had landed was hardly a great catch despite his title.

The groom in question, Lord Lucan Sempter, was also clutching at his coat collar. The wind ruffled what little hair he possessed and his lips were blue with cold beneath his pencil-thin moustache.

"Really," Lucan said, in his aristocratic British drawl, "I don't see why we should both be out here. Sophie is your cousin. Your grandfather appointed you as chaperone but there's no reason for me to stay here and catch my death of cold."

Sophie saw the irritation on her cousin's face. The new marriage, she thought, was not going well. Maxine had not found her white knight. The only thing

Lucan brought to the union was his title. She wondered what Maxine brought to the union except, of course, American money.

"Sophie is intending to accost a young man out here," Maxine said, "and her intentions could very well be misunderstood. I have not been able to prevent her from doing this, but the very least I can do is to make sure that nothing inappropriate occurs."

"Oh, Maxine," Sophie said, "you haven't understood anything I've said, have you? I am waiting out here to meet Dick Williams and his father. I have to meet them and make my case. We've been three days on board this ship and I have not found any other way to do this. I can't just rush up to them at dinner, and I certainly can't go into the gymnasium or the smoking room, or knock on their cabin door, but I'm not going to let this opportunity pass. I need to talk to them and they will be here shortly."

"How do you know?" Maxine asked.

"I talked to a steward and —"

"Bribed a steward more likely," Lucan sniffed.

Sophie nodded, rather proud of herself for the way she had handled the obtaining of information. "Money changed hands," she said. "The steward told me that Mr. Williams and his son are in the habit of taking the air before they retire for the night."

"Bloody cold air," Lucan muttered. "Ice everywhere. I'm surprised we're still moving."

Maxine turned impatiently toward him. "I've told you, Lucan, that the *Titanic* is unsinkable. A little bit of ice is not going to hurt her." She turned back to Sophie. "And all you want to talk about is tennis?"

"Of course," Sophie said. "I'm not husband-hunting, Maxine."

Maxine flinched. Sophie's jibe had struck home. It was obvious that Maxine's mother had sent her to England to find a husband with a title – anything to impress old Aidan Paxton, the man with all the money. Maxine had found what she could and in just two days' time, the family would meet Lord Lucan Sempter. In Sophie's opinion, Lucan was not much of a catch.

Sophie felt a moment of sympathy for her cousin who thought that any husband was better than no husband. Sophie knew she would rather die an old maid than be married to someone like Lucan.

"So far as I'm concerned," Sophie said, "this is the most important moment of my life."

"Don't exaggerate," Maxine said.

Sophie clutched her cousin's sleeve, overcome for a moment by the memory of a younger, softer, Maxine who had always had time for Sophie, the lonely young heiress. "Max," Sophie said, "it's the Olympics! It's tennis. I have a really good chance of being Dick Williams' partner in the mixed doubles. I just have to meet him and tell him about all of my awards and —"

"Are you really that good?" Lucan drawled.

"Yes," Sophie said firmly. "I am that good. I've been seven years in England at a progressive school for girls where sport is emphasized."

Sophie felt a sudden stab of pain at the thought of those seven years. *How could her grandfather have done this to her? How could he send her, a child still grieving the loss of her parents, to that faraway school? Had he known that the Howell School for Girls would take that lost child and mold her into an independent woman, or had he just wanted to rid himself of the responsibility of raising the child of his dead son?*

Sophie shrugged off the pain of the past. "I have discovered that I am a gifted tennis player," she said. "I have my own coach." *Had my own coach. Had everything I wanted until Grandfather decided to send for me.* Sophie shrugged again. She would not dwell on that grudge. "I've won titles and I want to represent my country."

Lucan shrugged. "Seems inappropriate," he said, "for a young lady of breeding, but of course you are American – it's not the same, is it? I know you were educated in England —"

"Wales," Sophie corrected.

"Very well then, Wales. Wherever it was, it makes no difference. Breeding is in the bones, and your grandfather was ... well ..."

Lucan allowed his voice to trail away. Perhaps he was having second thoughts about insulting the heritage of Aidan Paxton who had left Scotland as a penniless boy and, by hard work and cunning amassed one of the greatest fortunes in an age of great fortunes.

Sophie was not about to let Lucan's unspoken insult remain unspoken. Maybe he was Maxine's husband, and maybe Grandfather Paxton would welcome him and his title with open arms, but Sophie already despised him.

Before Sophie could devise an appropriate response, she was distracted by a sudden movement of the deck beneath her feet. She clutched at the rail. The night was calm, and for days the *Titanic* had ridden smoothly on the long, slow Atlantic swells, but now it seemed to hesitate.

The pause was momentary. Almost immediately the deck steadied and the moment passed but Sophie saw that Maxine was also clutching the rail, and even

Lucan's hooded eyes were wide with surprise as he huddled against a bulkhead. So she hadn't imagined it. Something had happened. Sophie was suddenly acutely aware of the vastness of the ocean around them and the great distance that lay between them and dry land.

At that moment she was glad of the memory of Henrietta Pattison, the physical education teacher of the Howell School. Miss Pattison was not with her in person, but she was always with her in spirit. She embodied the ethos of the Howell School and every lesson that Sophie had learned during her seven years in Wales. Of course, no one else could see Miss Pattison or even guess as to her existence. She was Sophie's secret companion The memory of Miss Pattison's cropped hair and broad-shouldered competence was the one thing that Sophie had been able to keep with her, and she clung to it tenaciously, but secretly.

Her thoughts were interrupted by the sound of a door opening from the smoking room. Light flooded out along with the odor of cigars. Three men stepped out onto the open deck speaking anxiously as they opened the door.

"What the devil was that?"

"Felt like we hit something!"

Sophie's heart skipped a beat. She forgot about the *Titanic's* sudden hesitation - that was nothing, but this was something! These were the men she wanted to meet. Charles and Dick Williams were not alone. Three men were bathed in the orange glow of the deck lights. Sophie recognized Dick Williams from his newspaper photographs. He was on his way to play tournaments around the United States before he returned to Harvard. The gray-haired man was his father, Charles, chairman of the tennis federation, but also the man who would eventually choose a mixed-doubles partner for his son. The third man was a little older than Dick, maybe thirty years old. He did not have Dick's athletic build but he was broad shouldered and strongly built.

All three men seemed puzzled and concerned about the ship's alarming behavior, but Sophie couldn't waste this important opportunity. She had planned this conversation and she needed to put forward her case.

Miss Pattison reminded her that here her future hung in the balance as to how she used the next few minutes. It has to be no coincidence that Dick Williams and his father were on board the Titanic and were now standing in front of her. This moment would determine Sophie's destiny. This was a clear sign that she could be an Olympian and she would let nothing stand in her way.

The three men were still speaking.

"I've never seen the ice this far south," Charles Williams said.

Dick shrugged. "The captain doesn't seem concerned."

8

"There's been talk of putting Captain Smith out to pasture. He's not as keen-minded as he used to be," said the third man.

"They wouldn't have given him this ship if they didn't think he was up to it," Dick said.

Sophie reluctantly clasped Maxine's arm. She did not like that her cousin had been foisted on her as a chaperone, but Maxine had a title and she might as well make use of it. The men were distracted by the ship's sudden movement and, if the men were concerned, might a young lady and her aristocratic cousin be afraid?

Sophie, having decided that being afraid and being in the company of a titled lady, would play to her advantage, dragged Maxine forward into the light. She put an agitated flutter into her voice. "Oh, thank goodness you're here," she said to the three startled men. "Please, you have to tell us what's happened. My cousin and I were just standing here talking and suddenly... well, suddenly the ship, made this sort of... hesitation. It was very strange. I'm sure I have no idea what it was. Do you think something's happened? Have we struck something?"

"Struck something?" Charles said. "Oh, I should doubt that very much. I'm sure it's nothing to worry about. You know that this ship is unsinkable."

"Oh, yes, of course," Sophie said, remembering to keep a note of hysteria in her voice even as she saw her chance to become acquainted with her quarry. "My cousin and I ... please allow us to introduce ourselves..."

She turned and beckoned aggressively to Lucan. "This is Lord Lucan Sempter, and his wife, Lady Maxine, and I am Sophie Paxton." She forged ahead without giving anyone else a chance to speak. "You're Charles Williams, aren't you, and this is your son." She fixed Dick Williams with a clear-eyed gaze, abandoning her hysteria. "I have been so wanting to speak to both of you."

Charles said nothing, not even to acknowledge the introduction. He seemed preoccupied, as if he had not yet recovered from the shock of that small movement that the *Titanic* had made - that momentary hesitation that surely meant nothing.

"It's about the possibility of my being Dick's mixed doubles partner," Sophie said.

Charles waved a dismissive hand. Sophie was acutely aware that this was not the right moment, but she had to take her chance. "I've written to you, Mr. Williams," she said. "I've been playing in tournaments in England for four years and I'm being coached by Gloria Cooper, the Olympic Gold Medalist. She has very high hopes for my future. I could give you a list of all the matches I've won. I have a whole shelf of trophies and I want to represent the United States in the Olympics. My family is American. We're the Paxtons of Paxton Steel, my grandfather is Aidan Paxton, I'm sure you've heard of him."

Charles shook his head. "Not now. Please, not now!" He looked at his companions. "I think we've reversed engines."

Dick moved away from Sophie and leaned over the rail to look back toward the stern. Sophie, her heart pounding and determined not to miss her opportunity, rushed to join him, pulling Maxine with her.

"If you would just give me a chance," Sophie said. "I'm going to be in New York and ..."

Maxine pulled at Sophie's arm and pointed in the direction Dick was looking. "Sophie," she whispered, "what is that?"

Looking back along the rail Sophie made out a grey ice mountain rapidly receding into the distance. It was the shape of the Rock of Gibraltar and massive enough to make her draw in a sharp breath. They had been seeing icebergs in the distance all day and had even seen some small ones close up but they had seen nothing like this.

Dick stood back from the rail and spoke to his father. "How could the lookout miss something that size?"

"I don't know," Charles said, "but it's the only explanation I can offer for what just happened. We didn't hit head on. It must have scraped along the starboard side. That's why we reversed our engines, and I think we are still making an attempt to turn."

"Dammit," Dick said.

Charles shook his head. "Watch your language, son, and don't alarm the ladies. We all felt it. It was just a little bump. There's no damage done." He gave a hearty, if unconvincing, laugh. "No need to rush for the lifeboats just yet. The *Titanic* is better than any lifeboat. She's double-hulled so it would be impossible to put a hole all the way through the hull and even if..."

Sophie somehow felt the weight of words he had not spoken. She looked back at the iceberg. Even from a distance it seemed to exude menace. The starlight that danced blue-white on the small ice floes, failed to reveal any charm or beauty in the berg's mountainous presence.

Charles turned to the third man. "What do you think, John?"

"I think we have stopped engines," John said. "We're drifting."

Charles uttered a curse, a strong one that Sophie had only ever heard used in the steel mills. An expression of serious concern settled over his face and he made no apology for his language.

"I think I'll go and have a word with the stewards. They should know what's going on, and, in the meantime..." he hesitated for a moment and when he resumed speaking, his words belied the comforting smile he had pasted onto his face. "Do you all know your lifeboat stations?"

Lucan stepped out of the shadows. "I think we have had enough of this alarmist talk," he said. "We will return to our cabins. We have no need to stand around here in the cold. Miss Sophie has accomplished her purpose." He gestured to his wife. "Maxine, will you please accompany me."

For a moment Maxine looked dubious. Lucan repeated his request, although now it was a command. "Maxine, you and Sophie should come with me."

Sophie shook her head. If she knew anything, she knew that now was not the time to go inside and hide in her cabin. Some problems were best faced head-on and this was one of them.

"Sophie," Maxine repeated.

"No."

"Well, leave her be," Lucan said. "I'm sure she would be safer inside, but if she insists on remaining out here all night, and risking pneumonia, it's up to her"

Maxine tried to protest, but now Lucan seemed to be exerting his controlling personality over his bride. Up until then Sophie had wondered if he even had a personality. Now he had a determined look in his eyes. Sophie suspected that as Lucan's true personality emerged, her disregard of him could possibly turn to dislike.

An unwelcome thought attempted an invasion, although Sophie could not bring herself to give it a home. She, Sophie, only child of the oldest son, was the sole heir to Grandfather Paxton's fortune, but if she died, the Paxton millions would go to Maxine, the only child of a younger son. Did Lucan know this? Would he like to see Sophie dead and his wife in possession of a fortune?

Lucan held his arm out for his wife. Maxine looked pleadingly at Sophie who shook her head and Maxine took her husband's arm and walked away.

Sophie now found herself in the company of three men – all total strangers.

Charles was first to speak. "A wise decision, Miss Paxton. My son and Mr. Alder will keep you company while I go and see what I can discover." He looked at Dick. "Perhaps you can speak to Miss Paxton about her tennis triumphs."

Charles went back into the smoking room while Dick and John Alder stood at the rail, both of them looking worried and neither one of them looking approachable. Sophie hesitated, uncertain what to do or say next.

She was rarely unsure of herself. Her parents had died when she was an infant and she had become a ward of her grandfather and heiress to a large fortune. The staff in her grandfather's Virginia mansion had treated her like a princess. She had been gifted with stunning blue eyes, coal black hair, and a small curvaceous body that was able to perform remarkable athletic feats. The fact that her appearance usually drew the attention of men of all classes was something she took for granted, but now, apparently, she did not have the attention of the only two men within reach.

Although this was the opportunity she had hoped and planned for – a chance to speak to Dick Williams about her tennis ambitions, she knew something more important was at hand. She had read the expression on Charles's face as he went inside. She wished she had insisted that Maxine wait with her.

She stepped toward the two men tentatively aware that they were deep in conversation. She couldn't interrupt but she couldn't just stand there alone on the ice-cold deck of the drifting ship.

Dick's companion turned as she approached. "Miss Paxton," he said, "we have not been introduced. I am Jonathon Alder, but my friends call me John."

Sophie decided that she liked John Alder, and the way he had smoothly put her at ease in an uncomfortable situation. "And you should call me Sophie," she said.

Dick Williams had not turned his head or even acknowledged her.

"Don't worry, Sophie," John said. "I'm sure everything is under control."

Dick shook his head. "I don't think it is."

Sophie failed to suppress a cry of alarm. "What are you saying?"

Dick held up his finger for silence. "Listen," he said.

Sophie listened. Earlier, when Sophie, Maxine, and Lucan had taken up their position outside the smoking room, the *Titanic* had been virtually asleep. Dinner, the social event of the evening, was long over. The great liner had no ballroom – it's passengers - at least the first-class passengers - did not expect to dance their way across the Atlantic. A few of the ladies engaged in after-dinner games of bridge. Some of the men gambled or played billiards, or frequented the bar, but now it was after midnight and the ship should have been silent. It was not – the silence had been replaced by a low hum of activity.

Sophie told herself that there was nothing here to cause alarm - no bells, no whistles, no blasts of the ship's horn, nothing but a brightening of the lights, and a strangeness in the way the ship was moving. Drifting! Jonathon Alder – John – had said that it was drifting.

She leaned over the rail and looked down at the deck below where the lifeboats were suspended in their davits. Something was happening down there. Deckhands were scurrying about but with no obvious purpose, like befuddled ants from a destroyed nest. A few minutes passed and then a swarm of more purposeful deckhands appeared and began pulling back the canvas covers on the boats.

Charles Williams' question echoed in her head. *Do you know your lifeboat station? No, I don't. The steward said there was a note in the cabin. I didn't read it. Are we going to sink? No, no, no, we can't sink. We can't. We just can't.*

She felt John Alder's hand on her arm. Had she spoken aloud? She didn't think she had. "Miss Paxton - Sophie, there's no need for alarm. You're in good company. As your ... er ... as Lord Sempter has taken his wife below, Dick and I will take good care of you. You were wise to stay on deck."

The lifeboats lay uncovered for several minutes and then, with rising panic, Sophie saw the first reluctant passengers beginning to appear on deck, some fully dressed, some in night clothes. Their voices drifted upward in a babble of impatient shouts, and complaints aimed at the seamen who stood by the boats. Was this even possible? Were the passengers being put in lifeboats? Why?

She turned away and stared at the door of the smoking room. Where was Charles Williams? Had he found out what was happening? Where were Maxine and Lucan? Were they obstinately locked in their cabin while something – who could say what – was happening outside?

At long last, Charles appeared carrying an armful of life jackets. His face was white with concern. He thrust a jacket at Sophie and two more at Dick and John.

"Put these on and take Miss Paxton down to the boat deck."

"What's happening?" Dick asked.

"There's no general alarm been given," Charles said, "but the stewards have been going from cabin to cabin waking the first-class passengers and telling them to take to the lifeboats."

Sophie clung to the lifejacket for a long moment, hugging it as though it had the same ability to comfort as an old well-worn teddy bear.

John approached her, already wearing his lifejacket. "Miss Sophie, shall I help you with that?"

Sophie took a deep breath. She was a graduate of the Howell School, a progressive institution that graduated purposeful young women able to take control of their own lives. Now was the time to put her training to the test.

"I'll do it myself," she said. She turned to Charles and looked him in the eye. "Are we sinking, Mr. Williams?"

Charles did not even hesitate or try to hide the truth. "Yes, I think we are. There's water in the mail room and on the squash court, and it's rising in the stairways. Most of the passengers are still unaware, but it will not be long before the water rises into the cabins and then we will hear from the third-class passengers."

Sophie was still capable of additional shock. "Has no one told them?"

"No," Charles said grimly. "They will find out for themselves soon enough but, in the meantime, you must secure a seat in a lifeboat."

She tried to resist. "Surely someone should tell the third class."

Charles' face was cold and expressionless. "What would be the point? I don't mean to be unkind, Miss Paxton, but the fact is that there are nowhere near enough lifeboats."

"But they should still be given a chance..."

"It's not up to me," Charles said stiffly. "In situations like this, it is our duty to obey the captain and I'm sure that he is doing everything he can to keep the ship afloat for the benefit of all the passengers. Perhaps I am exaggerating the danger. Perhaps there is another solution."

Sophie knew she was grasping at straws. "Do you really think so?"

An unexpected voice thrust itself impatiently into her mind. Miss Pattison spoke with a strong, Welsh accent, and her usual disdain for girls who could not make up their minds. *Don't stand there dithering, Sophie. It's up to the captain to save his passengers and there's nothing you can do to help him except to get into a lifeboat. You should not need a man to tell you that.*

Sophie made one last attempt to make sense of the situation. "If there are not enough lifeboats," she said, "how will they decide..."

Her thoughts trailed away because she knew the answer and she knew she could not force Dick, Charles or John to speak the words aloud. *Women and children first.*

Charles caught her arm as he pushed open the smoking-room door. "Stay with me," he ordered as he pulled her inside. He looked at Dick and John, "Stay together."

As they exited the smoking room and emerged into the carpeted first-class companionways, they encountered only a handful of passengers with ladies dawdling and protesting petulantly, and gentlemen offering bland reassurance.

"My jewel case. I have to have my jewel case."

"Don't worry, you'll row just a short distance away while they make repairs. You'll be back by breakfast."

"Will we need a ticket to return? How will anyone know who we are?"

"Don't make me laugh, darling, everyone knows who you are."

"Are they really saying it's just women and children? This is really too beastly."

"What will you do, darling, while I'm gone?"

"I shall go to the bar, of course."

Sophie was relieved to step out onto the boat deck where a general hub-bub of noise drowned out the fatuous individual comments of privileged passengers who had not been told the truth. It was not their fault that they didn't believe. They had not seen the iceberg. They had not felt the ship's moment of hesitation. They had believed the ship was unsinkable. In fact, they still believed.

"Sorry about this," Charles said as they forced their way into a milling crowd of confused passengers. "We should have been here sooner, before everybody realized..."

Realized? Realized what?

Sophie hesitated, looking around for a glimpse of Maxine and Lucan, but now John had hold of her hand and was pulling her forward. Sophie stumbled behind him until they found a boat that was preparing to launch. Although the boat was not fully loaded, no one in the group of bystanders seemed anxious to go aboard and one woman who had already entered the boat was now on the point of exiting. The gunwale was still aligned with the deck and it was a simple matter for her to step out. It would be an equally simple matter for others to step in and take the empty seats but the ladies were tearful and hesitant and the men were all standing back.

It seemed to Sophie that the crew had abandoned common sense, a highly valued commodity at the Howell School. Despite the obvious need to load more passengers, the sailors were already beginning to free the ropes that would control the lifeboat's descent to the water. Surely Sophie and her three companions should be allowed to go aboard and be lowered down to the ocean where several other lifeboats boats were already floating away from the ship. She had been wrong about this. There was plenty of room for men in the boat.

She was stunned when one of the sailors leaped in front of John as he attempted to hand Sophie into the boat. The sailor's face was taut with a mixture of fear and officiousness. "Women and children only," he said.

"But your boat is almost empty," Sophie protested.

The sailor shook his head. "We have our orders."

John stepped back, almost as though he had expected the rebuff. "Of course." he said. "Just take the women."

Sophie looked into his face, realizing for the first time how handsome he was, with his broad, open face and wide brown eyes. Surely, he didn't intend to give up and just ... die! There had to be another solution. Perhaps they would all be rescued. Perhaps a rescue ship was already on the way, ploughing at top speed through the ice field. The alternative was absurd. These men could not be left to drown!

Someone grabbed Sophie's arm, pulling her away from the lifeboat and she was relieved to find Maxine was beside her. So, Lucan had come to his senses and come out of his cabin.

"Is this our lifeboat?" Maxine asked.

"It is now," Sophie said. "We can go aboard, but Lucan can't and neither can —"

Lucan dismissed Sophie with a wave of his hand. "I'm going with my wife."

The sailor who had blocked John, now blocked Lucan. "Women and children only."

Lucan pushed the sailor aside. "Don't be absurd - I'm going with my wife."

Suddenly Sophie was in the midst of a brawl - a tangle of pushing and shoving. Someone stamped down hard on her foot and she fell backward. She caught sight of Maxine tumbling into the boat, still calling out for her husband. Ignoring the pain in her foot, Sophie sprang upright and came eye to eye with Lucan. She read desperation and malevolence on his face.

Sailors were calling out now. "Lower away. Lower away" The boat was not full - how could they do this? How could they leave people behind? She felt Lucan pushing her away from the boat, pushing her toward the rail and the yawning darkness of the ocean. She pushed back with every scrap of energy she possessed, knowing only that the sea was cold and unforgiving and that she wanted to live. Balance and athleticism that she had learned on the tennis court, gave her the strength to hurl herself sideways over the gunwale of the lifeboat. She landed in a heap in the bottom of the boat.

When she looked up, she saw Lord Lucan Sempter being led away by Charles and Dick Williams.

The sailors began to lower the lifeboat, and then suddenly they were still again. Had they changed their minds? Had someone come to their senses and agreed to let the men into the boat? No, their stillness was caused by the sudden arrival of Captain Smith himself. His face within its frame of neat white beard and moustache, was contorted as if in agony and he was incongruously holding a loaf of bread. He leaned forward and tucked the bread into a locker at the bow of the boat and then stood back and looked at the passengers.

"No time to waste," he said urgently. "Lower away, sailors. If you think it safe, you can pick up women from the lower decks, but do not delay. There is a light out there. It's another ship. Row toward it. Unload your passengers and return. Go now. Go! "

As the captain turned away, a gunshot rang out from somewhere toward the bow. In the shocked silence that followed, the captain simply repeated his instruction. "Row toward the light."

CHAPTER TWO

Sam White
On board the Leyland Liner *Californian*
Midnight, April 14, 1912

Sam White shivered as he stepped out onto the deck of the *Californian*. The night was clear and cold with not a breath of wind. The ship's engines were at full stop and the *Californian,* drifting with the current, was in no danger from the jagged ice field that stretched as far as Sam could see.

Captain Lord had sent Alfie, the cook's boy, to inform Sam that the *Californian* would be stopped until daylight. Sam had greeted the message with impatience as his mind dwelled on his need to reach the United States without delay.

His trip to England had been an expensive and impetuous risk, following the tenuous threads of a story involving big names – really the biggest names. Putting those names in print by selling his story to a major newspaper would give his career the boost it so needed.

He had paid an exorbitant price for his passage on the *Californian,* and Captain Lord was giving him very little value for his money. The *Californian* was crossing the Atlantic at an almost leisurely pace. They were already one week out from Liverpool and still five days away from Boston. Sam had been taking his meals in the officers' mess where a silent Captain Lord presided over a taciturn group of officers. Apart from that small social contact, he had seen no one but Alfie, a ragged young Cockney boy who claimed to have been at sea for five years although he looked no older than fifteen.

Alfie brought him hot water to shave, clean towels for his bath, and occasional messages from Captain Lord. Sam wasn't confined to his cabin, of course, but for the past four days that was where he had remained. He had a story to write and no time to waste. He wanted it finished before he went ashore in Boston. He wished that the *Californian* had been heading for New York instead of Boston, but passage on the *Californian* had been better than crossing the Channel to find a ship in France. Britain's national coal strike had wreaked havoc with the shipping schedule and, for him, it was the *Californian* or nothing.

Now he stood out on the deck and allowed the frigid air to cool his impatience. However much it rankled, Sam knew that Captain Lord was wise to stop and wait. The *Californian* was a modest ship, with none of the safety features of the new White Star liners. The *Titanic* and the *Olympic* were said to be unsinkable. The *Californian* made no such boast and Captain Lord had every right to be cautious.

According to Alfie, who had apparently made the transatlantic crossing many times, it was unusual to see icebergs so far south at this time of year, but here they were, blue and menacing on the horizon and uncomfortably close. Captain Lord had stopped his engines and he would wait until daylight.

Sam buttoned his coat. He had not brought a hat but his thick thatch of brown hair was sufficient to keep his head warm. He strode toward the foredeck to get a better view of the ice field.

Later tonight, he would occupy himself and his impatience by writing a word picture of what he had seen. He did this every night, as a commitment to the future – a future when he would use his fame as a reporter as a stepping-stone to fame as a novelist.

He had a notebook filled with fragments of ideas and word sketches of interesting personalities. Elements of Captain Lord's character would contribute to the perfect antagonist - cold and grasping and driving a hard bargain. He was already writing in his mind, trying to find the words to describe the haunting sensation of being aboard the *Californian* on such a night – stopped and surrounded by ice – silent beneath a blanket of stars.

He was not alone on deck. Two crew members were standing by the rail and staring into the distance across the ice field. He recognized McGregor, the ship's Scottish carpenter but not the young, grease-stained crewman who stood beside him.

McGregor turned at his approach. His bearded face, aged by many years at sea, wore a puzzled expression.

"Evening, Mr. White. What brings you out of your bed?"

Sam shrugged. "I'm not sure. Maybe the lack of movement."

"Us engineers are glad of it," the young man said. "Gives us a chance to make repairs."

Sam felt renewed anxiety. He had a story to follow and he had paid for a speedy passage. Was the *Californian* really going to be delayed for repairs?

McGregor grinned at him. "Nothing to worry about, Mr. White. This here is Ernest Gill, our donkey man. He's been down below working on the donkey engine. We'll be moving at first light even if we canna get it working."

"We'll get it working," Gill insisted.

Sam nodded and set his anxiety aside. He stood for a moment gazing out across the vast expanse of ice and thought he saw a faint flash of light. He blinked and refocused his eyes.

He turned to McGregor. "Is that a light over there?"

McGregor nodded. "It could be. We're not the only ship adrift in the current. Before he went to his bed, Evans, the radio officer, said he's heard from a half dozen ships stopped one side or the other of this damned ice."

Gill pointed out across the water. "Is that the light you saw, Mr. White?"

Sam followed his pointing finger and focused on a glimmer of light. "That's the one. What is it?"

"Well," Gill said, "it's a ship but I don't think it's stopped. I think it's still moving."

McGregor squinted. "Hard to tell," he said. "But if he's got any sense, he'll be waiting for morning."

He studied the light a little longer obviously seeing and understanding far more than Sam could see or understand. "It's a passenger liner," he declared. "Could be the *Frankfurt*. She's around here somewhere."

Gill squinted at the fuzz of light. "You're right. It's a big one. I'd say there's maybe two rows of lights or maybe three?"

"Or maybe it's four," McGregor suggested. "That would mean it's the *Titanic* making for New York."

"That would be something to see," Gill said. "A floating palace with all the rich and famous on board."

"They're not all rich and famous," McGregor said. "Third class is filled with immigrants."

"Well, good luck to them," Gill said. "I might try that myself someday. I could go west. Be a cowboy."

Sam let their conversation drift over him. He knew about the *Titanic,* of course. In fact, he was certain that one of his aunts was on board. Aunt Ella, wealthy through her deceased husband, John Stuart White, was always on the move and Sam had heard his mother say scornfully that if the maiden voyage of the *Titanic* was the newest noteworthy event, then Ella Stuart White would be on board.

Ever since she'd found a young woman as a traveling companion, Aunt Ella had been spending her money on luxury travel and luxury living. None of that money had ever been offered as support for Sam - not that he'd ever asked for it. He was making his own way in the world. He had a degree from the University of Pittsburgh under his belt, and he'd kept himself alive for years now as a freelance reporter. He turned his attention back to the arguing seamen.

"I'll not say it's the *Titanic,*" McGregor said. "It could be anyone. Could be a trawler or a sealer, or some other small boat going about its own business. Hard to judge distance on a night like this. It's either something big about four miles off, or something small and much closer. She's none of our concern."

"I think she's moving away," Gill said.

"Then she has a fool for a captain," McGregor replied. "Our Captain Lord is nae the best captain I ever sailed under but at least he has the sense to stop when he sees icebergs."

Sam continued to stare across the ice trying to shake off a sense of unreality. The ocean was vast and land was far away and yet here was a friendly glow of light as evidence that they were, in fact, traveling the unmarked highway between Europe and North America.

As he watched the distant glow, a streak of light separated from the hazy outline. It shot upward, blazed for a moment against the starlight and then died.

Sam turned to his companions whose eyesight was so much better than his own. "Was that a rocket?"

"Most likely a shooting star," Gill said.

"No," Sam said firmly, "it wasn't a star. It was a light that went up from that ship."

McGregor's gaze turned away from the distant ship and he punched Gill in the arm. "Look lively, lad, officers on deck. Come to look at her."

Sam saw the two watch officers arrive on deck accompanied by a seaman. He remained in place at the rail. As a passenger, he should not be here on the foredeck but Sam was not a man who paid attention to rules. He should be asleep in bed, but then he would have missed this strange encounter. He had gone out onto the foredeck in the hope of finding something to take his mind off his obsessive impatience, and it seemed he had found what he was looking for. Something was happening out there and he wanted to know what it was.

The watch officers took no notice of him as they trained their binoculars on the horizon. After a few moments, Captain Lord himself appeared. He took the binoculars and focused them on the lights of the distant ship. He shook his head and handed back the binoculars.

Sam was not close enough to overhear their conversation, but he saw that a seaman had uncovered the big Morse lamp on the foredeck and had begun to signal.

Even without binoculars, Sam could see that the glimmer of light from the distant ship was fading. The unidentified craft was drifting away beyond the horizon.

Gill shook his head and gestured to the seaman working the shutters on the lamp. "What's the point in signaling with the lamp?" he asked. "Seems to me that if they really want to know who he is and where he's going, they could wake the radio officer and send a message."

"Why don't you go and suggest that?" McGregor asked.

"Not me," Gill said. "That's none of my concern."

"Nor mine," McGregor said. "I'm for my bed." He nodded to Sam. "Good-night, sir."

Sam cast a final glance across the horizon. The only light now was the flickering of the Californian's Morse lamp. Whatever ship had been out there, it was not there now.

⫷◆⫸

John Alder
On board the *Titanic*.

John Alder kept a firm grip on Lucan Sempter as Lifeboat #8 was lowered slowly toward the ocean. The *Titanic* had begun to list and as the boat was lowered it swung out and away from the hull offering no possibility for anyone else to board from the lower decks. He kept his eye on Sophie Paxton who appeared to be struggling to hold onto Lucan's wife. What was her name? Ah! Yes – Maxine.

"I don't know who you think you are," Lucan said as John finally released him. "You're not in control of this ship."

"It seems that no one is in control of this ship," John replied.

"We'll see about that," Lucan said over his shoulder as he stomped away.

The crowd was thinning now that there was no other lifeboat in the davits. Some men were already moving purposefully away in search of other boats, some moved aimlessly with no idea where to go, some wiped tears from their eyes. They were, no doubt, the men who had handed their womenfolk into the lifeboat, now choking back the knowledge that there would be no further hope of rescue. Several of the men appeared to be servants. John did not know whether to admire them for their loyalty or curse them as idiots. Maids and nannies were allowed into the boats, valets were not. It was all a form of utter foolishness and he had, like a gentleman, played along.

He felt Dick Williams hand on his shoulder. "Well, old man," Dick said, "I think I just found and lost my ideal mixed-doubles partner."

"You mean Miss Sophie?"

"I do. I saw you admiring her yourself."

"I'm no tennis player but I know a pretty girl when I see one," John said, choosing the desperation of the moment to be completely honest. Sophie Paxton was the prettiest and spunkiest girl he'd seen in a long time. If he lived, and he probably would not, he would find her hard to forget. If he died, well, he was glad to have met her.

Charles Williams joined them, his face set in a passive mask of gentlemanly courage. "Come along, fellows. No point in standing around here. Let's go and get a drink."

"They needed us in the boat," Dick said.

"We would have started a riot," Charles replied. " *"Noblesse oblige.* "

"Not in the case of Lord Lucan Sempter," John said.

"The very worst of his breed," Charles agreed. "I need a drink to wash the taste of him out of my mouth."

As he turned to follow Dick and his father, John heard the woosh and thunder of a rocket and looked up to see a white starburst high above the ship. The crew was firing distress rockets from the roof of the officers' quarters but was any ship close enough to see them? Captain Smith had shouted something about rowing to a light. Was there another ship close by? John had not seen a light, but perhaps it could be seen from the bridge. How odd that Captain Smith should be handing out bread for the lifeboats. Bread was the last thing anyone needed. Why not bring water? Who could say how long the lifeboats might be out there alone on the ocean? They would need water.

What had happened to the captain? Had shock robbed him of his senses?

The atmosphere on the deck was rapidly turning from disbelief to panic. John had a suspicion that some of the men who had been told to stand back would very soon be changing their minds. There was something almost criminally absurd about making the men wait while half empty boats were lowered down to the water. The absurdity may not occur to the first-class passengers schooled from childhood in the ways of chivalry, but everything would change when the second- and third-class passengers finally realized what was happening.

John followed Dick and Charles into the first-class lounge. Despite the situation outside and the inevitability of disaster, the room remained a sanctuary. Something in the quiet luxury of the oak paneled room, soothed him. He joined Dick and Charles at the bar where a white-coated steward waited as calmly as if nothing out of the ordinary was happening outside.

Charles set his silver hip flask on the bar. "Be good enough to fill this for me. You can charge it to my cabin. Charles Williams."

John could not hold back a burst of laughter. For all he knew Charles's cabin was already under water. Charles turned to look at him. "Keep it together," he said softly. "We can't falter now."

The steward flicked a duster along the bar and announced that the bar was closed. "At midnight, sir. The bar closes at midnight, so as not to disturb the passengers who are sleeping."

Charles's hand shot out and caught the front of the steward's jacket. He pulled the man toward him until they were nose to nose across the bar. "No one is sleeping," he said, "and we are all very disturbed. Fill the damned flask or I'll do it myself."

So much for keeping things together, John thought.

The steward fell back as Charles released him. "It's open," he croaked. "The bar is open." He raised his voice. "You gentlemen may order drinks."

Looking around, John realized for the first time that they were not alone in the lounge. Men, some in evening dress, some in coats over their pajamas were arranged singly and in groups around the room. They sat in stupefied silence like mourners at a funeral. They were gentlemen who had done the right thing and now all they could do was wait for the inevitable. They did not even move to accept a drink from the steward. They were nothing but waiting dead men. John was glad that he was not waiting alone. He was glad of the friendship of the Williams men.

Charles accepted his replenished flask and gestured to Dick and John. "We'll have a while to wait. Let's take a walk."

"A walk?"

"Yes, let's go take a look at the chart on A deck. It would be good to know where we are."

Dick raised his eyebrows. "Wherever we are, it's too far to swim."

"Humor me," Charles said. "I'm not staying here with these walking corpses, and I'm not going outside. We'll wait for the outside to come to us." He held out his flask. "Take a drink, gentlemen. It'll keep the cold out."

They walked companionably along the corridor and did not remark aloud on the fact that they were now forced to keep hold of the handrail. The deck was at an increasingly acute angle both to starboard and downward. It was obvious that time was running out for the *Titanic* and she was well on her way to sinking by the bow.

John found some relief in the fact that the lights were still burning. He spared a thought for stokers down below who were keeping them alight and wondered when the captain would dismiss them. Smith had seemed like a decent chap even if he had lost his common sense. He couldn't imagine that the captain would leave men down in the hold to die. They at least deserved to see the sky and try to swim for it - whatever that meant or however hopeless their swimming would be.

They found the chart tacked to the wall outside the dining room along with figures of yesterday's run. John noted that they had not been updated, and the chart marker had not moved, but what difference would that make? The chart showed clearly that the nearest point of land was Cape Race in Newfoundland more than three hundred miles away across an icy ocean.

Charles rubbed his hands together. "It's getting cold in here. What do you say we go down to the gymnasium and get our blood pumping."

Dick shook his head. "No, Dad. Let's just go and find a quiet place on the deck. You don't have to treat me like a child, and try to distract me. I know what's ahead. This ship is going down. It won't take long and then we'll be in water too cold for survival. We can swim, but if we're not picked up immediately by a lifeboat, we won't stand a chance."

John intervened. "I know it looks bad but don't give up hope. You heard what the captain said. There's a light on the horizon. It must be a ship. It can't be anything else. If the lifeboats can reach it, unload and come back again, we all stand a chance of getting out of this alive."

"What if there isn't a ship?" Dick asked.

Charles took a long pull at his flask. "If there isn't a ship, no one will survive, not even in the lifeboats."

He handed the flask to John. "What do you say, Alder?"

"It's a matter of timing," John said. "Right now, the sea is calm but if a wind gets up, they won't stand a chance, and if there's no ship just over the horizon, they'll freeze to death."

He took a long pull from the flask and drank to the death of his dreams. He would not return to Washington and continue to climb the ladder of success, first as a senatorial aide and eventually as a senator. More importantly, at least for this moment, he would not have another chance to talk to Sophie Paxton or to see her play tennis in the Olympics.

He looked back at the chart. They had been so close. In another day and another night, they would have seen the distant smudge of coastline. New York city had been almost within reach. Now their fate relied on the illusion of a distant light and the slim possibility of another ship.

⸺◆○◆⸺

Lord Lucan Sempter
On board the *Titanic*. 2:00 a.m.

Chaos! Discipline was collapsing and the crowd had taken on a new voice – a voice with many languages. The third-class passengers were finding their way onto the open deck. Whatever gate or barrier that had been holding them back had given way and they came in a flood - men, women, children finally understanding the truth. – that the lifeboats were leaving without them.

Lucan fumed with anger. An aristocrat from birth, he had no patience with the absurd *nouveau riche* dignity of the men who had ushered their wives and daughters into lifeboats and now waited to die like gentlemen. Lucan knew what it really meant to be a gentleman, albeit an impoverished one, and a gentleman had a responsibility to his family line. He had already undertaken marriage to a plain and unremarkable woman for the sake of his family line and for the sake of an infusion of cash into the family coffers.

The discovery, on his wedding night, had come as a shock. Apparently, there would not be an infusion of cash.

The bride and groom were in bed. Lucan had finally managed to complete his marital duty. It had not been easy with the bride about as animated as a shop window dummy. He rolled off her and into a sitting position. He stared down at her shocked face.

"Well, that was no fun," he said.

Maxine, whose hair was not even rumpled, had tears streaming down her face.

"I didn't hurt you," Lucan said.

He reached for his clothes and began to dress. He reminded himself that he was doing this for the money – Maxine's inheritance. To inherit, of course, someone would have to die.

"How old is your grandfather?"

Maxine gulped away a sob. "Why do you need to know?"

"Just wondering how long I ... we have to wait for your inheritance."

"I already have my inheritance."

"What?"

"Grandfather settled a trust on me when I was a child. I can live well on it for the rest of my life. It's a very generous sum."

"But when he dies..."

"The estate goes to my cousin, Sophie. Her father, now deceased, was the oldest son. She will have it all."

Lucan knew that, for the moment, he would have to set aside his righteous anger. Now he must concentrate on the lifeboats but when they reached dry land, and he was determined to reach dry land, the situation with Maxine would have to be resolved. However generous her trust fund, it would not be generous enough and something would have to be done.

He turned his attention back to his current situation and the need to save his own life. There would be no saving the *Titanic*. The deck had taken on a steep angle. The White Star's floating palace was obviously doomed and so were the people milling around on the deck. Tempers were rising and scuffles were breaking out between people of various races. Lucan heard another pistol shot. It had to be one of the crew. He was willing to believe that there would be any number of sharp knives among the immigrants, but not pistols.

The crew was still gallantly fighting to maintain order. Idiots, he thought. Why not just get themselves into a lifeboat and row away? There was no one left to hold them responsible.

He pushed through the mob. He needed a better view – a way to survey the entire scene. He found a service ladder and climbed upward until he was well above the crowd.

The Sempter family had not endured for five centuries by being dullards. Lucan made a quick, but intelligent, survey of the situation and understood what was needed. The *Titanic* was listing to starboard which meant that unlaunched lifeboats on the port side were too high up in the air. Any attempt to lower them would be futile as they would simply be smashed against the hull. Although this was obvious to him, the panicked passengers were still crowding the port side, fighting for a place in those boats. Absurdly enough, even though the boats could not be launched, the crew were still turning away men and calling for women and children.

Lucan turned his attention to the starboard side of the ship where water was beginning to wash across the deck and he found what he was looking for. At the semi-submerged bow, very close to the point where waves were breaking, a deck crew was preparing to launch a collapsible lifeboat with canvas sides. It was still hanging in its davits but the water was rising to meet it. It had hardly any distance to drop. It would be in the water within minutes.

Lucan dropped down from the ladder and began to push through the crowd. Natural instinct was taking over and, without even meaning to, people were moving away from the bow, climbing upward toward the stern – away from the water.

Lucan went downhill - down toward the bow and the one remaining means of escape - and soon reached the collapsible. Although it was smaller than the big wooden lifeboats, it was not small. It currently contained about forty people, and Lucan could see quite clearly that there would be room for more. The passengers were mostly women or children, and even a baby crying in its mother's arms. From their clothing, Lucan concluded that most of the passengers had come from third class but he was amazed that they were sitting patiently and silently. On the port side they were fighting for their lives, but here was an oasis of quiet.

A man wearing an overcoat over pajamas was calling loudly for passengers, but no one else responded. The man, whose nose and hands were blue with cold, seemed to be in despair as he looked around. His eyes were wide and panicked. He called out desperately.

"Women and children. Women and children."

No one moved. There was no one to move. No one was paying attention to the canvas boat perched so dangerously at the bow. Primitive instinct had taken over sending the passengers scrambling uphill toward the stern that was rising steadily as the bow dropped.

The sailors working the ropes on the davits began to lower the boat. Lucan waited, his eyes on the face of the pajamaed gentleman who was calling out for women and children. He read panic in that face – panic and frustration. Any moment now the man's instinct for self-preservation would take over. Any moment now, that man would step into the boat. He could read the intention on his face. Lucan stepped forward. He had listened to the man's voice and judged him to be an Englishman. "Well, old chap," he said. "Looks like it's just us."

"This boat is for women and children only," the man said.

Lucan heard nothing but desperation in the man's voice – desperation and a loss of intention. He was going to break and when he broke, the final barriers of discipline would come tumbling down.

"No one would blame you for stepping into the boat," Lucan said. "You've done your best, haven't you?"

The man shook his head. "This was my best" he said bitterly. "This ship was my best. She was mine."

"Yours?" Lucan queried.

The man suddenly extended his hand as if he were meeting Lucan at a club or an office. "Bruce Ismay," he said, "Chairman of the White Star Line."

"Lord Lucan Sempter," Lucan said, accepting the handshake. "Do you mind if I step into the boat?"

Lucan congratulated himself on the smoothness of the moment. Not a hint of panic, just a simple, almost offhand, request. *Do you mind if I step into the boat?*

"You might as well," Ismay said. "There's no one else."

Lucan stepped into the boat. The sailors let out another notch in the rope and the boat dropped abruptly, stopping with a jerk just a few feet above the water. Lucan studied Ismay. The man was about to break. His dark eyes searched for passengers. No one came forward. At last, he came to an inevitable decision. He ducked his head, unwilling to meet Lucan's eyes, and scrambled hastily over the gunwale. He did not look up as he took a seat.

Lucan was not sure if the boat dropped down to meet the water, or if the water rose to meet the boat. It no longer mattered. The lifeboat was leaving the ship, that was what mattered.

CHAPTER THREE

Dick Williams

On board the *Titanic*, 2:05 a.m.

For the moment he was warm, and dry and comfortable and then someone interrupted his sleep.

"Excuse me."

Dick opened his eyes to harsh reality. He was on the *Titanic* and she was sinking. He could not believe he had actually fallen asleep with his head on his father's shoulder like a small child. He sat up abruptly. Beside him John Alder stirred and stretched his arms. Apparently, he too had been asleep.

Two figures, a man and a youth, lurched clumsily toward them, grasping the handrails for balance.

Dick's mind instantly registered that they both looked familiar and that they were first-class passengers. He wondered why that gave him a sense of relief. What would it matter now if the second-class passengers, or even the immigrant third-class passengers, invaded the luxurious hallways of first-class? Why hadn't they done that already? Was something or someone keeping them down below? How could the corridors be so empty in the midst of such chaos.

The youth was making an obvious attempt to keep his voice steady. "I'm looking for...I mean, have you seen...do you know..." The voice turned from questions to a desperate statement. "I can't find my father."

"You're Jack Thayer, aren't you?" Dick said. He turned to his father who was blinking owlishly. So, he had also been asleep. Well, no one would say that the Williams men were not cool in a crisis.

Dick made the introductions. "Dad, John, this is Jack Thayer. We met on the squash court this morning, or I suppose I should say it was yesterday morning."

Charles nodded. "I know your father," he said. "He's a fine man."

"President of the Pennsylvania Railroad," Jack said. "I think everybody knows him, but I can't find him."

"Where did you last see him?" John asked.

"We were on the deck," Jack said. He indicated his companion. "This is Mlton Long and we've been trying to help each other. My mother and her maid went in a lifeboat but my father and I couldn't go with them."

"No men were allowed in the lifeboats," Long added.

"It was a terrible scene," Jack said. "The women were crying. They didn't want to leave their husbands. We watched until the boat rowed away and then we heard that boats on the port side were allowing men and so we tried to make our way over there. It wasn't easy. When we started there were only a few people willing to get into the boats but now there are hundreds and I lost sight of my father. I don't know where he went."

Charles rose to his feet and laid a hand on Jack's shoulder. "I wish I could help you, lad, but I haven't seen him. Why don't you stay alongside us. We may yet find a way out of this mess."

"I doubt it," Long said. "There are obviously not enough lifeboats and a great many people are going to find themselves swimming for their lives."

Swimming where, Dick wondered, and for how long?

John Alder was on his feet now. Even with a lifejacket belted over his swallow-tail evening coat, he managed to look elegant. That was his special gift. That was why he would one day be a splendid diplomat – if he survived.

Even now his tone carried a measure of comfort. "I know that we won't swim far in freezing water," he said, "but we have to swim clear of the ship, or she'll take us down with her in the undertow. After that it's just a matter of staying afloat long enough for one of the lifeboats to take us aboard. We know they were launched with empty seats, so when the panic subsides, they'll come back for people in the water."

"You'll have to defend yourselves," Charles said. "It'll be every man for himself."

"It's that way already," Long said. "Discipline is failing. The last lifeboats have been launched and the crew has lost control."

"Is there any sign of a rescue ship?" Dick asked.

"I heard that the *Carpathia* is coming," Jack said, "but she's hours away." His voice trembled slightly. "We don't have hours."

"What about the other ship?" John asked. "We heard the captain say that there was another ship. They could see a light on the horizon."

"There's no light on the horizon," Long said. "I don't know what the captain saw, but it's not there now."

"I don't want to die in here," Jack said with sudden passion. "I don't want to give up. I want to try."

"We all want to try," Dick said. "We..." His words caught in his throat as the deck shifted abruptly beneath his feet and he began to slide. As he grasped the handrail to save himself the lights flickered momentarily and when they came on again, they reflected off water welling up from somewhere far below. They were out of time.

They hauled themselves upward, hand over hand on the polished oak railing. Dick refused to look back but he felt the water as a malevolent presence rising inexorably behind him.

Charles went first, forcing open a service door and holding it open until they were all on the deck. They were out now in the frigid air with the uncaring stars looking down on a scene of chaos. The starburst from a distress rocket momentarily lit the night and Dick saw his fellow passengers as nothing but a desperate amorphous mass.

The *Titanic* had already buried its bow in the water and its stern was rising slowly. The mob moved as one to climb upward and escape the inevitable. Dick lurched from the doorway to the railing and held himself in place with John Alder and Jack Thayer beside him. Milton Long released his hold on the door but as he attempted to cross the deck, he was impeded by the sudden arrival of a barking, squealing, shrieking pack of dogs and pigs, with chickens fluttering above them. Obviously, someone had decided that even the animals deserved to die in the open - not that the animals knew they were about to die. There was in fact something joyous in this, their last chance to stretch their legs and flap their wings.

Long lunged forward only to have his feet swept out from under him by a small terrier trotting at the back of the pack. Dick could only watch helplessly as Long flailed his arms and slid downward into the mass of people churning helplessly in the rising water. In moments he was gone from sight.

Dick clung to the rail but Jack began to haul himself upward joining the mass of humanity who were headed toward the stern - climbing up and away from the water to gain just a few more minutes of safety. John made a desperate lunge across the deck. He caught the railing with one hand, and caught Jack Thayer's jacket with the other. The boy turned with angry desperation on his face. He wanted to do the only thing possible, he wanted to climb away from the rising water, but John held him in a strong grip and dragged him back, bellowing instructions.

"We have to swim clear of the ship or we'll go down with her. We have to go now."

Dick's heart hammered in his chest. Swim! How? Must they slide down the deck into the mass of struggling, flailing, humanity? He turned to look at his father.

Charles gesticulated wildly. "Don't wait. Dive!"

Dick didn't know if he could do it. He wasn't sure that his panicked brain could force his knees to bend and his legs to thrust him out and away from the ship. It was a dive he could do on a summer day, but this was not a summer day and he couldn't make himself move.

While he hesitated, Jack broke free of John's grip and flung one leg over the railing. He was going to do it. He was going to do what Dick was failing to do. Without a moment's hesitation, Jack flung himself out and away and disappeared from sight.

Now John climbed over the railing and turned toward Dick urging him to move. Dick's legs finally obeyed him and he climbed over the rail.

As he stood outside the rail, poised and ready to hurl himself into the water, the lights of the *Titanic* flickered and then abruptly died. As though a curtain had dropped on a stage, darkness enveloped them. For one moment a stunned silence hung over the *Titanic* and then the noise returned louder than ever and with it came something even more terrifying. Above the noise of the people in the water, the screams, the curses, and the prayers, Dick heard a great rumbling sound, rising from deep below, shaking the deck plates and starting a grinding sound from high above their heads.

He looked at the *Titanic's* funnels silhouetted against the ceiling of stars and saw that they were moving. As he watched in stunned horror, the forward funnel broke loose and crashed onto the deck landing in a shower of sparks that gave a brief moment of light. In that momentary brightness Dick saw his father throw up his hands to shield his face. He saw him fall, and he saw the funnel slide forward toward the water, carrying everything with it.

He turned toward the vast ocean. The sea was black as ink, and two miles deep. The nearest land was 400 miles away, and the rescue ship was beyond the horizon. He looked up and saw a starburst as a rocket shot up into the sky and flung its light out across the water to reveal the flailing arms and legs of those who were still alive, and the white life jackets of those who only drifted, all consciousness gone. With a cry that was made up of rage and despair, he leaped out into the darkness.

Sophie Paxton
Lifeboat #8, 2:18 a.m.

A shower of sparks, a rocket flung up into the night sky, and then sudden darkness. The grinding, groaning, mechanical death moans of the *Titanic* itself ended abruptly with the extinguishing of its lights and its final descent beneath the waves. The *Titanic* was at long last silent but the ship's silence made way for a rising chorus of human voices wailing in despair.

Maxine had collapsed with her head in Sophie's lap, her shoulders heaving with great gulping sobs. Sophie shivered, not just with cold but with horror. What was happening over there in the dark? How many people were in the water? Where were the other lifeboats? What were they to do now? Where were Dick and Charles and John?

She didn't realize that she was babbling her questions aloud until she felt the firm grip of a woman's hand on her shoulder. "Shush, dear. Just be still."

"Still?" Sophie said impatiently, glad to find a target for her questions. The woman beside was little more than a shape in the darkness. The starlight could not compensate of the loss of light from the *Titanic*. "How can we be still?" Sophie demanded to know. "We have to go back. We have to help the people in the water."

Maxine lifted her head from Sophie's lap. "We have to find my husband," she said uncertainly. Sophie realized that Maxine had already accepted the inevitable.

"We're not going back," said a rough masculine voice. The feeble glow of the lifeboat's navigation light showed Sophie a sailor resting on his oars. "If we go back, we'll be swamped," he declared.

"But my husband..." Maxine whimpered.

The woman beside Sophie laid a soothing hand on Maxine's head. "Everyone left someone behind, my dear, but we can't go back."

"Why?" Sophie demanded. "Why can't we go back?"

Another woman spoke up. Her chinchilla coat and feathered hat marked her as a woman of wealth. Her firm expression marked her as a woman who was used to getting her own way. "Turn this boat around," she demanded. "There are people drowning out there. We have room in our boat. Look at all the empty seats."

"By my reckoning," the rough-voiced sailor said, "there was more than a thousand people what didn't make if off the ship before she went down. Granted some of them are already dead, but not all of them. There'll be hundreds of people in the water what ain't dead. You take this boat back there and they'll turn it over trying to get in."

"We can't just stay here listening to them," the wealthy woman protested.

The woman beside Sophie continued to pat Maxine's head as she spoke. "I think we should do what the seaman advises."

Another man spoke from the darkness. "Hey, lady, don't be calling Hale a seaman. He ain't no seaman. He's a dining room steward, he can't row to save his life, and he's a coward. I say we go back."

"I say we don't have to listen to you," Hale said.

Sophie was surprised by a sudden flare of white light from the seat in front of her. The light, bright and steady revealed the faces of the shocked survivors. All were women except for four sailors - two on the oars and two facing each other angrily in the stern of the boat. The light itself glowed from the head of a cane held by a heavy-set woman in a fur coat.

"That's quite enough," the woman said. "Arguing will not help. If you men are not in charge, then just who is? Who did the captain place in charge of our welfare?"

A tall woman rose from one of the seats and made her way forward. "Mrs. White, may I borrow your cane?"

Mrs. White squinted, blinded by her own light. "Who is this?"

"You know me, Mrs. White. I'm the Countess of Rothes. Let me have the light."

The light changed hands and now it was held aloft so that its light fell on all of the passengers. Sophie, faced with the reality of who was in the boat felt a shiver of fear. The women in this boat were rich and angry but they were also powerless.

The four men were not the courteous crew members they had been on board the *Titanic*. They were leaning on their oars, surly and obviously frightened. Sophie could not help thinking that they would have been better off with Charles and Dick Williams, and John Alder. The Howell School taught girls to be independent but Sophie could not deny the fact that the crewmen would not have been so surly if they had male passengers to deal with. That was just the way of the world.

The countess spoke again, her voice strong and confident. "Our fate is in our own hands now. We have four men on this boat and I would like to know who is responsible to row us."

One of the sailors spoke up, "We don't have to listen to you."

"You'll listen to whoever I tell you to listen to," the countess said sharply. "Which one of you is in charge?"

"I'm Thomas Jones," said the second man. "And I want it put on record that I think we should go back."

"Morally, I agree with you," said the countess, "but this is more than a moral question. There is no point in going back if we are going to be swamped."

"We could wait a bit," Jones said, "until the noise dies down. No one will last long in the water. If you ain't never been in water that cold ---"

"On the contrary," said the countess, "I have indeed been in water that cold and because of that, I understand what you're saying, Mr. Jones. I'm afraid we will have to be practical." She raised her voice commandingly. "My maid is here with me and she will row."

A woman in a dark coat lifted her head to look at the countess. "You will row," the countess said firmly. The maid nodded, her face expressionless as she moved forward. "Mr. Jones and I will take care of the tiller and we will need two more ladies to assist with the oars. We are going to hunt down that light. We are going to reach that other ship. They will have lifeboats to send out. Maybe they have already done so. We will not give up hope."

Sophie raised her hand. "I'll row."

She tried to move Maxine from her lap but Maxine clung to her, sobbing. "No, don't leave me. You don't even know how to row."

"I know how to row," Sophie said firmly. "Why don't you come and try. It'll take your mind off ..."

Maxine's sobs cut off any further speech and also the possibility that Maxine could be persuaded to row.

"Miss Young, my companion, will row," Mrs. White said. She turned to the woman at her side. "You will, won't you, dear? It will help you to keep warm."

Moving forward to take an oar, Sophie was surprised by a sharp pain in her left foot. She had stumbled when the boat was abruptly lowered. Could she possibly have broken a bone? *Miss Pattison immediately invaded her thoughts with brusque encouragement. "Press on, Sophie. Excelsior, my girl. Only losers stop to cry."*

By the time she reached the seat and took up an oar on the starboard side of the lifeboat, Sophie's pain had diminished to a mere throbbing in her big toe. Icy water filled the bottom of the boat. She gritted her teeth and lowered her foot into the water. The pain receded as her foot went numb.

The oars were long and heavy and Sophie began to feel warm inside her heavy coat. She paused, intending to take it off when the woman had initially been sitting beside her, and who now had Maxine's head in her lap, leaned forward to speak to her.

"Don't take you coat off. I know you're perspiring but taking off you coat is the best way to catch pneumonia."

"Is it?" Sophie asked incredulously. "Are you a nurse?"

"I'm a doctor, dear. Alice Leader."

"A woman doctor?" Sophie said disbelievingly.

"A woman can be anything she wants," Dr. Leader said and Miss Pattison's spirit agreed with her.

Sophie took a firm grasp of the oar. *A woman can be anything she wants.* They would find the light and they would be saved. The lifeboats would return and Lucan would be found and reunited with Maxine. Perhaps he was with Dick and Charles Williams and the third man, John. Yes. they would all be saved together. She would still have her chance at the Olympics.

Fueled by ambition and a hope she knew to be false, she pulled hard on the oar and ignored the throbbing pain that had returned to her left foot. Ahead of them was only darkness broken occasionally by the rhythmic flashing of a faraway light.

A signal. It had to be a signal. She had been taught Morse code at the Howell School. *Always be prepared. You never know when you might need to send up a message. Maybe you've been kidnapped, or stranded on a desert island. You never know what might happen if you throw yourselves into an active life. No shrinking violets here. So, you will learn your Morse code. It may save your life.*

Now she read the message that flashed brighter than the stars.

QRZ – Identify Yourself.

CHAPTER FOUR

John Alder

Night on the North Atlantic

John Alder and Dick Williams leaped together into the unknown. John felt himself drawn down deep into the icy water before his lifejacket dragged him to the surface. Even as his head broke the surface, his lungs rebelled. The cold water held him in a vice-like grip and he could not draw a breath. Fight! He had to fight! He drew in a small amount of air. His lung expanded. He began to breath in short desperate gasps fighting his body's intention of shutting down.

He had to get out of the water, but how?

He floated for a moment while his eyes adjusted to the starlight reflecting on the white of the life jackets. The ship, of course, was gone. John believed that they had gone part of the way down together - the ship giving up the fight and diving bow first toward the ocean floor, and John fighting his way to the surface.

The night was no longer filled with the rumbling death throes of the *Titanic*, but it was far from silent. All around him screams rose up into the night air. He knew why they screamed. The water was agony, like the piercing of a thousand sharp needles.

He struggled to breathe, well aware that it was in his power to end this agony. All he had to do was to stop struggling. The lifeboats had already left. There would be no rescue. The captain had spoken of a rescue ship but it was hours away. If John could not heave himself out of the water very soon, he would not have hours, not even minutes.

A man in a life jacket bumped up against him. John could not see his face but he made out the shape of a bowler hat on his head. How strange! In those terrible moments when passengers scrambled for their lifejackets, their nearest and dearest, and their valuables, this man had chosen to retrieve his bowler hat.

John assumed that he was an Englishman. The English had a strange affinity for bowler hats.

He tugged at the man's life jacket, wanting to see if he was alive. Perhaps the two of them could do something if they worked together. He was too late - far too late. The man was dead, a frozen, startled corpse held on the surface by his life jacket.

John knew what he had to do if he planned to stay alive. He was disgusted at the idea of desecrating the dead but Jesus himself had said "Let the dead bury the dead." He held onto that thought as he placed both hands on the dead man's life jacket and pushed the corpse down, using it as a step to heave himself a little way out of the water. Even a little helped. But how could he do more?

Voices came from close by - not screams but words. The words were angry and desperate but John realized that somewhere nearby, people were alive. He released the corpse and swam in the direction of the voices.

He bumped up against something - not a floating corpse but a solid object. He stretched out his hand. His frozen fingers grasped something firm and hard. A lifeboat? He pushed against it and heaved himself upward until his upper body was out of the water.

"Wait your turn, John. We both have to wait our turn."

The sound of Dick's voice from somewhere close by lifted his heart. So, Dick had survived the initial leap, but where were they now? He looked about, trying to make sense of what he could see. He seemed to be holding onto the gunwale of a semi-submerged lifeboat. The lifeboat was filled with standing figures, he could not discern whether they were men or women, but their voices were coming from somewhere above him – somewhere out of the water.

A man spoke sternly. "Don't try anything or you'll put us all under."

John managed to gasp out a few words. "What's happening? Is this boat sinking?"

"Not if we're careful. If we get rid of the stiffs, we can take both of you."

John discerned movement from the pack of people standing in the boat. Why were they standing? What had happened to the boat?"

Something dark and heavy seemed to slide out from the midst of the people. The shape fell into the water and John saw it for what it was - a corpse in a lifejacket. He clung to the gunwale, half in and half out of the water and waited while the action was repeated three more times. The corpses floated away.

"You can climb on now."

Climb on! How was he to do that? He waited for a hand to be extended to help him but no one came to help. He knew, of course, that it was every man for himself. If he was to claim his place on this fragile island of refuge, he would have to prove himself capable.

The boat was so low in the water that it took very little strength to heave himself over the gunwale and flop helplessly into the water collected in bottom of the boat. Standing was the problem. His legs were numb but as he tried to make them take his weight, they protested with stabbing pains. For the first time he screamed aloud as he finally regained his feet.

He had no time to wonder what was happening to his legs. He was absorbed into the midst of a pack of people all standing in water that came up above their knees. He was dimly aware that Dick Williams had also climbed on board – so far so good.

John thought he had been cold in the water but this was worse. He shivered and groaned as the rising wind blew across his soaked clothing. He imagined ice forming on his hair and face, even on his eyelashes.

A voice beside him spoke sharply. "Don't move. You'll turn us over."

"What is this boat?"

"It's one of the collapsibles," the voice said. "It was on the roof of the officers' quarters. They never got it launched. It just washed off the deck. I saw it go and I thought here's my chance." The man actually gave a brief snort of laughter. "Fat chance!"

"Better than nothing," John said. "Can we bail her out."

"No, we tried. She'll turn turtle if we get her out of balance."

"So, what are we doing?"

"Damned if I know," the man said. "Waiting, I suppose, for her to get a bit lighter."

"How?"

"How do you think? We're all going to die. Some are going faster than others. If we let them off and don't take anyone on, we'll be lighter in the water." The speaker drew in a sharp breath. "Damn. my legs are killing me."

John heard Dick's response. "Me too. Not sure how long I can stand."

He felt movement at his side and felt his hand taken in a firm grasp - a handshake of sorts. "William Mellor," his companion said.

"Jonathon Alder," John replied. He waited for Dick to introduce himself and heard only a groan. "Richard Williams," he added.

He felt a ripple of movement through the tight press of bodies.

"Another one gone," Mellor said. "We had at least thirty at one point. They don't last. There's one poor Swedish chap down on his knees in the water holding onto his wife. No one has the heart to move him and she's too weak to climb in and stand up. Actually, I think she's dead but he won't let her go."

John shuffled aside as an inert body was pushed past him and into the water. No one climbed aboard to take its place. He strained to see what was happening in the water around the boat. The screaming was over. The ocean was littered with people. He amended his thoughts. No, not people - just life jackets. The ocean was littered with life jackets but the people were no more. The sea had taken their lives.

The pathetic semi-submerged lifeboat that was his only haven, drifted among the bodies, barely rising to ride the ever-increasing waves. The sky was beginning to show a hint of dawn light. Another body slid past him into the ocean. They were a mere handful of people now but at least Dick was holding his own. John could see the Swedish man, up to his waist in water as he knelt in the bottom of the boat and held his wife's hand.

"I'm sure she's gone," Mellor said, "but he's not hurting anyone down there. If he wants to hold her, well, let him."

John felt Dick trembling beside him. "What is it?"

"The pain in my legs. Not sure how much longer I can stand."

"I'll hold you up."

The sea was no longer calm and waves were beginning to break over the gunwales of the lifeboat. Dick seemed to grow weaker with every wave that rocked the boat. John scanned the horizon and saw nothing but icebergs. They were all around them now, as if they had come to see the place where the *Titanic* had foundered. Some of them were massive, far bigger than the iceberg that had brought the *Titanic* to its doom.

The little lifeboat was drifting helplessly with the current. They had no means to steer her. She would be no match for even a small berg. Even a splinter of floe ice would destroy her.

Two sharp whistle blasts broke the unnatural silence. Mellors gave a great whoop of relief. "That's an officer's whistle. They've seen us. Someone's seen us."

Dick began to sag and John dragged him upright. Looking over Mellors' head, he saw a splash of white.

"It's a sail," Mellors said. "That's a lifeboat under sail. He's seen us. He's heading straight for us."

Excitement threatened to capsize the submerged collapsible as discipline fell apart among the handful of survivors. As the lifeboat approached, some of them sank to their knees. A woman, the only female survivor John had seen, began to sob. All eyes turned to the Swedish man who still held his wife's hand.

As the lifeboat came alongside and the officer on board began to issue orders. The Swede slowly removed the wedding ring from his wife's hand and, at long last, he released her and allowed her to drift away on the current.

The new craft seemed like a luxury liner as compared to the horrors of the submerged collapsible. It bowled speedily along with the sail filling in the fresh breeze. Its officer, a Welshman with a naturally commanding presence, brought the survivors to a rendezvous point where they found a gathering of lifeboats. John draped Dick's arm over his shoulder and they staggered together into the comparative safety and stability of Lifeboat #2.

Before he collapsed onto a seat, John managed to stand for a moment and look round at the other boats. Where were Sophie Paxton and her cousin Maxine? He had helped them into Lifeboat #8, but where were they now? In fact, where was Lifeboat #8?

Lord Lucan Sempter
Collapsible Lifeboat C

The lights of the *Titanic* were now only a distant memory. The lifeboat drifted on the current, leaving behind the dead and dying, and soon it was as though the *Titanic* had never been. There was only the dark, cold sea, the bright, hard starlight and the towering grief of the shivering survivors.

Lucan kept his eyes on Bruce Ismay. He was the owner of the damned ship so surely he would now take charge of what little was left of the *Titanic* - forty passengers and one collapsible lifeboat. Ismay did not move. He sat with his eyes wide and unfocused, staring at nothing.

One of the sailors was apparently a quartermaster and, when Ismay failed to act, it was up to Quartermaster Rowe to take charge and to order the sailors to row away from the thrashing, groaning people who called out from the water.

"They'll sink us," Rowe said. "We'll keep clear and wait until the noise dies down."

They waited and the noise did indeed die down, but Rowe gave no orders to turn the lifeboat. Ismay lifted his head and focused his eyes for just a moment. "We had word of a rescue ship," he said. "The *Carpathia* is coming at full steam."

Hours passed and the starlight faded. Lucan closed his eyes and allowed his thoughts to drift until they ran into the jagged rock of his unfortunate marriage.

Maxine Paxton had come to London as part of the "fishing fleet." That was what society had named the influx of wealthy young American women who arrived on the social scene every fall in search of husbands. The *quid pro quo*, although unspoken, was shamelessly obvious. The ruthless robber barons who had made their fortunes in American steel and coal, were now looking to the social status of their obscenely wealthy descendants. It was time to create an American aristocracy and what could be more aristocratic than a title? London in the "season" was a little more than a market – rich Americans buying titles for their daughters.

Lucan's title, although low in the social scale, had the advantage of being hereditary which meant his son would one day be a lord, and his wife would be Lady Sempter. In return for this title, Lucan would have wonderful, abundant, American money.

He and Maxine had found each other on the fringes of the social scene – Lucan with his title and very little else, and Maxine Paxton almost too old to be eligible, but still looking for a title to take home.

Even now, adrift in a lifeboat on the North Atlantic, he could still find the energy to be angry. He had been deceived into taking Maxine Paxton as his wife by the promise that she was an heiress.

Heiress to what?

Heiress to nothing.

And who is the true heiress?

Sophie Paxton, Maxine's younger cousin.

The voyage on the *Titanic* was a chance for Maxine to introduce Lucan to the heights of American wealthocracy. He realized now that Maxine had been unable to afford the tickets herself. She had persuaded her grandfather or maybe her grandfather's lawyers, that her young cousin Sophie, the heiress, should not be allowed to embark on the *Titanic* without an appropriate chaperone.

Lucan knew now that Maxine and her mother survived on handouts from old Aidan Paxton, and handouts only came if Maxine stayed in the old man's good graces. Maxine had managed to snatch a title – the reward was their voyage on the *Titanic* accompanying a young cousin she scarcely knew.

Lucan knew one thing - if anything happened to Sophie, Maxine would be next in line for the fortune. Lucan could wish for Lifeboat #8 to sink and drown pretty Miss Sophie, but that would also drown Maxine, and without Maxine he was nothing. It was a conundrum.

He was brought back from his bitter reverie by the sound of a whistle.

"That's an officer's whistle," Rowe said. "Now maybe we'll see some action."

Ismay lifted his head and focused his eyes, but said nothing. The sailors pulled on their oars and the lifeboat turned clumsily in the direction of the whistle. Before long, hope and discipline arrived in the form of Harold Lowe, *Titanic's* fifth officer. Lowe had rigged a sail on his lifeboat and now, with the sail billowing under a rising wind, his boat was skittering among the scattered lifeboats.

For a while at least, the survivors had something positive to think about. As Lowe rounded up the lifeboats and brought them together, there were occasional moments of reunion, a wife finding a husband, a mother finding a child. For Lucan there was no reunion. Lifeboat #8, containing his wife and her cousin, was nowhere to be seen.

Officer Lowe's face twisted as he came alongside the collapsible and spotted Ismay, unmoving and unfocused. Their eyes met briefly and, when it was obvious that Ismay had no ability to give orders, Lowe took charge of what was left of Ismay's passengers, moving them from one boat to another like pieces on a chess board. He took shivering, despairing men and women from frail sinking crafts and put them into the relative safety of the sturdy, clinker-built lifeboats. Many boats had rowed away from the *Titanic* with only a handful of passengers. Lowe filled the empty seats.

Closeness lent comfort but only for a short while. The wind was rising and waves were breaking against the ice shelf. Time was running out for those who were in Lowe's sheepfold. And what of the other boats? Lowe was obviously unsure as to how many boats had been successfully launched but Lucan was quite certain that Lifeboat #8 had survived the drop into the water and had been rowed clear of the undertow as the *Titanic* sank. So where was it now?

As starlight began to give way to dawn, the rescue ship *Carpathia* heralded her arrival with rockets rising from beyond the horizon, and then the Cunard liner itself came into view. Hope banished despair, but Ismay did not even raise his head.

The *Carpathia* was fully prepared to receive them with rope ladders, cargo nets, and a canvas bucket to haul up those who could not climb. The process was slow and could have given way to chaos at any moment as the lifeboats clustered around the waterline of the *Carpathia* and survivors yearned for the safety of the ship's deck high above them. Officers of the Cunard Line controlled the processes and passengers had little energy left to resist.

When it was his turn, Lucan opted to be taken aboard in a canvas bucket and he was hauled up and spilled out onto the deck and into the arms of a welcoming committee. One of the *Carpathia's* doctors was examining each of the survivors as they were brought up from the lifeboats to the deck. A girl stood with him, taking names, and pointing and gesturing to show where the shivering survivors could find warm drinks, blankets and shelter.

Lucan took second-hand British pride in the work of Captain Rostron and his crew. Rostron was an Englishman – one of the best of his breed. He should be given a medal – maybe a knighthood. He had obviously worked all night to prepare for the influx of survivors. Of course, no one, however efficient, could prepare in advance for the outpouring of grief from bereaved women and children or the level of injuries sustained in the escape from the *Titanic*.

Lucan kept his eye on Ismay. Now that they were safe, passengers would have time to ask questions and he knew what one of those questions would be. How had Ismay, owner of the ship, found a seat in a lifeboat when so many of his passengers had not? With men being excluded from the lifeboats, how had Ismay managed to save himself? They could ask the same question of Lucan, but they would not. In this scenario Lucan was a nobody. Ismay was the man at the center of the storm and he knew it.

Ismay had been brought up ahead of Lucan and he was still on deck, leaning against a bulkhead. His head was down and frost had formed on his dark hair and moustache. An officer from the *Carpathia* approached him. He spoke softly but Lucan could hear him. "Mr. Ismay, will you not go inside and get some soup, or something to drink?"

Ismay shook his head. "No, I really don't want anything at all."

"But you must get something. You can't stay out here."

Ismay lifted his head and Lucan studied his face. He was a broken man – and not just broken, but also terrified. And why not, Lucan thought. Now that the full scale of the disaster was revealed, the survivors would be looking for someone to blame. Ismay was the obvious scapegoat. Captain Smith had not survived but here was Ismay, safe and sound – the rat leaving the sinking ship.

Ismay snapped at the Cunard officer. "If you will leave me alone, I will be very much happier. Just find me a room where I can be quiet and out of sight."

The officer considered for a moment, looking around at the organized hustle and bustle of the deck. "Come with me. I'll find you somewhere."

As Ismay was led away, Lucan turned his attention back to his most pressing concern. Where was his wife? If Maxine had not survived, how was he to have any kind of life in the United States? He had been relying on Maxine for his future security. There was still the problem of Sophie, but that would have to wait. Well, really, it would all have to wait. There was nothing he could do. Ideally, he would have liked for Maxine to survive while cousin Sophie perished.

Well, there was no point in shivering out here on the deck. He would go below and see who would be keeping him company on the *Carpathia*. There would be gamblers, of course - there were gamblers on every ship, and there would be new widows – wealthy ones. Perhaps he should not concern himself so much with the fate of Lifeboat# 8.

CHAPTER FIVE

Alfie Blackwell, Galley Boy
On board the *Californian* , 6:30 a.m. April 15.

Blimey this was tricky. Alfie Blackwell balanced a tray with tea, milk and sugar and tried to make his way from the galley to the passenger cabins. The *Californian* was underway, ploughing determinedly through the rollers, and Alfie was watching the teacup and saucer with an eagle eye. He weren't going to break another dish and have the cook in fits and calling him a clumsy little bastard.

Well, Alfie was some things, but he weren't no bastard and he'd told the cook that straight out. "My dad and mum didn't make no bastard. My mum died of the coughing and my dad went down at sea, but he were a good man and they was married."

The cook had cuffed him round the ear. "Maybe you ain't a bastard, but you're the clumsiest kitchen boy I ever seen."

"That's on account of me broken leg," Alfie said.

"Well, whatever it's on account of, take that tea tray to Mr. White and tell him there's no breakfast this morning."

Alfie balanced the tea tray on one hand and knocked on the door. One passenger this trip, a strange bloke the captain took on all sudden like in Liverpool - sudden and secret and nothing said until the *Californian* had cleared the harbor.

Then it was "*Hey you, boy, we got a passenger and no steward. You look after him.*"

Mr. White was a good enough kind of bloke, Alfie thought, but a bit untidy and in need of a haircut. Not to mention that he didn't care about his boots. What kind of man don't care about his boots? You can be poor, but you don't have to have dirty boots.

"You want me to polish your boots, sir?"

"If you want to."

Alfie had polished the boots just as his dad had taught him, but Mr. White didn't seem to appreciate the effort. He was busy in his cabin writing in a notebook. Always writing.

Alfie knocked again and then tried the door. It weren't locked. Mr. White was a trusting kind of bloke and that was a mistake. Alfie didn't trust anyone on the crew, except maybe Evans the Marconi man, but none of the rest.

Alfie opened the cabin door. Gray dawn light was seeping in through the porthole and he could see Mr. White still snoozing in his bunk. Mr. White didn't have no night shirt. Alfie thought all toffs had night shirts, so maybe Mr. White wasn't no toff. He had money though. Word among the crew was that Captain Lord had made him pay well over the odds for his sudden passage on the *Californian.*

It was a rum do all around, but Alfie had bigger things to think about this morning. He edged inside with the tea tray and set it down on the small, paper littered desk. He skipped any kind of formal greeting in favor of an announcement. "There'll be no breakfast in the mess this morning. I can bring you some toast."

Mr. White came fully awake and stared into Alfie's face. "What's the matter? What's happened.? You look like you've seen a ghost."

Ghosts! Blimey, there was going to be thousands of them. Would they stay down there at the bottom of the ocean or would they rise up and haunt the ships that passed over them? He'd heard stories. All sailors told stories.

"Alfie," Mr. White said. "What's happened?"

Alfie turned away from the tea tray. "Everyone's busy. We're all at sixes and sevens. When Evans signed onto the Marconi this morning, he picked up the news." He took a deep breath as if to steady his voice for the announcement. "The *Titanic's* gone down, sir."

<hr />

Sam White

Sam studied the boy who was pouring tea with a shaking hand. Alfie was small and sharp featured but usually he was relentlessly cheerful and talkative – but not this morning. He said what he had to say and then just stood as if he could not believe the words from his own mouth.

Shock and a fleeting thought for his Aunt Ella who might possibly be on that ship, made Sam's voice shaky. "The *Titanic*?" he repeated. "Are you sure?"

Alfie nodded. "Quite sure, sir."

Sam shook his head. "That's impossible," he said firmly. "Where did you hear this?"

"Early this morning – got it straight from the radio officer. He said the *Titanic* had been sending CQD all night but, of course, he didn't know about it because he was off-duty and asleep. She's struck ice. We're going now to ... uh ... render assistance."

Sam's intuition told him everything. The light that streaked across the night sky was not a shooting star as McGregor had insisted. He knew the truth. The light had been a distress rocket. The glow in the distance was no longer a mystery – it was the *Titanic* and he had been witness to her distress.

Sam swung his legs out of bed. "What else do you know? Where are the survivors? Surely there are survivors." He thought again about his aunt and thinking of his obstinate aunt with her love of luxury put a face on the disaster. Alfie shook his head. "Ain't no way of knowing how many survivors, sir. She's gone quiet. Last message from her was at two in the morning and nothing since. She said she was putting women and children into lifeboats. We don't know what we'll find."

"How far away are we?"

"Close, sir." Alfie looked around as if to check the cabin door was closed and lowered his voice. "There's another ship, the *Carpathia*, what was fifty some miles away. They heard the CQD and they've gone to the rescue. They were headed for the Mediterranean but they've turned around. They've been full steam ahead all night, so they say. They'll get to the *Titanic* before we do but ..."

Sam waited, studying Alfie's face and seeing his internal struggle. "But what?" he said at last.

"There are them what say we were closer than the *Carpathia*," Alfie said softly.

"Closer? What do you mean?"

"Our ship was the closest to the *Titanic* when it struck. That's the whisper."

"Who's whispering?"

"The crew, sir. There's people saying that we was really close and the captain knew about it. There was rockets going off in the night and we didn't do nothing about it. If someone had woken the radio officer, we could have been there before it went down, couldn't we?"

Sam closed his eyes and recalled the glimmer of light across the water and the rocket shooting high into the starry sky. A chill ran down his spine. He remembered McGregor's words. *It's either something big about four miles away, or something small and much closer. She's none of our concern.*

Sam remembered the dismissive way Captain Lord had handed back the binoculars and turned his back on the light across the water. He knew that he should not drag Alfie into whatever was going to happen next, but he needed to speak to someone. He had to say what he knew.

"I think your captain is wrong. I think we were very close. I was on the deck and I saw lights, and something that could have been a rocket."

Alfie nodded. "Second officer reported rockets. That would be about two in the morning."

Sam shook his head. "No, this was much earlier. About midnight, and it was just one rocket. Mr. McGregor saw it."

'Well, he ain't admitting it now," Alfie said. "Down in the mess, he said he saw lights, but now he says he didn't."

"But I was with him," Sam said. "How can he deny it? He pointed out the lights to me. He said it could be a German ship or it could be the *Titanic*. There was a man with him, an engineer, I suppose. He said he was the donkey man."

"That would be Gill," Alfie said. "He was talking about it at first, but now he says he ain't seen nothing."

It was happening already. The story was changing. Well, maybe the crew had cause to lie, but Sam was a passenger. Captain Lord had no hold over him. "McGregor's lying," he said.

Alfie looked at him bleakly. "You should be careful sir. Maybe you shouldn't say nothing to anyone about the lights. Best to be quiet, if you get my drift."

"No, I don't get your drift. What are you trying to say?"

"Captain Lord's a hard man and, well, it won't look good for him if some people were to say what they've seen."

"I'm not a crew member," Sam said, "and I'll say what I damned well please."

Alfie nodded. "That's right, sir. You can say what you please, but ..." He paused and glanced at the door as if to make sure that it was still closed. He spoke softly. "Maybe you should wait."

"Wait for what?"

"Until we reach Boston. You're the only passenger on board, sir, and well... you're traveling alone."

Sam ignored the chill that was, once again, creeping up his spine. "That's ridiculous," he said.

Alfie glanced at the door again. "Look, sir, on this ship I'm not ranked as a seaman, I'm stuck in the galley, but I ain't forgotten what I learned under sail and steam before I broke me leg. I know a thing or two about navigation and I know there's something going on. Right now, we're steering a very strange course and we ain't going straight to the rescue. *Carpathia* is full steam ahead, and us ... we're wandering."

Sam shook his head. "Surely not. The Marconi message said they were putting women off in lifeboats, how could anyone ignore that? Maybe we're just slowed down by avoiding ice."

Alfie laid his finger beside his nose in a knowing gesture and lowered his voice. "Or maybe we don't want to arrive too soon because then it would be obvious that we were very close."

Sam shook his head. "Don't be ridiculous."

"I ain't being ridiculous," Alfie protested. "I'm saying, that maybe our officers are all cowards." He tapped his nose again. "Last night we was safe and snug wasn't we? Ice all around but we was stopped and drifting. Think about it, sir. The watch reported rockets but no one woke the radio officer. Maybe the captain didn't want him woken. Maybe he didn't want to know what was happening and why a ship was firing rockets – not if it meant he had to move his ship at night through the ice. The captain of the *Carpathia* is going to be a hero, what will our captain be?"

Before Sam could react, a blast of the *Californian's* horn jarred his nerves, and Alfie looked around nervously. "That's all crew on deck," he said. "You don't have to come, you being a passenger."

"I'm coming," Sam said, reaching for his clothes.

"You won't tell no one what I said?"

"No," Sam said, "I won't, but I'm coming up on deck to see and hear for myself."

Alfie scuttled away leaving Sam to finish dressing. He wasted no time and simply flung his overcoat over his undershirt.

He went up on deck. The sky was a leaden grey and the wind cut like a knife. *We are putting the women off in lifeboats. God help them.* Pack ice was visible off the starboard bow but the *Californian* was nosing through clear water. Sam noticed a double watch in the crow's nest and a double watch on the bow. Lord was taking no chances.

He caught sight of McGregor leaning on the rail, peering forward.

"Mr. McGregor."

McGregor did not take his eyes off the horizon. "Mr. White."

"We saw her, didn't we?" Sam said.

McGregor shook his head. "Canna say for certain, sir."

"You sounded certain last night. Four rows of lights, four miles away."

"I said maybe it was a passenger liner - maybe the *Frankfurt.*"

"You said that maybe it was the *Titanic.*"

"Maybe," McGregor said. "Maybe it was a steamer. I didn't know."

Sam felt the heat of a rising, righteous anger. "It was the *Titanic.* You knew it was."

"It's not up to me to know anything," McGregor said. "I don't give the orders."

Sam stood for a moment staring down at the white foam pushed aside by the *Californian's* bow as it ploughed through the ink black waves.

"Captain on deck."

Sam watched as Captain Lord and his senior officers made their way onto the foredeck. Captain Lord was silent. It was the First Officer who conveyed the news.

"We have a Marconi message from the *Carpathia.* She has arrived at the *Titanic's* last reported position. The *Titanic* is gone. The *Carpathia* is taking up survivors from lifeboats."

Sam spoke because it seemed that no one on the crew dared to utter a word. "How many survivors?"

"The *Carpathia* reports twelve lifeboats, so far. Mostly women and children."

Sam fixed his eyes on Captain Lord's face and caught a fleeting glimpse of bleak despair before it was replaced by cold determination.

PART TWO - RESCUE

Stanton Coit

Carpathia **passenger**

At 5:30 Monday morning last, our bedroom steward reported that the ship had stopped to rescue the passengers from the *Titanic*, which had sunk the night before. I hurried on deck, saw great icebergs about, and looking over the railing, saw some fifteen rowboats approaching us, full chiefly of women. These were drawn up on board and passed us by, most of them so stiff with cold and wet that they could not walk without being supported. Soon the tragic news spread among us that some fifteen hundred people had been drowned, and for the most part only women had been saved. My first and lasting impression was the inward calm and self poise--not self-control, for there was no effort or self-consciousness--on the part of those who had been saved. I said to one woman, whose dress, but not her face, betrayed that she was one of those who had undergone tragic experiences: "You were on the *Titanic*?" She answered, "Yes, and I saw my husband go down."

CHAPTER SIX

Sophie Paxton
  Lifeboat #8 - 6:30 a.m. April 15
Sophie was warm. She could feel sweat trickling down her back, but Dr. Leader had told her to keep her coat on, and so she did. Her arms felt leaden with the effort of pulling on the long, heavy oar designed for a sailor's grasp and not the grasp of Sophie's small hands. Well, at least she had strong arms. Four years of sporting activity at Howell had given her unladylike strength and agility. If it were not for the throbbing pain in her left foot, she would be able to say that she was quite comfortable.

She couldn't say the same for the other ladies in the boat. Maxine was silent. Her eyes were closed and Sophie thought that she was sleeping. Perhaps that was for the best. Nothing Maxine could say would improve the situation.

The stars that had been so brilliant were now hidden by drifting clouds. The first hint of dawn light appearing in the east had been merciless in revealing their desperate situation. They were alone, surrounded by menacing icebergs and no other lifeboats were in sight. Sophie 's confidence was fading fast and she wondered why she should continue to pull on the oar. She had been rowing all night, but why? Where were they going? What was the point? Although she had watched all night, she had not seen the flashing light again.

They had all been silent for some time. There was nothing left to say. It was Mrs. White, owner of the electric cane, who broke the silence. "I don't think we're going anywhere. You're all wasting your time with those oars."

The Countess of Rothes, a commanding figure at the tiller, contradicted her immediately. "We are maintaining our heading."

"But where is the light?"

"I cannot tell you. I haven't seen it."

"Of course, you haven't" Mrs. White said. "The captain lied to us. Goodness knows what he intended by his actions, probably just to make us get into the boat. It is my belief that there was no light."

Sophie thought of speaking up and saying that she had seen the light, but how would that be helpful? It had been a momentary glimpse as the lifeboat was being launched. That was hours ago, and maybe Sophie had been mistaken. Maybe there was not a ship out there sending querying demands across the ice. *Identify yourself!*

She turned to study the countess and read a look of despair on her face. The night had been so long and they were so alone. The presence of the formidable Countess of Rothes had offered some meagre comfort but if she had lost her courage, Sophie was not sure what would happen next. There were twenty-two women in the boat and four crewmen and beyond that there was nothing. The *Titanic* was gone. The other lifeboats were not in sight. What would happen if they stopped rowing, because eventually they would? They couldn't do this forever. What would they do next? What would they even say to each other.

Thomas Jones stood up and put his hand on the tiller. "Sit down, your ladyship. You need to rest. You've had a long night."

"We've all had a long night," the countess replied, "but that's no excuse. We need to keep rowing. We can't give up."

Sophie pushed her doubts aside. The countess needed her support. "I saw the light. It was a signal light. We have to keep rowing. If we have to row all the way to Newfoundland, then that's what we'll do."

Mrs. White shook her head. "Don't be absurd."

Miss Young, who had been rowing all night, suddenly sprang to her feet. "Look! Look! Rockets! I see rockets.

Sophie joined in the great gasp of relief. They were not alone. A ship was coming. She followed Miss Young's pointing finger and saw streaks of light blazing across the dreary dawn sky, bright but very far away.

Her heart sank. She blurted her fear aloud. "They're so far away. Will they see us?"

The countess was cool and in control again. "Of course, they will. Mr. Jones, I suggest we fire a signal flare to let them know where we are."

Jones leaned down and opened the locker beside the tiller. He rummaged around and brought out the loaf of bread Captain Smith had so perversely placed aboard. "No flares," he said.

The countess uttered a rude word that was totally unsuitable for a lady of her social standing and Sophie echoed it in her own mind.

"So now what do you suggest?" Mrs. White asked. "The light from my cane is almost extinguished and we can't count on the other lifeboats to say where we are. We've been rowing all night and obviously we've rowed far away from them."

"We don't know that there are any other lifeboats," Jones said. "We were one of the first boats away. We don't know how many more were launched or how they fared during the night. If that's a rescue ship, it's going straight to the last known position of the *Titanic* and they're going to find nothing but bodies. They won't sink, you know, not the ones with lifejackets. There'll be hundreds of them floating. They'll be in the shipping lanes. They'll be everywhere."

The countess reached out and touched Jones on the shoulder. "Mr. Jones, this is not helpful. Let the dead bury the dead. We are alive. Think, Mr. Jones. What can we do?"

Jones rested his head in his hands. "No one checked the lifeboats," he said wearily. "There should be flares."

"Yes, there should be," the countess agreed, "but they are not here, so what else can we use?"

"Bloody White Star Line," Jones muttered. "They thought they could build a boat that would never sink. We didn't need lifeboats. We didn't need anything. We had it all. Now look at us. There's a rescue ship over there and they won't even see us because we don't have any bloody flares."

Alice Leader, the woman who had told Sophie that she was a doctor, rose to her feet. "There is something we can do," she said. "It will soon be full daylight and that ship will most certainly have a lookout in the crow's nest. We are low in the water and our lifejackets are white. We must show some colors. Ladies, you must show your brightest colored clothing. Does anyone have a bright scarf or well ... anything?"

"Are you suggesting that we remove our clothing?" Mrs. White asked. "You must be aware, Dr. Leader, that there are men in this lifeboat. What will they see if we shed our coats? Some of us are in our night attire."

Sophie turned in her seat. "They'll see nothing if we all die of cold," she said. "I'm willing to take my coat off. I'll take everything off if it means we can be seen. I'll do it now."

Miss Young spoke up immediately. As Mrs. White's travelling companion, she was obviously accustomed to pouring oil on troubled waters. "I have a red scarf and a red —"

"Never mind what else you have," Mrs. White said firmly. "Just your scarf. Wave your scarf." She fixed her gaze on Nellie Bisette, her personal maid who had been by her side all night, "Nellie," she said firmly, "you will row and Marie will wave her scarf."

Nellie moved obediently, and Miss Young made her way to the bow of the boat. With Hale to hold her steady, she waved vigorously.

She was still waving, but less vigorously, when the sun broke the horizon and they saw the smoke of the rescue ship.

The countess continued to steer toward the ship. The exhausted women pulled on the oars, and Miss Young waved. Their progress was slow but at last they were able to make out the ship itself, a liner with just one funnel. It was stopped.

Dr. Leader grasped the significance of what they were seeing. "They must be stopping to take people up from a lifeboat. They have no other reason to stop."

Sophie's heart lurched with sudden relief. All through the long terrifying night she had feared that they were alone - that these few women represented all that could be saved of the *Titanic*. Now it seemed that the rescue ship had found others. She thought of Charles and Dick Williams and John Alder - was it possible that they were still alive? Was Maxine's husband still alive? Her cousin was awake now, sitting up straight and studying the ship. Hope gleamed in her red-rimmed eyes. Sophie had no liking for Lord Lucan Sempter, but she could not wish him dead – not when Maxine so obviously wished him to be alive.

Of course, Mrs. White was quick to see the dark side of their situation. "If they pick up people way over there," she said indicating the distant ship, "they won't come looking for us. Why should they? They won't know that we were sent on a fool's errand rowing toward a light that never existed. They'll think we were lost. We're still miles away. It's not enough for Miss Young to wave her scarf if they're not even looking for us."

Sophie's patience, never her strong point, failed her completely. "Why don't you come over here and take Miss Young's place? The faster we row, the more likely we are to be seen."

Mrs. White shook her head. "I wish I could. I turned my ankle when we were boarding in Cherbourg. I couldn't put any weight on my foot. Miss Young will tell you that I did not even leave the cabin."

"Well, you've left the cabin now," Sophie said. "And your feet don't hurt any more than anyone else's. We've been up to our ankles in freezing water all night."

"I'm afraid frostbite is a very real possibility," Dr. Leader said. "It will become more painful before it gets better...if it gets better."

Mrs. White opened her mouth to speak, but the countess interrupted her. The ship was moving again. "It's turning. Look! It's turning! They've seen us!"

Sophie slumped forward on her oar. *We're saved.*

John Alder
On board the Carpathia 8:30 a.m.

John sat on an upturned box with Dick beside him. Together they huddled under a borrowed blanket and watched the crew of the *Carpathia* as they brought the survivors on board. The sun, now well above the horizon, offered no warmth and hours seemed to have crawled by since they had each climbed the rope ladder onto the *Carpathia's* deck. John saw that Dick, a trained athlete, had struggled with the climb. He should have gone in the canvas bucket, but John knew his friend. He would never give in to pain and he was in considerable pain.

"It's only frostbite," he said, "but it's like my legs are being prodded by a demon with red hot needles."

"You should go below to the doctor," John said.

Dick shook his head. "Not much a doctor can do. Ice crystals in the blood. The only cure is time. I'm not going below. I'm waiting for the ladies we put on the lifeboat. It's what my father would want me to do."

A Cunard officer approached them. "Gentlemen, I have to ask you to go below," he said. "We prefer that you don't remain out here on the deck."

"And we prefer to wait here," Dick said

The officer was politely insistent. They had shed their life jackets revealing damp evening clothes. No doubt the officer had recognized that they were, or had been, first-class passengers. Somehow a first-class ticket on the *Titanic* was enough to buy them courtesy from the officers of the *Carpathia*, but not patience.

"Gentlemen," the officer said, "you're setting a poor example for the other survivors. They all want to watch as the lifeboats come alongside. They're all hoping to find their loved ones but it's hopeless. It's increasingly obvious that most of the passengers were not saved and having the survivors out here will create chaos. The scale of this disaster is becoming evident and we fear a riot. We have to get all survivors below and secured."

"Secured," Dick said. "You mean locked up?"

"If necessary. If they remain on deck there will be chaos every time we bring another boat on board. These women are praying that their husbands have survived, but it's obvious that very few men made it into the lifeboats."

John noticed a change of expression on the officer's face. It had shifted from entreaty to a lightly veiled contempt. "I am told that the gentlemen stood back and allowed the women to be saved."

"Yes, we did," Dick said grimly. "I stood back with my father. We made no attempt to get into a lifeboat."

The contempt was still on the officer's face. John guessed that the officer would have heard the news from the bedraggled survivors who were hauled on board. He would know that Jacob Astor, Ben Guggenheim, John Thayer, Isidor Straus, some of the richest men in the world, had stood aside and allowed the women into the lifeboats.

John knew that he was not required to explain himself to this essentially unimportant officer. He also sensed that he would have to get used to offering an explanation for his own survival if he didn't want to be branded a coward.

"I went into the water without a lifeboat," he said. "I jumped. I was fortunate enough to be picked up." It was a poor explanation for what had happened, but it was enough to change the officer's expression. John took advantage of the moment. "We put some ladies in a lifeboat, but we haven't seen them come aboard. We just want to make sure they are all right."

"What boat?"

"Number eight."

"You're in luck. We're bringing them on board now. You can stay here for the time being until we have them listed and then you can take them below. In the meantime, please don't get in the way."

John watched the officer walk away before he spoke to Dick. "Where's the husband?"

"What husband."

"Lord Lucan Sempter, husband of Miss Sophie's cousin. I saw him come aboard, but where is he now? You'd think he'd be out here waiting for his wife."

"I wonder how he managed to save himself," Dick said.

"He was in the lifeboat with Ismay," John replied. "Dry as a bone from what I can tell."

"We haven't heard the end of that," Dick said."

"Meaning?"

"Meaning Ismay didn't go down with the ship."

"He wasn't the captain. He wasn't even an officer. He didn't have to."

"So you think it's fine for him to save himself?" Dick asked.

"We saved ourselves," John said.

"We went into the water. Ismay didn't."

John shrugged. "From what I saw, half the lifeboats were launched with empty seats in them. Ismay didn't steal anyone's seat. I feel sorry for the man. He did nothing wrong but he's going to be shamed just for surviving."

"He's already shamed," Dick said, "because instead of facing up to what happened, he's hiding. He's locked himself in the doctor's office. He should be up here apologizing."

Alder looked down at Dick's righteous expression and thought of the difference in their ages. Dick was twenty-one, an athlete used to making snap decisions. It was no surprise that he would rush to judgment. John, at thirty, had been building a career in senatorial politics, where judgment was always delayed, and often ignored. He was reserving judgment on Bruce Ismay.

A flurry of activity on the deck told him that Lifeboat #8 was now secured and passengers were being brought on board. They'll be in better shape than some, Alder thought. The survivors in Lifeboat #8 had been loaded from the deck of the *Titanic* and launched well before the time that chaos had erupted. Its passengers had endured a long night, but they would be dry, unlike John and Dick and so many others who were chilled to the bone and shivering beneath their borrowed blankets.

As the first passengers from Lifeboat #8 were hauled up onto the deck, John saw Lucan Sempter emerge from the saloon doors with a brandy in his hand. His face was flushed. John wondered how many brandies the Englishman had imbibed while he waited below, uncertain whether or not Lifeboat #8 would be found. He gave Dick and John a sly sideways glance. John imagined that his lordship would not easily forget that Dick and his father had held him back when he insisted on accompanying his wife. Lucan looked like the kind of man who would carry a grudge.

He looked away from Lucan in time to see that Sophie Paxton had just been hauled up onto the deck. For a moment she seemed dazed. Her eyes slid past Lucan as though she did not even recognize him and landed on John and Dick. She flashed a brilliant smile, and took a hesitant step toward them. She took only two more steps before she stumbled and was held upright by the young lady who had been listing names of passengers.

John rushed forward and put a steadying hand on her. Together they watched the arrival of Lady Maxine Sempter. John had serious doubts about Lucan's attachment to his bride, and his doubts were not assuaged by Maxine's greeting of her husband.

"Oh Lucan, I thought you were gone. When they turned you away from our boat, I ... I..." Words seem to fail her and yet she seemed reluctant to hurl herself into his arms, standing at a short distance and asking the obvious question. "How did you manage?"

"It seemed foolish to die," Lucan said. "I decided to join the Chairman of the White Star Line in displaying some simple English common sense."

As he had kept vigil on the deck, John had witnessed moments of despair as survivors had been brought aboard. Women who had lost sight of their husbands still hoped for a miracle – that they would find a husband or son who had not gone down with the ship but was simply in another lifeboat. Mostly they were doomed to disappointment.

There had been a few good moments. Jack Thayer had found his mother, a little girl had been reunited with her sisters, and Washington Dodge had found his wife and son. Lady Maxine's eventual embrace of her husband, seemed to lack the emotion of these other reunions. Something, he thought, was very wrong with the marriage.

Sophie took John's arm and turned her back on her cousin. Sophie's attention was fixed on Dick Williams and John seemed to be no more to her than an inanimate crutch. He guided her to Dick who had managed to stumble to his feet. "Your father?" she asked immediately.

Dick shook his head.

"I'm sorry."

Before she could say more, a loud cry went up from a group of survivors who had, apparently, managed to make their way back onto the deck

"A ship! There's another ship."

John managed to protect Sophie from being trampled as a wave of wet, ragged people poured out from the interior saloons of the *Carpathia*, ignoring all attempts to restraining them.

"It's a ship."

"It's our husbands."

"They've picked up people from the water."

For a moment even John embraced an absurd hope. Could it be that during the long night, another ship had come upon the *Titanic* survivors struggling in the water, and somehow brought them aboard? Could Dick's father be on that ship? No, of course not- no one could have survived more than a few minutes in water so cold. They could not have survived long enough for another ship to find them. As for Dick's father – he could not forget what he had seen – Charles Williams had been directly in the path of the falling funnel.

The survivors milling around on the deck were now filled with unreasonable hope, most of it expressed in languages John did not understand. He knew French and German, the languages of diplomacy, but the women who were now pleading with the officers, spoke another language. He thought, possibly, Scandinavian. Surely immigrants from so far north would understand the death sentence of water so cold. It didn't matter. Logic had no place in the sudden, unreasonable resurrection of hope. The bereaved survivors yearned for a different outcome to the night of April 15 and for a short time reason gave way to wild hope.

The deck crew forced the pleading, crying survivors back inside, ignoring their protests. *No more. No more survivors. Men not coming. Go below.*

John stayed back watching as Dick and Sophie hobbled together into the warmth of the ship's interior. In the quiet that followed the departure of the women, a young man appeared on deck. He wore a uniform jacket with no markings of rank. He pulled a crushed pack of cigarettes from his pocket and then turned to look at John.

"Smoke?" he asked.

John shook his head. Much as he wanted a cigarette, he knew that his fingers were too cold and clumsy to take hold. They were frozen and gray. He recognized the threat of frostbite. There was, as Dick had said, nothing to be done except wait and see.

John gestured to the approaching ship. "What ship is that?"

"That's the *Californian*, a freighter bound for Boston. They said they'd be coming along. I should go down and talk to them."

He smiled at John's puzzled face. "Harold Cottam," he said, "Radio officer for the *Carpathia*. I send Morse code but I call it talking. I talked to the *Californian* last evening. They said they were stopped and surrounded by ice and the radio officer was going off-duty."

"Did they know about the *Titanic*?"

"No. At least, I have to assume they didn't or they would have been here much sooner. They were close last night, much closer than we were."

"You mean they could have arrived before you did – before we..."

"I don't know," Cottam said, "all I know is that they were close – very close. Stopped and surrounded by ice." He looked across the expanse of dark water and sized up the approaching ship. "It's taken a long time for him to get here from where the captain said he was."

John was too tired and too bemused to try to interpret Cottam's words. Was he hinting at something? Probably not, but they were words worth remembering.

Cottam took a long pull on his cigarette. "It's only the grace of God that brought us here," he said. "You should thank God, you're alive."

"I do," John said.

"I was off duty," Cottam said, "and getting ready for bed when the message came through. I had put on the headphones for a final check and there it was. *Titanic to all ships. Come at once. We have struck ice.*"

"What did you do?"

"I went to the bridge. No one there would believe me. I don't blame them. *Titanic* was supposed to be unsinkable. The ice shouldn't have mattered. I double checked the message and then took it to the captain."

He threw the stub of his cigarette overboard, allowing the wind to carry it away.

"After that it was all go, all night. I'm pretty much worn out. Fortunately, there was a Marconi man traveling on the *Titanic*, headed for the Marconi station at Cape Race. He's in pretty good shape so he's spelling me for a moment while I get my breath back. Even between the two of us, it's not going to be easy. We're getting constant wires from newspapers. We're ignoring them, but we can't hold them off forever. They're hounding us for a list of survivors but we don't have one – not an official one. If we release some of the names, there will be a run on the stock exchange. Companies will fail."

John nodded. He had seen them for himself - men who were now dead. Captains of industry stepping back and allowing women into the boats.

"And then there are the immigrants," Cottam said. "They've lost the bread-winner in their family." He shook his head. "Now we don't even know where we're taking them."

"What do you mean?"

"The *Carpathia* was bound for the Mediterranean. The question is, do we keep going and drop them in Gibraltar, or do we turn around? Closest land is Halifax, but we don't know that the Canadians want them. Sure, there are some rich widows who survived and they can go anywhere, but there are more than a hundred third-class survivors – immigrants."

"Shouldn't you take them to New York?" John said, "that's where they were intended to go."

"There's a lot of ocean between us and New York," Cottam said. "I don't make the decisions. I just send the messages. All I know is that, whatever is decided for us, it's going to be pretty grim. We have food and facilities for our original seven hundred passengers and now we have fourteen hundred passengers, half of them sick or injured, and all of them out of their minds with shock."

He shrugged. "I'd best be off. The captains will want to talk to each other on the Marconi."

CHAPTER SEVEN

Sam White

On board the Californian, 10:00 a.m.

The crew of the *Californian* stood in silence as the *Carpathia* steamed away westward. They had arrived too late to be of any assistance.

The captain of the *Carpathia* had brought his ship through the ice field and arrived in time to rescue survivors, but what had Captain Lord done? Sam didn't know what to make of Alfie's suspicion that the *Californian* had taken a long slow route toward the *Titanic's* last reported position. Perhaps it no longer mattered. The *Carpathia* had done what needed to be done and the *Californian* would be no more than a footnote in history. Other ships that had steamed all night would soon be arriving, but there was nothing for anyone to see. The wind was picking up. White caps were forming on the waves and the *Titanic's* grave had no marker.

The *Californian's* horn emitted one long mournful farewell blast which was answered by the *Carpathia* as it passed beyond the horizon, leaving the *Californian* alone among the ever-looming icebergs and drifting ice floes.

Without asking permission, Sam had taken up a position on the foredeck joining the crew in searching the cold gray ocean. Why were they searching? What could they hope to find? Here on this patch of ocean, the *Titanic* had met its fate but it had left nothing behind except thirteen lifeboats and some seven hundred survivors. Of the remaining fifteen hundred there was no sign. Of the great ship itself there was nothing to be seen but a few deckchairs and floating scraps of wood. Nothing! Not even bodies held up by lifejackets.

Where were they? Where were the men, women and children who had not found a seat in a lifeboat? Surely, they should be here, buoyed up by their lifejackets - waiting for rescue or at least for recognition.

As the *Carpathia* steamed away, the *Californian* remained behind, circling the unmarked grave, searching for something, anything that would give them hope.

Was it possible that another lifeboat was somewhere in the vicinity? Thirteen was a very small number and the *Titanic* had carried twenty boats. What had happened to the other seven? The lookouts in the crow's nest of the *Carpathia* had searched the ice field with their binoculars and there had been no sign of other lifeboats or survivors. Now the *Californian* took up the search.

Although the *Carpathia* and the *Californian* had been almost alongside each other for a while, communication was still limited to Marconi messages. So much *should* be said, but only very little *could* be said. The story of the *Titanic* could not be told in the blue sparks of the Marconi machine, or the shuttering and unshuttering of the Morse lamp.

"Sir"

Sam turned to find Alfie standing behind him. He wore the same stunned expression that Sam was seeing on the face of every crew member. No doubt his own face was equally stunned. The truth was almost impossible to accept. The *Titanic* had vanished. He wasn't sure what he'd expected to find, but it certainly was not this... emptiness. The sea had swallowed the *Titanic* whole and left nothing to mark her place. A few more hours and the sea would have swallowed the lifeboats and then there would be no one to tell the tale.

A few more hours? Sam could not help thinking of the midnight lights and the lone rocket. Had they really been that close? Was it possible that he had seen the lights of the *Titanic*? It would be a story to tell his grandchildren. Grandchildren? No that was not going to happen. He could not imagine a future life in which he would be a husband, father and grandfather. There would always be secrets to unearth and he would always be there. He would die with his notebook in his hand.

"Sir," Alfie said again, interrupting Sam's musing on the future.

"Yes?"

"Captain's compliments and would you meet him on the bridge. I'm to escort you."

"I don't need an escort," Sam said. "You keep watch. I'll go alone."

Alfie shook his head. "The captain's called off the search."

Sam's response was visceral. "No! Suppose there's still someone out there."

"The *Franconia* and the *Celtic* are coming up. They've been steaming all night. They'll take over. We're to return to our original course."

Sam followed Alfie into the interior of the bridge deck. His face and fingers tingled in the warmth. He was not aware of how very cold he had been, facing into the wind as the *Californian* steamed in endless, pointless circles. He wondered about frostbite. Surely, he had not been long enough outside but what about those poor devils in the lifeboats?

Alfie stopped abruptly at the door that led to the bridge itself. "Before you go in," he said hesitantly, "could I just say something?"

Sam could only think of meeting Lord face to face. He had things he wanted to say to that man. Questions were already forming in his mind. He dismissed Alfie. "Not now. Tell me later."

"But sir—"

"Not now."

Sam stepped onto the bridge where daylight flooded in through a broad sweep of windows. The atmosphere was hushed. An able seaman was at the wheel with several officers hovering beside him. Lookouts lined the windows. Obviously, Lord did not intend to relax his vigilance until the *Californian* was well clear of the ice field.

Captain Lord, immaculately dressed, greeted Sam with a frosty smile. "Sorry to disturb you."

"You're not disturbing me. I'm told you no longer need me on deck to look for ... debris."

"That is correct," Lord said. "There was no need for you to be involved. You are a passenger. We do not normally put our passengers to work."

"I was glad to help."

"Of course."

Lord was obviously distracted and merely going through the motions of polite conversation. On such a day, polite conversation seemed pointless.

Sam cut the conversation short. "You asked to see me."

"Yes, I did. Come into the chart room. I need a private word with you."

Sam followed the captain into a wood-paneled room located just behind the bridge. He noted a sofa and comfortable chairs and a plotting table where a chart lay unrolled. The chart showed a disconcerting amount of sea, colored in light blue, and only a small amount of white where presumably the land touched the edge of the chart. What he could take from this quick glimpse was the fact that they were very far from land and also the chart had been assiduously studied resulting in lines, numbers and scribbled notations. Next to the chart lay the *Californian's* log book, currently closed.

"In all my years at sea, I have never seen or even imagined a tragedy such as the one we have witnessed," Lord said as he lowered himself into one of the chairs. "Take a seat, Mr. White. As a passenger and not a member of my crew, I feel I can talk to you man to man. I can admit to you that I am quite devastated. Of course, we must all press on. We are back on course for Boston, but ... well..."

Lord seemed to have run out of words and he spread his hands as if momentarily helpless. Sam had trouble reconciling this troubled man with the man he had met in Liverpool. With the *Californian* ready to sail and every other ship in the harbor delayed by the coal strike, Lord had been cold and uncompromising in driving a hard bargain for the price of Sam's passage to Boston. Sam had found nothing likeable about him then - not that it mattered - all he needed was passage to the United States.

"The *Carpathia* is returning to New York with seven hundred and five survivors," Lord said. "That is the final number. There is no possibility of anyone else having survived."

The reporter in Sam wanted to ask questions.

How many of America and Europe's richest men have died?

What are their names?

What about Guggenheim, and Astor, and Thayer?

And one final question. *Was my Aunt Ella saved?*

How absurd. He had no idea if Aunt Ella was even on the Titanic.

He realized that he had no need to ask so many questions. There was an easy way to find the answers for himself. "Captain, do you have a list of survivors?"

Lord shook his head. "No, I believe a list has been sent to Cape Race and, therefore, to New York. My Marconi man did not have time to take it all down. We will find out soon enough, I am sure."

"And what about..."

Again Sam hesitated. This was an impossible conversation. There was no easy way to speak of a thousand or more dead people – people who had been alive just twenty-four hours ago.

He started again. "What about the bodies? We have seen none."

"Well," Lord said, "that is easily answered. Many of them would have gone down with the ship. She kept her lights on until the last moment which means that the stokers stayed below and ..."

It was Lord's turn to hesitate. Sam replayed his words. Had Lord really meant to say that the *Titanic* had kept her lights burning? How would he know that unless he had seen them?

Lord overcame his hesitation and moved on. "As for the people who went into the water – well, their lifejackets will hold them up for a while and keep them on the surface."

"But we didn't see any bodies."

"They're out there," Lord said. "They've drifted with the current. The Labrador Current is strong hereabouts and it's carried them away. I'm afraid they'll soon be clogging the shipping lanes. We've been told not to pick up any that we see. The president has ordered a cable-laying boat out of Halifax to round them up and identify them where possible. The *MacKay Bennet* is built for a task like that and we're not."

"And what will be done with them?"

"They're to be taken to Halifax or buried at sea," Lord said, "depending on their condition and whether they can be identified."

They were both silent for a moment. These were hard words to even say - hard questions to ask.

Lord finally sat back in his seat, his mouth set in a grim line. "Mr. White, I understand you are a newspaper reporter."

"Yes, I am."

"Which newspaper do you represent?"

"I am a freelance journalist."

Why was that so hard to say? Nothing wrong with being freelance. Freelance did not mean failure, it meant that he had not chosen to commit himself to just one newspaper.

"So, you will wish to sell the story of what you have seen here today to the highest bidder and, therefore, you may be thinking that you can use our Marconi man to send reports of what you've seen. This would be something of a scoop for you, wouldn't it?"

Sam shook his head. "No, Captain, this would not be a scoop. I would not be able to beat the New York papers and if we are still headed for Boston..."

"We are."

"And the *Carpathia* is going directly to New York?"

"She is."

"The New York papers will have the story long before I can do anything. The story will be over before I have time to write about it. The newspaper business moves fast these days. This tragedy will be old news after a week or so, replaced by some other excitement."

While he spoke, Sam thought of the financial story he had captured in Scotland. That was a story with legs. That was a story that would affect the lives of every man and woman in the United States who had a bank account. The *Titanic* was a tragedy, but it would be forgotten, subsumed by other stories of other tragedies. In fact, his financial story when he released it could drive the *Titanic* from the headlines.

"Well, it's just a friendly warning," Lord said. "We have only one operator and he is busy. He will not be able to send messages for you."

The captain rose abruptly and extended his hand. "Thank you, Mr. White, for your assistance." He gripped Sam's hand. Their eyes met. Sam found that he could not take the measure of the man. Stanley Lord's nature was shrouded in mystery.

"I doubt we'll speak again," Lord said. "I am a busy man."

He turned away and opened the door for Sam, making it clear that Sam was not welcome to linger on the bridge.

As soon as he was off the bridge, Sam found Alfie waiting for him.

"Well?" Alfie asked.

"Well what?"

"What did he say to you?"

Sam considered the question. What did Lord really say? Was there a warning contained somewhere in that strange conversation?

"He said that the Marconi man is very busy."

Alfie's eyes lit up. "Ah, well, yes ... the Marconi man."

"What about him?"

"He says that he's been given instructions not to send any messages you give him. He's to take them straight to the captain. The captain will decide what messages you can send, if any."

If any! Sam's first instinct was anger, but anger turned to curiosity. Lord wanted to keep him quiet. If Sam tried to send a story, it would not be transmitted.

Why?

Sam thought of the man who had just shaken his hand. Was he a cold-hearted monster who had refused to help a ship in distress, or was he a man who had made a terrible mistake?

CHAPTER EIGHT

Sophie Paxton

On board the *Carpathia*, April 16

Sophie and Maxine stood arguing outside the door of the ship's makeshift hospital. Maxine was, for once, without her husband. Lucan had found a place where men were playing cards. Sophie was glad to be free of his obtrusive presence, but she couldn't resist the opportunity to comment.

"So, he's playing cards," Sophie said. "Is he playing for money?"

"I suppose so."

"Your money?"

"You don't like him, do you?"

"I don't trust him."

Maxine closed her eyes for a moment as if she could only utter the truth if she did not have to look at Sophie. "Neither do I," she whispered.

Sophie could hardly believe her ears. Maxine didn't like Lucan! Then why did she...? "Why did you marry him?" she asked aloud.

"You don't understand about us," Maxine said. "You've been away and no one has ever told you the truth about your fortune. My mother is Aidan Paxton's daughter but that counts for nothing because she had an older brother who was heir to the family fortune. When your father died, Grandfather made an irrevocable trust that you, the daughter of his favorite child, would receive his entire fortune. At the same time, he grudgingly created a trust fund for my mother and me and ..."

Sophie interrupted. There was something she had to know.

"If I was the child of his favorite son, why would he send me away?"

"I remember what he said at the time," Maxine replied. "My mother and I were at the house. Your father had scarcely been buried before Grandfather made his announcement. He would give you into the care of Nanny Bess until you were old enough to be sent away to boarding school. He chose the Howell School because it promised to teach you to be strong and independent. You were a weepy child —"

"I had just lost my parents."

"I know that," Maxine said, "and so did Grandfather, but your grief wasn't important to him. He wanted you to be as close as possible to being a boy, and that's what the Howell School promises."

"No, it doesn't. We're not taught to be boys. We are taught to be independent women."

"Taught to be stubborn," Maxine said.

"All right, maybe I needed to be sent away for my own good so I could learn to cope," Sophie said, "but I don't see why that has anything to do you with you marrying Lucan. It's obvious you're not in love with him."

"I tried to be," Maxine said.

"And now?"

"Now, I don't trust him, but I need his title."

"Why?"

"To make our grandfather happy. We live on grandfather's charity, and he's expressed a desire for one of his granddaughters to marry into the aristocracy. I was determined to get there before you did. I may not be grandfather's heir, but I've done my duty. My son will be the next Lord Sempter."

Sophie looked at her cousin. "Maxine, are you ... "

"Possibly," Maxine replied archly, "and that's the reason that I don't care what Lucan does now. He's done what needed to be done."

A blush suffused Maxine's sallow face and she turned away for a moment. Sophie considered what her cousin had said. *He's done what needed to be done.* Apparently, Maxine was embarrassed by whatever Lucan had done. Teaching at the Howell School had been very straightforward on the how, when and why, and very encouraging about the potential for enjoyment. *Don't be silly and shy. You have a right to enjoy this as much as he does.*

Sophie wished their conversation was taking place in a more private place. Maxine had persuaded her to hobble down to the second-class saloon that had been turned into a hospital. People constantly came and went along the corridor, pushing past in the confined space.

Maxine turned back with her face set in its usual sour expression. "We're not talking about this anymore. This is neither the time nor the place. You have to face facts, Sophie. Your foot is turning black and you are running a fever. You need to see the doctor."

"You're making a fuss about nothing."

Maxine gave Sophie a grim smile. "I hope I am, but you have to show your foot to the doctor. You can't die, Sophie. I won't let you."

"I'm not going to die from hurting my foot,"

"Your life is at risk," Maxine said, "but I won't let it happen."

Sophie shook her head. "I don't understand."

"And I don't want to explain. I don't want to say words that I can't take back."

Sophie studied her cousin's face. "What words? Just say them."

Maxine looked down at the floor, refusing to meet Sophie's eyes. "If I let you die, I would inherit our grandfather's fortune. It is a temptation, Sophie. It really is. Lucan ... No, I really can't say it."

Sophie had trouble finding her voice. "You said that you don't trust him..."

"At first, he thought that I would inherit the money. He didn't know about you."

"Because you didn't tell him."

"I didn't tell him everything. Not until I was sure of the title."

A chill ran down Sophie's spine. She wanted to blame it on her fever, but it was not that kind of chill. "So now that he understands that I'm the heir," she said, "what will he do?"

"I hope he will settle for living extremely well on the money that grandfather has already settled on me. It is better than anything he had in England. He has no money of his own."

Sophie took a deep breath. "I think he tried to push me out of the lifeboat."

Before Maxine could speak, the double doors of the saloon opened and Dick Williams exited and hobbled toward them. His face was set in a mask of pain. "Miss Sophie," he said, "welcome to hell."

Maxine bridled. "Mr. Williams, that is no way to address a lady."

"Sorry," Dick said, "I'm not quite myself." He pushed past them and took several steps along the corridor. He beckoned them toward him. "Please, I have to talk to someone."

Sophie and Maxine stepped toward him.

"What is it?" Sophie asked.

Dick spoke as though he could hardly believe his own words. "There are doctors in there who want to amputate my legs."

Sophie was lost for a meaningful response and could only stutter in disbelief "What? Why?"

"Frostbite." Dick said. "Very severe frostbite."

Sophie gasped. "You're not going to let them do it, are you?"

"No, of course not. I'd rather die which, they say, may happen."

"I don't understand this," Sophie said. "Haven't we been through enough?"

"Yes, we have," Dick said, "and that's why I've come to a decision about something else."

"I don't want to hear about something else," Sophie insisted. "Tell me about your legs. You can't lose them. How would you play? How would we ..."

She stopped speaking, suddenly realizing what she had said. Her concern was not Dick's legs it was her tennis career. Here was her cousin Maxine telling her that just possibly Lord Lucan Sempter was a threat to her life, and here was Dick Williams on the verge of spending the rest of his life in a wheelchair, and still her mind was fixated on what all of that would mean to her tennis career.

She suddenly hated herself. Hated her obsessiveness. Hated her insistence on winning. Where was her compassion? Maxine had been forced into marrying a man she despised, and Dick had lost his father and now he was going to lose his legs. What business did she have to feel sorry for herself?

"Let me speak," Dick said. "I want to tell you my decision. I've decided that if I make it to the Olympics, you, Sophie Paxton, will be my doubles partner. Are you willing to do that? Will you join in my dream and give me some reason to keep going?"

Sophie's heart skipped a beat. Never mind Dick's dream – her dream was about to come true.

No, it's not. He's going to lose his legs and what about your foot?

There's nothing wrong with my foot.

Oh, yes, there is.

But this is my opportunity.

Don't hide from the truth. Go and see the doctor and don't lie to him. It hurts like hell and you need to say that. Get at least one thing right.

"I'm willing if you're willing," Sophie said, "but is it realistic? Would you really rather die than lose your legs?"

"I don't intend to do either," Dick said. "It's just frostbite. My legs were frozen. They've turned black, and the tissue is dying, but my blood is still circulating, and while it circulates there is some hope that I can be saved from gangrene."

Sophie shuddered. His legs had been frozen! Is that what had happened to her foot? Did she have a broken bone or was it this ... this horrible destruction of flesh?

"There's a doctor in there," Dick said, "Doctor Lengyel, he's the only one with common sense. He tells me that if I keep walking and if I don't allow the blood to settle in my legs, there is still hope. I just have to keep moving. I can't rest. I'm going to do it, Sophie. I'm going to beat this and I'll be at the Olympics and you'll be with me. We'll make my father proud."

"Of course, we will," Sophie said with a sudden remembrance of Charles Williams, of his courtesy and his insistence on seeing her into the lifeboat.

"If you're going in to see a doctor," Dick said, "ask for Doctor Lengyel. He's Hungarian and he was an army surgeon. He's rough but he knows what he's doing. There's another doctor taking care of the first-class survivors but their problems are mostly grief and shock. Lengyel has the broken bones, and gashes and ... well, it's all awful."

Maxine interrupted by pulling on Sophie's arm. "Thank you, Mr. Williams. I don't think we need to discuss this any further. Come along, Sophie."

Dick turned to Maxine. "I see that your husband was saved."

"No thanks to you," Maxine said.

Sophie studied Dick's face. There was something he wanted to say, but couldn't say. What was it? What did he know about Lucan Sempter?

"You should warn him," Dick said.

"About what?"

"The men he's playing cards with are professionals. My father knew who they were. He'd seen them on other ships."

"I am quite sure my husband knows what he's doing," Maxine said. She tugged at Sophie's arm. "Come along, Sophie. Good day, Mr. Williams."

When they entered the makeshift hospital, Sophie suddenly forgot everything that had been on her mind. Maxine gasped and clasped Sophie's hand tightly.

Sophie thought she had seen enough horror on the *Titanic*, but in this cramped medical ward, the horror continued to mount. The background noise was coughing - dozens of people coughing, intermingled with groaning. There was weeping, and to go with weeping, the occasional childish shriek. They were all in here – the people with pneumonia, the people with broken bones, the women who had been overcome with hysteria, and the victims of frostbite watching their ears and toes and fingers turning black.

Women bustled about between the beds. Not nurses, Sophie thought, volunteers from the *Carpathia*n's passengers. Women who had paid for a cruise to the Mediterranean were now doing the work of hospital orderlies.

As soon as they entered, they were approached by a weary-looking man in a very good quality suit. Sophie made a rapid judgment. If this man was a doctor, he was doctor to the first-class passengers. He was not Doctor Lengyel.

"Ladies," he said, "I'm Doctor McGee. What can I do for you?"

Sophie was right. This was not Doctor Lengyel. "We want to see Doctor Lengyel," she said.

"Doctor Lengyel? Are you quite sure? If you ladies are having problems, maybe you need something to soothe your nerves or —"

Sophie did not hear his words. Miss Pattison had come to put things right. *Howell girls do not take potions to soothe their nerves. Howell girls face the world head-on.*

Sophie faced Dr. McGee head on.

"I believe I have frostbite and I would like to speak to Dr. Lengyel."

McGee rubbed his hands together. "Well, yes, Lengyel certainly has a good way with frostbite. Unfortunately, he treats all patients as he would treat his soldiers. I will stay with you. He can be very... er ... direct."

Dr. Lengyel was in his shirtsleeves. He was a tall wiry man, with a large moustache and pale blue eyes, red-rimmed from lack of sleep. Sophie perched on a high stool and Lengyel unlaced her boots. They were the high heeled, leather and lace bootees that she had put on as she prepared to go outside and meet Dick Williams. That was no more than thirty-six hours ago but so much had happened in those thirty six hours, that she felt it to be a lifetime ago.

She was very much in the present now. Lengyel drew the boot from her left foot and pain sprang from every toe and every bone. Her big toe was black and the rest of her foot was bluish-white with the skin crumpled like paper. It was a dead thing and yet alive enough to create agony.

Lengyel explored with long nicotine-stained fingers, watching her face as he probed. The pain was diminishing slightly as her bones settled into place without the constriction of the boot. Perhaps there was nothing really wrong. The thought lasted no more than a second and then Dr. Lengyel's fingers found what he was looking for. He pressed on her big toe. She screamed.

"Broken," Lengyel declared. "A broken toe."

"That doesn't seem like much," Sophie said. "I can see that all these people in here are horribly injured. A broken toe is nothing."

"It would be nothing," Lengyel said, "if there was not also this."

His fingers touched a patch of broken skin on her toe. If it was a cut, it had not gone deep. It looked unreal. There was no blood. Perhaps, Sophie thought, because there was no blood in her foot. She was beginning to panic and drew her foot away from him.

"It's frostbite, isn't it," she asked.

Dr. McGee intervened heartily. "I'm sure the frostbite is nothing serious. And the rest is just a broken toe. It will probably heal on its own."

"It could," Lengyel said, "but it may not."

"But nothing serious," McGee prodded, obviously attempting to elicit some encouraging remark from Lengyel. Like every survivor of the disaster, Sophie needed good news, not more bad news.

Lengyel abruptly placed his hand on Sophie's forehead. "Warm," he said. "Too warm You have a fever."

"No, I don't. I feel fine."

"You have a fever. It is nothing now, but you must take precautions." He looked at Maxine. "The skin is broken and that is where infection has entered. You were all night in cold water??

"Yes, I was, or at least my foot was," Sophie said. "The water collected the bottom of the boat. I couldn't move. I was rowing."

Lengyel nodded. "Well done. I am sorry for what is going to happen to you."

"Nothing is going to happen to me."

"We hope," Lengyel said. He looked at Maxine. "Who is this?"

"My cousin," Sophie said.

"Lady Maxine Sempter," Maxine added.

Lengyel was not interested in Maxine's title. "You will watch her," he said. "We have no room in here, so you must watch her."

He drew a broad graphite pencil from his pocket, studied Sophie's foot for a moment and drew a line across the arch of her foot, the pencil making a broad black mark against the disturbingly pale skin. His pale eyes flicked from Sophie to Maxine and back again. "You will watch this line," he said. "If a fever develops, sepsis will follow and this foot will swell. There will be red lines. If any red line crosses the line I have drawn, you will come to me immediately."

"Why?" Sophie asked

"So that I may remove your toe."

"What? You can't remove my toe."

"If you come at once," Lengyel said, "I will remove only your toe. If you delay, I will remove your foot, maybe your leg."

Sophie stared at her foot in horror. "Why?"

"So that you do not die."

Sophie rose from the stool holding her boot in her hand. *So that you do not die!* She was emphatically not going to die – not from a broken toe, or some scraped skin. Her bare foot challenged her with its obnoxious black line. She could not wait to wipe it away.

She crashed out through the double doors and into the corridor. She wanted to be alone but solitude could not be found anywhere on the *Carpathia*. The number of passengers had doubled overnight and the *Titanic* survivors with no possessions, no dry clothes, and no private cabins, milled about, lost, bewildered, and very, very afraid. If the *Titanic* could sink, any ship could sink.

Maxine followed her, calling her name and Dr. McGee followed Maxine. "Lady Sempter, Lady Sempter."

Sophie had only angry thoughts. Dr. McGee had latched onto Maxine's title immediately. Did he even remember Sophie's name? Perhaps Maxine had not been so foolish after all in marrying an English lord. Having an aristocrat in the family would bring prestige to this family of a runaway Scottish nobody. Maxine had done what she could to please their grandfather but it was a poor effort. Would Sophie be expected to do even better? Was she supposed to snag a duke or maybe a prince? That would be hard to do if she was confined to a wheelchair and missing a leg.

Maxine caught hold of Sophie's dress and dragged her to a halt. "Stop running - you can't run away from this."

"I can try," Sophie said. "Didn't you hear what that butcher said. He's going to cut off my toe." Suddenly the *Carpathia* was too small. There was nowhere for her to run to - nowhere to hide from the doctor and his knife.

"Stand still, Sophie," Maxine said firmly. "You're jumping to conclusions. That's not what he said."

Sophie couldn't receive the words. Her mind was racing ahead of the present to a future where she had only half a foot. How could she play tennis with only half a foot? It wasn't going to happen. She wouldn't allow it. Dr. Lengyel had said there would be fever, well, she wasn't hot. She was in fact cold. *Take that, you Hungarian butcher.*

Dr. McGee was in front of her now. "Miss Paxton, come back into the hospital and let me give you something for your nerves."

"I don't have nerves."

"Well, come back anyway and let me explain. Dr. Lengyel is very direct, but he's not always correct."

"He said I'm going to die!"

Sophie felt Maxine giving her arm a vicious shake. "Just stop it, Sophie. You were wonderful in the lifeboat, don't fall apart now."

Dr. McGee was in front of her again. "Miss Paxton, please calm yourself. I can assure you that I will not allow Dr. Lengyel to cut you. In three days, we will be in New York—"

"Has that been decided?" Maxine asked.

"Yes, we have already altered course and we will bring you all to New York. It will be a difficult three days. There's a storm blowing in from the north, so we will have rough weather, but the *Carpathia* is a good old ship. We'll get you safely to New York and you will be able to consult a specialist."

Sophie calmed her racing mind. She should know better than to give way to hysteria. It was only three weeks since she'd graduated from the Howell School as a modern young woman ready to face the world with an independent spirit. Just three weeks and she'd already given in to feminine weakness – not that she didn't have a good excuse.

She straightened her spine. "Thank you, Dr. McGee. I am quite steady now."

McGee nodded. "I will find a stewardess and arrange for clean clothes for you, and a cabin. We are fitting people in wherever we can and our passengers have been very obliging. If you would wait in the first-class saloon, I will make the arrangements. We have managed to keep the first-class areas free of other ... er..."

"Free of immigrants?" Sophie suggested. "I imagine that was not too great a problem. Not many were saved."

McGee corrected her. "There was a surprising number saved, and we are doing what we can for them. Some will not even come inside. They sit on the deck, terrified of being ... well ...

"Being locked in," Sophie said. "That's what happened. They were locked in."

McGee sighed. "Miss Paxton, you are on a Cunard liner now. Whatever happened on the *Titanic* is not our concern. We are going to get you safely to New York, that is our concern. An American senator, I think his name is Smith, has already announced a full inquiry to be convened in New York without delay. The truth, whatever it is, will come out at the inquiry."

"Really, Sophie," Maxine hissed, "the immigrants are none of our business."

"We were immigrants once," Sophie snapped.

"Grandfather Paxton was an immigrant," Maxine corrected, "and things have turned out well for him ... and for you."

"For you too," Sophie said. "You're not exactly poor, Maxine."

As the two cousins glared at each other, each probing for the other's understanding of the situation, Dr. McGee opened the etched glass doors of the first-class saloon. "Here we are, ladies," he said heartily. "I'll send a steward to fetch you when your accommodation has been arranged. Meantime, I suggest tea to soothe your nerves."

"I don't have nerves," Sophie responded.

Whatever else she wanted to say to McGee was halted by a stentorian voice calling from the other side of the room. She knew that voice. Mrs. White.

"Sophie, come here. Come over here. We've all been looking for you."

Sophie slowly accustomed herself to the low light in the saloon. The day was not yet over, but the impending storm had sent a blanket of dark clouds to warn of its imminent arrival. The light through the large windows was grey and dreary and full of foreboding.

Even in the dim light, it was possible for Sophie to recognize her boatmates gathered in a corner on sofas and chairs, and drinking tea. During the long night in Lifeboat #8, Sophie had concentrated on rowing. She knew very few names, although she recognized the Countess of Rothes, Miss Young, and Dr. Leader. Of course, the women gathered here were only the first-class passengers, and not even all of them. The maids and servants who had followed their employers onto the boat were somewhere else on the *Carpathia* as were the second-class passengers and the handful of immigrants.

Mrs. White's eyes swept over Maxine. "Lady Sempter, I hear that your husband was saved."

Maxine nodded, understandably overawed by Mrs. White's formidable presence.

"He was in a boat with Bruce Ismay," Mrs. White added.

"Yes."

"Well, you must be very pleased to have him restored, although I wonder how that came about. It was highly inappropriate for Ismay to save himself while the ship sank."

Maxine looked down at the floor. "I can't comment on that," she said.

"No, of course not," Mrs. White said with something like glee in her voice, "but someone will. So many gallant gentlemen stood back and then there are others like Ismay, Sir Cosmo Duff-Gordon and the list is growing longer as we speak – men who did not do their part. Their names will be revealed."

Dr. Leader spoke up suddenly. "I think that Sophie is unwell. Come over here, dear, and let me look at you."

Mrs. White turned on her. "Not now, Alice. Let us get our important business out of the way first. Come sit down next to me, Sophie and bring your cousin with you."

Sophie and Maxine found a path through the crowded room and entered the circle of seats that, more or less, represented Lifeboat #8.

"Let me come straight to the point," Mrs. White said. "It is my ... our ... belief that there is something the White Star Line is not telling us."

Sophie decided not to be intimidated by Mrs. White. She was just another wealthy bully. Well, Sophie had money of her own – far more money than anyone else in the room. All Mrs. White had was determination. She took a seat in the circle of ladies and spoke to Mrs. White. "White Star is telling us nothing because they have no representative here on the *Carpathia*."

"They have Ismay," Mrs. White countered, "but he has locked himself in the doctor's cabin and refuses to come out. I went with a deputation of ladies to talk to him and he has a sign posted, *Please do not knock*. The arrogance of the man! Please do not knock, indeed! She looked at Maxine. "Perhaps your husband could talk to him, Lady Sempter. It seems they may be friends."

"I'm not aware of any friendship," Maxine said.

"They were in the boat together. They must have had some kind of agreement to take a seat when the boat was only for women and children."

Sophie had a headache and a throbbing pain in her foot. She told herself that if she did not have these distractions, she would stand up for her cousin. Maxine had not been to the Howell School. She did not have Sophie's perspective on the rights of women.It was obvious that Maxine had been tricked into marrying a feckless, penniless man she could not love. In fact, the trick had gone both ways, because Lucan was equally tricked and this had all been done for the sake of an old Scottish man in a lonely mansion in Virginia.

Sophie turned the conversation away from Lord Sempter and back to Mrs. White's original remarks. "What is it you want from the White Star Line?" she asked.

"Compensation of course, and an admission of blame."

"I understand there is to be an inquiry," Sophie said.

"Senator Smith from Michigan," Mrs. White sniffed. "It's political grandstanding, and it won't help us. I am thinking of something else entirely."

"I see," said Sophie, although she did not see. She did not want to see. She wanted to lean back in her seat and close her eyes.

"We were told to row toward a light," Mrs. White said. "We all heard what Captain Smith said, didn't we ladies?"

The ladies agreed, although the Countess of Rothes had something else to say. "We heard him Mrs. White, but now that I've had time to think, I'm not sure I believe him. He was acting very strangely. Why did he give us a loaf of bread? That was not rational. It seemed to me that he was not really in charge of his senses. He could have imagined a light."

"No," Sophie said. "It was there. I saw it and it was a signal light, sending Morse code."

"Hah" said Mrs. White triumphantly. "Well done, Sophie. How can we find someone who knows what it was signaling? Perhaps one of the sailors..."

"I could read it," Sophie said. "I can read Morse code."

The Countess of Rothes looked at Sophie admiringly. "Well done."

Mrs. White had no time to waste on admiration. "What did it say? Tell us what it said."

"It said QRZ which means *Identify Yourself.*"

A murmur of surprise rippled around the circle of ladies. Mrs. White waved them into silence. "So, it was not a random signal, or a trick of the light. It's obvious that another ship was out there on the ice and it was very close by. Captain Smith had seen it. It was not a product of his imagination, and I believe a crime has been committed."

"Many crimes were committed," the countess said. "It was a night of unspeakable violence and failure of compassion and we will hear all about it if we wait for the senate hearings. We can say nothing until then."

"If we say nothing now," Mrs. White said," we will not be believed in the future. I wish to speak now, although I don't know who will hear me. Do any of you understand what I'm saying? The captain of the *Titanic* is not alone in shouldering the blame for our sorry condition."

"The other ship," Miss Young said tentatively.

"Exactly. Thank you, Marie. I am talking about the captain of that other ship. If he was so close that we could see his light, why didn't he come to our aid? Why didn't he lower his lifeboats and come to us?"

Sophie could not prevent her thoughts from spiraling into anger. She thought of the hours that her broken foot had been immersed in freezing water. She imagined the ice crystals forming in her flesh and her foot slowly dying. How long had that taken? Could it have been avoided if the mystery ship had come to them immediately? Was there truly a ship's captain who had seen their lights, signalled with his Morse lamp, and then sailed away leaving thousands of people to drown?

"Ladies," Mrs. White said, "if no one else will do this, then we will do it. As soon as we reach New York, I will find out the name of that ship and together we will point the finger of blame at the man who truly hurt us."

Sophie thought of the ship that had come up on the *Carpathia* as she was taking up the last of the lifeboats. Where had she come from? How had she managed to be the second ship on the scene? What was her name? Oh yes, *Californian.*

CHAPTER NINE

John Alder
On board the Carpathia, April 17

The storm heralded its arrival with a crack of thunder that sent many of the traumatized survivors to their knees. *Had they hit another iceberg? Was this new ship going to sink.* The survivors who had refused to go below decks for fear of being locked in again, were now forced to concede defeat and take shelter. Waves broke across the *Carpathia's* bow, and the dangerously overloaded ship rolled and pitched as the storm churned the deep, cold water.

Through the hours of turmoil, Dick Williams continued to walk, and John walked with him. They traced a path through the public rooms, observing women who had paid for a cruise to the Mediterranean now cutting up their spare clothing and sewing dresses and shirts for the immigrants who left the *Titanic* with nothing. They walked the mattress-strewn corridors where hollow-eyed women and children crouched in terror of the storm. They ascended to the deck and saw that the surviving *Titanic* officers and crew were taking their turn at standing watch. They even walked through the galleys where food was carefully apportioned to feed twice as many people as planned at each meal. They heard rumors and rumors of rumors.

John, using his senate credentials, managed to tease some information from Cottam, the Marconi officer, although Cottam was circumspect.

"Mr. Marconi reserves the right to my story," Cottam said. "I'm his employee and I do what he says but..."

"... but what?" John asked. "Tell me what you can."

"Rumors, that's all. The newspapers have it all wrong. Some say no lives were lost, some say all lives were lost. Some say it was sabotage. I've sent the list of survivors but it's not good enough. Some people are convinced there are survivors elsewhere – maybe trapped on the ocean floor in a watertight compartment —

John interrupted him with a contemptuous snort. "Even if that were possible, they would be dead by now. No one can survive at that temperature."

"I know that," Cottam said, "but I'm not responsible for the rumors. I'm sending messages all the time on behalf of Captain Rostron but until we arrive in New York, no one is going to believe the scale of this disaster or the wealth and standing of the people who died. Even your American president is asking questions. He's planning on sending a gunboat out to meet us."

John, who had met President Taft on several occasions could only shake his head in disbelief. "A gunboat! How is that going to help?"

Cottam would not meet his eyes. "I shouldn't have said that. Some of the messages are highly confidential."

John could see the strain and weariness on the young man's face. He gripped Cottam's shoulder for a moment. "Don't apologize. You didn't sign up to be the go-between in presidential politics, or the center point of such a disaster. Is there anything else you can tell us without compromising yourself?"

Cottam nodded. "It's general knowledge now that Senator Smith from Michigan has formed a committee to investigate." He looked at John. "You work in the senate, Mr. Alder, do you know the senator?"

"I've met him," John said. "He's ambitious. He has his eye on the presidency. This will put him ahead in the race."

"Good for him." Dick said bitterly. "Someone should find out what the hell happened."

"Yes, they should," John agreed. He glanced down at Dick's feet. "Someone should answer for this because it was not an Act of God. It was a terrible man-made mistake. Let's leave Cottam in peace. He's already told us more than he should." He extended a hand to Cottam. They shook hands and Cottam walked away, presumably heading for the radio shack perched on the bridge deck.

John looked at his exhausted friend. "Let's walk a little longer," he said. "Does Dr. Lengyel think it's working for you?"

"He's holding out hope," Dick said, "and I still have my legs. I have faith in him. That's what I told Sophie Paxton. I told her not to waste time with the other doctors and to go straight to Dr. Lengyel."

John kept his tone casual. He was not ready to betray his special interest in Sophie Paxton. "Why did Miss Paxton need a doctor?"

"Frostbite," Dick said. "Or at least I think that's what it was. We didn't have much of a conversation. I had just discovered that, unless I did something about it, I was going to lose my legs and my mind was all over the place. You know me, John. You know I'm not usually impulsive but there had been so much bad news, so much tragedy that I suddenly wanted to brighten someone's day and I wanted to reassure myself that I would make it to the Olympics."

"So, what did you do?" John asked.

"I told her I wanted her to partner with me at the Olympics. It was a stupid thing to do, but I did it anyway. I don't even know if she's really good enough. If my father was here, he would..."

John recognized his friend's silence. Surrounded by so much death and so much pain, Dick had pushed aside his grief, but it was still there, traveling with him as he walked the deck. There was no point in pursuing that grief now – that would have to come later when they were ashore – better for him to concentrate on other things.

"What did Miss Paxton say?" John asked. "Did she say that she would do it?"

"She couldn't talk," Dick said. "She had that sour cousin of hers with her, and they were looking for a doctor. I said that if she had frostbite, she should see Dr. Lengyel and no one else."

"But she didn't actually say frostbite?"

"I don't think so, but I was not really in a state to remember. I think I actually swore, not at her, but definitely within earshot."

"No one can blame you for that," John said. "You had really bad news, and, anyway, she seems to be an independent kind of young lady, and not easily shocked."

Dick looked at him. "You like her?"

"I don't really know her," John said.

"But nonetheless..." Dick teased.

"She is going to be one of the richest women in America," John said. "She will have plenty of choice."

"But you saved her life."

"No, I think that it was your father who saved us all by recognizing what was happening."

Dick shook off the mention of his father. "Well, I'm worried about her," he said. "If she had frostbite and if it hasn't been treated, it would be manifesting the worst symptoms just about now.

When I went in to see Dr. Lengyel this morning he was performing surgery. The ship was rolling and pitching but his hands were steady and he had his patients lined up, all men, and mostly crew. He was cutting off ears and finger tips and parts of noses that had already turned back. It wasn't pretty and it was obviously painful. He says he has very little in the way of anesthetics and he is saving that for more serious surgery. The small surgeries he's doing will prevent gangrene and sepsis and possibly death."

John's heart was suddenly pounding. He could not imagine that Sophie, who would soon be the darling of society, would have to submit to a Hungarian army surgeon nipping off her ears or fingers. Suppose the frostbite was not limited to her fingers. Could she possible be as damaged as Dick and about to lose her legs, or could the frostbite have attacked her face? Her nose?

Surely not. Not while he... *No, that train of thought was completely inappropriate - Sophie Paxton, heiress to a fabulous fortune, and Jonathon Alder, aspiring politician with nothing but a modest salary and a good education – not likely. Sophie could snag a duke, maybe even a prince. On the other hand, fate had thrown them together. Perhaps fate would keep them together.*

Dick pushed open the door of the smoking room and John tamped down his spiraling worries. They were greeted by a fog of cigarette and cigar smoke and a distinctly masculine odor emanating from a crush of unwashed men. These were not poor men unaccustomed to bathing, they were men who had previously prided themselves on their immaculate evening wear. Now they were sea-soaked and salt-stained. Their expensive watches no longer worked and their gold fountain pens were at the bottom of the ocean, along with their shaving materials, pomades, and moustache brushes. And also their valets.

Thunder cracked and the *Carpathia* dove into a wave, rolling as she plunged. Dick, swept off his unsteady feet, stumbled and fell against a table and John lunged for a chair, missed and ended up sprawled on the floor with men shouting angrily above him. It seemed that he and Dick had got themselves into the middle of a card game and tempers were running hot.

John had no fear for his personal safety. He knew how to look after himself, but Dick was vulnerable as he tried to regain his footing. John sprang up, ready to take on all comers. Some of these men were fools. Having just won at the greatest lottery of all by surviving the *Titanic*, they now seemed intent on testing that luck again against one of the greatest social hazards of ocean travel - card sharks.

It was no secret that professional card sharks traveled on every ocean liner. The shipping lines could warn the passengers, but they could not prevent their presence. It stood to reason that there had been card sharks on the *Titanic*, and they were, no doubt, the kind of men who would find a place in a lifeboat. No doubt the *Carpathia* also had a couple of home-grown card sharks on board. Now John and Dick seemed to have literally landed in the midst of them. John was disgusted. How stupid could these men be? The fact that Lord Lucan Sempter was in their midst came as no surprise.

The melee resolved itself without anyone resorting to fists or pistols. The players resumed their seats and John helped Dick to find a chair where he could sit and rest his legs – not for long – not long enough for the blood to pool in his veins.

The bar in the smoking room was open for business, presumably operating on an IOU basis. John could hardly blame the survivors for taking to drink, but drinking combined with gambling was a foolish occupation for foolish men, and the most foolish seemed to be Lucan Sempter.

John could hear the quiet conversation of two men who stood at the bar. From the fact that one of them sported a bandage around his head, and they both wore salt-stained evening clothes, John knew them to be *Titanic* survivors. From the way they observed the cards, he thought they could be professionals, but they were obviously not about to join in.

The blond stocky man shook his bandaged head. "I thought we had an agreement. We agreed not to do this," he said.

"No Charlie, you and I agreed," the other man said, "and Towson agreed, but it looks like the small fish won't give up the game."

"Haven't these people lost enough?" Charlie asked.

"Apparently, they're hoping to make up for their losses. Look at that damned fool English lord, I know his type. He's up to his eyebrows in IOUs. He's well and truly hooked."

"He's good for it," Charlie said. "Seems he's married money. His wife is an heiress and he says she's about to come into her fortune."

John edged closer. They were obviously talking about Lord Lucan Sempter, but John had understood that Sophie was the Paxton heiress, and Maxine was merely a relative, so how did Lucan plan to come into a fortune? It was a troubling question. The only way Maxine could become the heiress would be if Sophie... *Where was Sophie now? Why had he not encountered her in the dining room or any of the public rooms?*

"Lady Sempter is heiress to old man Paxton and he's worth millions, if not billions," Charlie said. "She married his lordship for his title, and I assume he married her for her money."

John considered informing them that Maxine was not the heiress, but he thought better of it. These two men were not at risk from Lucan. Apparently, they had agreed not to con the survivors and they were staying away from the card tables. It was a small point in their favor. *Honor among thieves.* No doubt that they would replenish their wardrobes and be back on board another liner before the end of the month, but, at least these thieves had some decency. As for the men who were playing now - let them play. Let Lord Lucan write his worthless IOUs, and let him take the consequences. John had better things to do. He needed to find Sophie.

He looked back at Dick Williams who had slumped into one the chairs that were bolted to the floor. The storm was playing havoc with anything that was not bolted down, but Dick seemed to be securely in place. John, once again checked his watch, and, once again remembered that it was not working. The hands pointed to 2:15. The watch had stopped when he leaped from the deck of the *Titanic* and went down into the bone-chilling water. He would buy a new watch in New York, but this one he planned to keep. Something to show his grandchildren.

Would they care?

Probably not. By the time I have children, the *Titanic* will be forgotten.

He tapped Dick on the shoulder. "I'm going to find Sophie. Are you coming with me?"

Dick groaned.

"How bad is it?" John asked.

"Like walking on hot coals," Dick said.

Maxine Paxton, Lady Sempter
On board the *Carpathia*, April 17

"My leg is on fire," Sophie whispered. "Help me, Maxine. Do something."

Maxine hesitated with a cold cloth in her hand. She had been wiping her cousin's brow for hours as the fever mounted and Sophie tossed and turned on the narrow bunk in the tiny cabin. It was a cabin designed for a lady's maid, so the maid would be close to her mistress in the first-class cabin nearby. Now it was a sickroom.

Maxine resumed her futile wiping. Sophie was burning with fever and this was all that Maxine knew how to do.

Sophie's hand shot out and caught Maxine's wrist. "My foot," she whispered. "Look at my foot."

"I've looked at it," Maxine lied. She had not been the one to look at Sophie's foot. It was Lucan who had looked just about an hour ago as he was making his way to the smoking room to play cards.

"This is nonsense," Lucan had said. "Who ever heard of a doctor drawing lines on his patients? You say the man is Hungarian?"

"Yes, that's what I heard."

"Then this is some kind of Magyar folk magic," Lucan said. He took the cold cloth from Maxine's hand and swiped it across Sophie's foot. "There you are," he said, "all gone. Just keep bathing her. That's what my nanny always did for me when I had a fever. There is absolutely no point in taking her to the hospital and putting her in the hands of an ignorant butcher."

"There's another doctor," Maxine said. "Doctor McGee is the doctor for first-class."

Lucan dropped the sheet back over Sophie's foot. "She doesn't need a doctor." He paused and Maxine felt his eyes assessing her. Before they were married, he had assessed her this way and had always seemed delighted with what he saw. Now his assessment was critical. "Don't question my judgement, Maxine. I know what I'm doing."

"But you're not a doctor..."

"I'm your husband and I'm looking out for our interests. I know what I'm doing. Bathe her with cold water. She'll be fine."

Maxine moved from the one and only chair and sat at the foot of Sophie's bunk. The *Carpathia* dropped into a trough in the waves, and her bow pitched down in a sickening remembrance of the *Titanic's* final moments. *No one has said the Carpathia is unsinkable.* The sudden movement tossed Maxine against Sophie's foot. Sophie screamed as Maxine's weight fell on her foot.

The *Carpathia* leveled out and resumed her course on an even keel. Maxine sat back and stared down at the sheet draped over Sophie's foot. She should look for herself. Grandfather Paxton had made her responsible for bringing Sophie home. She had won the old man's approval by marrying into the British aristocracy, but she could lose it very easily if anything happened to Sophie.

What do you mean by "happened"?

Well, if this fever...

Killed her?

No, not that.

That's what you're thinking. That's what Lucan is thinking. If anything happens to Sophie, you'll inherit the old man's money.

I would never harm her.

Then look at her foot!

Maxine lifted the sheet. This was a maid's room. It had no porthole and only a single light fitting hanging from the ceiling on a short chain. As the *Carpathia* wallowed through another wave, the light swung wildly, casting a light on the foot and then swinging away. Even so, Maxine could see that Lucan had not entirely wiped away the line that Dr. Lengyel had drawn across Sophie's foot.

"There will be red lines. If any red line crosses the line I have drawn, you will come to me immediately."

"Why?"

"So that I may remove your toe. So that you will not die."

Maxine studied Sophie's foot. The big toe had turned completely black with the skin cracking open like a sausage cooked on a grill. The foot was no longer shrunken and deathly white, it was pink and swollen. The small scrape that Dr. Lengyel had noticed was livid with a thin tracery of red lines reaching out across the foot. As the light swung toward the bunk, Maxine saw the shadowy marking left by Lucan's attempts to erase Dr. Lengyel's line. One red line, more pronounced than the others, was there already, nudging the line – nudging Maxine's conscience. What should she do? Sophie herself had sworn that she would not lose her toe.

She looked down into her cousin's flushed face. "Sophie…"

"My leg is on fire."

"It's your toe. Remember the doctor drew a line and said that if the infection passed that line, he would have to cut off your toe. Do you remember that, Sophie?"

Sophie's eyes were wide and unfocused. Maxine leaned down close. "Sophie, your toe is black and split like a burnt sausage."

"Fire," Sophie whispered.

"I think the doctor will have to take it off."

Sophie sat up in the bunk. Her hair was wild and unbound. The fever sweat had molded her shift to her body. Her cheeks burned with two red fever spots but her eyes were suddenly in focus "Butcher," she hissed. "You wouldn't dare." She stared around the cabin, seeing something that Maxine could not see – perhaps it was the tennis courts of the Berlin Olympics. Perhaps it was her dream dying here at the hands of an army surgeon.

As suddenly as she had returned to clarity, Sophie slipped away again, throwing herself back against the pillows. Her eyelids fluttered closed. Maxine rose and went to the cabin door. She needed to speak to someone. Not Lucan – she could not trust his judgment, or anything else about him. She should find Dr. McGee. Dr. Lengyel was harsh and slightly crazed, but Dr. McGee had a way of putting her mind at rest. She should go and look for him.

And leave Sophie alone?

That would be almost a relief.

She opened the cabin door. Despite the storm, there had been an illusion of quiet and privacy in the cabin with the door closed. Opening the door brought her out into the chaos of the *Carpathia* – the passageways crammed with wild-eyed survivors, and the shocked but compassionate passengers who had expected to be at Gibraltar by now. She assumed that Dr. McGee would be in the hospital. She would have to go and fetch him, although that would mean leaving Sophie alone. How long would it take? How fast was the red line moving. Could anyone stop its progress?

As she stepped out into the passageway, she realized that she recognized one of the people approaching her. It was Dick Williams, and despite the rolling of the ship and the need to hold onto the handrail, Dick appeared to be making progress with his walking. Perhaps he was going to recover after all.

Maxine was happy for him, and happy also that he was here. He could help her. "Mr. Williams."

Dick was not alone. He was accompanied by a man who looked to be a few years older than Dick. It took Maxine a moment to place him. She had last seen him on the deck of the *Titanic*, standing back so that women and children could enter Lifeboat #8. What was his name? Oh, yes, he was Jonathon Alder and he was what she needed. She could send him to fetch Dr. McGee. Dick was still moving slowly but Mr. Alder looked perfectly fit.

She was not prepared for the look of utter relief as Mr. Alder recognized her. He did not bother with the niceties of polite conversation. "Lady Maxine, thank heaven we found you. Where is your cousin? Where is Sophie?"

Maxine gestured to the cabin. "In there. She's... she's..."

"She's what?"

"I think she is very ill. I'm very concerned. I need someone to fetch the doctor."

Maxine was taken aback as Alder swept past her and into the cabin. Had he no sense of propriety? He should at least ask if she was receiving visitors. *She's not dressed. She's in her shift.*

"We've been looking for you," Dick said. "I was concerned because frostbite has been turning to gangrene in some of Dr. Lengyel's patients. I had to know if Miss Sophie is having any symptoms."

"I don't like Dr. Lengyel," Maxine said.

"He' a good surgeon."

"He wants to remove her toe."

Dick was silent but Maxine could read everything in his face. He knew what it would mean, even if she did not.

"He drew a line on her foot," Maxine explained. He said that if she had fever, and if the red line from her toe crossed the line he had drawn, I must bring her to him."

"And has that happened?"

Maxine nodded dumbly.

"Then we must take her."

"She doesn't want to go."

Alder appeared in the doorway. He had wrapped Sophie in a blanket and he carried her in his arms. "We're going now," he said. "You must come with us, Lady Maxine, to give permission."

"For what?"

"For the amputation."

CHAPTER TEN

Sophie Paxton
On board the *Carpathia*, April 18

Sophie reluctantly emerged from a deep, brain-dead sleep. She lay still for a moment, unwilling to open her eyes as she gathered up her scattered senses. She was still on the *Carpathia* - she could feel the pulse of the engines. It seemed the storm was over and the *Carpathia* was riding smoothly.

She was in a bed, but not the bunk in her borrowed cabin. She was in a large room and she could sense movement all around her. Fire! Her leg had been on fire. How had ice turned to flame and burned her skin until it was black and split open?

Someone had put out the fire and replaced it with a throbbing pain. She chased the flash of memory and found Dr. Lengyel in a white coat with a tray of instruments and a tool that looked more like it should be used to prune roses. Someone pressed a cloth to her nose. Ether, and then nothing – no memory at all until the first awakening. She had screamed. She didn't mean to. She was a Howell girl and Howell girls do not scream. But this Howell girl screamed a scream that was made up of many things that could not be contained...

The death of a great ship,

A night of despair,

Pain, of course,

Realization – there would be no Olympics.

Anger – who had given permission for this?

Fear that someone would try to kill her – she could not put a face on that person.

Could not or would not?

After the scream had come a soothing voice and an injection. She had spiraled down into sleep. Now she was clawing her way out of that comfortable well and back into reality and a world that had surely changed for her, but by how much? She had to know.

Despite his poor English, Dr. Lengyel had made himself very clear, even shouting at the man who had carried her into the hospital suite. Who was that man? She was not sure, but he had been strong and she had felt safe with him.

"Fools!" Lengyel shouted. "I told you what to do. Why do you wait so long? Now we have gangrene, next we will have sepsis. You have left me no choice. I will have to amputate below the knee."

Sophie remembered hearing the words, felt herself physically shriveling. This could not be true. The leg was on fire – let it keep on burning. Let the burn spread to her whole body. She would not lose her leg. She would rather die!

A man had spoken. His voice was faintly familiar, but she had no name to go with the voice. He was bargaining with Dr. Lengyel – bargaining for Sophie's leg. "Take the toe. Only the toe."

And Maxine's voice, hesitant and tearful. "Only the toe. Yes, only the toe."

The memory was clear now and the question was pressing. What had Dr. Lengyel taken? Had the unknown man won the argument? Did Sophie still have her leg? She could feel pain in her leg and that must be a good sign. A leg that was not there could not hurt, but what about half a leg – could that hurt? She opened her eyes. Her legs were covered with a sheet. She moved her left leg. Although movement ratcheted up the throbbing pain, she saw her shape beneath the white sheet. She still had two legs. So, what had Dr. Lengyel taken with the garden pruning shears? Her toe? It had to be her toe.

She closed her eyes again and tried to find the morphine-induced peace of just moments before. She had not lost her leg, but she had lost her big toe. What did that mean? How would she function? Would there be tennis? Dick Williams had invited her to be his partner. She held onto that thought and grasped at the wispy tendrils of sleep.

For a moment she was able to drift and then she heard a familiar voice. Maxine was close by, probably standing next to the bed.

"She's not awake yet."

"Does she still have a fever?"

That voice came from the other side of the bed. Maxine's husband was here. Sophie kept her eyes closed.

A hand brushed Sophie's forehead. "She feels cool. I think she is all right."

Lucan seemed less than thrilled by Sophie's lack of fever. "There you are then. It was probably nothing in the first place. You all panicked. None of this was necessary. You should never have given permission. I told you not to bring her here."

"Her toe was black and splitting open," Maxine protested. "The infection had moved beyond the line the doctor drew on her foot."

"That was ridiculous" Lucan said. "I don't trust that foreign fellow for a moment. If you had just waited until we got to New York, we could have taken her to a specialist."

"I'm sorry Lord Sempter but delay was impossible." That was Dr. McGee speaking and soothing the first-class patient with his first-class bedside manner. No doubt he'd been sent in to explain what marvelous feat of entirely necessary surgery the foreign doctor had accomplished with his pruning shears.

"You had no right to mutilate her," Lucan said.

"We saved her life, your lordship," McGee said. "This was the best we could do."

"So will she live?" Lucan asked.

"Oh Lucan," Maxine said, "how can you ask such a question? Of course she will live."

"I'm just making sure," Lucan said. "Her life is in your hands, Maxine. You gave permission for this ridiculous surgery and I'm just finding out if any more surgery will be needed."

"We think we have caught the infection," McGee said, "but one can never be certain. These are extreme circumstances."

"My wife will not be giving her permission again," Lucan said. "Is that understood?"

"Of course," Dr. McGee said. "Now, if you'll excuse me, I have other patients."

Sophie heard the doctor's retreating footsteps and then Maxine was speaking again in feeble protests. "Lucan, what if...?"

"No, Maxine, you will not give your permission again. Leave this up to me. I'm responsible for your cousin. I'm the man of your family on this ship."

Sophie bit down on words of protest. *You're not the man of our family. Grandfather is the man of our family.*

Now Lucan was urging his wife to leave. "We'll go before she wakes up. You don't want to be here when she finds out what's happened to her foot. Your cousin seems to be very quick tempered, and no doubt she'll blame you."

"I had to do it," Maxine said. "I couldn't find you, and Mr. Alder and Mr. Williams said ..."

Mr. Alder – so that's who had carried her into the hospital – John Alder, Dick Williams' friend.

"I was in the smoking room and that's where I'm going now."

"Oh, Lucan, must you really go back there? My income is not —"

"Your income is not what I was led to believe," Lucan said. "I am attempting to make up the difference."

"By gambling?"

"Do you have a better suggestion?"

"I'm not poor. I'm just not as rich as Sophie."

"And how is your grandfather? How long will it be before Sophie comes into her inheritance?"

"Really Lucan, I don't think that is a polite question."

"How long?"

"Grandfather is not well. He's usually confined to a wheelchair."

"He and Sophie should make a good pair," Lucan said.

Sophie kept her eyes shut and listened carefully to their voices. Lucan's voice was filled with irritable impatience, but Maxine's tone had changed. She could recall scraps of a conversation she'd had with Maxine. When was that? Oh yes, when they made their first visit to the doctor. Had Maxine really said that she did not trust her husband or was that wishful thinking on Sophie's part?

A woman's voice interrupted the marital squabbling between Lord and Lady Sempter. "I shall have to ask you to leave now. I need to take care of Miss Paxton."

Sophie assessed the voice. English, and even more aristocratic that Lord Sempter. It was the voice of a woman who was completely in control of the situation and it held not even a hint of deference to Lord Sempter's title.

Sophie heard a rustle of clothing. Someone, it had to be Maxine, planted a light kiss on her forehead and the footsteps retreated. Sophie opened her eyes. She was in a large, brightly lit room, the light coming from electrical fixtures in the ceiling. Gymnastic equipment had been pushed to one side to make room for maybe fifteen beds. A tall, sandy-haired young woman was standing by her bed. She wore a dark dress and a starched white apron embroidered with the Cunard logo. A nurse?

The woman smiled and answered the unasked question. "Hello, Miss Paxton, I'm Poppy Melville, I'm a first-class stewardess from the *Titanic*. We are all back on duty again, wearing borrowed aprons. Dr. McGee has asked me to make sure that you're comfortable. I'm not a nurse, but I'm afraid we're very short of nurses. I will do my best for you."

"From the *Titanic*," Sophie queried weakly. "You were saved from the *Titanic*?"

"Yes, we were all saved, all the female staff. We were given a few days to rest but White Star wants us back on duty. I come from a big family, and I'm quite used to taking my turn in the sickroom.

"This is the *Carpathia's* gymnasium and it's been set aside for women. Fortunately. there are not as many sick and injured women as there are men. Very few women took to the water and survived. Most of us were in lifeboats."

Sophie was still teasing at the question of the woman's voice. She knew that by wondering about the woman in the apron, she was only delaying the inevitable moment when she would have to look at her foot. *Well, why not delay the inevitable?*

"You don't sound like a stewardess."

"Nonetheless, that is what I am. My name is Poppy, and I am here to help you. It looked as though you were not enjoying the company of your visitors."

"I kept my eyes closed. How did you know what I was thinking?"

"I was thinking that I would not have enjoyed their company," Poppy said. "I'm afraid there has been considerable dispute about your surgery and many questions about your condition. The two gentlemen who brought you in have been asking to see you."

"I don't want to see anyone."

"I understand."

Poppy allowed a long moment to pass before she spoke again. "Do you want to see it?"

"See what?"

"Your foot."

Sophie cringed. "No!"

"Are you sure? It may not be as bad as you think. It was very neatly done."

"You've seen it?"

"I was present during the surgery. As I said, we are very short-handed and I am not squeamish."

"They took my toe?"

"They were going to take your entire foot," Poppy said. "Dr. Lengyel had to be dissuaded."

"By whom?"

Poppy smiled. "I spoke up for you, Miss Paxton. You are still young and I imagine that you enjoy dancing, and —"

"Tennis," Sophie said. "I was going to play in the Olympics."

Poppy's face fell. "I am so sorry."

Sophie looked at Poppy's face and realized that the stewardess was pitying her. She pulled herself together. *She could almost see Miss Pattison's windburned face and cropped hair, and hear her shouted instructions to any unfortunate Howell girl who showed fear. Animus omnia vincit, young lady. Courage conquers all. Excelsior, girls. Onward and upward.*

Sophie levered herself upward into a sitting position. "All right, Poppy. Let me see how bad it is."

"You have to remember how bad it was before," Poppy said

"I didn't see it clearly," Sophie admitted, "but I know how much it hurt. I thought my leg was on fire."

"I shouldn't take the dressing all the way off," Poppy said, "just enough for you to see the shape of your foot."

Sophie held her breath as Poppy unwound the bandage that encompassed her entire foot. Slowly the foot began to emerge and she could see her small toes. She wiggled them, and they moved – all four of them – and where a big toe should exist, nothing but cotton padding.

Sophie stared down at her truncated foot and pushed Miss Pattison and her calls for courage aside. She didn't want to be brave. She wanted to be angry. Who had done this to her? There was a list, of course.

Dr. Lengyel, with his pruning shears.

Maxine, who given in to the doctor and permitted the surgery.

Mr. Alder, a man she hardly knew, who had carried her against her will to the hospital.

But if she chose to be angry with any of these people, then she could not be angry with Lucan Sempter who had tried to stop the surgery. No, that was not right. She was going in the wrong direction. Go back. Go all the way back.

Captain Smith, who had run his ship into an iceberg. He was dead, so her anger at him could never be satisfied.

Bruce Ismay, who owned the ship, or at least some part of it, but he hadn't been in charge of the ship.

Was there anyone else, or would she have to just accept her loss as an Act of God? No. Perhaps no one could have prevented the ship from sinking, but frostbite had not come from the sinking. It had come from the long hours in the lifeboat. It was not God who held the responsibility for that, it was the captain of another ship, - the one that had sent signals across the ice field and then had failed to move.

Now she remembered Mrs. White and the committee of women who had already assigned blame for what had happened. She felt a warm bubble of righteous anger forming around her heart and pushing all else aside. Now she knew what to do. She would get out of this bed and she would find that captain – the man who had abandoned the *Titanic's* passengers to their fate. She would find the man who had destroyed her dreams.

A small voice in the back of her mind prompted her to be reasonable but reason was not as warm and comforting as pure anger. She settled back against the pillows and allowed rage to take the place of all other emotions.

John Alder
On board the *Carpathia*

Fog! The *Carpathia's* horn sounded its warning into the grey unknown as she made her way cautiously toward New York Harbor. First a storm, and then a fog – John Alder wondered how much more the weather gods could throw into the path of the *Carpathia*.

He stared blindly into the gray mist, his thoughts bitter and full of foreboding. How long could Dick Williams continue to walk the deck? He needed to see a real doctor in a real hospital. What about Sophie Paxton? What kind of recovery would she make now that Lengyel had amputated her toe? Would she blame him for taking her to the hospital?

He hadn't seen Lady Sempter again. She seemed to be in hiding although her husband was most certainly making his presence known. He was still spending his time in the smoking room, and still writing IOUs. The professional gamblers knew they had him truly hooked.

John knew something that the gamblers didn't know. He knew that Lucan Sempter had no money. Sempter's wife was not the heir to a great fortune and the true heiress was Sophie Paxton. In normal circumstances, the gamblers would not make such a rookie mistake. Usually, they set their goals in advance, knowing the wealth of every gambling man on the ship. They had made a mistake this time.

John could not help thinking that Sempter was hoping that Lengyel's surgery would not be enough to halt the sepsis and Sophie would succumb to her injuries. The doctors were now very short of medicines of all kinds. The *Carpathia's* passengers had been asked to surrender any patent medicines that they had been carrying for their own use, but painkillers were in very short supply. John was certain that Sophie was in pain but there was little he could do about the situation except to pace the deck and curse the weather.

His troubled thoughts were interrupted by the arrival of a crew member carrying a message from Captain Rostron. *Would Mr. Alder please meet him in the chart room at his earliest convenience.*

John allowed the crew member to lead him up to the bridge deck. Unlike the rest of the ship, the bridge was a place of ordered calm. The instruments glowed in the dim light and the windows were shrouded in fog. It was as though the *Carpathia* was drifting in a world of her own except, of course, for the sound of the fog horn – as lonesome as a train whistle in the night. *"I am here. Where are you?"*

Captain Rostron met him as he entered the bridge. This was the first time that John had spoken personally to the man who had saved his life – saved all their lives. Arthur Rostron was a tall, upright man, and John judged him to be around forty years old. He had shouldered an enormous responsibility in racing to the rescue of the *Titanic* passengers, but he carried the responsibility well, showing few signs of the tension he must be feeling. He was immaculately dressed in his Cunard uniform, and he greeted John with a firm handshake.

"Mr. Alder, you must be wondering why I have asked to meet you."

"I am glad to have the chance to shake your hand," John said truthfully. "I am indebted to you for my life."

"I have done what any sailor would have done," Rostron said. "This fog is keeping us busy, and I have little time to spare, but I have a pressing problem with one of your fellow passengers. According to information I have received, you hold a position in the U.S. Senate, is that correct, Mr. Alder?"

"I am senior aide to Senator Eldridge of Ohio."

"So, you are familiar with the workings of the U.S. Senate?"

"Of course."

"In that case, I would appreciate your assistance. As you are most probably aware, Mr. Bruce Ismay, Chairman of the White Star Line, is on board."

"I think that many of us are aware of that fact," John said.

He did not add that he also knew that Ismay had locked himself away and refused to speak to any of the survivors. He had even turned away a deputation of the richest and most powerful women on board. His steadfast refusal to interact with the survivors had sparked resentment that would no doubt boil over into fury by the time the *Carpathia* reached New York.

"He has asked me to find someone on board who can assist him in communicating with the U.S. Senate. I am hoping that you can speak with him," Rostron said. He gave John a self-deprecating smile. "Mr. Ismay and I are Englishmen and we don't fully understand the workings of your Government, but Mr. Ismay has received several worrying communications."

"If someone will take me to him, I'll certainly do my best to explain things," John said. He kept his voice steady although he was actually burning with curiosity.

Captain Roston was not yet finished with him. "Mr. Alder, were you familiar with Major Archibald Butt. Did you see him on board the *Titanic*?"

'Oh yes, of course. I knew him already as a special envoy for President Taft, and he's a sociable fellow. He certainly made his presence known on board."

"I have received a communication directly from your president," Rostron said, "inquiring about Major Butt. His presence has not been registered here on the *Carpathia*. Is it possible that he is here under another name?"

When John frowned, Rostron gave a slight shrug. Underneath his stiff, official exterior, he was obviously concerned.

"No," John said, "he's not here. I would know him at once. The last I saw him, he was on the *Titanic* helping to load the lifeboats. I haven't seen him since."

"Your president," Rostron said, "is sending a gunboat, the *USS Chester*."

John winced. It seemed that Taft had decided to employ Roosevelt's threat-filled gunboat diplomacy, but why? The *Carpathia* was a British passenger liner and Britain was a friend of the United States. There should be no need for a gunboat to be sent out.

"It seems," Rostron continued, "that your president is very seriously concerned about Major Butt, or maybe there is some other reason for his concern. The reason currently given is that the presence of the *USS Chester* within Marconi distance, will allow for better communications with the White House. At the moment our messages are being passed through whoever is in hailing distance, and then on to Cape Race, and eventually, to the president, or the senate, and, of course, the press."

John decided to keep his own counsel. He had heard rumors around the senate offices that Archibald Butt's mission to Europe had not been as innocent as it appeared, but he could see no point in repeating the rumors to Rostron. Perhaps the *Chester* had been sent for no reason other than the one that had been given.

"I didn't see Major Butt enter the water," John said.

He queried his own use of words. *Enter the water!* What a feeble way to describe the horror of diving into that deep, cold maelstrom. The memory brought an involuntary shudder.

He pulled himself together. He could not allow this memory to haunt him for years to come. It must be dealt with now. "I have not seen him here on board the *Carpathia*," he added. "There is nothing else I can tell you."

Rostron nodded. "You've told me enough. I will convey the information to the *Chester* when she comes within range. Meantime, I'll have someone escort you to Mr. Ismay."

John had no need of an escort to take him to Ismay. His location was now well known. One of the doctors had vacated his cabin and that was where John found Ismay. When he knocked, ignoring the notice that asked him not to knock, Ismay ushered him inside and closed the door firmly behind him.

Although Ismay wore clean, probably borrowed, clothes there was nothing of ease or comfort about him. His eyes were bloodshot, his upper lip – adorned with a dark moustache – twitched and he constantly ran his fingers through his hair. He was older than John – maybe in his late forties, and appeared to be on the edge of hysteria. He was, John thought, a broken man.

The cabin was sparsely furnished. Ismay sat at a small desk and John sat on the bunk. Ismay fixed John with a concentrated gaze. "You are familiar with the workings of your senate?" he asked.

"I will do my best to tell you what I know," John said.

Ismay nodded. "We are informed there will be a senate inquiry."

"I have heard the rumor," John said, "but we have all heard too many rumors."

"Oh, this is no rumor," Ismay said. "My office in New York has sent me messages. There is a resolution in the senate to hold an inquiry into what happened to my ship and Senator William Alden Smith has been made chairman. I want you to tell me who this man is. Do you know him?"

Senator Smith from Michigan – yes, John knew him. He was a man who had risen from poverty to the heights of political influence. It was no secret that Smith had his eye on the presidency, and there could be no doubt that this inquiry would be a political coup.

"I know him," John said.

"What do you think he wants?" Ismay asked.

"I suppose he wants to know what happened," John said. "We all want to know what happened."

Ismay rolled his eyes. "What happened is nothing to do with the American Senate. We, the British, will hold our own inquiry, but I'm damned if I can see what this has to do with a pack of American senators!"

"I assume it is because so many American citizens were lost," John said mildly. He sensed that Ismay was in danger of losing control.

"Don't assume," Ismay snapped, "ask!"

John was momentarily stunned into silence. What was Ismay suggesting?

"Ask your senator," Ismay said. "You're on his staff, aren't you? Ask him what is going on."

John thought about Senator Eldridge. He could not imagine the senator being involved in any way with Senator Smith. Smith was a Republican. Eldridge was an Independent. Considering the speed with which Senator Smith had grabbed the chairmanship of the Senate Inquiry, John suspected that he had consulted very few senators. He could only imagine that Smith's behavior was now being discussed behind closed doors. Alliances were being formed. Smith had stuck his neck out and someone would be sharpening an axe – maybe it would be Eldridge. John would know nothing until he was back in Washington, in the thick of the political fight.

John knew that he should not refuse Ismay's request outright, but he could point out Ismay's lack of wisdom. It was very obvious that Ismay was still in a state of shock and, from the dilation of Ismay's pupils, he suspected that the doctors had been giving him something to calm him – maybe an opiate.

"I could send a Marconi message to my senator," John offered, "but I assume that it would not be confidential. Anything I say could be picked up by the newspapers. It would draw attention to you, sir, and that would not be wise."

"Well," Ismay said on a note of rising hysteria, "what do you think *would* be wise? Am I just to sit here while American politicians plot against me? They're going to blame me, aren't they? I wasn't in charge. I was a passenger." He looked at John. "I was no more in charge of that ship than you were, Mr. Alder, but no one is going to believe me. I know it already. Captain Smith went down with his ship and I didn't because ..." Ismay was now sweating profusely. "Because," he said, "I was not in control. It was not my place to be a hero and die with the ship."

He swiped a hand across the perspiration on his forehead. "I am completely innocent. There were no women or children waiting for a seat in that lifeboat. If you don't believe me, you can ask Lord whatever-his-name-is."

"I'm not sure who you mean."

"Young fellow, losing his hair. I told him to get in the boat. Couldn't see any point in us both standing there like statues waiting to be drowned."

"Lord Lucan Sempter?" John asked.

"Yes," Ismay said, "that's the fellow. I told him to get in and he wasn't the only one. There was another fellow – Carter was his name, and there were four Chinese men hiding in the bottom of the boat and I allowed them to stay." Ismay's voice rose in loud complaint. "There was no one else! No women, no children – no one

-and so I stepped in. What would be the point of me dying? Isn't it better for me to live and do what I can for the survivors?"

There was something wishful in Ismay's tone. John suspected that this was the first time Ismay had attempted to justify himself and he was looking to John to gauge his reaction.

In his time with Senator Eldridge, John had learned the value of silence, and now he remained silent. As he suspected would happen, Ismay could not stop talking.

"I will not be talking to any senators," Ismay said. "In fact, I don't intend to set foot in the United States, neither me, nor my crew. I have sent a message to my New York office and they're holding a ship. The *Cedric* will take us all home and we will leave immediately."

John could not suppress a shudder. At that moment, tired and heartsick, he could not imagine voluntarily setting foot on a ship ever again. He wondered how Ismay's crew would react. Surely, they had the right to refuse.

Ismay looked at him with narrowed eyes. "There'll be no jumping ship," he said. "The crew won't get their pay until they get back to England. That'll keep them in line."

John had been nursing a certain amount of sympathy for Bruce Ismay with the terrible weight of responsibility resting on his shoulders. Now that he heard Ismay's cavalier dismissal of his crew's needs, his sympathy dissipated. He considered what he knew of Senator Smith and the power of the Senate. He doubted very much that Ismay would be allowed to simply board the next ship for home.

PART THREE - NEW YORK.

Thomas Andrews
Managing Director, Harland and Wolff (Builders of the *Titanic*)
You weren't there at my first meeting with Ismay. The first thing I thought was "Now there's a man who wants me to build him a ship that's going to be sunk." We're sending gilded egg shells out to sea.

CHAPTER ELEVEN

Maxine, Lady Sempter
On board the *Carpathia*, New York City, April 18.
After a storm at sea and a nerve-racking journey through fog, the *Carpathia* had not found welcoming weather even in New York harbor. As the harbor tugs brought them up the Hudson, they were met with drenching rain. Night had already fallen but the darkness of the rain-soaked night was pierced with the constant flashing of cameras whose bright flickering lights revealed the presence of thousands of people awaiting the arrival of the survivors.

Maxine wondered about the photographers behind those flashes. When they developed their film, what did they expect to see? How could their pictures ever convey the horror behind the eyes of those who had been saved?

She stood beside Lucan on the deck of the *Carpathia* as the harbor pilot nestled the *Carpathia* up against the Cunard pier, and the attendant tugs took their leave. She thought she heard a collective sigh of relief from the people who stood with her at the rail. It was as though everyone on the *Carpathia* had been holding their breath as the tired ship battled everything the Atlantic could throw at it. Now, at last, they were in New York.

Dry land was just a stone's throw away, but Maxine could not join in the sighs of relief. She wondered about many things but mostly she wondered if she would ever feel safe again. If she had not been safe on the unsinkable *Titanic*, how could she be safe anywhere?

She knew now how very short a life could be. It could end at any time, and she had seen it end for hundreds of people. She was not the same person who had boarded the *Titanic*, triumphant in her acquisition of a titled husband, but still jealous of her beautiful young cousin.

A gangplank was lowered briefly to admit an elegant gray-haired man, accompanied by a small entourage and several New York City police officers. When the entourage was safely aboard, the gangplank was lifted again. It seemed that no one would be going ashore immediately.

"Policemen!" Lucan said staring down at the newcomers. "What do they want?"

Maxine turned to study her husband's suspicious face. "I don't know," she said. "Perhaps there are criminals on board."

"Why would you say that?" Lucan asked.

"Perhaps some of the men you played cards with are to be arrested," Maxine suggested, feeling no need to hide her venom. Since she had admitted to herself that marrying Lucan had been a terrible mistake, it had become harder and harder to play the dutiful, respectful – even grateful – new bride.

"You may be right," Lucan said. The flashing bulbs revealed his hopeful expression. "They should all be arrested. I told you that they were cheating. It's tantamount to outright stealing money. I should file a complaint and get my money back."

"Have you given them money?" Maxine asked.

"Not yet," Lucan said. "I'm assuming that your family money will —"

"We can't assume anything," Maxine said – not for the first time. "I don't have immediate access to family money. I have my allowance, of course, but that's all."

"At the moment," Lucan said.

"Everything depends on my grandfather. He may have made an additional bequest," Maxine said, "but really, Lucan, I wish you hadn't gambled away so much money. It won't make a good impression on grandfather if the first thing we do is ask him for money."

"I thought my title was sufficient to make a good impression," Lucan said.

Maxine hesitated, unsure how to tell him how very unimpressed her grandfather had been when he learned that she planned to marry Lucan. His telegram was brief and straight to the point but it had arrived after the wedding.

LOOKED INTO HIS FINANCES STOP

NO MONEY STOP

NO WEDDING STOP

Maxine's mother, Agatha, the only daughter of Aiden Paxton, had fought hard against the idea that so much of Aidan's fortune would go to his son, Robert, and so little would go to his daughter.

Matters became even more difficult when Robert and his wife died leaving behind an infant daughter. Aidan Paxton, grieving the loss of his only son, found no comfort in Agatha, and decreed the money he had planned to leave to Robert, he would now leave to Robert's child, Sophie, and nothing but a pittance for Agatha.

Although the will was still in place, Agatha had railed against it for years. Surely there was a way into the old man's granite heart – a way to gain his approval and edge Sophie out of the way. Agatha thought she knew a way into the old man's granite heart and tightly-closed purse. Maxine's marriage was to be the key.

"We'll go to England for the season, and we'll make a spectacular marriage for you. Your grandfather grew up as a poor crofter's son, looked down on by the English. Nothing would please him more than having a fine old English title in the bloodline, then no one can look down on us. We'll find someone for you. He doesn't have to be rich, or handsome, but he has to have a title. Give the old man a titled grandson and you'll have anything you want."

Maxine, who thought her allowance was already quite generous, had not really wanted anything other than to be left in peace. Of course, what she wanted had never mattered.

It had not been easy. The social competition had been fierce. Maxine, tall, ungainly, unwilling and almost thirty years old could not attract the attention of even the lowest of viscounts, or the ugliest of earls. There had been only one contender – Lucan Sempter, fifth son of a baronet but bearing a hereditary title of Lord. He was not persuaded by Maxine's looks, but he was persuaded by her money. Somehow, he was given the impression that she, Maxine was the heir to the Paxton fortune. Maxine had not lied to him herself, but she knew that her mother had made misleading statements delivered with an airy wave of the hand.

My daughter is well provided for in her grandfather's will.

Yes, he's chosen to leave his money to his granddaughter.

An estate in Virginia and a townhouse in Washington and, of course, a townhouse in London is always a possibility.

I'm afraid he's in poor health. He won't be with us much longer.

The wedding had been in a small chapel on the Sempter Estate and the telegram had arrived too late. Agatha had laughed it away.

Your grandfather will come around, dear. Don't worry. Besides, I have arranged for him to give you the honeymoon of your dreams.

I don't dream about honeymoons, mother.

"You will dream about this one. It's all arranged. You and Lucan are to travel to America on the new Titanic, all expenses paid by your grandfather.

Really?

Yes, my dear, really. There's just one small snag, but it won't be a problem. You and your husband will be chaperoning your cousin, Sophie. Your grandfather is recalling her from that horrible school in Wales. She's past the age for schooling and he wants her back in the United States as soon as possible. It will be first-class all the way, dear. I will return to America ahead of you and make sure my father understands that you have grasped a prize. You will spend time here in England and in April you will board the Titanic. What a joy for you both.

A blast of rain-soaked wind from the shore and a muttered curse from Lucan drew Maxine's mind away from the problems with her marriage and her fear that Lucan was, in fact, a far worse man than she had at first suspected.

"What's the matter?"

Lucan jerked his head. "Those two fellows. They're following me."

Maxine turned her head to see Dick Williams and John Alder looking over the rail at the activity on the dock. "I don't think so," she said. "Why would they follow you?"

"I think that Alder fellow has appointed himself as your cousin's guardian angel. He thinks she's in danger from me."

"But why?"

Lucan's expression changed swiftly. Maxine had the feeling he had said more than he intended. "Alder's the one who persuaded you to take her to the doctor. It's his fault that Cousin Sophie will be in a wheelchair for the rest of her life... if she survives."

"If she survives?" Maxine said. "Of course, she'll survive and she'll learn to walk again."

"If she doesn't lose her whole foot or her leg, or, of course, her life. You said she still has a fever. Obviously, the infection is still spreading."

"No, it's not. She just needs rest and to get off this ship," Maxine said.

She spoke with as much confidence as she could muster. She knew full well that Sophie's surgery was not to be laid to John Alder's account. She, Maxine, had given permission. It was all her fault.

"Lady Sempter." John Alder had edged closer to her. "How is Miss Sophie?"

"She's going to be just fine," Maxine said. "My grandfather is arranging for her to be treated as soon as we are ashore."

My husband thinks she'll die.

Thinks she'll die or hopes she'll die?

John Alder seemed about to make another comment but Lucan interrupted. "Mr. Alder – any idea why the police have come aboard? Are they making arrests? There are some fellows who have been playing cards – I should say cheating at cards."

Alder's face was grim. "I doubt if anyone is interested - card sharks are small potatoes. The police are escorting Senator Smith of Michigan, Chairman of the U.S. Senate sub-committee. Tomorrow morning, he will open an investigation into what exactly happened on the *Titanic*. He has subpoenas for the *Titanic's* crew and for Mr. Bruce Ismay."

"You mean Ismay's being arrested?" Lucan asked.

"No, not exactly, but they are all being detained. It's not quite the same thing, although I imagine the British will not see it that way."

Maxine saw her husband raise his eyebrows as his expression became supercilious. "The *Titanic* was a British ship, she's none of your damned American business."

Maxine set her hand on her husband's arm. "Lucan, I don't think this is the time..."

"I just hope no one expects me to give evidence to this wretched inquiry," Lucan said.

"You were in the same lifeboat with Mr. Ismay," Alder said.

"What about it? The man's entitled to save his own life. We're all entitled to save our own lives." Lucan glared at Alder. "You saved yours."

Whatever reply Alder intended to give was interrupted by the arrival of two men, talking loudly as they came out onto the deck. Maxine did not recognize them, but she'd had very little contact with the other passengers as she tried to take care of Sophie.

Although these men were not known to Maxine, they were definitely known to Lucan who abruptly turned and walked away. *Walked away? No, he scuttled away. He was afraid of these men. These must be the card sharks – the men to whom he owed a great deal of money.*

The two men approached her. One was stocky and blond and wore a bandage around his head, the other had unusually boyish features that contrasted strangely with his graying hair. As they approached, John Alder and Dick West shifted their positions. Maxine, abandoned by her husband, had a feeling that she still had two protectors.

"Lady Sempter?" This was from the man with the boyish features. "May we have a word?"

They were Americans and their faces were not unfriendly.

Alder stepped up as if to send them away, but Maxine ignored him. "What do you want?"

"To give you a warning," said the other bandaged man.

Maxine took a deep breath. These were the men who had taken Lucan's money – her money – at the gambling tables. She clung to the rail, her knees suddenly weak. They wouldn't do anything to her, not now, not in front of so many witnesses. She should let them speak.

The bandaged man smiled at her, and there was no menace in his smile. He seemed to be offering comfort. "Charles Romaine," he said, "and this is Kid Homer." He had a comfortingly familiar Viginia accent.

John Alder intervened. "What do you want?"

"You traveling with this lady?"

"What I'm doing is none of your business," Alder said. "What do you want with Lady Sempter."

Romaine ignored Alder and fixed a steady gaze on Maxine. "Me and the Kid," he said, moving his head to indicate his companion, "we stayed away from the tables. We're all lucky to be alive, and we agreed to leave the survivors alone, but I can't say the same for everyone. Your husband is involved with some dangerous people, and they want their money. He's been saying that they'll get paid when you go ashore. He says that you, Lady Sempter, have the money."

"He says you have expectations," Kid Homer added. "You are expecting money."

"No," Maxine said, "I'm not expecting anything. You tell these people, whoever they are, that I have no intention of paying them. So far as I'm concerned, they're criminals. If they come near my husband, I'll have them arrested."

Romaine shook his head. "It doesn't work that way, Lady Sempter. Your husband wrote his IOU. Me and the Kid, we just came to give you a friendly warning. This is none of our business, but we sympathize. Everyone on this ship has been through enough. Just know that you need to find a way to pay off your husband's debts, or it will be the worse for you."

Maxine was aware of Dick Williams and John Alder moving closer, but she could feel no threat from these two men. They seemed honest enough – for the moment.

"You've warned her," Alder said. "Now leave her alone."

Romaine seemed almost nonchalant. "Sure thing, Mr. Alder. We've said what we came to say. Her ladyship's in no danger from us." He hesitated before speaking again. "Keep an eye on your cousin," he said, "the one in the infirmary. Keep an eye on her – that's all I wanted to say."

Maxine saw activity on the pier. The gangplank came down again and this time it stayed down. Glancing the length of the ship she saw that additional gangplanks were being lowered. Officials in brass-buttoned uniforms were being taken aboard. Maxine looked around for Lucan. He had not yet returned. She turned away from the rail. Obviously the *Carpathia* was ready to discharge her passengers. Sophie would need her. She would have to forget about Lucan for the time being.

Sophie was still in bed in the gymnasium. Those patients who could walk, even on crutches, had already left the makeshift hospital. Those who could not walk were sitting up in bed awaiting the arrival of wheelchairs – except, of course, for Sophie who still lay in a bed of tangled sheets.

Maxine recognized Poppy, the harried stewardess who was attempting to brush Sophie's hair, although Sophie seemed unwilling to even lift her head from the pillow. As soon as Maxine arrived, Poppy handed her the hairbrush. "Dr. Lengyel has given her opiates to keep her calm. I think perhaps he gave her too much. She just doesn't want to sit up. I'm sorry your ladyship, but the *Titanic* crew are required to assemble. I can't stay here with her."

Maxine took the hairbrush. "You've been very kind," she said. "Of course you must go. Will you be returning home now on another ship?"

Poppy shook her head. "No, I'm staying here in America. My sister is with me." She grinned. "We're planning to go to California and Daisy is determined to be a Hollywood movie star. I'm just going along to make sure she behaves herself. "

"Good luck," Maxine said, suddenly envious of this young woman's freedom. Hollywood! California! Just imagine.

As Poppy hurried away, Maxine looked down at her cousin. She thought of Poppy's ambition – she was going to California. Sophie had once had ambition, but it was gone now. There would be no tennis and no Olympics for Sophie. What would Sophie do now with all that energy and determination held hostage by Dr. Lengyel's amputation?

I had to agree, or she would have died.

Lucan had wanted her to withhold permission. She pushed that thought away. He could not possibly...

Maxine slipped her arm under Sophie's shoulders and pulled her into an upright position. Sophie was as limp as a rag doll, her head lolling forward as Maxine ran the brush through her tangled hair. She could see now that someone had dressed Sophie in a loose cotton dress. She wondered briefly what had happened to Sophie's original clothing – the dress and coat that she had worn that last night on the *Titanic*. Perhaps they had been dried and given to someone else. She thought about the photographers waiting eagerly – some would say ghoulishly – to take pictures. It would be a coup, wouldn't it, to take a picture of the Paxton heiress with tangled hair and an old cotton dress?

Maxine set to work again to braid Sophie's hair, and had just completed her task when Dr. Lengyel arrived at the bedside accompanied by a man with a wheelchair.

"Enough now," he said. "This man has come with an ambulance to transport your cousin."

"The attendant took a step forward and Maxine waved him hurriedly away. "She's not properly dressed."

The attendant was dismissive. "You wrap her in blankets."

Maxine set down the hairbrush and watched Sophie flop back against the pillows. She looked at Dr. Lengyel. "What did you give her?"

"Something for the pain." Dr. Lengyel said. He looked at Maxine sympathetically. "And something to calm her." He rested his hand on Sophie's forehead. "This one is a fighter. She has fought me every day. She calls me a butcher. I shall be glad to be rid of her."

Maxine nodded. "I understand, Dr. Lengyel. I cannot imagine what she's going to call me. I'm the one who gave you permission to operate."

"You saved her life," Lengyel said. "That is what I have told her. I am no butcher, I am a lifesaver. You must be firm and give no sympathy. There is no reason she should not walk."

He gestured to the orderly with the wheelchair. The man was large and Sophie was small. It was easy for him to wrap a blanket around her and lift her from the bed into the wheelchair. Sophie opened her eyes and looked at the man and then at Maxine.

"Wha...what... what?"

"We're in New York and we're going ashore," Maxine said firmly.

"Hmm," Sophie mumbled. "Identify Yourself."

"I'm your cousin, Maxine."

"No, not that," Sophie mumbled. "Lights. Dot, dot, dot."

"I don't know what you mean," Maxine said.

"But I do," Sophie mumbled. Her gaze flickered from Maxine to Dr. Lengyel. "Butcher," she said.

Lengyel shrugged. "She's fine," he said. "She'll be awake and fighting in a couple of hours. Where are you going to be staying?"

"I've had only brief messages from my grandfather on the Marconi," Maxine said, "you know how busy the operator has been. We are to go to the Waldorf Astoria where he will have people waiting."

She set her hands on the handles of the wheelchair but before she could set the chair in motion, the door crashed open and Lucan was suddenly at her side.

He looked balefully at Sophie and then turned his attention to Maxine. "You have to come with me. They won't let me in."

Maxine stared at her husband. "Who won't let you in? What are you talking about?"

"I'm talking about getting off this damned ship and entering the United States. I can't leave without you."

For a moment, Maxine was reassured. *I can't leave without you.* That was almost romantic.

"Obviously, I don't have my travel papers," Lucan said, "being that they are at the bottom of the ocean with everything else I possessed. I'm obviously a first-class passenger, but they say they need you to vouch for me. It's utter chaos up there. None of the steerage passengers have papers and most of them don't speak English. I don't know why anyone would think I belong with them. I need you to come – Now!"

Maxine's heart sank. *I can't leave without you* - these were not the words of an anxious bridegroom – they were the words of a man impatient to go ashore and escape the men to whom he owed money. The marriage was hopeless. She had known it all along. It had been formed by her mother's lies. Lies that she had gone along with.

Maxine adjusted Sophie's blankets. She did not want Lucan to see the expression on her face – the mixture of utter disappointment and sheer anger. He had tried to leave without her!

Lucan was now irritably impatient. "Are you coming? Do we have to bring her with us?"

Dr. Lengyel stepped in "You go ahead, Lady Sempter and take your husband through Immigration. The orderly will bring your cousin. You can take the stairs. He will take her on the elevator."

Lucan returned his attention to Sophie, slumped in the wheelchair with her chin resting on her chest. "She looks bad."

"She's much better," Maxine said, "but Dr. Lengyel has given her something for her pain."

"She looks sick to me."

"She will get better," Maxine insisted.

"Who is that with her?"

"An ambulance attendant. Grandfather has sent an ambulance."

"'And what has he sent for me... for us?" Lucan asked.

"I don't know," Maxine said. "I am sure he's sent someone to meet us and take care of everything. We'll all go together."

"I go different way," the orderly said. His accent was guttural – German perhaps.

"Yes, I understand that you will need to use the elevator," Maxine said to him, "I'll come with you."

"No," said Lucan, "you're coming with me now. The orderly can bring the wheelchair, but I need you at Immigration. We're going to put those petty officials in their place. Just because they have a few brass buttons, they think they can order people about. This is a British ship, dammit and I'm a Peer of the Realm."

"But now you are in America," Maxine said with a feeling of quiet satisfaction. *You're in my realm now and I'm the only friend you have. Let's see how you behave now.*"

She turned to the orderly. "I will meet you at Immigration."

Doctor Arped Lengyel
On board the *Carpathia*, New York City

Dr. Lengyel watched as the orderly took control of the young lady's wheelchair. He didn't like that this particular young lady had called him a butcher. He'd done what needed to be done and he'd saved her life. Considering the circumstances, the removal of her toe had been a very fine piece of surgery.

He sighed in relief. The nightmare rescue of the *Titanic* survivors was almost at an end. All that was left for him to do was to write a report for Cunard. He walked over to his desk and picked up his pen. Now that the excitement was over, he allowed himself to feel tired. Of course, Cunard wanted the report written in English. His eyelids began to droop.

He was startled awake by the arrival of Frank McGee. The first-class doctor, impeccably dressed as always, was looking toward the closed doors.

"I see you've discharged your patient. I saw her come out of the elevator up on deck."

"Which patient?" Lengyel asked.

"The one with the gangrenous foot."

"Not her foot," Lengyel corrected. "The sepsis was confined to her big toe and I have taken care of it. There was no question of gangrene."

McGee nodded. "I agree. I saw you at work. You did a fine job."

"She does not think it is fine," Lengyel said. "She calls me a butcher."

McGee sighed. "That's what happens when you have patients from first-class. It's not just about pills and tonics, it's all about telling them what they want to hear. She didn't want to hear that she was going to lose her toe."

"Better than losing her foot," Lengyel said, "or her life."

"You were correct about her condition," McGee said, "but you were wrong about young Dick Williams. You told him he would lose his legs, but he still has them. I've just seen him going ashore – walking on two legs."

Lengyel stiffened, feeling a need to justify himself. "I did not tell him that he would lose his legs."

"I believe you did."

"I told him it was a possibility."

"You should have left it to me," McGee said. "I would have been more tactful."

"No! You would have been kind to him and you would have let him lie in a bed and rest his legs. That was not what he needed. He needed to be made afraid. He needed to believe that he was truly in danger of losing his legs."

"Are you saying that he was in no danger?"

"No, I am not saying that. There was a very real danger for him. He needed to keep moving and so I gave him a reason to move."

"You scared the living daylights out of him," McGee said.

"But I saved his legs. Full recovery may very well be available now. He was a first-class passenger – he has money. He will see a specialist. He will continue to walk. As for the young lady – without her toe she will still live a fine life. She will tell everyone that she was ruined by an ignorant Hungarian butcher, but that makes no difference to me. I will never see her again."

"I hope to see her, and make her my patient," McGee said, "After what we've been through on this voyage, I don't see me spending the rest of my life as a ship's surgeon. This was a nightmare from beginning to end, but as a result, I've helped some of New York's wealthiest at the worst time in their life. Now I have contacts and people to vouch for me. I'm going to set up my own practice in New York."

"I would not enjoy that," Lengyel said.

"Maybe you like the excitement," McGee said, "but it's not for me. I have made a point of being highly sympathetic to Sophie Paxton and she will remember me. She's a wealthy young woman, and well connected. Her cousin even has a title and that is rare but valuable in New York"

"Her cousin may have a title, but she's still a foolish woman," Lengyel said. "She was afraid to do what needed to be done. As for her husband ..."

McGee nodded. "A dreadful man. It seemed to me that he didn't care whether your patient lived or died. In fact, I suspect..."

Lengyel was impatient to return to his desk and complete the formal report Cunard was requiring him to make. He waited impatiently for McGee to voice whatever it was he suspected.

McGee chewed his lower lip for a moment and then finally voiced his suspicion. "I suspect that Lord Sempter would not be unhappy if young Sophie had succumbed to sepsis. If she dies, then Lady Sempter inherits."

Lengyel forgot about his report for a moment. He remembered Lord Sempter's aggression and Lady Sempter's hesitation. These people had been saved from drowning - how sad that simply being alive was not good fortune enough for them and they must still pursue money.

"Are you suggesting that he deliberately neglected to get treatment for her? Do you think he would really have let her die?"

McGee shook his head. "I don't know. I hope I'm mistaken. Lord Sempter's a strange fellow, naturally unpleasant, and rumor on board is that he owes a great deal of money to some very unpleasant people. Perhaps I should look in on the young lady and make sure that she is being properly attended. I'm glad to see she's going to a good hospital."

"No, not a hospital," Lengyel said. "She'll have a private nurse at her hotel."

McGee frowned. "Are you sure of that?"

"Yes, that is what I was told. The orderly said that he had an ambulance waiting."

"The orderly wore a hospital smock," McGee said. "He was not from a private agency. He was from Mount Sinai."

Lengyel shook off his weariness. Of course this could be nothing. Perhaps the man had been contracted from Mount Sinai - no doubt every hospital in New York had been put on alert. On the other hand, he didn't disagree with Dr. McGee's dark suspicions about Lord Sempter.

Snap decisions were Lengyel's strength and now he made one. "Dr. McGee, you go to Immigration. If all is well, Sophie will be there and you will make sure she stays with Lady Sempter and does not enter an ambulance. I will attempt to follow the wheelchair, and we will see what is going on."

The two doctors left the gymnasium and rode the elevator up to the crowded promenade deck. The last of the *Carpathia's* passengers had already left the ship, and now the survivors of the *Titanic* presented themselves for processing – a task made almost impossible by the lack of travel documents. Even women who had saved their jewel cases had not thought to save their credentials.

The line inched toward a barrier, with the first-class survivors leading the way as they would be easier to process and harder to please. Lengyel saw the scale of the tragedy in the way the line moved - a mixture of eagerness and reluctance. For these survivors, landfall would become a time of reckoning. Their time on the *Carpathia* had been a time of unreality, but now they would all have to face their losses, and money and class made no difference to their grief.

Perhaps, he thought cynically, it was easier to grieve when there was food on the table, but in the end, Mrs. Astor's loss was the same loss as any penniless Irishwoman. They had each lost the man who defined them.

He could spot Lord and Lady Sempter making their way through the line. Was Lady Sempter wondering what had happened to her cousin? Lord Sempter, looking casually around, didn't seem concerned but perhaps he already knew.

Frank McGee shuffled his feet. He had sprung into action at Lengyel's command but now he seemed lost. Lengyel took command. "You go and stop Lord Sempter from leaving the ship."

"How?"

"You will think of something."

Lengyel was already scanning the pier. Lights blazed from the ship and from light poles on the dock while the constant flash of camera bulbs created a confusing dazzle of light and shadow. Survivors from the *Titanic* were leaving the *Carpathia* by the gangplank at the bow where Immigration and Customs had set up a processing station, but there were no wheelchairs or stretchers in that line. The sick were leaving some other way. He looked toward the stern. Yes, there they were – steerage passengers and stricken crew members in wheelchairs and on stretchers. They would not be required to pass through Immigration here. They would be taken directly to St Vincents Charity Hospital and given time to recover ... or die.

He spotted the orderly pushing Sophie Paxton. His patient, wrapped in blankets appeared to be completely unconscious. He knew he had given her a very generous dose of opium, but he felt justified in what he had done. She had needed something. Her fever would never break while anger raged like a furnace in her. Her body and mind required a rest from the strain that she exerted on herself.

Lengyel set off at a brisk run. The passageways within the *Carpathia* were almost deserted save for the Cunard crew who would now attempt to prepare the vessel for an almost immediate departure. Despite everything they had seen, the majority of the original passengers still wanted their Mediterranean cruise. Captain Rostron would be allowed no more than two days to turn the ship around and head back to Gibraltar.

Lengyel exited by the stern gangway and raced along the dock. If he was attracting attention from the passengers looking down from the *Carpathia*, he would not know about it. The crowds of onlookers on the shore were making enough noise to drown out any minor disturbance and he didn't have time to look up. His attention was focused only on the tall orderly with the wheelchair.

The orderly looked behind him, took note of Lengyel's approach and started to speed up. There was a paved road just ahead with a line of vehicles. Presumably the driver of one of those vehicles was not waiting to pick up just any patient. He was here for one purpose only – to take Sophie Paxton. Why? What was the plan? If murder was planned it could have happened long before this. In the chaos of the *Carpathia*, anything could have happened.

He wondered is someone intended to hold Sophie as a hostage. Was this some wild plan put forth by Lord Sempter? It seemed a possibility. Whatever it was, it had to be stopped.

Lengyel shouted. He didn't realize that he was shouting in his own language. That he spoke Hungarian made no difference. The orderly heard the tone of his voice, looked quickly over his shoulder and then picked up his pace. It was some years since Lengyel had done his basic military training but he still remembered how to bring a man down, even a big man. Once on the ground, height wouldn't matter.

He flung himself forward and grasped the orderly's knees. They hit the cement dock together, with Lengyel scrabbling to come out on top and hold the big man down.

It was an uneven contest. Lengyel was outweighed and the orderly had no problem throwing him off. He broke free in moments and Lengyel found himself lying flat on his stomach, gasping for breath as he watched the orderly retrieve the wheelchair as it rolled toward the edge of the dock. Desperation had made the orderly stupid. With the brake off and Sophie unconscious while the two men wrestled, there had been nothing to stop the wheelchair from rolling straight into the water.

The orderly was running now, with Sophie slipping sideways in the chair. Lengyel sprang to his feet and set off again, but the orderly was wary and looking over his shoulder. A disturbance rippled through the immigration line and a figure broke free, heading straight for the orderly and the wheelchair. Lengyel forced his pace. He didn't know the man who was now tackling the orderly but he knew that someone would have to catch the wheelchair.

He had his hands on the chair before the newcomer had completed his take-down of the orderly and he could only stand and watch the two men, one in an orderly's smock and one in a dark suit. They were evenly matched and were soon locked together, each grunting and grasping as they rolled on the rain-soaked ground. As each scrabbled to rise, their efforts brought them closer and closer to the edge of the dock. Lengyel could do nothing while he held Sophie in the wheelchair. He watched helplessly as the two men, still locked together, tumbled into the dark waters of the Hudson River.

Now there was no time to waste. He had to make a decision. He pushed the wheelchair up a ramp and onto the road. A row of motorized ambulances waited at the curb. Lengyel by-passed the private ambulances, and the Red Cross ambulances. He knew what he wanted. He wanted a place where no one would look for Sophie Paxton and he needed an ambulance that was ready to depart. He ran with the wheelchair until he found an ambulance with its engine running and obviously ready to leave.

"Do you have room for one more?" Lengyel shouted.

An attendant, who had already closed one of the back doors, turned to look at Sophie slumped in the wheelchair.

"We've room for her, but not the wheelchair."

"Which hospital?"

"St. Vincents. It's charity. We're taking the people who can't pay for anything better, and the crew, of course."

"She can't pay," Lengyel said. "She's a poor woman, an immigrant. We've amputated her big toe for frostbite. Also she has a fever."

The attendant produced a clipboard. "Name?" he asked.

"Matild Gutfreund," Lengyel said, giving Sophie the name of his own mother. "Can she walk?"

"She should try," Lengyel said. "Make a note. She should try to walk."

"She doesn't look much like walking now,"

"She has been given an opiate," Lengyel said. "She will not wake up for several hours."

He could not begin to imagine what Sophie would do when she emerged from her drugged sleep and found herself in a charity hospital with a name that marked her as an Hungarian Jew.

The attendant pushed the clipboard toward him. "Sign."

Lengyel signed his own name. He was not ashamed of what he had done. He had saved Sophie Paxton's life for the second time.

———◄○►———

John Alder,

The Hudson River

Paralysis! He could not move. Where was the ship? He should swim. His lifejacket should keep him up. It wasn't working. He was going down, sinking deeper. Down like the Titanic. He was going down with her. Instinct forced him to kick. He was going up now. Where were the people? He had dived into a sea of people but now there was no one. He remembered the press of bodies, the desperate thrashing of arms and legs. Where was Dick?

His head broke the surface. He gasped for air and his mind cleared. He was alone in the water. Not the ocean. Not the Atlantic. The Hudson. He was in the Hudson River caught in a strong current.

He had survived the *Titanic* but it seemed he was destined to drown one way or another. Now that he was thinking clearly, he realized that he could see the lights of the *Carpathia* and behind that the lights of New York City, but they were all receding. The current was taking him out into the center of the river to join the outflowing tide. He tried to swim against the current but there was no progress to be made. He stilled his arms and legs and floated with the current while he tried to think. He knew that he couldn't last long. The water was not as cold as the water of the North Atlantic, but it was cold enough to kill him.

Why was he here? Oh, yes. He had tackled the orderly with the wheelchair and they had gone together into the water, and the water had taken his mind back to the *Titanic*. That curse would probably follow him all the days of his life, but for the moment his mind was clear. He had gone into the water of his own free will to take down the man who had Sophie in a wheelchair. Where was that man now? Well, he was not here. John was alone.

A light flashed red just ahead of him. He tried to ignore it. It was just a fragment of memory – an instruction from Captain Smith to "row toward the light. Unload your passengers and come back." Nonsense, utter nonsense. There had been no light. On the other hand, this light was real and he didn't have to row. He was drifting straight down on it.

The buoy revealed itself in flashes of its own light. It was draped in weed and rolling with the current and each wave that passed. The light on the mast swayed tracing red semi-circles across John's vision. He was moving quickly now, the current carrying him down on the channel marker. He would have one chance. He cleared his head of all other thoughts and questions and then he collided with the unforgiving surface of the buoy.

For a moment the current pressed him into place. He stretched out his arms feeling for a handhold on the slimy metal surface. His right hand found something, a protuberance of some kind. He clung with one hand as the current tried to wrench him free. He pulled himself backward, his shoulder joint shrieking as it threatened to leave its socket, but he was finally close enough to hold on with both hands. He took a deep breath. He couldn't stay here. He couldn't fight the current until day light. He had to get out of the water.

The buoy was a circular platform with a navigation light enclosed in a cage welded to the canter of the platform. The climb was difficult but at last he managed to lever himself out of the water and flop onto the platform. The buoy rolled with the waves and standing was not easy but he managed to get on his feet and pull himself upright, clinging to the cage that surrounded the light mast.

In his wet clothes, he was miserably and thoroughly cold but this was not the same as clinging to the semi-submerged lifeboat. He had to relinquish all comparisons to the *Titanic*. His position was far from hopeless. He was not adrift in the North Atlantic, he was in the middle of a busy harbor. He was surrounded by the buildings of New York City. Safety was a simple matter of surviving until morning when he would, surely, be seen..

A wave, higher than the other waves, maybe the wash from a ship entering or leaving the harbor, broke over the platform and threatened to shake him from his precarious perch. He tightened his grip on the bars around the light, but his fingers were numb. He couldn't stay like this all night.

CHAPTER TWELVE

Maxine, Lady Sempter
Waldorf Astoria Hotel, New York, Early morning, April 19

Maxine had a secret. It had been whispered in her ear by Dr. Lengyel. He had chosen the moment when just about everyone on the pier had been thrown into a frenzy with the realization that Sophie Paxton was nowhere to be found.

While Cunard officers searched the ship, and police searched through the crowds on the shore, Dr. Lengyel had taken Maxine aside.

"She is safe."

Maxine tried to break away to report this news, but Lengyel held onto her. "You tell no one until morning, and then you go alone to St. Vincent's Charity Hospital and find a woman named Matild Guttfreund."

"Why?"

"Because that is the name I have given to your cousin. She is safe for tonight."

"But the orderly —"

"Was not sent by your grandfather."

Now it was morning and Maxine was in the sitting room of the suite of rooms that had been reserved for the Paxton family and she was very much awake. She assumed that Mr. Ponsonby, the lawyer her grandfather had sent to meet the ship, was already out of bed and making telephone calls – probably hiring Pinkerton men to investigate and intimidate. She knew that Lucan was asleep, as was her mother, Agatha, who had been a surprise passenger in the Cadillac *"I had to come, my dear. After all you've been through, you need your mother."*

Although Mr. Ponsonby had kept them all awake with his questions and his fretting until late into the night, no trace of Sophie had been uncovered. At midnight with all the passengers debarked and the crowd dispersing, the Paxton party had been advised to go to the Waldorf Astoria and wait.

Maxine's mother, initially hysterical, had taken a sleeping draft. Maxine's husband, not even momentarily hysterical, had climbed into bed and almost immediately fallen asleep. Maxine had spent the night sitting on a spindly chair in the sitting room of the suite, waiting for the first light of day and wondering why Dr. Lengyel thought that Sophie had needed to be taken to a safe place.

They were in New York now, in the trustworthy hands of Mr. Ponsonby. What did Dr. Lengyel know that Maxine didn't? She couldn't answer that question. No! Wait...she knew something. Somewhere, buried deep among a myriad of disappointments was the answer to her question. She would not admit it, even to herself, but it was there – it was the reason that she would not lie in bed next to her husband – not tonight and maybe not any night in the future.

The carriage clock on the mantelshelf, chimed discreetly six times. The hour was still early, but daylight was already creeping across the city, and Maxine had waited long enough. She had not undressed and she still wore a gown donated to her by a passenger from the *Carpathia*. It was not a good fit, but it was of good quality. She could certainly pass for a lady of means in this dress. A lady of means could take an early morning taxi without causing a scandal, but only if she had money to pay for the taxi which, of course, she did not.

Maxine already had a plan. It would rely on the assumption that women who had spent a night together on a lifeboat in the North Atlantic had formed a bond. They had relied on each other in Lifeboat #8 and Mrs. White had certainly held them together on board the *Carpathia*. Maxine was now going to test that bond.

She had hoped to find the corridors of the great hotel empty at this hour of the morning, but instead they bustled with life – not with guests of course, but maids, housekeepers and bellboys. Maxine found the door of Mrs. White's suite and knocked, timidly at first and then, remembering her purpose, loudly and firmly. The door was opened by Mrs. White's maid, Nellie Bessette, who had rowed alongside Sophie in the lifeboat. Nellie was in a wrapper with her hair done up in curling rags. For a moment she seemed not to remember Maxine and then her face lit up into a broad smile.

"Lady Sempter. So early in the morning."

"Yes, I know it's early. Good morning, Nellie. I wonder if I may come in."

"*Mais oui*, yes, of course." Nellie was from Quebec, more French than Canadian. Mrs. White enjoyed that Nellie's habit of speaking in French gave rise to rumors that Ella White had found herself a French lady's maid.

"I regret that I have to answer the door myself," Nellie said. "You know that Mr. Ringhini went down with the ship."

"Who is Mr. Ringhini?" Maxine asked.

"Sante Ringhini, Mrs. White's manservant. He escorted us to the lifeboat but, of course, he couldn't come with us."

"Of course," Maxine muttered, but something inside her rebelled at the thought of Mrs. White's Italian manservant - she assumed from his name that he was Italian - doing his duty right up to the end and then simply turning away from the lifeboat. She had thought that such acts of nobility had only been performed by gentlemanly first-class passengers. She had not thought of manservants and valets performing obediently right up until the last minute.

As Nellie was still lingering, nonplussed in the doorway, Maxine asked again. "May I come in? I must speak urgently with Miss Young or Mrs. White."

"I'll call Miss Young. Mrs. White will not wish to be disturbed."

"I am already disturbed," said a voice behind Nellie. Mrs. White limped into view, leaning heavily on her marvelous electric cane. Evidently Mrs. White had kept an entire wardrobe of clothing in her permanent suite here at the Waldorf. On the *Carpathia* she had stubbornly refused to take advantage of the clothing offered to her by the passengers but here, in her own home, she wore an ivory silk wrapper trimmed with marabou feathers with a matching sleeping bonnet.

At the sight of Maxine, Mrs. White's eyebrows lowered fiercely. "Lady Sempter, to what do we owe this honor?"

"I'm sorry. I know it's early. It's my cousin, Sophie Paxton, she —"

"I know who she is. She's a very stubborn young woman. What about her?"

"She's disappeared, or so they say."

"Oh yes, my maid told me something of that sort last night," Mrs. White said, "but I didn't give it much credence. There are so many reporters and so many rumors." She considered Maxine for a moment. "Are you saying it's true?"

"Very true," Maxine said, "except that Sophie hasn't exactly disappeared. No one knows where she is except that —"

"If no one knows where she is, then she's disappeared," Mrs. White argued.

"*I* know where she is," Maxine said desperately, "and I need your help to fetch her here."

Mrs. White looked up and down the hotel's corridor. "Don't raise your voice. In a place like this, even the walls have ears. Come inside. I don't know why Nellie left you standing on the doorstep."

Maxine stepped inside the luxurious suite crammed with furniture, and expensive bric-a-brac. Over the many years that Mrs. White had occupied the suite, she had furnished it with souvenirs of her travels, and the sitting room gave the impression of a Turkish bazaar somehow transported into a roomful of *Louis Seize* furniture.

126

Mrs. White raised a beckoning finger to Nellie. "Fetch Miss Young and order coffee."

Maxine took a seat on a small brocade sofa and sat in silence for a moment under Mrs. White's scrutiny.

"You really know where she is?" Mrs. White asked.

"Yes, I do, but I can't go and get her, not dressed like this and with no money."

"Money! Why don't you have money? I'm told your mother came to meet you. Surely, she brought money and clothing – that dress is quite horrid."

"My mother didn't think to bring me anything." Maxine said. "She really didn't understand how rapidly we left the ship. My mother assumed that I would have my steamer trunk and my jewels from the purser's safe. She... they ... don't understand that we have no more possessions than the poorest immigrant – just the clothes we stood up in."

"Lady Sempter!" Miss Young was in the room now in a bright silk Japanese kimono, her hair loosely braided and her face creased with worry. "Have they found her?" she asked.

"Lady Sempter says that her cousin is not really lost," Mrs. White said, "but she needs our help in retrieving her."

Maxine looked at Miss Young. "Please," she said.

"Of course we'll help you," Miss Young said impatiently. "Young Sophie kept us all alive in that lifeboat. I could never have kept rowing if she had not encouraged me. So, if you know where Sophie is, do you also know where Mr. Alder is? Are they together?"

"Mr. Alder? No, I don't know anything about him. Is he also missing?"

"Is it possible that Sophie and Mr. Alder are together?" Mrs. White asked. "I realize that it would not be proper, but this disaster has turned the world on its head and I thought I detected a certain ... spark between them."

Maxine dismissed the suggestion. "My cousin has been sick almost from the moment we were taken on board the *Carpathia*. I am sure there has been no opportunity for any ... sparking. Besides, Sophie is too young."

"Nineteen is not too young," Mrs. White said dourly.

Forgetting for a moment that she needed to stay in Mrs. White's good graces, Maxine took offense at the suggestion. "My cousin is a respectable young lady, she would not —"

"Then where is she?" Mrs. White asked again.

"She's at St. Vincent's Charity Hospital," Maxine said. "She was taken there on the instructions of Dr. Lengyel."

Mrs. White seated herself on a white brocade armchair and gave Maxine a piercing stare. "This is very strange. Why would the doctor send her to such a place and why would he ask you to keep it secret while the whole harbor front is being searched for the poor girl?"

"I don't know," Maxine said, unwilling to voice her suspicions."

A knock at the door heralded the arrival of a bellboy with a coffee cart. Maxine breathed in the aroma of freshly brewed coffee, realizing that there had been no coffee on the *Carpathia* – only tea, and very little of that.

Mrs. White accepted a coffee cup from Nellie and sipped thoughtfully. "The light," she said. "It must be because of the light we all saw. Now they want to deny that there ever was a light, but we know what we saw."

Miss Young laid a hand on Mrs. White's shoulder. "Now Ella, really, don't upset yourself and don't go jumping to conclusions. No one knows anything about that light. Senator Smith is starting his investigation this morning and calling his first witnesses. Everything will be revealed at the proper time."

"It was a ship," Mrs. White declared, "a ship that could have saved us all. No doubt someone is trying to hide that information from the Senator. That's why Sophie was kidnapped."

"If that was the reason, then we would all have to be kidnapped," Miss Young said, her hand still on Mrs. White's shoulder. "You heard what Lady Sempter said. She said that Dr. Lengyel sent Sophie to St. Vincent's. That has nothing to do with what we saw from the lifeboat. I am sure it has something to do with the injury to her foot."

Mrs. White ignored Miss Young's attempts to soothe her. "In that case," she said, "why is Mr. Alder also missing – a senatorial aide no less, and his senator is a member of the sub-committee investigating what happened to the *Titanic*. Why would he be missing?"

Maxine had been biting her tongue as she watched Mrs. White concoct a baroque plot involving the U.S. Senate in Sophie's disappearance. This was not a matter for the U.S. Senate. This was simply a family dispute and one that she herself had created. Sophie was heir to a great fortune and Maxine was not. Add to that the fact that Lucan Sempter was an obsessive gambler who would like to see his wife inherit that fortune, and you had a good enough reason for Sophie to be kept safe.

Nellie, who had been arranging coffee cups, spoke without being invited. "I heard that Mr. Alder fell into the harbor."

"Nonsense," said Mrs. White.

"That is what I heard," Nellie repeated. "The harbor patrol looked for him last night, but it was too dark."

"I think the two incidents are not connected," Miss Young said. She withdrew her hand from Mrs. White's shoulder and accepted a coffee cup from Nellie. "There is nothing we can do for Mr. Alder, but we can certainly help Lady Sempter and Sophie." She looked at Maxine. "What is it that you need?"

Alfie Blackwell
On board the *Californian* April 19

From the first day that he went to sea, Alfie had learned not to draw attention to himself. *Do what you're told. Don't talk back. Don't play cards.* Now he was just Alfie the crippled galley boy, too low to be noticed, and so he heard things he was not supposed to hear. It was happening now. Standing under the companionway, still as a statue, he overheard a conversation. As he listened, his heart had begun to pound. It had been beating so hard, he was sure they would hear him, but they didn't. Now they'd gone on their way, and he was alone and terrified.

He's a reporter.

Captain won't let him use the radio, but it will all come out when he goes ashore.

Captain can't stop him after he leaves.

But Captain can stop him now, for good and all. No one will even know he was aboard.

The galley boy knows. He's been taking him his meals and he's a nosey little perisher.

Same thing then.

What about the Captain? We ain't been given the order.

He will!

Sam White
On board the *Californian,* April 19

The skyline of Boston was clearly visible as the *Californian* slowed to take on a harbor pilot. Sam watched the pilot boat coming alongside. He saw the skillful way the small boat was held against the hull of the *Californian* and the agility with which the pilot stepped from the pitching and tossing deck of the pilot boat onto the rope ladder sent down for him.

He had not seen how the *Carpathia* had taken up the *Titanic* survivors. They were already aboard when the *Californian* came up to her. The *Californian* had agreed to remain on station, searching for additional survivors, but what would have happened if by some miracle they had found someone? Sam could not imagine how a survivor, in a lifeboat or in the water, could be brought aboard the *Californian*? A half-drowned man or woman would not be able to climb a rope ladder the way that the pilot had just done.

Sam asked himself what would have happened if the *Californian* had arrived ahead of the *Carpathia*? What if it had arrived in time to see the *Titanic* go down? What could the *Californian* have done about the thousands of people who would still be in the water, kicking, screaming and drowning? What orders would Captain Lord have given? How would he have organized them or brought them on board?

Sam was loth to think any kind thoughts of Captain Lord, but he wondered if the dour captain had imagined a scenario well beyond his ability to handle, with two thousand desperate people fighting to climb aboard the *Californian*. By comparison, the captain of the *Carpathia* had arrived hours after the tragedy had resolved itself, and the survivors, subdued and semi-frozen were in lifeboats.

Sam remained on deck until the pilot had pulled himself up the ladder and disappeared into the bridge housing. The pilot boat skimmed away, and the *Californian* began her cautious approach into Boston Harbor.

Sam returned to his cabin and sat on his bunk. His bag was packed and he was ready to go ashore and finally be able to buy a newspaper. What he wanted most was a list of survivors. He was curious about Aunt Ella?. Had she survived? She was not the most likable of women, and he was not close to her, but she was family. He didn't like to think of her floundering in the icy water, calling out for her maid, or her manservant, or Miss Young, *to do something*.

Of course, he couldn't fool himself that Aunt Ella was the only reason he wanted the list of survivors. He wanted – needed – to know which of the world's richest men had been swallowed up by the sea. Some of those men were important to the story he had been chasing for months – the story that had taken him to England and then on to a house party in Scotland. He already had the headlines in his mind.

Secret agreement will change American banking forever. Every American will be affected. Read all about it!

Ten New York bankers, dressed as duck hunters, board a private train to a remote island off the coast of Georgia. Crisis in American banking! Read all about it!

He would insist on a byline. He would not be an anonymous reporter. He would have his name in print. He would set the financial world on its head.

No – most surely that had already happened. Maybe Sam didn't know the names of the millionaires who had died, but other people did. Other reporters already had that story. His story, his scoop, wouldn't hold a candle to what had already happened as rich men lost their lives. He would have to wait and he hated waiting.

He sprang to his feet, ready to kick himself for his stupidity. He already had a replacement story. It was right here, and he was the only one who knew it. The machinations of J.P. Morgan and his cabal of financiers paled into insignificance beside the events he himself had witnessed on board the *Californian*.

He had seen the grave of the *Titanic*. He had witnessed the *Carpathia* taking up the lifeboats. And he knew what no one else knew! He knew that the *Titanic* had not been alone on the ice. She had not gone down unseen. He, Sam White, had seen her lights and her distress rockets.

Forget about financiers – he would take care of them later. This was the story of a lifetime. This could change his whole future.

He rummaged in his bag, took out his notebook, flipped past the story of J.P Morgan and the bankers, and found a blank page. He poised his pencil ready for a headline. Where would he begin?

He was still poised, still thinking when Alfie slipped in through the door with a worried frown on his face and a finger to his lips. Sam thought it overdramatic of the boy but he kept the thought to himself and remained silent while Alfie closed the door.

"I don't want to alarm you, sir," he said, "but I don't like the way the wind's blowing."

Sam raised his eyebrows. Alfie had been at sea for most of his life, maybe he was speaking literally and not dramatically.

"Captain called a meeting," Alfie said, "and if I was you, mister, I'd be worried."

"I don't think your captain can do anything to me," Sam said.

Alfie shook his head. "You don't know the half of it. You gotta watch your back." He glanced at the door as if to make certain it was closed before he continued. "Captain's instructions are that we didn't see nothing – no rockets, no lights, well, not lights from a liner. He says maybe a small boat, someone out sealing or going after cod, but we didn't see no liner, and we sure and for certain didn't see the *Titanic*."

Sam paused, measuring the meaning of Alfie's words. He had no doubt the boy was telling the truth – why would he lie? On the other hand, why would Captain Lord order his crew to lie?

"And what do you think of those instructions?" Sam asked.

"I dunno know, sir. I know I didn't see nothing, but you said you did, and so did Gill and so did McGregor and so did half-a-dozen others."

"What are Gill and McGregor saying?"

"Nothing, sir. They know what side their bread is buttered, if you know what I mean."

Sam shook his head. "Your captain isn't buttering any bread for me, Alfie."

"I know, sir, and that's what has me worried. Captain says he wants a quick turnaround in Boston and then back out to sea, and a bonus for every man who stays aboard and don't take shore leave. To be honest, sir, I think that if we didn't need to take on coal, we wouldn't be putting into Boston at all."

Sam felt as though the temperature in the cabin had dropped several degrees, but he couldn't bring himself to agree with Alfie. "Don't you have cargo to unload?"

"True enough, but talk down below is that Leyland Line might thank us for not stopping and not giving anyone a chance to talk to a journalist."

Now Sam was certain that the temperature was dropping. "I'm a journalist."

"I know."

"Does your captain think I can be kept quiet?"

"He didn't mention you, sir, not directly, not while I was listening."

A shiver ran down Sam's spine. It was absurd, of course, but he knew the old saying - *Strange things happen at sea* – but surely not this strange.

"Sir..."

Sam looked at Alfie's anxious face. "What is it?"

"I'm not sure you'll get a chance to go ashore."

"What do you mean?"

"I heard something. I ain't saying where I heard it or who said it, but it were something to think about. So I thought of something."

"I'm not sure I understand what this all means."

Alfie gave Sam a sharp anxious look. He seemed to be trying to make up his mind about something. "Well, sir, it's like this. I don't know if anyone knows you're onboard – anyone at the head office. You came aboard at the last minute and we wasn't supposed to be carrying passengers on this trip, so if your name ain't been recorded ... well..."

Sam drew in a long breath, realizing that Alfie was no fool, and he had made a good point. *Strange things happen at sea, particularly to passengers who are not on the manifest – passengers who have seen something that should not have been seen.*

"Do you see what I mean, sir?" Alfie asked.

"Oh yes, Alfie, I see."

"Did you tell anyone that you was coming on the *Californian?*"

"No, I didn't have time."

"And you ain't been sending messages on the Marconi."

"No, your captain would not permit it."

"So, no one knows," Alfie said.

Sam needed to think. He held up a finger for silence but Alfie would not be silenced. "The pilot ain't a company man."

"What do you mean?"

"Pilots ain't company men. Pilots are employed by the Harbor Master so that pilot don't answer to no one else."

"You mean he doesn't answer to Leyland?"

"Right sir, that's what I mean. So, what I think, sir, is that you have to let the pilot know that you're on board."

"But this has nothing to do with him."

"That's it, sir. You got it."

Sam stared at the boy astounded by the devious mind hidden behind the dirty face and ragged clothes. "Yes," he said. "I've got it, Alfie. The pilot doesn't have to know me, he only has to know that the *Californian* is carrying a passenger."

Sam's thoughts were racing now putting together the scattered fragments of Alfie's story. The crew had been told that, whatever they thought they had seen, they had not seen the *Titanic.* They were being bribed to stay on board and say nothing.

"The *Californian* would make a quick turnaround – just long enough to unload the cargo but not to take on another. That meant the *Californian* would be sailing in ballast back to her home port – a loss of money for Leyland. Someone was taking this very seriously. On the other hand, Lord and the Leyland Line had no hold over Sam. No one could stop Sam from going ashore, or could they? There was one way, of course, but was that really believable?

Sam chose to believe.

"So, if I can reach the pilot, I could get him to take me ashore on his boat," Sam suggested. He didn't like the idea of scrambling down the ladder, but it seemed a better choice than the exit that Alfie was hinting at.

"The pilot won't need his boat to go ashore," Alfie said. "He'll bring the *Californian* into her berth and then step ashore. If you go up on the bridge now and stay there, you can step ashore with him, and no one to stop you."

"Alfie," Sam said, "you are brilliant."

Alfie's cheeks flamed scarlet beneath its covering of dirt. "Thank you, sir."

Sam snatched up his bag. "I'll go now. Sooner the better."

Alfie stood hesitantly in the doorway. *Tip, Sam thought. I should give the boy a tip, a really generous one."* He reached into the inside of his coat. "Alfie, I'm really grateful —"

"Can I come with you, sir? I can't stay here. They'll know who warned you and I'm the one who'll disappear – not that anyone cares about me."

Sam laid a hand on Alfie's shoulders and felt the boy's tremor of fear. This wasn't right. This boy shouldn't have to fear for his life. "You're right, Alfie. You should come with me. We'll go up to the bridge together. We'll go now."

Alfie hesitated. "I can't go with nothing, sir."

"I'll take care of you. Buy you whatever you need."

"I'll need my papers and my paybook. I can't just go waltzing into America with no papers. Even if we go ashore with the pilot, we'll still go through Immigration. It won't take me long, sir. I only have a few things."

Sam forced himself to take a deep breath and tamp down his impatience.

"Go ahead, Alfie. Go and get your bag. I'll wait for you here."

"No, sir. Don't wait in your cabin. Wait in the stairwell by the galley. I won't be more than a minute."

"Alfie, I think you're making too much of this."

"You didn't hear 'em, sir. Please don't wait in your cabin. We're almost over the harbor bar. They'll want to get rid of you where the tide will take you out. They won't want you floating around in the harbor."

Well, Sam thought, now he's said what he means and no playing around with words. He thinks that the crew of the *Californian* is willing to drop me into the harbor. He shivered. What kind of man was Lord that he could inspire such loyalty, or fear?

Alfie left for the crew quarters and Sam picked up his bag and followed at a distance, losing sight of Alfie before he reached the short, steep staircase from the galley to the officers' mess. It was a good spot, with very little electric light and a deep shadow where Sam could conceal himself. He felt foolish skulking in the shadows.

On the upper decks carpeting had been laid in the corridors and public rooms, but outside the galley, the *Californian* revealed her bare bones in riveted steel flooring. Footsteps here were not muffled, and Sam heard footsteps. He sank back into deep shadow and held his breath as two crew men walked past, heading in the general direction of the passenger cabins.

They're not coming for you. They're just going about their own business.

What business would they have down here?

I don't know.

So, they could be coming for you.

Stay where you are. Wait for Alfie.

Sam was ashamed of his initial instinct to flee. Alfie had taken a risk in warning him and he'd promised to see him safely ashore.

The two men moved away, their metallic footsteps fading into the distance. Sam took a deep breath, and told himself that he was being foolish. Alfie was being foolish. The whole idea of Lord wanting to be rid of him by dropping him into the ocean, was utterly foolish. The catastrophic loss of the *Titanic* seemed to have caused a kind of madness in those who had been at the great ship's grave. With the current mania, even among the intelligentsia for consulting mediums, he knew what some people would say. They would say that fifteen hundred ghosts now haunted the Atlantic. Sam did not believe in ghosts and he didn't intend to become one.

He thought he had his unreasonable fear under control, but when he heard more footsteps, his heart began to hammer.

It was not the same two men. Gill and McGregor passed him so deep in conversation that Sam could have stood in full view and not be noticed. He wondered what they found so engrossing – a junior engineer and a ship's carpenter who was an old salt with no interest in donkey engines. So far as he knew they had only one thing in common – they had both seen the light.

Alfie arrived, patting his pocket and grinning.

"Is that all you're bringing?" Sam asked.

"Don't want to give the game away. Besides I don't have much. Did you ... er ... see anyone?"

Sam shook his head, still refusing to give in to Alfie's fevered imagination. "Just people going about their business."

He didn't mention Gill and McGregor. Whatever they were up to no longer mattered. Sam had already decided on his story. As for the other two men – well, best not think about that.

He picked up his bag. "Let's go, Alfie."

Dick Williams
Pier 54 New York City, 6:30 a.m. Friday, April 19

The crowds had dispersed but Pier 54 was not deserted. It was hours now since the family of Sophie Paxton had been sent back to their hotel to await a police report. A few representatives of the press still loitered on the shore hoping to corner members of the *Carpathia's* crew, or maybe pick up a thread of the Sophie Paxton story, or even the John Alder story, but the main press corps had already moved to the Waldorf Astoria. Senator Smith was wasting no time - in just a few hours his investigation would begin. The world waited with bated breath. There had never been such a story.

Meantime, on the Cunard pier, the *Carpathia* was taking on supplies for a return to the Mediterranean. Captain Rostron would give his report to the Senate Committee and then he would return to his ship and depart from New York – next stop Gibraltar.

Life goes on, Dick thought, as he motored past the *Carpathia* in a rented boat. He knew he shouldn't be out here on the river. There were so many other places he should be. He should be at his grandmother's house on Fifth Avenue helping her with her grief at the loss of her son Charles, Dick's father. She had not believed it could be true, not until Dick told her himself.

Setting his grandmother aside for the moment, Dick knew he should be at the doctor's office, or maybe even in a clinic, where he could receive the first real prognosis on his legs. He was determined to play tennis again but determination did not always turn into fact.

Now that the sun was coming up and the chaos of the homecoming was over, he should be with the police, explaining that John Alder had not simply fallen into the Hudson. And he should have been with Lady Sempter whose cousin Sophie Paxton had somehow managed to disappear. He should, perhaps, be explaining to the police the troubling connection between the disappearance of Sophie Paxton and the apparent drowning of John Alder.

These were all places where Dick Williams was needed but he was in none of these places and he was talking to none of these people. He had kissed his grandmother's cheek, waved away the idea of a clinic, and roped his grandmother's chauffeur into returning him to the waterfront and helping him to rent a boat.

If no one else would believe him, he would have to do this himself. He had been standing in the immigration line with John Alder when John saw whatever it was that he saw, and went dashing off along the pier. The incident was over in moments and Dick's legs would not allow him to follow as John rushed to the edge of the dock where two men were fighting over a woman in a wheelchair.

Limping behind and cursing his frostbite, Dick had seen a flurry of activity but he was absolutely certain that he had glimpsed John and one of the men roll from the dock into the water. The third man had not paused to look. He had taken the wheelchair and started running toward the street. Perhaps he had called out in alarm but Dick didn't hear it among the babble of voices around him. He was, however, absolutely certain of what he'd seen.

Dick had tried to get the attention of the already overwhelmed police but only one constable would accompany him to the edge of the pier. The constable had reluctantly peered into the dark, fast-flowing water but, of course, he saw nothing. It was a wild night for the police and they could not spend time on an incident that Dick Williams may, or may not, have seen. The survivors, even the first-class ones, were in a sorry state. They were not reliable witnesses to anything.

He's a survivor, but they say he may lose his legs, poor chap.

Not thinking clearly.

Probably drinking. It would drive me to drink.

Now, with the sun beginning to lighten the sky, Dick, Regis the chauffeur, and Liam, a lively young Irish boatman, were searching the shoreline of the river for evidence of John Alder – alive or dead. The river had already presented them with one body, drifting face down on the ebbing tide. It had taken only a quick glance to know that this was not John Alder. The man was big. He wore rough shoes and workman's pants, coupled with an incongruous white medical orderly's smock. On Liam's advice they set the body loose to continue its lonely journey. *No need to involve the police.*

"Well," said Liam, as they passed the Cunard dock and motored out into the wide expanse of the Hudson, "where do you want to go now?" He indicated the drifting body with a flick of his head. "This one, didn't fare very well. Maybe your friend put up more of a fight."

"John's a good swimmer," Dick said.

"So, he probably swam until he was out into the channel," Liam said. "That would put him... well... just about anywhere."

Regis gave Dick a sympathetic smile. "We'll find him, Mr. Williams."

Dick felt a sudden stab of heart-pain. Regis had always called Dick's father "Mr. Williams" but Dick had always been "Mr. Dick". Apparently, Regis had already made the adjustment required by Charles's death. Of course, he hadn't seen the manner of the death – the great funnel groaning and screeching as it fell in a shower of sparks. Dick knew he would see it forever.

Offended, but ashamed of taking offence, Dick turned his back on Regis and looked downriver. "Is there a strong current?" he asked.

"There is," Liam said. "With the current and last night's ebb tide, your friend could have been swept out a long way. I suppose he wasn't wearing a lifejacket?"

Dick shivered. He remembered the pull of the lifejacket, dragging him up from down deep and keeping him on the surface. He realized how very fragile his emotions now were. He was home and he was safe, he still had his legs, but he had a new fight on his hands. He had to learn to control his reaction to random words, innocently spoken but capable of dredging up memories. Lifejacket was just one such word, but how many more would there be?

He wondered if his fellow survivors felt the same way. They had all been given a second chance at life but would they go through that second life suffering attacks of sudden, unspeakable memories?

Liam broke into Dick's thoughts. "Should we turn around?"

"No, not yet. Keep looking."

CHAPTER THIRTEEN

Sam White
On board the *Californian*, Boston Harbor

The pilot was in no hurry to leave. The *Californian* was snugged up against its berth in the inner harbor, and the crew was at work lifting the hatch covers ready for unloading of the cargo. The pilot lingered on the bridge and Sam and Alfie also lingered.

Sam was determined to wait. The gangplank had been extended and he could see the Customs and Immigration shed. He was not going to walk the gangplank until the pilot was walking behind him or beside him. He asked himself if he was being a paranoid fool and answered his own question. Probably - but better a live fool than a dead wiseman.

Alfie lingered just beyond the door to the bridge. When challenged he was happy to respond with. "I'm to carry Mr. White's bags. The captain made me his steward. I'm only doing me job."

Sam, offered no word of explanation and simply waited on the bridge. When he had first arrived, uninvited, he had made an excuse that he was interested in seeing the work of the pilot. Captain Lord frowned at him and said nothing while the pilot looked up from overseeing the helmsman and gave him a friendly smile. Sam now knew that his presence on board had been noticed. He could not simply disappear.

As soon as the *Californian* was safely nudged into her berth, Captain Lord left the bridge, favoring Sam with a scowl as he passed. The pilot, apparently in no hurry to leave, immediately engaged Stewart, the First Officer, in conversation.

"Did you see anything?"

Stewart delivered his response in a stiff, flat Liverpool accent. "Don't know what you mean."

"It's in all the newspapers. *Californian* was second on the scene. You must have seen something."

"When?"

"When you arrived on the scene. There must have been something to see."

Sam saw the tension leave Stewart's shoulders, and thought he understood. Someone carrying a load of guilt would have read suspicion into the pilot's first question *Did you see anything?* Stewart was instructed to deny that anyone on the *Californian* had seen the lights of the *Titanic*, or the rockets fired from her deck as she sank. He had taken the question as a challenge. Now that he understood, his tone turned from flat denial to an appropriate level of remorse.

"We came up on the *Carpathia* as she was taking up the last of the lifeboats. There was nothing for us to do. Not much to see really."

"Wreckage?"

"Very little."

The pilot busied himself with folding his charts and notebooks and stowing them in a waterproof bag. "Terrible thing," he said.

"Terrible," Stewart agreed. "I don't like to talk about it."

"You won't have much choice," the pilot said. "The U.S. Senate has convened an inquiry in New York."

Sam could not help himself. He had to speak. "What did you say?"

"It's all over the newspapers," the pilot said. "Senator Smith of Michigan has been appointed chairman of a Senate sub-committee. He's going to get to the bottom of what happened to the *Titanic*, because whatever it was, it shouldn't have happened. Some of the richest men in the world went down on that ship, and no politician worth his salt is going to ignore that fact. Enough rich men drowned that the stock market crashed – not to mention rumors that the immigrant passengers were locked below." He looked up at Stewart. "They'll want to speak to your captain."

Stewart shifted uneasily. "We're not staying. We have a twenty-four-hour turn-around."

"Seems like Smith won't take no for an answer," the pilot offered. "There's plenty who don't want to talk to him, but he's more than ready with a subpoena."

Stewart's shoulders tensed. "This is a British ship with a British crew, we don't answer to your senate."

"Tell that to Bruce Ismay," the pilot responded.

Sam listened incredulously. Banned from receiving Marconi messages, he had not been given any news of what was happening ashore. He knew that the *Titanic* would be headlines, but he didn't know that this was happening. He should have guessed that such a shocking tragedy would not soon fade from the news, but a senate inquiry? He had not expected that!

He could not remain silent. He had to find out whatever he could, beginning with the owner of the unfamiliar name. "Who is Ismay?"

The pilot was happy to tell him. "Bruce Ismay, Chairman of the White Star Line. The *Titanic's* captain went down with his ship, but Ismay saved himself. From what I read in the newspaper, Senator Smith is dead set on proving that Ismay was actually in command of *Titanic* and giving orders to the captain. He's holding all the surviving officers. The whole thing is turning into a circus. Smith has set up a hearing room at the Waldorf Astoria. He's not giving anyone time to get away, or change their story. From the pictures I've seen, everyone in New York is trying to get into the Waldorf."

Stewart shifted his feet again and Sam realized that the first officer was anxious to leave the bridge – anxious to report to his captain. Sam could not resist a moment of smug satisfaction. So, Captain Lord thought he could get away with saying nothing of what had been seen from the bridge of the *Californian* – the lights, the rockets. Even Lord would not be able to turn his ship fast enough if word leaked out, and Sam fully intended that word would leak out.

His plans evolved as he realized that he was now in reach of another piece of news. As soon as he stepped ashore, he would be able to buy a newspaper and, therefore, a list of survivors. He wondered if his hunch about Aunt Ella had been right. Would he see the name of Mrs. Ella Stuart White on the list? He knew one thing about his globetrotting Aunt Ella – she was a survivor. If there was a seat on the lifeboat, she would be in it.

And, if she survived, she would have a story to tell.

Don't get ahead of yourself.

I'll know soon enough.

You already have the story of the Californian. That's a coup. Aunt Ella is just icing on the cake.

Aunt Ella has a permanent suite at the Waldorf Astoria, and that's where the hearings are being held.

We've always liked Aunt Ella, haven't we? We should go and see her, first thing.

The pilot buttoned his coat. He was ready to leave. Sam followed him out onto the bridge deck and found Alfie waiting with his bags. When he attempted to picked them up, Alfie forestalled him.

"I'll carry them for you, sir."

"Yes, do that," Sam said, striding to keep up with the pilot. He didn't look behind him, but he heard Alfie shuffling along. He wanted to turn his head and give Alfie a smile or a wink to show that he remembered his promise, but he decided it would be best to ignore the boy and so give Alfie no excuse to set down the bags.

They went down the gangplank together. The pilot nodded a puzzled goodbye. No doubt he wondered why Sam had lingered on the bridge or why he now followed so closely behind him. Sam turned and took one of the bags from Alfie and together they went to the Customs and Immigration office. Before they went in through the door, Sam looked back at the *Californian*. Captain Lord was standing on the bridge wing looking down at Alfie, the only one of his crew to defect, and at Sam, the man who was going to tell the story.

St. Vincent's Charity Hospital
Sophie Paxton

Sophie knew she was dreaming. All she had to do was open her eyes, but that didn't seem possible. She had no control over her sleeping body, and she had little control over her dreaming brain.

Her dreaming had taken her to a climbing lesson on a mountain in Wales. The lesson was not going well. For some reason, Sophie was climbing without a rope and without shoes and now she was stranded. Of course, Miss Pattison was down below but there was nothing she could do except shout.

Sophie clung like a limpet. Her fingers had found a hold in the crevices of the sandstone cliff, her right foot had found a secure projection where she could curl her toes for security. Her left foot, scrabbling for a foothold, could find nothing.

Miss Pattison's voice came to her from below. She seemed to be very far away. Sophie wondered about the height of the cliff. She seemed to be very high up. How long had she been climbing?

"Stretch, Sophie," Miss Pattison ordered. "Stretch your leg."

Sophie stretched, but found nothing. The rock was smooth. Why had Miss Pattison set her this test? Why wasn't she roped? She didn't need Miss Pattison to answer that question - she already knew the answer. If she had been roped, she would have given up and allowed the cliff to defeat her, but if there was no rope, there could be no giving up. There was no safety in defeat and Howell girls were never defeated.

Miss Pattison was shouting again." Si nil conatum, nil acquisitum."

Sophie made an impatient translation. Nothing ventured, nothing gained. Oh really! What else was Sophie meant to venture, it seemed she had already ventured her life? "Abundans cautela non nocet," she replied. "A little caution does you no harm."

Why on earth was she arguing in Latin with Miss Pattison while her finger tips, jammed into minute crevices in the rocks were beginning to slip? She tried to lift herself with her right foot, and then, at last her left foot scraped something. A projection? It had to be. She planted her left foot on the step, curling her toes for security. She let her leg take the weight. Pain lanced through her foot and shot up her leg. She opened her eyes.

Where was she? This was not the *Carpathia* and it was not a cliff face in Wales. She was in a long, echoing room with a vaulted ceiling. Beds lined the walls, each bed with a white counterpane and a woman sitting upright against equally white pillows. Sunlight streamed in through tall windows and pooled on a green linoleum floor. A strong smell of disinfectant battled the odor of food, predominantly boiled cabbage.

Sophie was sitting on the edge of a bed, and it appeared that she had just tried to climb out of bed and set her left foot on the floor. That would account for the pain. She had been dreaming - the dream so real that she had been galvanized into action and into an attempt to stand up. She lifted her foot from the floor. She was not going to stand up. Hadn't she made that clear? Her foot had been mangled beyond repair. Her tennis career was in shreds, and she was not going to become a limping figure to be pitied. She would stay in the wheelchair.

Miss Pattison was back, just briefly. "Get up and get going, Sophie."

Sophie was relieved that Miss Pattison had abandoned Latin phrases and reverted to English, delivering in a sharp haranguing voice.

"Matild?"

This was a new voice – a woman's voice.

The name came again, and Sophie shed the last threads of her dreaming.

"Matild Guttfreund?"

So, she was in a hospital – with nuns - and one of the nuns was trying to get her attention.

"Matild, do you speak English?"

The nun had a broad red face, and dark, determined eyes and eyebrows. She wore a starched white apron over her black habit, and her sleeves were pushed up under white cotton sleeve protectors.

Before Sophie could reply, her cousin Maxine appeared beside the nun. "Yes, this is Matild. I'll take care of her."

Now Sophie was not sure that she was awake. Why would Maxine call her Matild? Maxine leaned down and kissed her on the cheek. "Oh, Matild, we were so worried about you. There must have been a mix up with the paperwork. Immigration was chaos, wasn't it? Dr. Lengyel certainly did not intend to send you to St. Vincents along with all the other steerage passengers."

When Sophie made another attempt to speak, Maxine leaned down again. She whispered to her under the guise of another kiss on the cheek. "Just be quiet. Don't say anything."

For once, Sophie had no trouble remaining quiet. Maxine was here, smartly dressed, and definitely controlling the situation which was very unlike her cousin and Sophie was not certain that anything that was happening was real. She half-expected Miss Pattison to put in an appearance and speak to her in Latin mottoes.

Maxine turned to the nun. "I've brought clothes for her. I know you're busy, so why don't I just help her dress and then we can be out of your way? I've brought a vehicle to transport her. I'm sure you have other things to do."

"Other things," said the nun. "Yes, we have many other things."

Irish, Sophie thought, and angry, very angry.

"We have the crew of the *Titanic*, poor devils," the nun said. "Burns, pneumonia, broken bones. Some of them are near to death. I suppose there were no lifeboats for them, left down in the boiler room to keep the lights burning and them saying White Star is not even going to pay their wages."

"Well, I don't know about that," Maxine said, "I was not there."

Sophie was startled. Maxine was saying that she was not on the *Titanic*? Why would she say that and why was she calling her Matild?

'I will be making a generous donation to your cause to thank you for taking care of Matild," Maxine said, extending an envelope "and to thank you in advance for not saying anything to anyone about this silly mistake."

The nun nodded a thank you. "And you'll take care of getting Matild dressed?" she said.

"Of course."

The nun turned to look at Sophie. "For a Hungarian woman, you speak excellent Latin." She looked back at Maxine. "She talks in her sleep. Says all kinds of things." She waved the envelope. "Ah well, we are grateful for your donation."

As soon as the nun had departed, Maxine opened her bag. "I didn't bring you a corset or any underthings. You'll have to manage without until we get to the hotel. It's just a day dress and a wrapper, but if you stay in the wheelchair, you'll be fine. We'll find you something better as soon as we can and —

Sophie interrupted Maxine's flow of speech. "Where am I, Maxine?"

"St. Vincent's Charity Hospital."

"How did I get here?"

"There was an ... incident on the dock. You were to leave by wheelchair and an orderly came for you. I had to go up on deck to help Lucan with his immigration. I don't know all that happened next but Dr. Lengyel told me a little. I don't think he told me everything. I mean, well, I don't know why... It's all a bit of a muddle."

"Maxine," Sophie said, "you weren't muddled when you talked to the nun. You were really very effective. Just pull yourself together and tell me what happened."

"We think someone tried to ... well, kidnap you. Take you away in the wheelchair."

"I remember," Sophie said.

"No, you were unconscious."

"I was awake enough to remember someone running with the wheelchair and me bouncing around. Do you know anything else? Do you know who did this?"

Maxine shook her head. "No, I don't know anything else, except Dr. Lengyel saved you and sent you here and gave you his mother's name. The police have been looking for you all night. No one really saw what happened to you. Dr. Lengyel took me aside and told me where you were but he said I should say nothing until morning, so I had to sit quietly while everyone else panicked. There was something else – some men fell into the river and ..." Maxine's voice trailed away. "We'll talk about that later. Perhaps it will resolve itself and I don't want to upset you."

Sophie thought that maybe her cousin had already said more than she intended, although why Sophie should worry about men falling into the river, she could not imagine. Thousands of people had been on the piers, and it was not surprising that someone would fall into the water.

Maxine held out a simple, but surprisingly stylish cotton dress. "Stand up and let me slip this over your head."

The memory of pain came immediately. "I can't stand."

"Just try."

"I can't."

"Sophie, you've done all kinds of brave things," Maxine said. "You rowed all night while I did nothing but cry. Come on, just put your foot on the floor. Dr. Lengyel says you'll be able to walk."

"Dr. Lengyel's a butcher."

"I told him to do it. I wasn't going to let you die of sepsis," Maxine said. "You can blame me if you want to."

Sophie shook her head. "No, I don't blame you. I don't really blame Dr. Lengyel."

The thought stayed in the back of her mind. *I'll find someone to blame.*

Sophie sat on the edge of the bed and Maxine slipped the dress over her head, and followed up with a wrapper with an empire waist and wide sleeves.

"Where did you get this?" Sophie asked.

"From Mrs. White, it belongs to Miss Young. Mrs. White and Miss Young have a permanent suite at the Waldorf Astoria and so they have clothes to replace the ones they lost. Mrs. White is anxious to see you. Let me braid your hair."

"What about the family?" Sophie asked as Maxine began to brush and braid her hair. "Who has come to meet us.? Is our grandfather here?"

"No, he's not," Maxine said, giving Sophie's hair an unexpected tug. "I really thought that, what with us having survived a disaster and the whole of New York having turned out to greet us, Grandfather would have come, but he didn't. It seems he's not even interested in meeting my husband. I brought home a title and he still doesn't care."

"Where is your husband?"

"At the Waldorf, I suppose," Maxine said.

Sophie waited but that was all Maxine had to say on the subject of her husband.

"Did anyone at all come from Virginia?" Sophie asked, "anyone else from the family?"

She supposed she should be disappointed that her grandfather had not come to New York but she was not surprised. Aidan Paxton rarely left his Virginia estate. Sophie was his heir and his responsibility, but he had fulfilled that responsibility first with nannies and Governesses and then with the Howell School. She had no special relationship with him.

"My mother came," Maxine said, "along with Mr. Ponsonby the lawyer, to ... well ... look over Lucan and they sent your old nanny, to look after you."

"Nanny Bess?"

"Yes, that's her."

Something that had been like a stone in Sophie's heart, softened. Nanny Bess – she didn't realize how much she had missed the old lady who had been her father's nanny and then returned to be nanny to the orphaned Sophie.

"Grandfather also arranged for a surgeon to visit you at the Waldorf." Maxine said. "He didn't come himself, but he is at least looking after us. To be honest, last night was awful, with all the crowds and the chaos, and you disappearing. I'm glad he wasn't here to make things worse."

Sophie turned her head to look up at her cousin. Tears streamed down Maxine's face.

"It's all right," Sophie said softly. "I'm here. I'm safe."

"I don't think so," Maxine said. "Dr. Lengyel had his reasons for sending you here last night. Mrs. White thinks that you were in danger because of the light."

Sophie scrambled to put two and two together. "What light?"

"The one we saw from the lifeboat. Have you forgotten already? When we were on the *Carpathia*, you were swearing to get to the bottom of it. We believe that there was a ship out there that could have saved us."

"Oh yes," Sophie said. Of course, that was the focus of the blame – the ship that ignored *Titanic's* rockets. She was silent a moment while Maxine finished braiding her hair and produced a pouch of hair pins. It was a long time since anyone had done her hair for her. The Howell School was of the opinion that women should be able to do their own hair.

"Did you come alone?"

"No, Mrs. White sent her maid, Nellie. She's waiting outside to help me get you into the taxi."

"What about Dick Williams and Mr. Alder?" Sophie put John's name second so that Maxine would not think that John was the center of her interest.

"I don't know where Mr. Alder is but Mr. Williams has gone to his grandmother's house. I'm afraid he's the bearer of bad news."

Sophie nodded. "His father."

"Yes," Maxine said. "From what he told me, he saw the ship's funnel fall on his father. There is no hope. There will be hundreds of families receiving bad news today. The list of survivors has been published in the newspapers already, but there was always the chance that a mistake had been made. Now there's no chance. The only people saved are the people who arrived here on the *Carpathia*. There is no one anywhere else, and the list is final."

Sophie's wall of anger opened a little to admit pity for the families of the crew members who had worked so tirelessly amid the chaos to launch the lifeboats. They had not entered the boats themselves and now their families would know for certain that they had lost a son, a husband, or a father.

"You will find the Waldorf Astoria very crowded," Maxine said. "The American senator who is leading the inquiry into what happened has taken up the East Room of the hotel and is calling witnesses already. He's not wasting any time. According to the newspapers, he wants to talk to people while their memory is fresh, and while they have had no chance to be influenced by anyone else."

"What do you mean by influenced?" Sophie asked.

Maxine gave a little shake of her head. "I'm not sure. I suppose there would be pressure to try to place blame on someone. Mr. Ismay is a very unpopular person, having saved himself."

"We saved ourselves," Sophie said.

"But we're women," Maxine replied. "We're supposed to be saved."

Before Sophie could respond to Maxine's remark, which was so very much against the teaching of the Howell School, an orderly arrived with a wheelchair. Maxine attacked the poor man with questions and insisted that Sophie would not leave the hospital, not even be placed in the wheelchair, until a nun was found to identify the orderly and follow them outside where Nellie Bessette waited with the taxi.

Sam White
Ashore in Boston

Once they were out of sight of the *Californian*, Sam hailed a taxi and gave the driver instructions to take him to the train station. Alfie picked up Sam's bags and placed them in the taxi and then stood back. Sam climbed inside and turned to look at Alfie, still standing on the sidewalk.

"Are you coming?" he asked.

"What, me?"

"Yes, you. Are you coming with me?"

Alfie's eyes widened. "Do you mean it? Do you want me to come with you?"

"Yes, of course I do. I said we'd go together, so let's go and make it snappy. We have no time to waste."

Alfie entered the cab cautiously and seemed uncertain whether to sit on the leather seats. Sam patted the seat beside him. "I don't bite. Sit down."

Alfie sat, and hastily wiped his eyes with the back of his hand. "Thanks, Governor," he said. "I didn't know where I was going. I thought maybe I'd find another ship here."

Sam realized what he'd done, or more specifically, what Alfie had done on Sam's behalf. Alfie could have kept quiet. He didn't have to warn Sam of his suspicions about the crew of the *Californian*. There was, Sam thought, something noble in this scruffy motherless boy.

Is he motherless?

He may as well be.

Is he fatherless?

No, that's not what I'm doing.

Alfie's eyes widened inquisitively when the taxi glided almost silently out onto the main road, without the usual rattle of chains, and the inevitable backfire.

"Blimey, Governor," Alfie said, "what's making this move?"

"The wonder of electricity," Sam said. "These days most taxis are electric."

"Ain't never been in a taxi," Alfie said. "Ain't never been beyond the docks."

Sam leaned forward and tapped the driver on the shoulder. "Pull over if you see a newspaper boy."

They sat in silence as the taxi made its way out of the dockyard. Sam felt a surge of relief as they left the bustle of the docks behind. He realized that his relief was premature. If someone from the *Californian* wanted to find him, they would be safe in assuming that he was making for the train station. He told himself that he was being ridiculous. He was in no real danger from the crew of the *Californian*. After all, what did he really know and how dangerous was that knowledge? Well, imagination or not, once he got to New York and put the story in the hands of, preferably, the New York Times, any danger real or imagined would be over. The story would be out and Captain Lord could deny it if he wanted to.

"Where we going, Gov?" Alfie asked.

"New York," Sam said. "You ever been there?"

"Yeah, I been there, but, like I said, only to the docks. I've been everywhere, Gov. Been to Australia."

"But only to the docks," Sam said.

"Yeah, Gov."

After a brief silence, while the driver negotiated a labyrinth of warehouses, Alfie spoke again. "I'll get a ship in New York," he said. "Lots of ships in New York."

"You're not getting a ship," Sam said. "You can't be a cook's boy forever. You stay with me, and let's see how we get along."

"What, like a sort of servant?"

"Assistant," Sam said. "Can you read?"

"Oh yeah, guv, I can read and I can do numbers. You see, I went to school, when I was little, before me dad... well, before..."

Alfie seemed unable to finish what he was saying and he was rescued from an awkward silence by the driver announcing that he'd seen a newspaper boy. Sam pressed some coins into Alfie's hand. "Go buy a newspaper. Make sure it has a list of survivors in it."

Alfie leaped out of the taxi to confront a boy who was only marginally less ragged than Alfie himself. After a brief conversational exchange, Alfie was back with a copy of the Boston Globe. The headlines screamed at him. NO HOPE LEFT 1,535 DEAD.

Sam rattled the pages impatiently, looking past photographs of the great ship and lurid pen and pencil impressions of the sinking. He paused to study the photographs of the rich and famous men who been been lost. What would the world do without Jacob Astor, John Thayer, Benjamin Guggenheim, George Wick, or Charles Hays? Stock prices were falling.

He turned another page and there it was – the list of those who had arrived in New York aboard the *Carpathia*. He traced his finger down the page, noting that even now, when death had become the great equalizer for so many, the list was divided by class – many more names in first-class than there were in third class. He knew where to find his aunt, and there she was, Mrs. J. Stuart White, known to him as Aunt Ella. So, his hunch had been correct. Aunt Ella, with money to burn, had boarded the *Titanic* in Cherbourg.

"You all right, Guv?" Alfie asked.

"I'm fine," Sam said. He was longing to read every single word of the newspaper and bring himself up to date, but there was something else he had to do first. Somehow, he had to find clothes for Alfie. He could not take him on the train the way he was.

After another conversation with the driver, the taxi delivered them to a crowded street, where trolley tracks halted their progress.

"There," the driver said, pointing. "Jordan and Marsh, best department store in Boston. You want me to wait?"

"Yes," Sam said. "You wait."

He looked at Alfie. He couldn't take such a ragamuffin boy into the store. He would have to go alone, and do the best he could to find a basic outfit that would allow the boy to go on the train. This was going to take time and it was most definitely not the way he had planned his escape from the *Californian*.

It's not an escape. You were not in danger. Don't be so dramatic.

All right, I'm not escaping but I need to get to New York before anyone else tells the story.

He turned to Alfie. "You stay here and look after my bags and I'll be back in a minute. Do you understand?"

Alfie grinned. "All right, Guv. Do you mind if I read your paper?"

"Go ahead, read it."

Sam climbed out of the taxi carrying only his wallet. There was something about Alfie that evoked trust and he knew that the boy and the taxi would be waiting when he returned.

It didn't take long. The department store was a crowded Aladdin's cave of scarves, dresses, shoes, tableware, even bedding and furniture. He pushed through the throng of shoppers and rode the elevator to the men's and boy's department and found a simple but serviceable set of clothes that would allow Alfie to board the train without suspicion.

When he returned to the taxi, he found Alfie hurriedly folding the newspaper.

"It's all right, I said you could read it."

"Well, I did and all."

Sam found it hard to read Alfie's expression, somewhere between truculent and sad. He handed him the brown paper bundle of clothing. "You can change at the railway station."

"Thanks, Guv."

Sam thought about his new name. Alfie had started by calling him "sir" but now he was simply Gov. He concluded that the name was a good compromise. He could be "Gov".

The taxi resumed its journey to the station but they had traveled no more than two blocks when Alfie suddenly burst into agitated speech.

"There ain't no one cares about them," he said.

"I'm not sure what you mean."

Alfie jabbed a grubby finger at the newspaper. "It's all pictures of toffs, ain't it? They tell about the lives of the rich, don't they but not about people like us. We're at the bottom. We don't count for nothing."

"Who, Alfie?"

"The crew."

"There's a list of the crew. Some of them survived."

Alfie picked up the newspaper. "Two hundred and twelve," he said, "and most of them were deck crew and stewards. What about the firemen, and the greasers, and all them what works down below? There ain't many of them still alive. They wasn't given a chance to go up on deck and take their chances. They just died down there in the dark, didn't they?"

Sam looked at the boy he had taken so carelessly from the *Californian*. Tears glittered in the corners of his hazel eyes and his bottom lip quivered. It seemed to Sam that there was only one question to be asked. "Alfie, what happened to your father?"

"He went down on the Hilda," Alfie said, "18th November 1905, just after my eighth birthday."

"Tell me about it," Sam said.

"Ain't nothing to tell. We don't know nothing. She were a steamship on the Southampton to Brittany run and she went down off the Channel Islands. My dad was an engine man. He weren't on deck to be saved."

"When your father went down, was anyone saved?"

"Six people out of a hundred," Alfie said. "She broke up on the rocks trying to get into the harbor at St. Malo. It were snowing and blowing and there wern't nothing anyone could do and no hope for the engineers – well, no hope for anyone really. Like I says, the sea always wins."

"It certainly seems to have won this time," Sam said.

Alfie sniffed. "I suppose we should be glad that we know what happened to me dad, and at least we know where he lies. We couldn't bury him, but I can put me finger on a map and say that I know where he is."

"I'm sorry, Alfie," Sam said. "Is that how you ended up going to sea when you were so young?"

Alfie nodded. "When we got word me dad was gone, me grandmother said I'd best go to sea. I didn't have no mum and me grandmother said she couldn't feed no more mouths without my dad's pay, so I should go down to the docks and find meself a ship."

Sam tried to imagine the eight -year-old Alfie wandering the Southampton docks, looking for a ship, any ship, that would take such a boy.

"Me dad had friends, you know," Alfie said, "on ships. Me first berth was under sail. She was a beauty, four masted steel barque sailing for Nova Scotia. I was gone from Southampton in two days, hardly time to say goodbye. Ain't seen anyone in my family since. I was a climber, up the rigging like a monkey, until I broke me leg and I couldn't be a deck monkey no more. So, I went out under steam, dogsbody in the galley. And now here I am, on land and in a taxi going God knows where."

"The Waldorf Astoria," Sam said. "That's where Senator Smith is holding his inquiry."

CHAPTER FOURTEEN

Sophie Paxton
Waldorf Astoria, Friday, April 19

"Stop!" Sophie said

The porter obediently halted the wheelchair and Sophie leaned forward until she was able to see from the lobby into the East Room of the Waldorf Astroria – the room where Senator William Smith was conducting his inquiry into the loss of the *Titanic*. A long table dominated the room with men in dark suits seated along each side. A dapper grey-haired man stood expectantly at the head of the table – the seat at the other end was vacant. For the prisoner in the dock, Sophie thought.

Apart from the sober-faced men around the table, the room was filled with onlookers crammed into whatever space could be found. Scanning the faces, Sophie realized that the audience contained at least a smattering of first-class survivors of the *Titanic* – men and women she had seen on board the *Carpathia*. Even Lord Sempter was present slouching against the far wall, his eyes darting nervously.

She turned to look up at Maxine who was walking beside her as the porter pushed the chair. "Your husband is here."

Maxine nodded. "I know."

"Is he saving a place for you?"

Maxine raised her eyebrows. "I hope not. I don't want to hear any of what they say. It has nothing to do with us."

"Don't you want to know what really happened?"

"It doesn't matter, does it?" Maxine said. "It happened and people died. We can't bring them back from the dead."

"Perhaps we can stop it from happening again."

Maxine shrugged. "They'll just tell lies. All men lie."

Sophie stared at her cousin. Of course, she and Maxine had been virtual strangers when they began the voyage – their difference in ages meant that they had never played together as children, but the disaster had brought them a little closer. She thought she had begun to understand her cousin, but it seemed that she had been wrong about Maxine's relationship with her new husband.

She looked back at Lucan Sempter. Something must have happened between the newlyweds while Sophie was sick and feverish on the *Carpathia,* and that something was now causing Maxine to look at her husband with utter scorn. Granted Lucan was not an impressive figure, but Maxine had previously shown every sign of being enamored with him. There was the money, of course, or rather the disappointment about the money. Perhaps that was truly out in the open now.

"I want to stay and listen," Sophie said.

"That's not appropriate," Maxine said. "You're not even properly dressed. Besides, there's no room. Look at all the people."

"They should make room for a survivor," Sophie said, "and especially one in a wheelchair. You go upstairs if you want to, and I'll ask the porter to take me in." She lowered her voice. "He's a big fellow. He'll move people aside."

Maxine looked at her waspishly. "Or you could just walk."

"I can't walk."

"Won't walk," Maxine responded.

"Whether or not I walk is up to me and not up to you," Sophie said.

"Do you ever think about anyone but yourself?" Maxine asked. "You're expected upstairs. Grandfather's lawyer is waiting for you, and Nanny Bess is here to look after you. Don't you want to at least see Nanny?"

Sophie's heart warmed at the thought of the woman who had been her father's nanny long before she became nanny to his little orphaned daughter. "Send her down," Sophie said. "She can sit with me."

"Very well," Maxine said, "have it your own way." She turned to the porter. "Miss Paxton would like to listen to the witnesses. Take her in and I'll send someone down to sit with her." She took several steps toward the elevators and then turned back for a final remark. "I thought the Howell School produced independent young women, not selfish malingerers."

As Sophie watched Maxine enter the elevator, the ghostly Miss Pattison made a sudden appearance and proceeded to assault Sophie's conscience with a jumble of Latin admonitions.

Noblesse oblige, Sophie. Quid infant sumus, you silly, selfish girl.

Sophie tried to shut Miss Pattison out of her mind. She was not interested in being nobly obliging and she was not behaving like a baby. All her dreams had been dashed to pieces against that iceberg and she could see no future for herself. Surely, she was entitled to a period of mourning for the life she had once planned to live.

Destitutus ventis, remos adhibe, said Miss Pattison.

Oh yes, Sophie thought, that was very apt. If the wind fails, use your oars. She had used her oars. She had rowed all night, and this was the result.

Fortunately, Miss Pattison faded away as the porter pushed the wheelchair forward, scattering aside the mass of well-dressed New Yorkers and placing Sophie just behind, and within earshot of, the gentlemen seated at the table. She was so close, in fact, that she could hear a whispered conversation between two of the seated men.

"Has there been any word, Senator Eldridge?"

"Not yet, Mr. Uhler," the senator replied. "I can't understand it. He was reported to be on the *Carpathia* and there's no way anyone left the ship before it docked, not with the *Chester* following its every move and lookouts posted to see if anyone was smuggled away."

"There's no doubt he was on the *Carpathia*," Uhler said. "I have confirmation from my own staff, not to mention the survivors who saw him on board. It seems that something happened last night. From what I hear he was involved in some kind of contretemps last night on the dock as the survivors were leaving the ship.

I don't have details. It was all very confused - you know how it was last night. But it seems that there was a disagreement at immigration about a woman in a wheelchair. I don't know how he was involved, but the result was that he fell or was pushed into the river."

The senator's face fell. "Let us hope that these are false rumors. This *Titanic* disaster has proven too much for the newspapers and they print nothing but lies and rumors while the survivors tell stories that are impossible to believe. I don't know how Smith is going to get to the bottom of anything."

"Well," Uhler replied, "let's hope that this is one of the false rumors. I wouldn't give anyone much chance of surviving in the Hudson this time of year."

"He's made of strong stuff," the senator said. "He's already survived the North Atlantic, he can survive the Hudson. I wouldn't want to lose him. He's a promising fellow. The party needs people like him. I could see him running for office. He has what it takes – charm, education and determination. I assume the harbor police are still looking for him, if not I'm perfectly willing to throw my weight around. I consider him essential to the nation."

Uhler shook his head. "They called off the search last night. It was too dark, and the police are shorthanded. I'm told that young Dick Williams, the tennis player, took a boat out this morning to look for him."

Sophie leaned as far forward as she could, feeling a shiver of alarm as Dick Williams' name was mentioned. Who were they talking about? Who had fallen into the Hudson?

The grey-haired man at the head of the table raised his voice slightly. "Senator Eldridge, are we ready?"

So this was Senator Eldridge. John Alder had said he was an aide to Senator Eldridge. Was it possible that John Alder was the person they had talked about. - the person who had fallen into the river?

What had happened on the dock? There had been a woman in a wheelchair - the flash of memory came as a shock. She had been drugged but not entirely unconscious. She remembered people pressing in around her, shouting, grabbing.

Sophie swiveled in her chair looking for the porter. She couldn't stay here. She had to find out. Had she been responsible for this? Was she the woman in the wheelchair?

When she tried to turn the wheelchair, she found that she was unable to move. The crowd, craning their necks to see the senators, pressed in around her. The porter was nowhere in sight. Maxine had promised to send down Nanny Bess, so where was she?

The man at the head of the table banged his gavel. The result a new surge from the spectators. Sophie's chair moved with flow, and spewed her out very near the front of the viewers.

The gavel came down once again and the crowd parted to allow a man in a dark suit to approach the empty chair at the foot of the table. He was of medium height with dark hair and heavy moustache. He walked with his shoulders back and his chest thrust out defensively, but his face was white with fatigue, or fear, and his eyes were red rimmed.

A whisper rustled through the audience. "It's Ismay, Chairman of the White Star Line."

Ismay took his seat. The crowd still whispered. Senator Smith wielded his gavel again, the sharp blows forcing the audience into an expectant silence. Before the echo of the last blow had died away, one of the men seated at the table rose to his feet.

Senator Smith, whose eyes had been fixed on Ismay, swiveled to recognize the interruption. "The chair recognizes Congressman James Hughes of West

Virginia. Do you have a procedural question, congressman? We are about to open our proceedings."

Congressman Hughes was a white-haired man whose round face was flushed with either embarrassment or determination. "In the interests of fairness, I need to make a brief statement," he announced. "A statement has been made in the press with reference to myself and, in the interest of justice, I wish to set the truth before this committee."

Senator Smith raised his eyebrows. "Please continue."

"'My daughter, Mrs. Eloise Smith, was on board the *Titanic*. She survived but her husband did not. It now falls to me as her father to protect her reputation along with my own. I have received a telegram." He pulled a yellow telegram slip from his pocket. "This has come to me from the Huntington, West Virginia *Advertiser*."

He unfolded the paper and read aloud.

Congressman Hughes, you are quoted in today's newspapers declaring that Ismay should be lynched. Please wire us, day press rate collect, 500 words, your view of the Titanic disaster.

The crowd seemed to react in unison, drawing in a sharp breath at the word "lynched" The man in the chair lowered his head.

The congressman pulled another paper from his pocket. "I have sent the following reply to the Advertiser."

"*Press reports untrue. My daughter said nothing that would bring any such statement from me. I may have said if investigation showed neglect of any officer, no punishment was too severe for him. Ismay was somewhat criticized by some for being among the men who were rescued. My daughter had no criticism of him.*"

"Thank you, senator," Smith said. "We understand your concern."

He gestured for the congressman to be seated, and gaveled again for silence. *Lynched!* Sophie could only wonder what the press had been stirring up while they awaited the arrival of the *Carpathia*. No more than twelve hours had passed since the survivors had stepped ashore and already rumors were flying and anger was building.

Sophie allowed her mind to wander as the unfortunate Mr. Ismay began to respond to questions fired at him by Senator Smith.

"Your name, sir."

"Joseph Bruce Ismay."

"And your place of birth?"

"Liverpool England.

"And your age?"

"I shall be 50 on 12th December."

"And your occupation?"

"Ship owner."

Sophie thought of the many failures of that night – the chaos on deck, the captain handing out loaves of bread, the lack of flares in the lifeboat locker, the surly attitude of the men who had been designated to row the heavy boats. But not everything had failed. Charles Williams had not failed in his perceived duty to care for her, the Countess of Rothes had not failed as she faced down the rebellious seamen. The crew of the *Carpathia* had not failed. John Alder had not failed.

Regret threatened to overwhelm her and she pulled her thoughts back from the brink of a cliff that she could barely comprehend. If she looked over the cliff she would see her own behavior - angry, selfish, whining, complaining and calling out for pain medicines. Well, Dr. Lengyel had given in to her complaints. He had drugged her but while she was drugged something had happened. What was it? What had John Alder done?

Ismay was reading a prepared statement. The words were devoid of passion - simple statements of fact issued in the voice of a man who'd had almost, but not all, of his Liverpool accent erased by his education.

"I presume the impact awakened me. I put my coat on, and went up on the bridge, where I found Captain Smith. I asked him what had happened, and he said, "We have struck ice." I said, "Do you think the ship is seriously damaged?" He said, "I am afraid she is.""

Even as Ismay continued to make what were, in Sophie's mind, reasonable and honest statements, she could feel the shadow of doubt that hung over the room, and the echo of that awful word – lynched.

"I assisted, as best I could, getting the lifeboats out and putting the women and children into the boats," Ismay said. "I stood upon that deck practically until I left the ship in the starboard collapsible lifeboat which was the last boat to leave the ship, so far as I know. More than that I do not know."

Sophie could see Lord Lucan Sempter on the other side of the room. He was following every word that Ismay uttered. In fact, as the questioning continued, there were moments when he seemed to be trying to make eye contact with Ismay. Sophie was puzzled. What did this man have to do with Lucan and why were his responses making Lucan so nervous?

Of course, now she remembered. Lucan and Ismay had shared a lifeboat. She remembered Lucan's words as he met them on the deck of the *Carpathia*. "*It seemed foolish to die. I decided to join the Chairman of the White Star Line in displaying some simple English common sense."*

Was that the reason why Lucan seemed so very determined to catch Ismay's eye? Was he fearful that Ismay would name names, and reveal to this committee that Lord Lucan Sempter had betrayed his aristocratic lineage and entered a lifeboat intended for women and children?

Sophie had little respect for Maxine's husband. In fact, she was still convinced that Lucan was planning to get his hands on the Paxton fortune by whatever means necessary. However, she had seen for herself the utter foolishness of lifeboats being launched half-empty. It seemed to her that the senate, or the public, or the newspapers were looking for a scapegoat. Bruce Ismay, with his red-rimmed eyes, the contemptuous curl of his upper lip, and his astonishing behavior on the *Carpathia*, would fill the bill very nicely and Lord Lucan would not be far behind.

Senator Smith's next words snagged her wandering thoughts.

"Mr. Ismay, what course was taken by the lifeboat in which you were after leaving the ship?"

"We saw a light some distance off to which we attempted to pull," Ismay said. "We thought it was a ship."

Sophie sat up straight in the chair. A light!

"Can you give the direction of it?" Smith asked.

Ismay shook his head. "No, I could not give that."

"But you saw a light?"

"Yes, sir."

"And you attempted to pull your lifeboat toward it?"

Sophie did not hear Ismay's reply. Someone bumped against her wheelchair. When she looked up, a small olive-skinned man stared unapologetically into her face.

"You Miss Paxton?" he asked.

"I am."

"Miss Sophie Paxton?"

"Yes."

"Huh. "He peered into her face and nodded. "Huh," he said again.

"Huh what?" Sophie asked.

The man's face turned from curiosity to alarm as the porter stepped from behind Sophie's chair and lifted him by the collar. Sophie thought she had been abandoned but apparently the porter had been watching. *Howell girls did not give tips because Howell girls did not require help, but this porter was obviously an exception. She would recommend a tip for him.*

The stranger broke free of the porter's grasp and straightened his jacket. "Just delivering a message."

"What message?" Sophie asked.

"Look over there. Look at his lordship."

Sophie looked across to the opposite side of the room. Lord Lucan Sempter was no longer lounging against the wall. He was in the grasp of two large men who appeared to be intent on escorting him from the premises.

"What's happening?" she asked.

"He had a plan," the stranger said. "It didn't work. Now we have a plan."

"What do you mean?"

"You'll find out. Tell her ladyship we're very sorry that she couldn't settle his debts"

"What debts?"

"Gambling." The small man shook his head. "It's a fool's game and his lordship is a fool." He gave Sophie a smile that was not unkind. "I think this was for the best. Looks like you got troubles enough, you didn't need the kind of trouble he was making."

"He deftly evaded the porter's grasp. "All right, all right, I'm going." He patted Sophie's shoulder. "Sorry about the business on the dock. That wasn't the plan."

Ducking another attempt from the porter, he slipped away into the crowd.

Sophie swiveled in her seat to look up at the porter. "Did you hear what he said?"

"I make it my business not to listen to the guest's conversation."

"You listened," Sophie insisted, "and you tried to throw him out."

The porter looked up at the ceiling and then down at Sophie. "I sometimes make exceptions, especially for young ladies in wheelchairs."

"So you heard what he said. They're going to do something to Lord Sempter."

"I don't know the gentleman."

"Well, I do," Sophie insisted, "and I don't care much for him, but I can't just sit here and do nothing. We'll have to call the police."

The porter returned his gaze to the ceiling. "I think," he said, "that whatever was going to happen has happened by now."

"What are you talking about."

"Your friend, Lord Sempter —"

"He's not my friend. He's my cousin's husband."

"You cousin's husband," the porter said ponderously, "has made some dangerous enemies."

"They said he was gambling."

"Yes, gambling."

"Do you know the man who was talking to me?

"I know who he represents."

"Are you saying I shouldn't call the police?"

"I'm saying it's too late."

The porter released the brake on the wheelchair and began to push Sophie out of the room where Senator Smith was continuing to question the hapless Bruce Ismay.

Sophie had never felt so helpless. A verse from the Bible echoed in her mind – a verse that surely did not apply to her. *When thou shalt be old, thou shalt stretch forth thy hands, and another shall gird thee, and carry thee whither thou wouldest not.* St. John had been speaking of old age, but here she was only nineteen and already she was being pushed, against her will, toward the elevators.

She turned her head to protest to the porter. "Where are you taking me."

The porter nodded toward an elevator. A man had just stepped inside. He was short and stocky, blond haired and with a bandage around his temples. A survivor! Sophie's memories of her time on the *Carpathia* had been fogged by her ever-increasing fever, but she remembered this man. She had seen him from the corner of her eye when she had been sitting with Mrs. White and discussing the still mysterious light. The elevator gates closed and he was taken out of sight.

"Who is he?"

"Charles Romaine," the porter said. "Normally he wouldn't be permitted in here, but it seems that today he has been allowed. I believe that he is on his way up to your suite. I will take you there as quickly as I can. I imagine he has something important to say."

"Why? What kind of man is he? Why isn't he usually allowed in here?"

"He's a professional gambler and well known in the mansions of Fifth Avenue. He can speak for himself."

"I don't even know where my room is," Sophie said. "I've come straight from the hospital."

"I know where to take you," the porter said. "The Paxton suite is adjacent to Mrs. White's apartment. We will go to the sixteenth floor."

The elevator was slow, and it had a long way to travel. Sophie fidgeted in the chair, suddenly impatient to be with people she trusted. The porter seemed trustworthy, but she didn't even know his name.

Maxine had said that Nanny Bess had come up from Virginia. That was who she wanted. She had not seen the old lady in seven years, but now she longed for her. She wanted someone who would put their arms around her and let her simply weep. *Howell girls did not weep, of course, but very few Howell girls had suffered what Sophie had suffered in the past five days. Sophie banished Miss Pattison and her Latin mottoes from her mind. She could not be brave any longer.*

The porter brought her along carpeted corridors to an elegant cream-colored door where he knocked discreetly. When the knock produced no result, he knocked a little harder and then much harder. Somehow the knocking, loud as it was, remained discreet. This porter, Sophie thought, was well trained. She wished she could keep him with her. If she was going to lead the life of an invalid – *you don't have to be an invalid* - she needed someone like him. She had money – a great deal of money – and she could make him an offer.

At last, the door opened and the porter wheeled Sophie inside. The sumptuous sitting room was eerily quiet. Only three people were seated on the velvet chairs. Sophie recognized Mr. Ponsonby, the Paxton family lawyer, white haired, walrus-mustachioed and wearing a strangling starched collar. Maxine, straight backed and with her hands clasped in her lap sat next to the lawyer. Maxine's mother, Agatha, was arranged on the sofa and was an older, thinner version of Maxine, with the same perpetual air of disappointment.

It was Nanny Bess who had opened the door and now she greeted Sophie with a broad, relieved smile. She had aged, of course, and grown more plump, but all Sophie saw was a familiar face and a shoulder she could cry on. But not yet. First there was the man with the bandage who stood in the center of the room.

The porter took a step back keeping his eye on the visitor. "I will wait outside to escort your visitor from the hotel. If there is trouble, just call me."

The visitor nodded to the porter. Understanding was established and the porter departed, closing the door behind him. Silence settled on the room for a moment. The visitor turned toward Sophie and gave her a slight bow.

"Charles Romaine," he said.

"Yes, I know."

"I am sorry for your troubles," Romaine said. "We are all sorry for your troubles. This should not have been allowed to happen. We had an agreement."

Ponsonby, the lawyer, cleared his throat. "Good morning, Miss Sophie. I have a great deal to discuss with you and, of course, messages from your grandfather, but it seems that we must first deal with this fellow. He informs us that he is a professional card player and a survivor of the *Titanic*."

"We know who he is," Maxine said. "He spoke to me as we were leaving the *Carpathia*."

"And I am sorry that I have to repeat myself," Romaine said. He nodded to Sophie. "I will come to the point as quickly as possible so that I can leave you to your family reunion."

"Leave Miss Paxton alone and speak to me, Romaine," Ponsonby said. "I am the family lawyer. I will handle whatever this is."

"Well," said Romaine, "you may know that we professional gamblers make our living traveling on liners and playing cards."

"Cheating," said Ponsonby.

"No," Romaine said. "I do not cheat. I am simply very good at what I do, and I am also very good at knowing who can be separated from their money. You may not approve of me, but what I do is not illegal. I was traveling on the *Titanic* with a small group of men who are, in my opinion, entirely trustworthy. Three of us were able to find places in the lifeboats and we were saved by the *Carpathia*. We knew that the survivors were all in a bad way and we had made an agreement among ourselves that we would refrain from playing cards until the ship arrived in New York. The judgment of the survivors was impaired. It was not right to take advantage of them."

"Honor among thieves," Ponsonby said.

"If you wish to put it that way, I will not argue with you," Romaine said. "I can assure you that I had no part in what will happen to Lord Sempter. There were other gamblers on the *Carpathia*. Men who had boarded in New York as passengers on the *Carpathia* to Gibraltar. Some of them did not honor our agreement, and Lord Sempter was easily drawn into their game." He looked at Maxine. "I explained this to her ladyship before we came ashore."

Maxine spoke again. Her voice was cold but composed. "Yes, I remember your warning. There was nothing I could do."

Sophie studied her cousin's expression. *No, Maxine, there was nothing you wanted to do.*

"So, what is to become of my husband?" Maxine asked.

"First, let me say that what is happening is none of my doing," Romaine said. "Your husband owed a great deal of money and he had made rash promises. Apparently, he was disappointed in the amount of money that you, Lady Sempter, brought to the marriage. He was expecting a great deal more."

Sophie looked at her Aunt Agatha, Maxine's mother, and saw the flush of guilt creep across her face. Aunt Agatha, determined to please Aidan Paxton, had created the deception. Now she was reaping the results.

"Our family affairs are none of your concern," Ponsonby said. "Say whatever you have to say, and be on your way."

"It's all right, Mr. Ponsonby," Maxine said. "He's only telling the truth. When I married Lucan, I was not aware of what had been promised to him." She glanced sideways at her mother. "Lucan was disappointed in me when he realized that Sophie will inherit the money."

"A misunderstanding," Agatha said.

Maxine waved her mother into silence and Romaine resumed his story. "Lord Sempter gambled heavily on board the *Carpathia*. He was warned but he could not be stopped. By the time we approached New York he was deeply in debt to men who do not tolerate debtors. I spoke to you, Lady Maxine, in a hope to avoid the inevitable, but it was obvious that you would not help him to settle the debt."

Romaine looked down at the floor for a moment, struggling for words. When he looked up, he was looking directly at Sophie. "I'm sorry to say, Miss Paxton, that he put forward a plan that would involve you. He suggested you could be kidnapped and held for ransom. He was convinced that Aidan Paxton would pay anything to get his granddaughter back and Sempter would have his debt forgiven."

"So that's what happened on the dock," Sophie said.

Romaine nodded. "The attempt failed, thanks to Dr. Lengyel and another man, we believe to be John Alder."

Sophie's heart skipped a beat. Her memory of the past few days on the *Carpathia* had been clouded by pain and drugs, but she knew that John had been a hovering presence. It was John who had picked her up and taken her to Dr. Lengyel. She should be angry about that. She had blamed Maxine for giving permission, and Dr. Lengyel for performing the operation, maybe she should blame John Alder for carrying her through the storm-tossed ship and into the hospital suite.

Or maybe you should stop blaming and start caring.

Who put that thought in her head? It had not come from Miss Pattison with an appropriate Latin phrase to back it up. This was her own thought, and maybe her own shame.

"Are you sure it was John Alder?" she asked.

"There were witnesses," Romaine said. "He was seen by the disembarking survivors and there is no doubt about what happened. He grappled with your kidnapper and they went into the river together. Neither of them has been found."

She wasn't ready for that. *Neither of them has been found.*

Romaine continued speaking unaware of the effect of the stabbing darts of guilt caused by his words. This was all her fault. If she had not demanded pain medications, if she had made an attempt to walk, none of this would have happened. She thought of the dark river, the crowds on the piers, and John Alder swimming somewhere amidst the chaos of small boats that circled the *Carpathia*."

"There was little that could be done to find them at night," Romaine said. "The police were busy with the crowds and the river was dark."

Sophie felt a hand on her shoulder. Nanny Bess handed her a handkerchief. Sophie had been unaware of the tears rolling down her cheeks.

Howell girls don't cry.

Well, I do!

Romaine had turned his attention to Maxine. "I have come, of my own free will, to tell you of Lord Sempter's plan to kidnap Miss Paxton and the result of its failure. Lord Sempter attempted to hold at bay some of the most dangerous men in New York." He looked back at Sophie. "Your safety was in doubt during the night, but I can see with my own eyes that you are here now, safe and sound, and the plan was a failure."

Now Sophie understood what had happened in the East Room. The man who had peered so intently into her face was simply confirming the failure of the plot. She had not been kidnapped. There would be no ransom.

Money! This was all about money – something that she had never lacked but something Maxine had always lacked. She turned her mind away from the thought of John Alder fighting for his life in the river. She could have prevented all of this if she had given Maxine money. Perhaps it was not too late. She could still change the situation.

She looked across at Maxine, sitting so upright and pale-faced. "Maxine," she said, "if you can't pay his debt, I will."

Surprisingly, Maxine shook her head. "No, you won't. If you pay this once, you'll be paying forever. Lucan is a weak man and he will never stop gambling." She looked at Romaine. "Isn't that true, Mr. Romaine?"

"I'm afraid it is," Romaine said. "His only value now is as an example to others who do not pay their debts. As I said, these are dangerous people. Lord Sempter's fate will be an example to others who choose to owe more than they can pay."

"Fate?" Ponsonby asked. "What exactly do you mean by that word?"

"I know what he means," Sophie said. "I saw him taken from the East Room just minutes ago." She looked at Romaine. "What should we do?"

"It's too late to do anything," Romaine said.

"But it was just a few minutes ago" Sophie said. "Are you saying that he's already ...

"He's beyond our reach," Romaine said. 'The decision has been made."

Agatha gasped, but Romaine ignored her, concentrating on Sophie. "It will be done quickly and quietly, and later today he will be slipped into the river. These men know the tides and the current. They will make certain that he washes ashore in some conspicuous place. The bullet hole will be a warning to others."

Agatha's gasp turned to a wail and Ponsonby rose from his chair to confront Romaine. "That's enough," Ponsonby said. "I won't have you talking like this and upsetting the ladies. I don't trust you, Mr. Romaine. How can you know any of this unless you were involved?"

Romaine shook his head. "It is because I was not involved that I have come here today. I felt that Miss Paxton and Lady Sempter deserved to know the truth. I have no wish to be involved and so I will leave it to you to tell Senator Eldridge what has happened to his aide. He will inform the family that their son died in a brave attempt to prevent a crime."

"Senator Eldridge's aide," Sophie said. "Is that John's position?"

"Yes," said Romaine. "I understand he had been on a fact-finding mission in Europe on behalf of the senate. Perhaps your lawyer would be the best person to speak on your behalf. No need for you ladies to involve yourselves."

Senator Eldrige's aide! John Alder was the senator's aide. Sophie sniffed and swiped a hand across her tears. Suddenly she realized the significance of the conversation she had overheard downstairs.

I'm told that young Dick Williams, the tennis player, took a boat out this morning to look for him."

"John's not dead," Sophie declared. "Dick Williams is out looking for him and I know he'll find him."

Romaine raised his eyebrows. Sophie realized that, as a professional gambler, Romaine was very accustomed to seeing and taking advantage of false hope, but this was not a false hope. Where Dick Williams was involved, there was always an opportunity for hope. She settled back in her chair. It was just a question of waiting.

Ponsonby, although obviously more accustomed to dealing with wills and trusts, seemed to have gathered his wits and was now ready to deal with this unexpected criminal element. "How do we know that anything you are saying is the truth," he asked. "I am going to call the police. They'll get to the bottom of this."

"This is New York," Romaine said, "and the police will do nothing. Lord Sempter crossed the wrong men. It is possible that a case file could be opened, after all the victim possesses an aristocratic British title, but no action will be taken."

Maxine interrupted in a small, tight voice. "Are you sure that his body will be found?"

"Absolutely. That is the object of the exercise."

Maxine nodded. "Good. I wouldn't want there to be any doubt." She pressed her hand to her abdomen. "The title is hereditary and it already has a new owner."

"Maxine, my dear," Agatha said, "you are in shock. We should call a doctor."

Maxine's smile was almost serene. "I have no need." She rose slowly. "So far as I'm concerned, you have brought me good news, Mr. Romaine."

A discreet but determined knock drew Romaine's attention to the door. "I believe that's my signal to leave. The porter grows impatient. I am not usually welcome at the Waldorf."

"How can we reach you again?" Ponsonby said.

"You can't," Romaine replied. "I'll be leaving New York on the next liner, wherever she may be headed. Lord Lucan has stirred up a hornet's nest. I don't wish to join him in the river."

Maxine moved ahead of him to open the door. She seemed revived and almost happy as she pulled the door open. "Thank you, Mr. Romaine."

CHAPTER FIFTEEN

John Alder
On the Hudson River
All he had wanted was to survive the night. Now it was morning and still no one came. He was too far from land. The current had swept him way out into the channel. If he had not climbed onto the buoy, he would be out in the Atlantic again.

He had spent the night in relative safety by pulling himself onto the buoy and finding a place to lie face down between the legs of the pylon that held the channel light. He was able to hold the struts with both hands. His position, under the channel light, had kept him out of the water and relatively hidden from view.

Now he heard the steady thrum of a small boat engine nearby. He knew what he would have to do. It was full daylight now and there was a chance he could be seen and rescued. The tide was on the ebb and flowing fast. The buoy leaned into the current and rolled with the waves. The boat was definitely approaching, probably coming down the channel for its own purposes – a fisherman perhaps. It would not be someone looking for him. After that long dark night there would be no one who would expect him to still be alive, but here he was. He told himself that John Alder was a hard man to kill. He had beaten death once, and he would beat it again if he could just stand upright and get the attention of whomever was in that boat.

He released the hand grip that he had held tightly all night. His fingers were cramped and his shoulders stiff but he forced himself to stretch upward, until he was on his knees. This was not high enough - he would have to stand on rubbery legs. His shoes, dress shoes he had been wearing that last night on the *Titanic*, gave him no grip on the slippery. weed draped platform. He locked his knees. He was doing it. He pulled himself upright and lifted his eyes toward the sound of the motor.

It was a small open boat, and he could make out three occupants. The motor was running slowly and all three men were standing. John's heart skipped a beat. This was no fisherman heading out for the day, this was someone looking for him. He released one hand and waved. He began to slip. His feet scrabbled for purchase but the smooth soled dress shoes offered no assistance. He waved, shouted, and clung precariously. He was starting to slip.

The engine note changed. Someone waved back. Sudden relief made him careless. He lost his grip on the pylon and slid inexorably across the platform, into the water and down again into the grip of cold memory. For one brief moment he gave in to inevitability – he was doomed to drown – but hands reached for him.

He was pulled to the surface. This was not like the night on the *Titanic*. This time friendly, willing hands pulled him into a sturdy boat. He was wrapped in a warm blanket and given a brandy flask. He opened his eyes to hopeful reality. It was over. The sea had not taken him.

John took a long pull from the flask and felt the brandy burning down his throat. He took in the fact that Dick Williams was seated beside him, and the other two men were strangers – smiling strangers – delighted strangers – congratulatory strangers. So congratulatory, in fact, that the brandy flask was taken from his hand and shared around.

"Here's to you," said the man at the tiller. "*Sláinte.*"

An Irishman, John thought. He turned to Dick. "How did you... How long have you been looking? Did you stay out here all night?"

"No," Dick said. "There was no point, but I've been out here with Liam and Regis since the crack of dawn. We were about ready to turn around when we finally saw you. Did you *have* to take another dive into the Atlantic? Haven't you done enough of that?"

"More than enough," John said. "What about the other man? The one who took the wheelchair?"

"He won't be troubling you again," Dick said. "He's on his way out into the Atlantic."

"And Miss Paxton?"

"She's fine," Dick said. "We received word that she was discovered this morning at St. Vincent's Hospital."

"But why?"

"Damned if I know," Dick said with a hint of impatience, "but I blame it all on Lord Sempter. He's got himself into deep trouble." He grinned at John. "Never mind. He gave you a chance to be a hero."

169

John shivered and held out his hand for the brandy flask. "Being a hero is overrated," he said.

"Find us a quiet place to land," Dick said to Liam. "We'll have to get Mr. Alder cleaned up before he faces the public." He winked at John. "Or Miss Paxton," he added.

The boat motor settled down to a steady pace, working against the tide and the current to return its occupants to the docks. They passed the bustle of the Chelsea piers and motored into a desolate area where the new construction ended and the old piers and jetties still remained.

"We can slide in here," Liam said, taking the boat past a series of rotting piers.

John glimpsed three figures standing on one of the piers. From what he could tell two large men, were dragging a limp, probably dead, body toward the water's edge.

"Liam," Dick said, "what's going on over there?"

"Best not to ask," Liam said, abruptly reversing his engine and pulling away from the shore. "Sometimes we have a little home-grown justice."

"But it's murder in broad daylight," John said.

"It's New York City," Liam responded. "Best to leave it alone."

No," John insisted. "We have to get in there and find out who that is."

Liam shook his head. "You're in no shape to take on anyone, and that, whatever it is, is not my fight."

The two men had reached the water now and, with one on the arms and one on the legs, they hurled the body into the river. The body entered the water with a loud splash and as it began to float away on the current, one of the men fired a single shot, causing the limbs of the dead man to jerk obscenely.

"Why in hell would they do that?" Dick asked. "Why shoot a dead man?"

"Just to make sure," Liam said. "I'll take you ashore now."

The body, caught in the current came close alongside their boat and Liam made no attempt to avoid it.

"Do you want it?" he asked casually. "If you're concerned, we can report it to the police. It's probably no one."

"Everyone is someone," John said, still shocked by what he had seen.

The body, floating face down, was now bumping into the hull, and Regis leaned down to snag its clothing. The body rolled and turned face up.

John stared for a long, long moment.

"Lucan Sempter," Dick said.

John could only nod – robbed of words.

Sempter's face was no more noble in death than it had been in life. The bullet – good shooting on the part of his assassin – had pierced his forehead.

"Do you want me to pull him in?" Regis asked.

He's been warned.

He wrote his IOUs.

He says that his wife is expecting money.

"Well?" Regis asked.

"Let him go.," John said.

Regis released the body and Lord Lucan Sempter rolled over as the current took hold and swirled him out into the ebbing tide.

Sam White
New York City, April 19

With the setting sun casting golden rays on the tall buildings along Fifth Avenue, Sam and Alfie approached the ornate exterior of the Waldorf Astoria Hotel. Sam was astonished at the size of the crowd gathered on the sidewalk at the corner of Fifth Avenue and 33rd Street. He saw that Alfie was open-mouthed in wonder at the magnificent Waldorf building with its arched windows, and columned balconies. The Waldorf was only outdone in splendor by the Astoria building's fairy tale roofline of minarets and domes.

Peacock Alley, joining the two halves of the hotel, was jammed with the fashionable denizens of New York. The public sidewalk was thronged with the working classes and around the edge of the confusion, reporters lurked, notebooks in hand.

Sam was relieved that, for once, he would not have to push his way in among the reporters. He had telephoned his Aunt Ella before he boarded the train in Boston. Her initial tone had been unwelcoming.

"Sam who?"

"Oh, Celia White's boy. Nephew by marriage then."

"What do you want from me?"

He had to speak sharply to break through her resistance. *"I saw the Titanic. No, Aunt, not at the dock. I saw her at sea. I saw the rockets."*

Now, he had her attention.

"Come up to my apartment. Miss Young is here with me. You'll have to fight your way through the crowds. It's a positive zoo here with Bruce Ismay as the main exhibit."

Sam and Alfie pushed through the crowd and entered the lobby of the Waldorf building. Although he knew that his aunt was expecting him, Sam was drawn aside, not by noise, but by a deep silence emanating from a large colonnaded room to his right. Alfie led the way, squirming between the standing, silent people, and making a path for Sam.

So, this was it. This was the room where Senator Smith was conducting his inquiry. The senator stood at the head of a long, polished table with committee members arrayed along each side. A handsome, square-jawed man in a Cunard uniform sat at the foot of the table. People, mainly men and mainly journalists, pressed in on each side but no one spoke above a whisper. All eyes were on the uniformed seaman who appeared to be reading from a log book.

"At 2:40, I saw a flare, about half a point on the port bow, and immediately took it for granted that it was the *Titanic* itself, and I remarked that she must be still afloat, as I knew we were a long way off, and it seemed so high. However, soon after seeing the flare, I made out an iceberg about a point on the port bow, to which I had to port my helm to keep well clear of. Knowing that the *Titanic* had struck ice, of course, I had to take extra care and every precaution to keep clear of anything that might look like ice."

Sam knew that this was not Bruce Ismay. This was Arthur Rostron, Captain of the *Carpathia*. Listening to Rostron's description of the risks he had taken on the night of April 15, Sam was filled with admiration. Rostron spoke without emotion but his actions spoke for themselves.

Sam, his Aunt Ella momentarily forgotten, realized that he, Sam White, had a unique view of the story that Captain Rostron was telling. He alone among the silent audience, had seen the *Carpathia* taking up the last of the lifeboats. He had seen the icebergs and the floe ice all around. Maybe he had, unknowingly, seen the singular iceberg that had caused the disaster.

"We picked up the first boat," Rostron said, "and the boat was in charge of an officer. I saw that he was not under full control of this boat, and the officer sung out to me that he only had one seaman in the boat, so I had to maneuver the ship to get as close to the boat as possible, as I knew well it would be difficult to do the pulling. However, they got alongside, and we got them up all right."

Rostron looked up from the log book. "I maneuvered the ship and we gradually got all the people up aboard by eight-thirty."

Rostron closed the log book and looked up as if surprised to see so many people listening to him. "Around eight o'clock," he said, "the Leyland Line steamer *Californian* hove up, and we exchanged messages."

Sam had fallen into a trance-like state listening to Captain Rostron but the mention of the *Californian* freed him. Rostron was now responding to questions. The man was obviously a hero. Sam knew this more than anyone else. He had seen the ice. Rostron's story would, no doubt, dominate the reporting alongside the story of Bruce Ismay, the man who had saved himself.

Sam had his own story to tell – a new villain to be exposed to the general public. He gestured to Alfie and they backed quietly out of the room, returning to the lobby and the bank of elevators that served the upper floors.

When they entered an elevator, the operator eyed Alfie suspiciously. Sam had done his best to transform the boy with clean clothes, but there was no denying that his hair was dirty, his finger nails were far from clean, and, despite the new clothes an odor of kitchen grease wafted into the air around him.

"Mrs. White is expecting us," Sam said.

The operator, a dark-skinned man whose suspicious gaze reflected years of protecting the sacred confines of the guest rooms, curled his lip scornfully. "All sorts of people coming in and out, day and night."

"I am not *all sorts of people*," Sam said stiffly. "I am Mrs. White's nephew."

"There'll be no peace until this *Titanic* business is over and done with," the operator muttered.

"Don't you want to know what happened?" Sam asked.

"Ships sink all the time," the operator said dolefully. "This one was full of rich people."

"And immigrants," Sam said.

"This fuss is not about immigrants," the operator replied. "This is because the stock market fell. If you ask me, it was an Act of God to show us our place in the world, and we have no business interfering."

The elevator jolted to a halt and the operator opened the gates. "Sixteenth floor."

Sam and Alfie made their way along the carpeted corridor to the apartment of Ella Holmes White. Sam had known Mrs. White, or at least known *of* Mrs. White, since he was ten years old. That was the year that the eccentric Miss Ella Holmes, had surprised the family and all of society by marrying Sam's uncle John White. It had been a short-lived marriage with John dying less than three years later. Fifteen years had passed and Ella Holmes White still clung to her widowhood, still called herself Mrs. J. Stuart White, and still acknowledged a tenuous relationship with her late husband's family.

There was, of course the mystery of Miss Marie Young, Ella's constant companion. For the past two years they had lived and traveled together, and Miss Young, a well-connected piano teacher, had abandoned her teaching practice. Why? Sam knew the nature of the speculation about the relationship between the two women, and he also knew it was none of his business. His business was the *Californian* and the rockets in the night.

Nellie Bessette, Aunt Ella's maid answered Sam's knock at the door. Sam had to admire her dedication. She had just been saved from a terrible death. Wouldn't she rather be at home hugging her loved ones instead of back in uniform and answering the door? Perhaps she didn't have a home.

Nellie gestured for them to enter the sumptuous room, but she snagged Alfie before he had taken more than three steps. Alfie was distinctly out of place in the extravagant sitting room and Nellie did not even hesitate.. "Come with me, young man. You need a bath."

Alfie threw Sam a helpless glance. "What am I supposed to do, Guv?"

"Have you ever had a bath?"

"Not since I went to sea."

"Well, you're not at sea now, so go along with Miss Bessette."

Sam turned his attention to his Aunt Ella who limped toward him leaning on a cane. He remembered her as a plump but kindly woman with a round face, apple cheeks and a ready smile. The passing years had turned her from plump to heavy, and the apple cheeks had become jowls that drooped wearily in an unsmiling face. He wasn't sure how to greet her. Should he bow, kiss her cheek or maybe shake her hand in the new style? Aunt Ella pre-empted any kind of familial greeting by brandishing her cane and informing him that he was late.

"I was drawn in by the inquiry downstairs," Sam admitted. "Captain Rostron of the *Carpathia*."

"A fine man," Aunt Ella declared. "We owe him our lives." She peered into Sam's face. "You look like your father. In fact, you look like my late husband. There's no doubting who you are."

"You thought I could be an imposter?"

"Reporters are getting up to all kinds of tricks to obtain an interview with a survivor, but I can see that you are who you say you are. Now, as for this story you told me on the telephone..."

"It's true – every word."

"You were on a ship named the *Californian*?"

"Yes."

"And you saw the *Titanic*?"

"I was on deck. I saw her lights and her rockets."

"How close were you?"

"No more than a few miles."

"And the *Californian* did nothing?"

"No. We did not move."

Aunt Ella suddenly tottered backward and slumped into an armchair. "Captain Smith did not lie," she said weakly. "There was a light." Her whisper rose to a sudden unladylike shout of triumph. "There was a light!" She called to Marie Young who had been standing at a discreet distance. "Marie, did you hear what he said?"

"I did."

She turned her attention back to Sam. "What do you intend to do with this story?"

"I intend to sell it to a newspaper. Captain Lord is attempting to take the *Californian* out of Boston without admitting to what we all saw in the night. I need to find someone who can help me reach the editor of the Times. If I could use your telephone..."

Aunt Ella's expression was shrewd. "I know someone, who knows someone. We'll get this story into the right hands as soon as possible." She glanced at the carriage clock on the mantelshelf. "There's no time to waste. Start writing your story and I will start talking on the telephone. Tomorrow the whole world will know that the women in lifeboat #8 were not imagining things – there was a ship out there, standing by and doing nothing while the *Titanic* went down."

Miss Young came to stand by Ella's chair and placed a comforting hand on her shoulder. "We have all suffered," she said, "and we demand justice."

Sophie Paxton
Paxton Suite, Waldorf Astoria
Evening, April 19

Mr. Ponsonby announced his intention of returning to his own room to make a report to Aidan Paxton, and Maxine and her mother had retired to their bedrooms. Sophie wondered how they could possibly sleep. She knew she wouldn't sleep, not until she knew, one way or another, if John Alder was still alive.

She was alone, apart from the comforting presence of Nanny Bess. With no one else watching, the old lady emerged from her chair in the corner and settled herself down onto the sofa, within whispering distance of Sophie's wheelchair.

"How are you, lamb?" she asked. Bess McNair's voice still held traces of her Scottish childhood and, even after so many years apart, the voice was in danger of returning Sophie to her helpless childhood condition. Her independence from sentimentality had been hard-won, and she would not throw it away just because this tender old woman was waiting to wrap her in sympathy and comfort.

"I'm not your lamb, not anymore," Sophie said. "I'm not even a little girl."

"You're still my little girl," Nanny Bess said, "and you've been crying."

"I'm fine," Sophie said.

"No, you're not. I know all about that terrible school where your grandfather sent you. and I see fine that you think it's turned you into a strong young woman. Maybe it has, but you're not strong enough to do this alone."

Sophie leaned forward in the wheelchair. "I am doing what the Howell School taught me. I am coping."

"You're not supposed to be able to cope with all that's happened to you these last few days," Nanny Bess insisted. "No school in the world can teach you to cope with such things, unless the school has taught you not to care. Is that what's happened? Has that school cut out your heart?"

"No, of course not. I care."

"Do you care about this man who has flung himself into the river to save you?"

"Yes, I do, and I can't bear the idea that he would die trying to save me. It makes me feel so helpless. I shouldn't need someone else to save me."

Nanny's voice was suddenly sharp. "Me, me, me! Is that all you can say? Listen to me, lassie. That school has ruined you. When you left my care, you were a kind and loving child and look at you now– so puffed up and full of yourself, you can't even cry for the man who saved you."

Sophie recoiled from the sudden attack. This was Nanny Bess, the woman who had comforted her when she had been brought as an orphan to Aidan Paxton's mansion. Nanny Bess had spoken soft Scottish words to her and fed her comforting puddings, and sweet cakes. Nanny Bess had loved her. How could she speak like this?

Miss Pattison emerged briefly to remind Sophie to trust no one but herself. Nulli credo nisi mihi. The Scotswoman is old and ignorant. Take no notice of her.

Sophie had no intention of repeating Miss Pattison's ghostly words to Nanny Bess. In fact, she was still wrestling with the possibility that there was some truth in Nanny's accusation of self-centeredness, when the candlestick phone on the desk rang...and rang...and rang. Sophie struggled with the wheelchair. She had not practiced moving it by herself. There had always been someone to push her. Now she needed to reach the phone. It could be news. Had a body been found? Lord Sempter maybe, or maybe John Alder. She had to know.

"Nanny, answer the phone."

"Get out of the wheelchair."

"I can't."

Nanny shrugged her shoulders. "I'm ashamed of you."

"Please, please, Nanny, answer the phone."

Nanny picked up the receiver and put it to her ear. She listened for a moment and then picked up the microphone. "Miss Paxton will require fifteen minutes to prepare for visitors. Please ask the gentlemen to wait."

Gentlemen? How many gentlemen? Who were they? Not police. Nanny would not have said "gentlemen" if they had been policemen and policemen would not have waited. Reporters? No, they wouldn't be permitted in the Waldorf. It could only be...

"Nanny, who was it?"

Nanny's face was wreathed in smiles, her previous anger forgotten. "Mr. Williams and Mr. Alder."

Sophie began to cry. It seemed that floodwaters had filled a deep well somewhere in her soul. Her memories and her fears now turned to tears that could no longer be contained. She gasped for breath as sobs shook her body. She cried for the dead, she cried for the living, she even cried for Lucan Sempter, and then, as the sobs turned to mere tears, she cried with relief. John Alder was alive.

Nanny was ready with a hairbrush and a washcloth. As she brushed Sophie's hair, she issued instructions.

"You will not say anything about your own abilities," she said.

"I don't know what you mean."

"All that nonsense about being able to save yourself. You'll do none of that. He saved you, and you will thank him, and..." Nanny paused with the hairbrush in her hand.

"And what?"" Sophie asked.

"Did that school teach you anything about courting?"

"Courting? No, Howell girls don't —"

"Don't what?" Nanny asked. "Don't need husbands?"

Husbands!

A knock at the door. Nanny bustled across the room, leaving Sophie to grapple with the word – husband!

Dick Williams was still limping but he was smartly dressed in, presumably, his own clothes. John Alder followed behind him. There was nothing smart about John's appearance. The suit he wore had been made for a smaller man, maybe for Dick Williams. His shirt collar was unbuttoned, his tie was loose, his hair was straggling down toward his collar and his chin bristled with beard stubble.

Husband material? Sophie asked herself. Too soon to tell, but at the moment he was definitely her white knight. He had flung himself into the river on her behalf. Her heart pounded at the notion of a man doing such a thing for her. She would have to do something special. How does one greet a man who has saved one's life? She couldn't kiss him - that would be too forward but what could she...

Wait! Miss Pattison was in residence again looking impatient. Too forward. What is too forward? Who says it's too forward? It's up to you, not up to anyone else. Kiss him if you want to.

Yes, Sophie thought. I want to – on the cheek.

She rose from the wheelchair, stood for one precarious moment, and then, instead of kissing his cheek, she simply collapsed, falling into John's arms as pain lanced through her foot.

CHAPTER SIXTEEN

John Alder
Waldorf Astoria Hotel, Saturday morning, April 20

John Alder and Senator Horace Eldridge sat in a quiet corner of the Palm Court Restaurant where no one would overhear their conversation. Senator Smith's picture could be found in every newspaper, often in company with Senator Newlands, but Senator Horace Eldridge kept himself to himself. He said very little as he sat in on the *Titanic* hearings, but he listened and he plotted and he planned.

John had been working for the senator for five years, rising rapidly in seniority and winning the confidence of the elderly man who was the key to John's future. Eldridge struggled with arthritis and walked with a cane, but his mind was as sharp as ever. Nonetheless, John was growing impatient for the senator to announce his retirement because he hoped that the retirement announcement would include an endorsement of John as the man who would stand for election in his place.

It was that hope that had brought John into the Waldorf on a morning when he would prefer to have remained in bed, sleeping off the exhaustion of the past five days.

Eldridge seemed to understand. "I won't keep you long. I don't need you to sit in on the inquiry. Smith is grandstanding, Newlands is toadying, and the witnesses are lying. If something doesn't happen very soon to change the *status quo,* this will all have been a waste of time. All I need from you is a quick report and then I suggest you go and do something about your appearance. I see that you have borrowed some clothes, but it appears that you borrowed them from someone who is several sizes smaller than you are."

"Dick Williams keeps clothes at his grandmother's house here in Manhattan. This is the best we could do for me on short notice."

"Then I suggest a visit to Macy's." Eldridge paused. "Speaking of Macy's - tell me the truth, John. The newspapers are printing so much sentimental claptrap that I am not sure what to believe, but Mr. and Mrs. Straus – the owners of Macy's – is the story true?"

John nodded. "I saw her, but I didn't realize what I was really seeing."

Confusion had not yet given way to chaos as John, Dick and Charles approached Lifeboat #8. The gunwales of the boat were still level with the deck and he could see that some ladies had taken seats, although many remained empty. One of the sailors was protesting loudly as an elderly woman who had been safely seated, decided to leave the boat.

At the time, he had condemned that woman as foolish but he had learned the truth on board the *Carpathia*. Dr. Alice Leader had seen and heard it all from her seat in the boat. Alice Leader, an eminently sensible woman, had shed tears.

"The sailor had told Mr. Straus, as he was so elderly, that he could go in the boat with his wife, but he would not. If the other men were not permitted, then he was not permitted. His wife sat in the boat for a few minutes. I could see how uneasy she was. Obviously, she was a woman of sense. She knew what would happen to her husband. Suddenly she stood up, took off her mink coat and draped it around the shoulders of her maid, and then she left the boat to be with her husband."

"I have not seen the newspapers," John said, "but I imagine they have managed to turn that short story into a page of drama."

"They have put words in her mouth," Eldridge said, "from the Book of Ruth – where you go, I go"."

"Perhaps they made up the words, but they didn't make up the story," John said. "I saw her leave the lifeboat myself."

"It's turned out well for the store," Eldridge said with the edge of cynicism John had come to expect from him. "I'm told that Macys is packed with shoppers – people who want to honor Mr. and Mrs. Straus. It may also have quelled some antisemitic feelings. Ida and Isidor were Jews, and yet they behaved nobly. Mrs. Straus may have done more for her race than she realized, and more for the future of her department store. You'd better get over there before they sell out of clothes."

"Are you sure I can't—"

"I've told you, you are not needed at the moment," Eldridge said. "In fact I'm not sure that *I'm* even needed. Smith is asking all the questions. He doesn't let me get a word in edgewise."

"If I were there to assist you —"

Eldridge cut him off abruptly by changing the subject. "I heard about Charles Williams. That's a great loss for tennis. How about Dick? I understand he came close to losing his legs and we came close to losing a national champion."

"He's doing remarkably well," John said. "He's learned of a clinic in France offering some very advanced treatment for the kind of injuries he suffered. He's determined to be ready for the U.S. National in August. He's disappointed not to be going to Berlin for the Olympics this year, but if I know my friend, he'll be ready for 1916 in Paris if —"

"Ah yes, Paris," Eldridge interrupted. "What do you think, John?"

"I think that Paris will not be in any condition to host the Olympic Games in 1916 – or that any of us will feel like attending."

Eldridge leaned back in his chair. "Is that your official report of your unofficial visit?"

"The rumors," John said, "are not without substance."

"Did you find out what Archibald Butt was up to on behalf of the president?"

"I know that his supposed personal visit to the Pope, somehow included visits to the Kaiser and several other European leaders, and a rumored visit to the Court of St. James."

Eldridge raised his eyebrows.

"King George," John explained, "or someone who has his ear. I planned to meet Butt on the *Titanic* where I could corner him informally. The man is...was...a social butterfly. I had not managed to catch him alone when..." John fought back a host of memories before he could speak again and still he stumbled. "Now, of course..."

"Are you sure he's gone?" Eldridge asked.

"Quite sure," John said. "There was only one way to be saved, and that was the *Carpathia* and he was not on the *Carpathia*."

"When you have rested, I would like a first-hand report of what you saw and heard on the *Titanic*," Eldridge said. "The truth is already giving way to lies. Senator Smith would be better off in Washington asking questions about what's going on in Europe instead of tying us up with this *Titanic* tragedy, although he thinks the two things are not entirely unconnected."

"I don't see the connection," John said.

Eldridge shook his head. "It's tenuous but Smith believes a connection exists. That's what we're doing here, at least, that's what *he's* doing. He's trying to find a chain of culpability that takes him all the way up to the ownership of International Mercantile Marine and a man whose money affects everything we do."

"J.P. Morgan," John said.

"Richest man in the world," Eldrige said, "with money enough to decide the outcome of a war, but even he can't afford to own this disaster, even though he owned the ship. I'll brief you later. You don't need to know everything now. Just be aware that the survivors of this disaster have become pawns in a political game of chess."

John could not hide his disappointment. He knew the cynicism of the political process, but he did not want to believe that the inquiry was anything other than an honest attempt at finding out what had happened to the *Titanic*. "I'm sorry, sir, but surely the purpose of this inquiry is to make sure that nothing like this ever happens again. I would expect us to write new laws regarding lifeboats and procedures so that every ship that carries Americans, and future Americans, is as safe as it can possibly be. This cannot be about Senator Smith's political ambitions."

"And that is what we will all say in public," Eldridge assured him, "but don't forget this is an election year – everything, even this disaster, has political meaning for all of us. Are you aware that the British have lodged an official protest against the fact that we are holding their citizens against their will? We'll have an international incident if we don't let the crew return home."

John caught the ghost of a smile on Eldridge's face. For Senator Smith to provoke an international incident would be bad for Smith, but could be beneficial for Eldridge. The matter would have to be handled delicately but Eldridge could come out of this situation smelling like a rose, and so would his successor.

"While you were in England," Eldridge asked, "did you get any hint of what our duck-hunting friends are up to?"

John shook his head giving the senator another disappointing answer. "Nothing, sir."

Eldridge grimaced. "There's something behind it, and rumor says that it will change the way Americans bank their money. These people are playing their cards very close to their chests. Are you sure you heard nothing?"

"A rumor, sir, of a house party in Scotland. I was unable to run it down as I had to be in Southampton. You needed me to board the *Titanic* and speak to Butt and I deemed that more important."

"It was," Eldridge said. "I know you did your best and no one expected the damned ship to sink. You can give me whatever you have when we get back to Washington. I'm expecting Taft is going to shut this farce down by tomorrow, if not sooner, and then we can get on with the work of the nation. Don't come back and see me again until you've had a shave and a haircut and found some clothes that fit you. I'm surprised you were even admitted into this hotel."

John thought he had been dismissed and was about to rise from the table when Eldridge introduced an entirely new subject. "One more thing, John. I think I deserve an explanation for the story that is currently circulating. Did you in fact dive into the Hudson on Wednesday night?"

John had hoped that this news would not have reached the senator, but, of course, Eldridge had ears everywhere. "I didn't dive," John said. "I was pushed, or maybe pulled."

"And were you involved in a brawl involving a young lady?"

"No, not a brawl, an intervention. The young lady in question was in real danger. I could not just stand by."

John could see that Eldridge was attempting to hide a smile. "And was Miss Sophie Paxton the young lady in question?"

"Yes, sir."

"Sophie Paxton," Eldridge repeated. There was no doubt now that he was smiling. "Heiress to the Paxton Steel fortune."

"Yes, sir."

"You aim high."

"Sir," John protested, "this has nothing to do with …"

Words failed him as memory sneaked in and caused him to feel a flush rising in his cheeks. She had tried to rise from her wheelchair and had collapsed in his arms. He remembered how she had felt in his arms, clinging so tightly that he could tell that she was not even wearing a corset. As he wrapped his arms around her waist there had been nothing but a thin layer of cloth between his hands and her naked softness.

He flushed again. *No, not naked. Don't even think of naked.*

Eldridge's smile was broader than ever. "It's a match made in heaven."

"It's nothing, sir. She was very grateful for what I did to help her on the *Titanic* and then again on the dock."

Eldridge waved his protests away. "No need to explain yourself to me. I see nothing wrong with the arrangement…"

John tried to protest but Eldridge had already corrected himself. "If there is an arrangement."

"There is no arrangement, sir."

Well," Eldridge said, "I would certainly support you in coming to an arrangement with her. Miss Paxton will never find a suitor who will match her in wealth, but marriage to a potential senator would be far better than marriage to a pauper with a title. We shouldn't be buying European titles. It's time we stood on our own two feet. I have great hopes for your future, John. If you were to marry Miss Paxton, I think I could almost guarantee you a seat in the senate by the time you are christening your first child."

John was at a loss for words. Confirmation! Eldridge saw him as a senator!

Eldridge consulted his watch and rose to his feet. "I have to take my seat at the table. With any luck, this will be the last day. So far as I'm concerned, there's very little left to say. Smith is intent on casting blame on Ismay and the White Star Line, and that is a dangerous intent that will soon be stopped, but not by me."

He gave John a thoughtful glance. "I trust your judgement, John. You were there. Smith will never call you to give evidence, he is afraid of what you might say, but just between us - who would you blame?"

Blame? John thought of the many things he'd seen from the moment the *Titanic* hit the iceberg, to the moment it slid beneath the waves. Two and a half hours of chaos filled with acts of bravery, despair, and utter incompetence, all taking place on a sea of glass under a canopy of stars.

"I cannot blame the officers or the crew," he said at last. "They did the best they could with the orders they had been given. There was so little time, Senator, so very little time."

"So would you call it an Act of God and cast no blame?"

"I cannot blame the iceberg, but I can suggest a scapegoat," John said, "if you need one, as a distraction."

Eldridge raised his eyebrows enquiringly.

"There was another ship," John said. "I do not blame that ship for the sinking but I blame it for all the hours that followed. He was very close. We saw his lights, and he must have seen our rockets, and yet he did not move. The captain of that ship broke every law of the sea. Search for him and you will have your scapegoat and a way to relieve international pressure."

"You saw this ship?" Eldridge asked. "Do you know its nationality?"

"No, sir, I do not."

"Well," said Eldridge, "with any luck it will be registered to some hapless small nation, and there will be an end to the current rattling of sabers – or better still, it will never be identified but searching will be a distraction."

Before John could reply, a shadow fell across the table. "Excuse me, sir."

John looked from Eldridge's thoughtful face to the face of a bellhop holding a message slip. "Mr. Alder?" he queried.

"Yes."

"Message for you, sir."

John took the message slip, wondering how anyone would know that he was here at the Waldorf. He smiled when he saw the name of the sender.

"Please come to Mrs. White's apartment. There is someone you need to meet. Don't delay. Very important."

John asked Eldridge's permission to leave. Eldridge nodded distractedly and John knew his mind was on the mystery ship and the way the presence of that ship could play into the politics of the inquiry.

He followed the bellhop across the lobby to the elevators and stepped into the open car. "Mrs. White's apartment," he said.

The operator closed the iron gates and the elevator began its journey upwards. John clutched the message slip. He had no idea why Sophie would want to meet him in Mrs. White's apartment but the reason didn't matter. What mattered was seeing her again. What also mattered was Senator Eldridge's words. *"Miss Paxton will never find a suitor who will match her in wealth, but marriage to a potential senator would be far better than marriage to a pauper with a title."*

Sam White
Ella White's apartment, Waldorf Astoria

Ella White's apartment at the Waldorf was spacious, but there was little room for the number of people who were now crowded in. Sam, who had been downstairs to listen in on Senator Smith's inquiry had been astonished to return and find the room filled with strangers.

Aunt Ella silenced the general buzz of conversation by proudly announcing Sam's arrival. She appeared to forget that Sam was her nephew only by marriage. In fact, she seemed to hold herself personally responsible for Sam's remarkable achievement.

"With my assistance," she said, "Sam has filed a first-hand report with the New York Times. We could not persuade the editor to stop the presses, so you will not read the report in the early edition, but you will read it in the mid-day edition." She paused for effect. "In just two hours," she declared, "the world will read Sam's report and will know that we, in the lifeboats, were not mistaken. We did see a light. There was a ship, standing by and not moving, while we fought for our lives! Now, thanks to Sam, we know the name of that ship. It is the *Californian* and its Captain is Stanley Lord."

She turned to Sam. "Sam, my dear boy, let me introduce you to the Paxton family."

He knew who the Paxtons were, of course - old Aidan Paxton had accumulated enough money to make his family one of the wealthiest and most notorious families in the United States. He surveyed them now, dismissing in his mind those who would be of no interest. The old nanny looked like something from a comforting children's book, and Ponsonby, the family lawyer, merely looked like a hundred other lawyers he had encountered.

Lady Maxine Sempter and her mother, Agatha, were both tall and somewhat homely. Lady Maxine, introduced as a survivor, had bulbous blue eyes set in a pale face that showed no sign of the trauma she must have recently suffered. If her face showed any expression at all, it was a sense of smugness that Sam found hard to explain.

There was some family resemblance between Lady Maxine and her cousin, Sophie Paxton. Sophie also had blue eyes, but rather than being bulbous and fish-like, they were wide and sparkling. Where Lady Maxine's hair was streaked with grey, Sophie's hair was midnight-black and arranged in loose curls around her face. Sam was not normally a follower of female fashion, but he thought it unusual for a well-bred young lady to be greeting a visitor with her hair loose.

Perhaps it was the fact that she was not sitting in a chair, but reclining on a sofa with a blanket over her legs that offered a dispensation. It appeared that she was an invalid and, as such, she did not have to meet the rigorous standards of high society. When she moved, he saw a bulky bandage on her left foot. She was a survivor of the *Titanic*. Obviously, she had sustained a serious injury.

Her face was flushed with delight and she was the first person to speak. "I knew it," she said. "I knew we saw a light. Now all we have to do is find where the ship is and have the captain brought ashore in leg irons."

Alfie, who had been standing beside Sam, tugged at his coat sleeve and nodded his head toward a tea trolly installed in a corner of the room. Sam saw the source of Alfie's interest – a teapot and a plate of pastries.

"Can I, Gov?"

"Yes, go."

Sam returned his attention to Sophie. "I'm not sure leg irons are appropriate."

"You were not on the *Titanic*," Sophie said bitterly. "You did not see what we all went through. I say that it's Captain Lord's fault that I'm unable to walk."

"I don't see how —" Sam ventured.

Sophie gave him no time to finish. "Frostbite," she said. "If he had come sooner and we had been taken from the water, this would never have happened. He's the reason my toe was amputated. It's his fault that I will never play tennis again."

"Tennis?" Sam said dubiously. He was assessing Sophie as a possible source for an in-depth interview, but it couldn't be an interview about tennis. On the grand scale of the *Titanic* disaster, the loss of Sophie Paxton's toe and her inability to play tennis, were minor inconveniences.

Apparently Sophie noted his surprise and she gave a hasty explanation. "I was going to play in the Olympics."

Sam looked away. He would not be interviewing this selfish young miss. Even if she spoke the truth, and even if she had the ability to play in the Olympics, didn't she understand that the disaster, and Captain Lord's role in it, could not be measured by her personal inconvenience?

A knock on the outer door caused Miss Young to rise from her seat and thread her way through the maze of chairs toward the door.

"If you were not taking up the entire sofa," Lady Maxine said to Sophie as Miss Young edged past, "there would be more room."

The invalid ignored her.

Miss Young opened the door and admitted a uniformed police officer. "This officer is looking for Lady Maxine Sempter."

"Oh!" Lady Maxine turned her attention away from Sophie and fixed her eyes on the young officer. Her pale face remained composed.

The lawyer, Ponsonby, pushed his way forward. "I'll take care of this. What do you want, officer?"

"I have to tell Lady Sempter herself."

"Go ahead and tell her," Ponsonby said. "She's right here."

The officer removed his hat and stepped into the room. Lady Maxine rose from her seat. "I'm sorry to inform you, ma'am, that a body was recovered from the river this morning. We believe it to be the body of your husband, Lord Lucan Sempter. He appears to have been shot."

Sam stood back and watched the scene unfold. Aunt Ella and Miss Young were obviously surprised by the news, but he could detect no surprise from Sophie, or Lady Maxine, or Maxine's mother. It took several long, uncomfortable seconds for Lady Maxine to finally register appropriate shock and grief and sink into a chair. Meanwhile, Sophie, oblivious to her cousins show of distress, was busy scribbling a note on a slip of paper.

The young constable looked hopefully at Sam and Ponsonby. "We'll need someone to identify the body," he said, "and perhaps one of you gentlemen..."

"Don't look at me," Sam said. "I didn't know his lordship." He was itching to pull out his notebook but he couldn't do it yet. Here was another story. Lord Sempter, English aristocrat and survivor of the *Titanic*, drowned. No, the constable did not say drowned – he said shot. Lord Lucan Sempter had been shot.

Why?

And why was Lady Sempter not reduced to hysterics? And why was Sophie Paxton writing distractedly as though this had nothing to do with her?

"I will come," Ponsonby said.

"Have you ever met the man?" Aunt Ella asked in a way that was typical of Aunt Ella. She could never resist an opportunity to interfere.

"Well, no," Ponsonby said, "but I have had him described to me."

"That won't be good enough," the officer said. "I'm afraid one of you ladies will have to come."

Lady Maxine, somewhat belatedly, produced a handkerchief to dab at her eyes. "I could not possibly," she said, "because of my ... condition."

"Condition?" the officer queried.

"For goodness' sake, man," Ponsonby muttered, "have you no decency? Can't you tell that her ladyship is with child?"

Lady Maxine and her mother exchanged glances. Sam's every instinct screamed out that there was a story here, but not for him. He was not about to dabble in society gossip. However, it did no harm to speculate. Lord Sempter was dead, but Lady Maxine already had everything she needed from him – an heir – someone to add a hereditary title to the Paxton family tree.

Maxine dabbed at her dry eyes. "My mother has met him," she said. "She can go with you. Mr. Ponsonby will accompany her."

The officer nodded his agreement. "Good enough. We should go now. It's going to be a warm day and – well, bodies that come out of the Hudson don't do well on warm days."

"I appreciate the need for speed," Lady Maxine's mother said, "but first I must go to my rooms and fetch my hat and my gloves. Nanny Bess, will you please, take Maxine to lie down. She's had a terrible shock - widowed after only a few weeks of marriage."

Lady Maxine does not appear shocked, Sam thought, but it might be best to take her away before she starts dancing a jig. Sam had seen tragedy before in the sudden loss of a loved one, but he had never seen the loss so willingly embraced. Oh, there was a story here, if he had time to follow it up.

"I'm staying here," Sophie announced. "I want to hear what Mrs. White's nephew knows about this Captain Lord." She turned to Maxine's mother. "Aunt Agatha, as you leave, would you please give this note to the porter. It's important."

Agatha took the note.

"No need to read it," Sophie added. "The porter will take care of it."

She settled back on the sofa and looked at Sam. "I am expecting a visitor at any moment."

Sam turned to look at her. For a few minutes she had not been the center of attention and it seemed that she did not like being overlooked. Now, instead of supporting her cousin, she was writing mysterious notes and squirming into a more comfortable position on the sofa, forcing Lady Maxine and her mother to push past her. Sam could find little liking for Lady Sempter and her mother, and absolutely no liking for Sophie Paxton.

Alfie, abandoning the tea trolley, edged over to speak in Sam's ear. "That's a rum go, ain't it?"

Sam laughed. "Do you mean that this is all very strange?"

"Yeah, it's a rum go. Seems like no one is going to miss his lordship. Good thing the wife already has a pea in the pod."

Sam took note that Alfie was a very good listener. He had been so silent, so unobtrusive that he had been overlooked, and so he had listened and drawn his own conclusions.

"What do you make of all this?" Sam asked.

"They already knew," Alfie replied. "Didn't need no copper to tell them about his lordship."

'What about the girl on the sofa?"

"Well," said Alfie, "I ain't no doctor, and I ain't no toff but it ain't like she's lost her whole foot, is it? It's one toe. If I can walk with what I done to my leg, then she can walk." He threw Sophie a disgusted glance and then beckoned Sam back into the corner by the tea trolley. "Cup of tea, Gov?"

Alfie poured two more cups of tea. "Gov," he said, "I was wondering, now that you've got your story in the newspaper, what's next?"

Sam sipped his tea. "I'll make what I can of this opportunity," he said. "It all depends on the president now."

"What president?"

"Taft, the president of the United States."

"The fat bloke," Alfie said.

"Well, yes, I suppose you could describe him that way."

"That's all right," Alfie said. "We got a fat king."

"Well," Sam said, "from what I understand, the president could put an end to these hearings at any time. I'm not sure that there is time for Senator Smith to find Captain Lord and bring him to New York to answer questions. I've managed to get the story in the newspaper, and the public will want answers, but you and I know that Lord is working to get his ship turned around and back out to sea as quickly as possible."

"Two days," Alfie said. "Can't turn around in less than two days and that's pushing it." He hesitated, staring into his tea cup. "It's nice here," he said at last. "I don't normally go ashore. Never been in a place like this. Your aunt is a nice lady, letting me sleep in the room she had for her manservant. I thought I'd have to sleep on the floor. It were a nice bed."

Again, Alfie hesitated and stared into his teacup. "Gov."

"Yes, Alfie."

"The manservant's name was Sante Ringhini. He's dead. Your aunt's safe, and the other lady, and the maid, but not him. He's dead and she don't seem to care."

"That's the way it was," Sam said. "Women and children first. I'm sure my aunt is sorry to lose him, but it was the rule."

"But she knew him. She's the one that took him on the *Titanic.* She saved the maid."

"The maid is a woman."

"Well, I'll bet that Sante Ringhini was a good man. "

"I'm sure you're right."

Alfie nodded. "It's all right, Gov, I just wanted to say what I thought and he shouldn't be forgotten. I wanted to speak his name. It made me think of me Dad, gone and no one spoke his name, and no one to bury him. I slept in that dead man's bed, Guv, and I just wanted to say that he shouldn't be gone like that."

"None of them should be gone," Sam said. "That's why Senator Smith is downstairs asking questions."

"But Gov, Alfie said, "it weren't Captain Lord's fault, were it?"

"It's Captain Lord's fault that I lost my foot," Sophie said loudly from her place on the sofa.

Sam turned around to look at her, surprised that she had been listening to their conversation. She pulled herself into a more upright position and spoke to Alfie. "It was absurd," she said. "I was in a lifeboat with Mrs. White and Miss Young, and there was plenty of room for Ringhini. He could have helped with the rowing, but he didn't even try to enter. It was all ridiculous."

Her face softened for a moment and Sam had a glimpse of the compassionate young woman who was hiding behind the angry face. Tears had gathered at the corners of her bright blue eyes. "You're right to speak his name," she said. "Tell me your father's name."

"Alfred Blackwell," Alfie said. "I'm named after him."

Sophie smiled. "Alfred Blackwell," she repeated. "See, now I have spoken his name."

Alfie nodded. "Thank you, miss."

"Well, Alfred —"

"You can call me Alfie."

"All right, Alfie. Would you mind pouring me a cup of tea. I can't do it myself, as you can see."

Alfie set about pouring the tea but stopped when someone knocked loudly on the outer door, and he took it upon himself to run to answer it.

A brown-haired man in an ill-fitting suit strode into the room as though he owned the place. Ella White and Marie Young were quickly on their feet to greet him, but he strode past them with his eyes fixed on Sophie.

"I received your note," he said dramatically.

Sophie's face was pink with blushing, and she shrank back under the onslaught of his approach.

Sam was not sure what to make of the situation until the newcomer made his intentions perfectly clear by taking hold of Sophie's hand and kissing it.

"Mr. Alder," Sophie said.

"Miss Paxton."

Alder continued to clutch Sophie's hand until Ella, brandishing her cane took back control of her sitting room. "Mr. Alder, you are very welcome," she said. "We were told last night that you had fallen into the Hudson River and that you were lost."

"Well, I'm not lost," Alder said with a forced heartiness. "If I could not be drowned by the Atlantic, I am certainly not going to be drowned by the Hudson." He looked at Sophie. "I had the pleasure of reassuring Miss Paxton last night that I was still alive and well. I am surprised that she did not let you know."

Sam was tempted to smile. Sophie may have been the first thing on Alder's mind, but he was not the first thing on Sophie's mind. Sam thought that the first thing on Sophie's mind, would always be Sophie.

"A great deal has happened since last night," Sophie said. She was no longer reclining but sitting upright and the blush had faded from her cheeks. Sam concluded that the relationship between Sophie and John was a tenuous thing, not yet fully born. "There has been little time to keep up with all the important news"

The implication was that John Alder's survival was just one thing on a list of important things. Sophie seemed blissfully unaware of how this dismissal was received by Alder.

"You have other important news?" Alder said.

"Oh yes. We have received news of Lord Sempter's death." Sophie spoke calmly without a hint of emotion. "He was found in the river. The police came to inform us, and so that someone would identify the body."

Alder turned toward her, contrite. "Oh, my dear, what a shock."

Shock? Sam questioned. No one here is shocked except maybe Aunt Ella – certainly not Alder. This news was no surprise to Alder.

"You must be devastated," Alder said. He seemed to be on the verge of offering compassionate, or maybe passionate support.

"We were warned," Sophie said. "A man came to see us – a professional gambler. He wanted to prepare us for what was going to happen. He said he couldn't stop it from happening. That ... er ... incident ... on the dock had been Lucan's plan for getting money to pay his gambling debts."

Aunt Ella pushed her way into the conversation. "Foolishness," she declared. "Gambling is a fool's game." She dismissed Lord Sempter with a wave of her hand. "He struck me as being a fool. Aristocratic inbreeding. I breed chickens at my place in New Hampshire and I see this kind of thing all the time." She looked at Sam for a moment as if suddenly remembering something. "I had chickens on the Titanic," she said.

"Why?" Sam asked. "Don't they have chickens on board for eggs and such?"

"I'm sure they do, but mine were a very rare French breed. If there had been time, I would have rescued them. I needed them for my breeding program. Oh well, there are worst things than a few lost chickens."

Sam took advantage of the sudden silence created in memoriam of his aunt's chickens. and he approached John Alder with an extended hand. "Sam White, Mrs. White's nephew."

Aunt Ella forgot about the chickens and paid attention to the introductions. "Sam is a journalist with the New York Times."

Sam winced at his sudden promotion but said nothing as the newcomer introduced himself. "John Alder, aide to Senator Eldridge of Ohio."

A senatorial aide. No wonder he was so sure of himself.

"Mr. Alder was with us on the *Titanic*," Aunt Ella said. "He's going to be very interested in what you told us." She clutched Sam's arm possessively. "Sam was coming from England on a cargo vessel."

"A last-minute passenger," Sam said. Why did he feel the need to explain his lack of a first-class ticket?

"And," said Aunt Ella, determined not to have her moment interrupted, "he saw the *Titanic*. He saw us, Mr. Alder, he saw our lights and our rockets and we saw his lights. Captain Smith told us the truth. There was a light and now we know the name of the ship. Sam's story will be published in the mid-day edition of the Times." She looked at Sophie. "Now we will have someone to blame."

Alder frowned. "Are you sure about this, Mr. White?"

"Of course I'm sure," Sam said. "If you won't take my word, you can take the word of someone on the ship's crew." He beckoned Alfie to leave his corner. "This young man was also on the ship."

"What was the ship?"

"The Leyland Liner, *Californian*, under the command of Captain Stanley Lord." Alfie said.

Alder was silent for an unusually long time. "Leyland Liner," he said at last. "Leyland." He straightened his ill-fitting jacket and snapped his hair out of his eyes. "You say this will be published at noon?"

"Yes."

"And have you published the name of the ship?"

"Of course."

Alder's face reddened – embarrassment, anger, frustration? Sam could not tell. He only knew that quite suddenly Alder was in a hurry. He made a sketchy bow toward Sophie and another to Ella White and was gone in an instant.

Sophie Paxton
Still in Mrs. White's suite

Sophie watched the door closing behind John Alder. Well, that was ... unexpected. If John was indeed courting her, he was doing it in a very strange fashion. Running off was hardly courtly behavior. Sophie wanted to look to Nanny Bess, but Nanny was not there.

Mr. Ponsonby and Agatha had gone to identify the body. Nanny had returned to the suite with Maxine – they had all left her behind. She was helpless on the sofa, in a roomful of strangers. No, she thought, not total strangers. The night she had spent in the lifeboat with Ella White and Marie Young had created a bond that would probably last a lifetime. They had suffered together, Marie rowing alongside Sophie, and Mrs. White waving the light of her electric cane.

Now they had news that totally changed the way that Sophie would remember that night. They had thought themselves alone on the ocean. They had thought that Captain Smith had lied when he told them to row toward the light. Sophie had disbelieved the evidence of her own eyes but everything had changed now. Now she knew they had not been alone. A ship had been out there just a few miles away, lurking in the darkness and that ship had a name - *Californian*.

She looked at the man who had brought the news of the *Californian*. He was ... she had only one word in her vocabulary to describe his appearance – raffish. Yes, Sam White was distinctly careless and casual- seeming rather in the style of heroes of the novels that graced the shelves in the Howell library. Bram Stoker with a touch of Solomon's Mines.

Howell girls are not afraid to read popular or racy books.

Howell girls do not censor.

Howell girls are not frightened by words in books.

Sophie, looking at Sam White, assumed that Howell girls should not be afraid of dangerously handsome, raffish men. The subject had never come up, even with Miss Pattison. Sophie had no Latin phrase to describe her feelings about this new man.

She studied Sam's face. He had light hair, hazel eyes and the beginnings of crow's feet around his eyes and frown lines on his forehead. He was not old, but he was definitely no longer young. Forty, she thought. Forty and still a wanderer. Why had he been travelling on a cargo ship? Where had he been? Where was he going? Where did the boy fit into the story?

Sam pulled out a pocket watch and tapped it impatiently.

"Noon," Sophie said. "Nothing will happen until noon."

"I should be downstairs," Sam said. "I want to be there when the senators find out that their job is only halfway done. What are they going to do about this new surprise – this ship that didn't move?" He looked at Sophie. "Do you realize, Miss Paxton, that when you were climbing into a lifeboat, I was only a few miles away? I could see your ship. She was a haze of lights on the horizon. We signalled."

"I know," Sophie said with sudden certainty. "Identify Yourself."

"What?"

"That was the signal. I can read Morse code, and that was the signal. QRZ Identify Yourself."

"Did anyone on the *Titanic* respond?"

Sophie shook her head. "I have no way of knowing, but I doubt it. It was all chaos."

Sam looked at his watch again.

"Veritas odit moras," Sophie said.

He looked up at her. "Truth hates delays," he said. "You are so right. Thirty more minutes."

Miss Young had been seated at the piano, shuffling through sheet music. Now she spoke up. "Perhaps you could pass the time in telling us why you were on a cargo ship. Are you an inveterate traveler, Mr. White?"

"It was the only berth I could find," Sam said. "The coal strike is having a serious effect on shipping and I needed to leave England in a hurry."

Raffish! Sophie thought. It was the kind of statement that would be made by a hero in the midst of an adventure – a man who had overstepped some social or political boundary and found enemies snapping at his heels.

"I hope you are not in any kind of trouble," Mrs. White said.

"No, no, aunt, no trouble," He winked. "Well, not really."

Sophie thought at first that he had winked at her, but then she realized that the boy, Alfie, had been standing behind the sofa. Sam's wink was aimed at the boy. *Who was that boy? Why was Sam traveling in the company of a London guttersnipe?*

"I've been following a story," Sam said, "listening at keyholes, talking to servants, criss-crossing the Scottish Highlands, in search of some of the biggest names in American finance. There is a cabal of ten men who are going to change the entire banking system of the United States and they are almost ready to make their move."

Sophie's heart sank. For a brief moment she'd had Sam White pegged as a swashbuckling hero and now it turned out that he was interested in banking. Banking! His need to cross the Atlantic on the *Californian* had been tied to a story about banking. It was just a stroke of luck that he had happened upon a much bigger story.

Only thirty minutes until the *Californian* story would break. Sophie knew she should go back to her own suite. It was really quite rude for her to be stretched out this way on Mrs. White's sofa, abandoned by her family. She didn't have her wheelchair. Someone had moved it after Sophie had been transferred to the sofa. That was hours ago, and she did not know what they had done with it. She felt utterly helpless. She would have to ask Mrs. White to call for a porter and a wheelchair. If she had ever thought of being an invalid in a wheelchair as romantic, she had now changed her mind.

"I think I'll go downstairs," Sam said. "The inquiry is still in progress and I would be interested in seeing the results of my revelations as the news filters into the room. I imagine it will be little like throwing a rock into a millpond."

"Good idea," said Mrs. White. "Perhaps you could escort Miss Paxton to her suite before you leave. We're both on the same floor."

"Happy to oblige," Sam said. He extended his hand. "May I help you up."

Sophie shrank back into the cushions. "I can't... I don't... I won't."

"You can walk, can't you," Sam said. "I was told your injury was minor."

"Minor!" Sophie exploded. "My whole toe is gone."

Alfie leaned over the back of the sofa, his face alight with interest. "Which toe?

"My big toe."

"Oh yeah, that's a tricky one. Hard to balance. You'll get the hang of it but you'll walk funny".

"How would you know?"

"Valparaiso," Alfie said.

"Spain?" Sophie asked.

"No, Chile," Alfie said. "I was cabin boy on a big square rigger, but Valparaiso's where I lost my ticket for sail. I ain't never going under sail again."

"What happened to you?"

"Me own fault," Alfie said. "Got careless. Got me foot caught in a winch. Broke me leg and crushed me foot. They had to put me ashore. Weren't no place for me in the rigging no more, and not much good as a cabin boy. After that I went under steam. Ain't done very well for meself there neither. Mr. White is giving me a new chance." He grinned at Sam. "Ain't that right Gov?"

"Wait a minute," Sophie said, momentarily forgetting her own problem. "Who put you ashore in Valparaiso, how old were you, and who looked after you?"

"Me shipmates put me ashore," Alfie said. "I was twelve. It was all right in the end. There was some nuns – nice ladies. I managed. I knew there was only one way out of Valparaiso, and that was on a ship. I had to walk, and so I did. I always manage. I look after meself."

Sam was still extending his hand. "Miss Paxton, take my hand and try to stand. I promise I won't let you fall."

It shouldn't be him, Sophie thought. It should be John. He's my white knight.

And what is this man?

Can there be two white knights?

Sam left her no choice. She could not stay forever on Mrs. White's sofa, and she was suddenly ashamed to ask for a porter. The boy, Alfie, had suffered a far worse injury, and he had survived. Alfie had been at such pains to tell her that her injury was not serious. The only lasting damage was that she would *walk funny*. Sophie didn't want to *walk funny*. She wanted to run, to sprint across the tennis court, to leap high for a ball she should not be able to reach and to stand on the medal podium at the Olympic Games. That was what she wanted. She wanted her old life and her old expectations.

"Miss Paxton," Sam said, "are you ready?"

Sophie nodded.

Sam gripped her hand firmly, his finger wrapping around her thumb and she surged to her feet as he pulled. Pain lanced through her foot but Sam's arm was at her waist, just as John's arm had been last night.

Take a step, she told herself. How bad could it be? She could feel her foot in contact with the floor. She took a step. Her body tried to find balance on the ghost of her toe. The ghost would not hold her. Her ankle turned inward, her knee buckled and she sank toward the floor. An unwelcome truth stared her in the face. She thought that refusing to walk had been her own choice and that, one day, when her anger had dissipated, she would get to her feet again. What if that were not true? Suppose the pretending had become reality. She was a cripple for life.

She took in a long breath and tried to calm her racing heart. She shouldn't cry. She was already a figure without any dignity, but crying would make it worse.

"I can't do it," she said.

'Well," Sam said, "I suppose we will have to find an alternative because I want to go downstairs and I can't leave you here. My aunt insists that I return you to your suite, so here we go."

He swept her up in his arms. It was not romantic although his hands were certainly where they should not have been. Her hair, unbound, was caught on the buttons of his coat, her loose-fitting morning dress worked its way up to her knees and he seemed to be grunting under her weight. She was not heavy! Was he actually staggering as he carried her along the corridor?

Nanny Bess responded to Alfie's knocking on the door of the suite. She stepped back in astonishment as Sam stepped inside and looked for a place to deposit his burden. Sophie, with her face almost buried in the shoulder of Sam's coat, mumbled instructions. "In the armchair."

Sam ignored the instruction and deposited her on the sofa and she was amazed to find John Alder leaping up to make room. Why was he here? Had he come back for her sake? What on earth would he think now?

Sam and John looked at each other and Sophie realized that she was not the subject of their inquiring looks.

"I told my senator," John said.

"Ahead of publication?" Sam said.

"He had to be forewarned. He's already told Smith. We cannot afford to have Smith look any more foolish than he currently does."

"I thought you were on opposite sides of the aisle."

"We are still Americans. We put our country first. Smith has already phoned the president.

"And..."

"Your story has changed everything," John said. "The president has authorized the inquiry to continue. The crew and the survivors who are witnesses are to be taken to Washington to face the full senate."

"And Captain Lord?"

"Smith has dispatched his special agent, Joe Bayliss, to Boston. The captain will face the full senate. I hope there are no holes in the story you tell."

"I have reported what I saw with my own eyes," Sam said. "My eyes did not lie. I will come to Washington myself and speak under oath."

John turned toward Sophie who was attempting to straighten her dress. "Miss Paxton, I had hoped to have the pleasure of your company here in New York, but I am told by my senator that we are departing for Washington this very afternoon."

Sophie could not find anything to say. She was still digesting an unpleasant truth. While she had not even tried to walk, she had found it possible to believe that she *could* walk. Now that she had actually tried, she found that she could not.

Nanny Bess leaned forward over the sofa and whispered in her ear "Tell him we're going to Washington."

Sophie said nothing. She could not recapture the anger that had given her strength on the *Carpathia*. She felt the return of hopeless self-pity.

Nanny Bess spoke for her. "The Paxton family has a townhouse in Washington. You will be welcome to call on Miss Paxton there... both of you."

PART FOUR - WASHINGTON

Robert W. Danial

Passenger on the *Titanic*

Not until the last five minutes did the awful realization come that the end was at hand. The lights became dim and went out, but we could see. Slowly, ever so slowly, the surface of the water seemed to come towards us.

CHAPTER SEVENTEEN

Sam White
Union Station, Washington DC
11:30 a.m. April 25

Sam and Alfie waited beneath the splendid new arched domes of Washington's Union Station. The train would be arriving at any moment now and Sam intended to be present when Stanley Lord stepped from the train.

Senator Smith, determined to complete his inquiry, had moved all his witnesses to Washington almost overnight. By Monday, April 22, the committee had reconvened in the Senate Office Building and Smith had recommenced his relentless search for the truth.

Meantime, Stanley Lord and Ernest Gill were making the long journey from Boston to Washington under the watchful eye of Joe Bayliss, Senator Smith's chief law enforcer. Sam imagined that Lord and his crewmen were dreading what lay ahead of them. In the absence of any scapegoat other than the hapless Bruce Ismay, the public could not wait to set eyes on Stanley Lord – the sailor who had not obeyed the first rule of the sea.

"Damn!" Sam muttered.

Alfie looked at him with interest. "What, Gov?"

Sam's eyes were fixed on the door of a first-class compartment, now being opened by a conductor. A stout middle-aged man in a very fine banker's suit descended. Last time Sam had seen Henry Davidson, Senior Vice President of the J.P. Morgan Bank and Trust, he had been buying clothing in the sporting department of Harrods in London. An assistant was fitting him with a tweed suit suitable for grouse shooting on the Scottish moors. The time before that, Davidson had been dressed for duck hunting.

Sam waited to see who else would descend from the carriage. He was not disappointed. Frank Vanderlip, the tall white-haired President of the National City Bank of New York, stepped out behind Davidson

"What are you cursing about?" Alfie asked.

"See those two men, stepping out of first-class?" Sam said.

"Two toffs?" Alfie asked.

"Yes, two toffs," Sam agreed. "They're two of the men I've been chasing after for two years. I followed them to England, but I never got this close. What, I wonder, are they doing now in Washington?"

"Come to hear the inquiry," Alfie suggested

"No," said Sam. "They have bigger fish to fry. I need to know where they go."

"Why?"

"Because their story is a way bigger story than the *Titanic*."

"Ain't nothing bigger than the *Titanic*."

"Not now, but the *Titanic* story will blow over. What these men are up to is not going to blow over any time soon. They are about to mess with the nation's money and the nation's banks and I want to expose their plan. The *Titanic* isn't my big break, but this is."

Before Sam could give any more explanation, a carriage door opened at the rear of the train, and Sheriff Joe Baylis, Senator Smith's enforcer, stepped out onto the platform. Bayliss was a tall, raw-boned man, with a grim face and hooded eyes. His presence, from the way he stood, to the gun belt at his waist, was pure threat. To Sam's surprise, Cyril Evans, the *Californian's* radio man stepped down alongside Ernest Gill. *Why Evans? What does he know? He was asleep.* The two men followed meekly behind Bayliss but Captain Stanley Lord kept them waiting before appearing in full uniform and placing his cap on his head as he took in the scene at the station.

One thing was obvious, Lord was here against his will. Lord would not be a co-operative witness. The question was – could Stanley Lord take the place of Bruce Ismay as the most hated man to appear before the senate?

"Alfie," Sam said. "We have to divide and conquer."

"What?"

"I can't be in two places at once. I need to find out why Evans is here and I also need to know where those two toffs are going." Sam hesitated. Alfie was a stranger to Washington – a boy who had rarely ever ventured inland from the many harbors he had visited.

"You promised Miss Sophie that you'd talk to Captain Lord," Alfie said.

"I know what I promised," Sam snapped.

"And she's letting us stay at her house," Alfie reminded him.

"Yes, yes, I know."

"And all she wants is to talk to the captain."

"Oh, she wants way more than that," Sam said. "But that would be a good start, I suppose."

"And," Alfie said, "if you let her down, well I expect Mr. Alder will get her what she wants."

"You leave Mr. Alder out of this," Sam said, surprised at how much he disliked the sound of Alder's name. The man had done nothing to him. In fact, he could well be a useful acquaintance but still his name rankled.

As Sam watched, the two financiers hailed a porter and were forced to wait while he went on board to retrieve their luggage. *Where were they coming from? Had they just come from Europe? Apparently, they were not traveling light.*

In the few seconds of delay that he had been granted, Sam made up his mind. Alfie was well able to look after himself – his story of being abandoned in Valparaiso was evidence enough. If the boy could manage to find his way back from Chile, he could find his way around Washington.

Sam hastily scribbled Sophie Paxton's address on a page from his notebook, and handed it to Alfie along with a dollar bill. "Find out where Evans is staying and try to talk to him. Tell him I'm ready to offer money for his co-operation and that I'll be in touch. I want to know why they've brought him to Washington. See where they go, try to talk to Evans and then come back to the house. I've written the address for you. Take a streetcar, and don't take any risks. Do you understand me? No risks, Alfie."

"All right, Gov. I understand. Where you going?"

"I'm going to keep my eye on those two toffs."

"They ain't the story, Gov."

"They are so far as I'm concerned."

"You're wrong."

"Don't stand there arguing, get after them.

Alfie nodded. "Leave it to me, Gov."

"Get going then."

"Right you are."

Sam watched as Alfie inserted himself into the crowd of departing passengers. Despite his limp, Alfie was quick and agile. Sam tried to convince himself that he had not set the boy an unreasonable task. The boy was familiar with London and New York, he should be able to cope with Washington. It held no more dangers than any other big city.

He had just about settled with his conscience by the time he caught a final glimpse of Sheriff Bayliss accompanied by Stanley Lord who was striding angrily with his head up and his jaw jutting defiantly. They disappeared into the crowd and Sam did not even see Alfie darting along behind them. That was good. The boy knew how to keep himself concealed. He would do a fine job and he'd be at the Paxton townhouse by evening.

Sam was ready to turn his attention to the two bankers, when he saw another two men forcing their way through the crowd. They were following in Bayliss's footsteps, or maybe following in Alfie's limping steps. Sam's heart dropped. He knew these men, or at least he knew what they were. They were Pinkerton men – no doubt about it.

Pinkertons! Sam had never personally run afoul of the Pinkerton Agency but he knew their story. From their bounty hunting in the old West to their infamous and murderous breaking of the Carnegie Steel strike in 1892, their reputation had only grown increasingly sinister. He knew what they were now – more than two thousand strong, they were the paramilitary wing of big business. They were mercenaries for the great industrialists – hired thugs without a conscience. They wore their dark overcoats and black hats as a form of uniform. They made no attempt to disguise themselves.

Now, they were on the trail of Joe Bayliss and Captain Lord. Why? Who had hired them? Surely not Senator Smith. He would never have Pinkerton men in his pay, but the same could not be said for J. P. Morgan and International Mercantile Marine, or even Aidan Paxton, Sophie's grandfather. He would not hesitate to use Pinkertons. He had already used them in Pittsburgh.

If Joe Bayliss caught sight of the Pinkertons, he would know what they were. Sam had a feeling that the sheriff would also know how to deal with them, but what about Alfie? Alfie was in the middle of this and ignorant of the nature of the men in black overcoats. Sam wished with all his heart that he had not sent the boy on such an errand but it was too late now - he couldn't call him back. Alfie was on his own.

Sam turned away. He was no longer interested in the two bankers, but apparently, they were now interested in him. He found his way impeded by a porter with a luggage cart, and beside the cart stood Davidson and Vanderlipt, their faces grim, their eyes hard.

"Mr. White," Vanderlipt said..

Sam affected a blank, uncomprehending stare. "Gentlemen. What can I do for you? Are we acquainted?"

"No," said Vanderlipt, "we have never been introduced, but we have long been aware of you, peeping through keyholes, sneaking around corners. Yours is a very low kind of profession, isn't it?"

"I can't imagine what you're talking about," Sam said.

For two years he had wanted to have a conversation with either one of these two men, but now the opportunity presented itself, he could only think of Alfie. He had to do something. He had to find out where Captain Lord, Evans and Gill were to be lodged and try to intercept Alfie. Someone would know. John Alder would probably know. Yes, the best thing would be to swallow a helping of humble pie and head over to the Senate Office Building to talk to John Alder.

"Mr. White!"

Sam turned back to the bankers. "Yes, I am a journalist," he said, "and proud to bring the truth to the world. Now, if you will excuse me ..."

"Not yet," said Davidson. "You may think you have a story but you don't, and you won't. Let me give you a word of warning. *Titanic* is not the only ship that can sink."

"What?"

"You understood me."

Sam could only stagger backward as the porter pushed past with the luggage cart. He sank onto the nearest bench, his legs unable to hold him, his ears hardly able to believe what he had heard.

The Titanic is not the only ship that can sink.

Sophie Paxton
Logan Circle Townhouse, Washington DC

Miss Pattison was very much in evidence this morning and, for once, Sophie welcomed her. The past hour had been hard – harder than anything she had ever done before. Only the echo of Miss Pattison's hectoring voice and misjudged Latin phrases kept her moving.

Excelsior, Sophie, reach for the heights.

Sophie wiped her sweaty hands against the pale ruffles of her morning dress. Miss Pattison approved of sweat. Whilst other schools may teach that horses sweat, gentlemen perspire, and ladies merely glow, such niceties did not apply to Howell girls. Sophie was not glowing; she was definitely sweating as she gritted her teeth and attempted to defy reality.

The early summer heat in her room would normally be unbearable, but Sophie had made it more so by having the maids close the windows. She did not want anyone to hear the noisy, if one-sided, conversation between herself and Miss Pattison.

Sophie's grandfather had sent a physician to the house to oversee Sophie's convalescence. The physician, eyeing Sophie enthroned in her wheelchair, suggested crutches. Sophie had protested. In fact, Sophie protested every suggestion made by her visitor even to the point of refusing to look down as he examined her foot.

"It's healing well. You had a good surgeon."

"I had a butcher."

"No, Miss Paxton, this is a fine piece of surgery. I could have done no better myself. You have sufficient bone to support your foot and perhaps a custom-made boot —"

"You expect me to go out in society and dance with boots?"

"Miss Paxton, it is too early to speak of dancing, but I am suggesting the various ways you can avoid being bound to this wheelchair. It is really not necessary for you to be confined here like an invalid. I will send you a pair of crutches. They will allow you to at least move around the house. Whether or not you dance is entirely up to you. In fact, Miss Paxton, it is all up to you now."

The crutches had arrived within hours and now they leaned against Sophie's bedpost waiting for her to tuck them under her arms. She had been tempted to try them. She was tired of being confined to her room. The Paxton townhouse was not equipped with an elevator. She had not been downstairs since she had arrived two days ago.

It seemed that the spectral Miss Pattison could read Sophies's thoughts. "Howell girls do not use crutches. Howell girls stand on their own two feet."

"What if I don't have two feet?"

Miss Pattison's face twisted impatiently. "You have two feet, girl. Now get on with it."

Sophie had been "getting on with it" for an hour now. She could only walk on the outside of her foot with her ankle buckling inward, her knee thrust outward, and her right foot splayed out to help her balance. Her whole body dipped with each step. She was not so much walking as lurching. She had adjusted her cheval mirror so that she had a view of her whole body from head to foot. For an hour now she had walked backward and forward trying to adjust the horrible dipping and collapsing gait - trying to maintain herself upright. It could not be done.

"Nothing wrong with a prosthetic boot," Miss Pattison said. "If the boot will improve your ability to involve yourself in daily life, why not try it?"

Sophie was suddenly waylaid by an image of John Alder as she had first seen him on the *Titanic*. Moments after the slight hesitation of the *Titanic* but before the chaos, before the night of terror, John had come from the smoking room immaculate in evening clothes. She had been so determined to speak to Dick Williams that she had barely noticed his companion, but now she remembered. Now she had a picture of how he would look at a ball or a dazzling Washington social event. Her position as Aidan Paxton's heir, could certainly put her at his side, if that was what she wanted.

She knew how *he* would look, but how would *she* look if she accompanied him. She could imagine it now. She had evening gowns – an entire wardrobe had been sent to the townhouse to await her arrival. For years she had worn only the Howell uniform, but obviously a new wardrobe had been prepared in advance of her summons to return home. She had already run her hands across the satins, and sequins of the gowns in her closet. There was a silk gown in a dazzling blue that would match her eyes. She could pin up her hair and slip into that dress and imagine herself accompanied by John who would be dressed as she had first seen him. There would be whispers, of course.

That's the Paxton girl. They met on the Titanic, you know.

They say she was a heroine. She rowed all night.

They make a handsome couple.

Yes, my dear, but have you seen her try to walk? She can barely stumble. It is so unattractive.

But she has money, I suppose that's some compensation.

Miss Pattison interrupted her thoughts. *"Why have you stopped walking?"*

"I was just thinking."

"Just feeling sorry for yourself."

"I have ball dresses, Miss Pattison, but can you imagine me at a ball.? How could I dance?"

For once Miss Pattison spoke hesitantly. "A prosthetic boot. If the dress is long enough it wouldn't be visible."

"Hems are rising, Miss Pattison. Ankles are on display."

"Howell girls are not slaves to fashion and —"

"Don't you understand? I'm Sophie Paxton, the heiress. I'm supposed to be fashionable. I'm no longer a Howell girl.

It happened in an instance. Miss Pattison simply disappeared and took with her Sophie's last line of defense. If Sophie was not a Howell girl, she was nothing, and nothing was expected of her. Without the thought of Miss Pattison to hold her up, Sophie sank to the floor and curled into a ball.

A tap on the bedroom door. Sophie looked up. The door opened and, for the first time in seven years, she saw her grandfather.

Aidan Paxton was a short, broad-shouldered man, built like a tree stump. His thick curly hair was white and his beard was prodigious, as were his sideburns. He presented a slightly gnome-like figure as he stood in the doorway of her room, looking down on her.

"Sophie."

Sophie lifted her face and sat back on her heels, ignoring the lance of pain through her left foot. She didn't know what to call him. If she had been a boy, she would surely have called him "sir" but she was not a boy – much to his disappointment.

"Grandfather," she said hesitantly.

"Well," Paxton said, "what's this all about? Why did I have to climb these stairs to see you and what are you doing down there on the floor?"

"I'm sorry. I have been trying to walk and I .. er... tripped."

Paxton had not lost the Scottish accent of his youth. "Looks to me like you've been greeting," he said.

"Greeting?" Sophie asked.

"Crying. Have you been crying, girl?"

"Just a little," Sophie said.

"I sent you to that school so you would learn not to cry."

Anger, her ever-present ally, brought Sophie to her feet in a sudden surge of pain and power. She stood as steadily as she was able. "You sent me to that school to get rid of me," she said.

"I sent you there so you could learn to stand up for yourself." Paxton's lips twitched. Was he about to laugh? Did he find something comical in this situation?

Oh yes, he was definitely grinning. "All that money spent," he said, "and I find you in a ball on the floor greeting your eyes out. Do you no see the humor in that?"

His words found a chink in Sophie's armor of resentment. She looked at her grandfather again, and this time she really saw him – not as a terrifying gnome-like figure, but as an old man who was fighting his disappointment just as hard as she was fighting her anger. He had come to this room to see what the Howell School had made of his granddaughter. He wanted to know if she was fit to carry the Paxton legacy, and he had discovered a weeping girl, crawling on the floor. He should have been angry but somehow, he had managed to put aside anger and find humor.

Sophie sniffed back renewed tears, and managed a smile. Her grandfather produced a handkerchief from the breast pocket of his linen suit. "Wipe your eyes, lassie, and sit down before ye fall down. Let's have a good old blether. It seems a lot has been going on. How much of your foot has been taken?"

"Only my big toe," Sophie said.

It was the first time she had used the word "only" to apply to Dr. Lengyel's amputation. Saying the word brought sudden perspective. She had lost her toe, but not her foot. She had lost tennis, but she had not lost her life. Something clicked into place in her mind, or maybe her soul. It was an unexpected surge of gratitude for the surgeon who had done what needed to be done, and for Maxine who had given permission.

"So, you can walk," Paxton said. It was not a question. It was a statement.

"Just about," Sophie admitted.

Her grandfather nodded his head. "Well, that's fine. I trust there will be no more crawling around the floor."

"I was..."

"Never mind. We'll talk about other things. Sit ye down,"

Sophie sat on the edge of her bed and her grandfather settled down beside her. She inhaled his scent. The mixture of tobacco, ghostly whiskey fumes, and the perspiration of a hot southern day brought back wisps of memory.

He was speaking soothingly now – telling her how she resembled her mother - but the words came from very far away and the wisps of memory solidified.

She was four years old, living with her parents in Pittsburgh where her father oversaw the Paxton Steelworks, a massive conglomeration of buildings on the banks of the Ohio River. Sophie and her parents lived in a spacious Sewickley Heights mansion high above the river where the air was clean. The mill only revealed itself at night in flames that lit the sky. When Sophie and her mother went into Pittsburgh to visit the department stores, she was aware that the stones and bricks of the building were painted black with soot. She had known even then that it was soot from the Paxton Mill that marred the buildings and it was choking smoke from those same mills that strained the faces of the immigrants who thronged the streets.

For her life was easy - a Governess to teach her, beginner tennis lessons at the Allegheny Country Club, and soon the birth of a little brother or sister – preferably a brother. It had all come to an end when a freight train, running on the Pittsburgh-Rochester line, sounded its horn at the Leetsdale Crossing and startled young Alex Paxton's team of finely-bred carriage horses. It was said that the horses ran for more than a mile up-hill from the river, before up-ending the carriage in Big Sewickley Creek and ending the lives of Sophie's parents.

Sophie still had a memory of that night. She remembered lights burning in all the rooms. People coming and going. Calls for a doctor, calls for a nurse, and then a sudden, stunned silence, and a question passed from one servant to another. "What about the child?"

"Gone."

"No, the daughter. What about Miss Sophie?"

It was all so long ago now. She had been carried to Virginia and handed over to her grandfather, a stranger who smelled of tobacco, whiskey, and grief. At the time, Sophie had thought that nothing else so terrible could ever happen in her life again. She had been wrong. Her grieving four-year old self could never have foretold another disaster in her life - the loss of the *Titanic* and the loss of her dreams.

Between those two terrible events there had been good years. Banished from Aidan Paxton's Virginia mansion, and sent to live a spartan life in North Wales, Sophie had found her true self as an athlete and the school had become her home as Virginia had never been. At the Howell School, she had found her courage, but on board the *Carpathia* that courage had deserted her. Where was it now, she wondered.

Her grandfather broke the silence that had settled between them. "About this newspaperman who is staying in my house..."

"He's just an acquaintance. He's not my ... anything...

"He's leading you into trouble."

"I'm a Howell girl," Sophie said. "We are not easily led."

Paxton gave a bark of a laugh. "You are your mother all over again. That girl had spirit."

Sophie's heart ached for her own lack of memory. She could recall little of Adelaide beyond a memory of rose-scent and fingers moving across a piano keyboard. There had to be more, but it had been blown away by the gusty winds of the Welsh coast.

Paxton was serious again. "Sam White, the newspaperman you brought here, was following a story."

"Captain Lord of the *Californian*."

"No, not that story, although heaven knows that's trouble enough," Paxton grunted. "No, he's on another trail."

"Something to do with banking," Sophie said. "It's nothing important."

"It's a story that could get him killed."

"How? Why?"

"He's caught wind of a secret. I canna tell you the secret because it is not one that concerns me. I know that it exists, but not all of the who and what and where and why. Do you know the name – J.P. Morgan?"

"I've heard of him."

"Some say he's the richest man in the world."

"Is he?"

"Possibly. He's far richer than I am. If you delve deeply enough into the network of finances behind the building of the *Titanic*, you'll find him. If you look behind the presidential elections, you'll find him. Morgan could swat me and my steel mills as easily as he could swat a fly. I've no wish to be on his bad side."

"I don't see where Sam White comes into this."

"Did you hear of the bank panic of 1907?" Paxton asked.

Sophie tensed. Was her grandfather testing her knowledge? Did he hope to find out what she had learned at the Howell School? Well, she knew nothing about 1907. Five years ago, she had been fourteen and whatever was happening in the United States had been nothing of interest to her.

Paxton shook his head. "Of course you didn't. It came to nothing because Morgan himself, used his own money to bail out the banks and keep America solvent. He did it once, but he won't do it again, so he and his banker friends are up to something and they're being very secretive about it. False names, disguises, secret meetings. Very few people are even aware that anything is happening but your friend Sam White has got hold of some information and he won't let it go."

"I don't care about banking," Sophie said. "Sam White has information about Captain Lord. He knows the *Californian* was close by. He saw everything himself. He wrote a story for the New York Times."

"That is very unfortunate for your reporter friend. He's drawn attention to himself now."

"And why shouldn't he? Everyone should know that he's shown Lord up to be a coward who left us all to drown."

Her grandfather shook his head. "No one can prove anything. You saw a light but no ship. A Boston newspaper paid a crewman five hundred dollars to say that he saw rockets. Your friend Sam White wrote a story that got him a byline in the New York Times. All these things are open to interpretation and Lord himself has said nothing."

"Well, he'll have to speak now," Sophie said. "Senator Smith will insist."

"Senator Smith will do whatever is expedient," Paxton said. "Everyone concerned is in someone else's pocket and the biggest pocket belongs to J.P. Morgan who is deeply invested in transatlantic shipping and determined to stay ahead of the competition. He's in danger of losing to the Germans and he'll do whatever it takes to win. There's a fortune to be made bringing European peasants westward to the new world and taking wealthy Americans eastward to marry off their daughters..."

Paxton paused for a moment and raised his bushy white eyebrows. "Speaking of that," he said, "I see your cousin managed to lose her new husband almost as soon as she found him."

"She still retains the title," Sophie said, suddenly feeling protective of Maxine.

"Best of both worlds," said Paxton. "I heard he was a gambler."

"Grandfather," Sophie prompted impatiently, "what about the *Californian*? "

"The *Californian*? Yes, well..."

Sophie saw something in her grandfather's face – a mental struggle. Aidan Paxton was no longer a young man. His attention had wandered and he was having difficulty returning to his previous thoughts. She was suddenly very aware that she was his heir. If his mental faculties were failing, then inheriting her responsibilities might come sooner than she had expected.

"The *Californian*," she said again.

"Leyland Line," Paxton said. "The ship and the line are also owned by Morgan."

Sophie stared at her grandfather. "Is there anything he doesn't own?"

Paxton grinned. His focus had returned. "As a matter of fact, lass, there is something."

"What?"

"Me."

"Oh."

"Morgan may hurt my fortune, but if he has hurt my family, he will have me to answer to. Show me your foot. Show me what Captain Lord did to you."

Sophie leaned down and removed her satin slipper to reveal her bare foot. There it was - the amputation in all its ugliness - misshapen, with puckered skin covering the end of the bone, the wound still red around the edges.

Aidan Paxton rose from his seat on her bed and looked down at her truncated foot. "So, that was the result of frostbite?"

"It was. This was what he did to me. I was going to be in the Olympics, and now I can hardly walk."

"Where's that newspaperman now – the one who wrote the story?"

"I don't know. He said he would go to the station and meet the train from New York that's bringing Captain Lord, but that was hours ago."

Paxton stared hard into Sophie's eyes. "Are you sure he's not your lad?"

Sophie thought about Sam for a moment, his unruly hair, his passionate energy, and, of course, the casual and dismissive way he had carried her in his arms.

"No, he's not."

"That's a good thing."

"Why?"

"Because Morgan is going to swat him like a fly."

CHAPTER EIGHTEEN

Sam White, Logan Circle

Afternoon had turned to evening by the time Sam stopped looking. He had spent hours scouring the streets around the train station searching for any sign of Alfie or any clue as to where Bayliss had taken the crew of the *Californian*.

Even as he searched, another part of his mind was occupied with Davidson's words - *The Titanic is not the only ship that can sink*. The words were meant as a warning but he took them as an invitation. He had to know more. He needed to find and follow Davidson and Vanderlip, but he couldn't – not yet. He was the one who had sent Alfie to follow Bayliss. He had sent a boy to do a man's job, and now he had to find him. Alfie had been abandoned once before. He would not abandon him now.

As the shadows lengthened, he had to acknowledge that his frenzied search for Alfie was hopeless. It was too late to find the boy this way. There was nothing to do but return to the Paxton house on Logan Circle. Perhaps his searching had been unnecessary. Perhaps Alfie, having dodged the Pinkertons, would be at the house waiting for him. If not - if Alfie had not made his way home - then the next step would be to find out who had hired the Pinkerton men, and for that he would require the assistance of someone with influence. His Aunt Ella had remained in New York, he needed another powerful friend.

As he turned his steps back to the townhouse on Logan Circle, he told himself that, although he was walking away from the last place he had seen Alfie, he was not giving up – he was going for help.

He rang the doorbell of the Paxton house and peered through the door's leaded glass panes waiting impatiently for a maid to answer. He needed to know if Alfie was here. He needed to be rid of his worry about the boy.

He could see movement behind the glass – someone in bright blue, so surely not a maid. Whoever it was, they were taking their time about answering. He rang again. The wavering blue outline approached and finally the door opened and revealed Sophie Paxton, neatly dressed in a high neck blue silk blouse and a form fitting skirt. Apart from the thickly padded bandage on her left foot, she was as elegant and fashionable as any young woman of wealth.

He took a step back in amazement observing the metamorphosis. This was not the traumatized young woman he had met in New York. Only one thing marred the picture – the expression of utter misery on her face.

Sam felt a surge of anger. Here she was, safe at home and back on her feet and yet still Sophie could not be happy. Poor little rich girl - why had he ever felt any attraction to her? John Alder could have her and the sooner the better.

At last, she spoke, her voice small and disappointed. "He's not with you."

"Who?"

"Alfie. He's not with you."

Sam's heart sank. "No. I thought he might be here."

"No, he's not here. There's a note."

"From Alfie?"

"No... well ... I don't know...."

Sophie took an ungainly step backward, resting her weight on her bandaged foot. "Come inside."

Sam stepped into the hallway. "What note? What did it say?"

Sophie was walking ahead of him now, her gait slow and painful to watch as she led him into the drawing room. The last rays of sun fought their way through the heavy lace curtain draping the tall windows. They traced a pattern of light on the rich furnishings of the room and on a man who was rising from the depths of a velvet wing chair.

"This is my grandfather," Sophie said.

Aidan Paxton's handshake was firm – almost too firm. It was not just a handshake, it was an invitation to a contest. The old man had the grip and the callouses of a man who had once worked with his hands. Studying Paxton's face Sam found signs of that early labor in a smattering of scars that could not be hidden by Paxton's prolific facial hair. These were the scars of a man who had worked among the searing sparks of a steel mill. Aidan Paxton was a self-made man.

"So ye're the one with the story of the *Californian*," Paxton said, his Scottish burr still in evidence. "Ye're the cause of all this trouble."

"Not the cause," Sam said defensively. "I reported what I saw."

"I'm nae talking about that damned ship that sat by while people drowned," Paxton said. "We'll save that talk for later. Ye're the one that brought the boy into the house."

"The boy? Do you mean Alfie? Do you know something?"

"I spent a fortune on sending my granddaughter to a school that would turn her close as possible into a man and —"

"That's not the Howell School's purpose," Sophie interrupted.

Paxton ignored the interruption. "Twice today I've found her in tears."

Sam mentally repeated his earlier thought. *Poor little rich girl!*

"First it's her foot," Paxton said, "and now it's some English guttersnipe."

"He's no guttersnipe," Sophie said. "He's a sailor and he's from the *Californian.*"

"He's nowt to do with us," Paxton said.

"He's to do with me," Sam said. "I brought him here. Do you know anything?"

"A note," Sophie said, giving her grandfather a defiant stare. "Two men brought a piece of paper. They gave it to the maid who answered the door." She looked at her grandfather again and then back at Sam. "That's why I answered the door myself this time. The maid couldn't tell me anything about the men who brought the note except that they wore dark overcoats and black hats, and demanded to know whose house this was. The maid told them and they gave her the note. When the doorbell rang just now, I wanted to answer it myself. I wanted to see if they had come again. Of course, it wasn't them, it was you."

"Where's the note?" Sam asked.

Sophie produced a familiar slip of paper from the deep pocket of her skirt. "It's about Alfie," she said.

Sam sighed. "That's my paper. That's a note I wrote so Alfie would have your address."

"Why did he need it? Where did you send him? I thought you went together to meet the train."

"There was something else at the station," Sam said impatiently. "a matter that needed my urgent attention. I sent Alfie to follow Sheriff Bayliss and Captain Lord but..." He stopped speaking. He had no time to explain everything. He held out his hand. "What did they write?"

Sophie walked toward him to place the paper in his hand. He noticed, with sympathy, the odd dip and lurch of her gait. Perhaps she had every reason to cry. She was out of her wheelchair, but there would be no tennis in her future, and probably no dancing. *Unless she has the right man to hold her up.* Sam did not even own an evening suit. He was not ... He pulled back his thoughts and studied the paper. Someone had added to the words in a round schoolboy hand. *I won't say nothing. Signed Mr. Alfred Blackwell, Esquire.*

Sophie retrieved the note from Sam's hand. "Alfred Blackwell." she said firmly. "We must say his name, the way he would want."

For a moment Sam was back in New York in his Aunt Ella's drawing room and Alfie was describing the loss of his father and the good ship *Hilda*.

"Tell me your father's name."

"Alfred Blackwell," Alfie had said. *"I'm named after him."*

Sophie smiled. "Alfred Blackwell," she repeated. "See, now I have spoken his name."

Alfie nodded. "Thank you, miss."

No, this was wrong. Sam wasn't going to remain here saying Alfred's name in a perverted litany for the dead. Perhaps Alfie was not dead. The Pinkertons had no reason to kill him. In fact, if they had killed him as some kind of warning, then they would have delivered his body and not his note.

"Did you see what was on the back?" Sophie asked.

Sam turned the note over. *The Titanic is not the only ship that can sink.*

On impulse, he passed the note to Aidan Paxton. "Do you know anything about this?"

"Kidnapped guttersnipes?"

"No, Pinkerton men."

Paxton took the note and retreated to his winged armchair where his face was partially hidden. "I have used them in the past ... in Pittsburgh. I would not use them on a boy."

Sam no longer cared whether or not his tone was respectful. He had little respect for anyone who had helped create the carnage of the Pittsburgh steel strikes. "What do you know about Henry Davidson and Frank Vanderlip?"

"As little as possible."

"They are the people who informed me, just a few hours ago, that the *Titanic* was not the only ship that could sink."

"Are they here in Washington?" Paxton asked.

"They came on the same train as Bayliss and the witnesses. I needed to know where they were going and I needed to know where Bayliss was going. So I decided I'd go after Davidson and I could send Alfie to follow Bayliss."

Paxton waved the paper. "This is all just blather," he said. "I know about Davidson and Vanderlip and their secret society. There's money there and power but all put together there's not enough to sink the Titanic, or anything other than a fishing boat.. You should nae have let them scare ye away."

"I wasn't scared."

Paxton gave him a long, cold stare. "Are you sure about that?"

"I had no idea the Pinkertons were here or I would never have sent the boy on his own."

"So," Paxton said, "what's the story you're following now? Is it the lights of the *Californian*, or the comings and goings of Henry Davidson, or is it just my granddaughter's money?"

Sam clenched his fists. He was ready to take on the belligerent old Scotsman. Sophie's money? No. He had never, even once, thought about her money except to pity her for what the money had made her.

"Grandfather," Sophie said, "you insult me."

"What?"

"You sent me away to learn to be independent – well I've learned and if you think the only reason a man would be interested in me, is because I have money, then you are wrong."

Paxton shrugged. "You still have much to learn."

Sophie's reply was fierce. "So do you," she said. She turned her back on the old man. "What do you intend to do, Mr. White? How will you find Alfie?"

"If he's alive, and if he hasn't come back here, he's still trying to do what I asked him to do."

"And what was that?"

"Talk to Ernest Gill and Cyril Evans."

"I want to talk to Captain Lord," Sophie said firmly.

Sam restrained himself and allowed the words to die unspoken. *It's not always a question of what you want.* He took a deep breath before continuing. "We all want the same thing," he said, "but I need Gill and Evans on my side. I have to know if they're going to lie to the inquiry – if, in fact, they will declare my story in the New York Times to be false. If all three of them tell the same story – that they never saw the *Titanic* —"

"Gill already sold his story to a newspaper." Sophie said.

"And, if he's offered enough money, he'll retract it. I have to reach him first."

The sound of the doorbell echoed through the house.

Sophie gave a small, ungainly jump. "Alfie's come back." She winced as her foot came down but, pain or no pain, she set off at a lumpy gallop toward the front door, with Sam following close behind.

They opened the door together and discovered John Alder on the doorstep. John's wide, honest face held a confusion of emotions. Sam could imagine that jealousy played some part in the expression but chiefly John's face showed concern.

"Is he here?" he asked. "Is Alfie here?"

Sophie didn't answer. A pink flush had suffused her cheeks. She took a step backward and lurched painfully to one side. Sam instinctively put out his hand to steady her. John's face lost the battle between anxiety and jealousy and jealousy was the winner.

That small moment on the doorstep reinforced Sam's intention of never, ever allowing his feeling for a woman to interfere with his pursuit of a story. There was a story here now, but it would have to wait while John Alder got over his jealousy and took his mind off the fact that Sam was staying in Sophie's house. Being in love, Sam thought, must be very tiresome. To care and fret about someone hour after hour, day after day, *till death us do part*, would be nothing but a burden.

You care about Alfie.

That's different.

John still hovered on the doorstep. "Where's the boy?" he asked. "Did he come back safely?"

"Alfie," Sophie said. "He's talking about Alfie." Now she reached for John to pull him in through the door. "Do you know something?"

John stepped into the hallway and Sam closed the door behind him. He deliberately stood with his back to the door, effectively barring John's exit.

"What do you know? Did you and your political bosses do this?"

"I have no political bosses," John said. "I quit."

"Why?"

"Because I went down with the *Titanic* and it's only by the grace of God I found a lifeboat. If Stanley Lord was out there and able to ignore our screams, I want him to own up to it. I won't waste my second chance at life kowtowing to liars whoever they may be and because, dammit, I know there was a light. Now tell me about Alfie. Who set the Pinkertons on him?"

Sam almost said the words he would have to hold back forever. *I did. The Pinkertons were coming for me.* He pushed the truth away. That truth would not help them now.

◆◇◆

John Alder
Senate Office Building, 5:00 p.m. April 25
John Alder was relieved to be home – not just home from his European trip, or home from the *Titanic* disaster, but also home from the clamor of New York City. The great advantage to being in D.C. was the proximity to his own apartment

and, therefore, the ability to obtain a suit that had been tailored to fit him, and to finally replace his waterlogged evening shoes.

Another advantage was his proximity to the townhouse of the Paxton family. Proximity made a simple excuse for calling at the house to inquire after Miss Sophie's health. What could be more natural?

The news that Sam White and the boy, Alfie, were actually staying at the Paxton residence, had come as an unwelcome surprise. Now after two nights of sleep in his own bed, he was ready to take on the challenge, if it was, in fact a challenge.

Unfortunately, Senator Eldridge, after giving him two days to rest, was now demanding his full attention. John could not, at this moment, pay a call on Sophie. That would have to wait until later. Now he was required in the caucus room to listen to the testimony of crewman John Collins.

The Senate Office Building gave the impression of being under siege. Crowds thronged the streets outside, even invading the landscaping and climbing onto the window sills so they could listen at the tall open windows. Inside the caucus rooms the people were packed in tight rows. Ladies fanned themselves, gentlemen perspired. Only the senators and officials, on a raised platform were free from invading elbows and stepped-on toes.

John Collins, a seventeen-year-old Irish scullion, stood alone. He seemed remarkably self-possessed for one so young, but John understood the nature of Collins' calm. For Collins, and for John himself, there was nothing left to fear. Life had thrown its very worst at them and they had survived. They were here now, safe and dry. They had seen things that no one should have to see, and they would never be the same again, but they were alive to tell the tale – that was what mattered.

Because the inquiry had now moved to Washington, any number of senators pushed to be present and to question survivors. They were so anxious, in fact, that they could not wait until the following morning. They were starting now, late in the afternoon and willing to work into the evening hours. The committee had split its responsibilities. Other senators were questioning other survivors in other rooms, but in this room, Senator Eldridge and Senator Bourne were asking the questions and John was forced to remain in attendance. Keeping notes was not a problem for John but keeping his own memories at bay as others recited their memories, took an effort of concentration.

Collins was a witness who had seen the disaster play out from its very first moments and it was obvious that the boy was no fool. Having seen stewards fitting life jackets on the first-class passengers, Collins had ignored orders to return to his bunk and lie down. He had kept his clothes and his wits and gone out onto the deck.

John made a note. Had the lower ranks really been given the orders that Collins described? Had they been told to return to their beds? If that was the case, then obviously they had been abandoned to their fate from the very first moments.

John remembered Charles Williams returning from the smoking-room carrying life jackets and he remembered the calm that had prevailed as the first-class passengers were quietly encouraged toward the life boats. At the same time, apparently, the unimportant crew members, scullions, cooks, and skivvies had already been written off and told to stay in their quarters.

Collins' testimony had not, so far, stirred the emotions of the spectators but as he continued his story, those who had managed to obtain a seat, began to move restlessly. Eldridge was allowing the young Irishman to tell his story without interruption. The words flowed over and into John. As Collins spoke, John was on the deck with him in the cold, cold starlight.

"We went up to the deck when the word came. Then I met a companion of mine, a steward, and I asked him what number my boat was, and he said sixteen so I went up to sixteen, and I seen both firemen and sailors with their bags ready and I said to myself, "There is no chance there."

John made a note. While some officers were loading boats with women and children only, whoever was loading Lifeboat #16 was admitting firemen – firemen who already had their bags packed. Bourne would be too wrapped up in the story to notice this anomaly but John made a note.

"We ran back to the deck," Collins said, "to the port side on the saloon deck with another steward and a woman and two children, and the steward had one of the children in his arms and the woman was crying. I took the child off of the woman and made for one of the boats."

John saw the spectators leaning forward in their seats. This was what they had come to hear – a child held in the arms of a kitchen boy. What would happen? Would the child be saved?

"Then," said Collins, "the word came around from the starboard side there was a collapsible boat getting launched and that all women and children were to make for it and we were just turning around and making for it when the wave washed us off the deck - washed us clear off it - and the child was washed out of my arms."

Collins made a small, helpless gesture, and John imagined the moment when the water, rolling up over the bow of the *Titanic*, swept the child from his arms. He heard a murmur from the onlookers. Perhaps they'd been holding out hope for that child even as Collins told his story but they had not been on that sinking ship. They could not imagine the force of that icy wave. There had been no hope for that nameless child. It had been gone in an instant. And what of the mother? Surely, she too had been swept away along with the other child. In its final moments, the *Titanic* had offered no refuge, only death.

"I went down," Collins said, "and wreckage and the people that was around me, they kept me down for at least two or three minutes under the water.

John stilled his pencil. No need to make a note of this. He knew how this felt. He remembered his own desperate struggle to reach the surface, trying to free himself from a tangle of arms and legs, all kicking frantically toward the surface

For a few moments he was engulfed by memory and Senator Eldridge's voice seemed to come from a great distance. In the heat of the packed hearing room, he shivered with cold. He returned to reality when he realized that now Senator Bourne was speaking.

"Mr. Collins, did you see any light in the distance?"

"Yes, I saw a green light".

A green light. Sophie had said a white light. What was this green light?

"Did you think it was one of your own boats?"

"No, sir; I did not really think of what it was until the firemen and sailors came up and said that it was a boat."

"A ship?"

"Yes, sir."

"What became of it"?

"It disappeared."

"How long was it visible?"

"About twenty minutes or half an hour, I am sure it was."

"How far away, would you think, from the *Titanic?*"

"I guess it would be about four miles ... I am sure, three or four miles."

Three or four miles! Was this true? John could hardly stay seated. So, Sam White had been telling the truth. Well, he had never really doubted him, but the story had been so outlandish that something in him had rebelled against blind acceptance. Or perhaps he was just unwilling to think anything good about Sam White. He did not like the way Sam had ingratiated himself with the Paxton family – specifically Sophie Paxton.

Senator Eldridge seemed intent on preventing Bourne from asking any more questions about the light nearby. In his attempt to re-establish dominance, and change the subject, he came very close to actually elbowing Bourne aside. "Mr. Collins," he said, "you say you were swept off the *Titanic's* deck by a wave?"

"Yes, sir."

"How long after the accident occurred or at what time would you judge it was that you were swept off of the deck?"

"Well, sir, I could not say; I am sure it was close on to 1 o'clock."

"Was the ship sinking when you were swept off?"

"Yes, sir."

While Eldridge continued his questioning, Bourne gathered his papers, rose from his seat, and walked out through the side door of the caucus room. His exit made no impression on the spectators as Collins launched into a description of his night in the lifeboat. While the spectators were held in thrall by Collins' description of night on the water, John was not. He made an attempt to concentrate but finally admitted that his need to question Senator Bourne was greater than his need to stay with Eldridge. It was, in fact, greater than his need to retain his position.

He caught up with Bourne in the long corridor that ran between offices.

"Senator."

"Mr. Alder, shouldn't you be in the hearing room?"

"No, sir, I believe that I should be here now asking you the meaning of your question to young Collins."

Bourne, a round-faced man with a bulbous nose and sharp gray eyes beneath sparse eyebrows, looked at John as though seeing him for the first time. "You were on the *Titanic*?

"I was."

"How are you now?"

"I am shaken."

"Must be hard for you to sit and listen to the retelling."

John shook his head. "No, I believe it's important that we find out what happened. I was there, but I could not tell you all of what happened. It is a very big picture, Senator, but we need to see all of it."

"I fear that may not be permitted," Bourne said.

John barely hesitated. He was about to betray his employer, put his entire future at risk, and probably destroy any chance he may have had with Sophie Paxton. An heiress might marry an up-and-coming senatorial prospect but not a glorified office boy who had deliberately destroyed his own prospects.

"Senator Bourne," John said, "why did you ask about the light? How did you know what Collins had seen?"

"I didn't know. It is my intention, contrary to my own interests, to ask the question of every survivor if given the opportunity."

"Why?"

"Because I believe the light existed. There's a reporter, a fellow by the name of Sam —"

"I know him."

"And you read his report in the Times?"

"Yes."

"Do you believe it?"

"I do. I have spoken to other survivors who tell the same story. Miss Sophie Paxton is adamant that she saw a light."

Bourne halted in front of his own office door. "Step inside, Mr. Alder. Walls have ears and we are both harming ourselves out here – although more harm to you than to me. If you want me to answer your question and if you plan to act on my answer, you will no doubt eventually lose your position, but we shouldn't let that happen prematurely. It is best that at least one of us remains within the tent."

"What tent would that be?"

"The one that is owned by J.P. Morgan."

John nodded and stepped into the senator's office. "What is happening, Senator?"

"Mr. Morgan may be the wealthiest man that the modern world has ever seen but even he can't afford what it would cost IMM to accept blame for the loss of the *Titanic*."

"The *Californian* had no part in the sinking of the *Titanic*," John said.

"We are beyond that now," Bourne said. "It is obvious that lives were lost that could have been saved. No general alarm was given, no ship's officers formally assembled, no orderly routine was attempted, or organized system of safety begun. It was pure chaos."

He looked at John. "I'm sorry. You are standing there, looking as you have always looked and I forgot for a moment that you were on the *Titanic*. You lived through this. I am preaching to the choir."

"It's all right. Please tell me everything."

"Very well," Bourne said, "I'll come straight to the point. This inquiry has revealed far more than was ever expected. We are well on our way to creating an international incident, not just with the British but with all the European countries who loaded their citizens onto the *Titanic*. According to many of my colleagues, this international incident has to be avoided. Political expediency trumps the truth, so the search for answers is over. The inquiry will now be shaped by political expediency. Senator Eldridge agrees and will act accordingly."

"But you will not?"

"I want the truth."

"And so do I," John said.

"And you are willing to act against the interests of your employer?" Bourne asked.

John hesitated over his final response – a response that would lose him his job – and his answer was interrupted by raised voices in the corridor outside Bourne's office.

"Pinkertons. You sent Pinkertons."

"No, Joe, I did not."

John looked at Bourne. Bourne spoke softly. "I know that voice. That's Joe Bayliss, Smith's personal lawman and that's Smith talking to him."

John nodded. Sheriff Joe Bayliss had been very much in evidence in New York, issuing subpoenas and rounding up witnesses. While some had doubted that a lawman from Michigan had the authority to detain foreign citizens, most had welcomed his willingness to cut through a forest of red tape and round up the officers and crew of the *Titanic* before they could take a ship back to England.

Senator Smith and Joe Bayliss were old friends but now it seemed that they were having a serious disagreement.

"Even in Michigan, we know a Pinkerton man when we see one," Bayliss said.

"I didn't send them," Smith insisted, "but what does it matter? Lord is here now, that's what matters. Where have you stashed him?"

"In a boarding house. It's across from the Capitol. I have Lord in there, along with Gill and Evans, and I have men watching them."

"What does Lord say?" Smith asked.

"Lord says nothing. Four hundred miles on that train and he didn't say a damned word. Gill is talking. You'll have trouble keeping his mouth shut, and Evans, the radio man, will do whatever Marconi tells him to do."

For a moment the two men outside the door fell silent, and then Bayliss spoke again, his gravelly voice full of concern. "Look here, Bill, I don't like this. I've stuck my neck out a long way already in detaining the crew but ..."

"I understand, Joe."

"No, Bill, you don't understand. I was more than willing to use my authority to stop the *Titanic* crew from being loaded onto the first boat back to England. That was plain and straight forward. I didn't mind going to Boston to pick up Lord, but this is the end of it. We've been friends for a long time and I thought I knew you, but I don't like what I'm seeing now – manipulating the truth, sending Pinkertons to threaten them -"

"Dammit, Bill, I didn't send them."

"Did you send a boy?"

"No! What boy?""

"Young lad, fourteen or fifteen. Walks with a limp. He was following us."

"Nothing to do with me," Smith said. "Why didn't you ask him?"

"I tried, but he gave me the slip. I'm hoping he had the sense to keep clear. Wouldn't want the Pinkertons to find him. I don't like the way they ask questions."

Inside Senator Bourne's office, John took a deep breath. "*Young lad, fourteen or fifteen. Walks with a limp.* Alfie!

A tap on the office door brought an end to John's eavesdropping. He heard footsteps fading – Senator Smith and Joe Bayliss walking away. He opened the door and saw the eager face of a senate page. "Compliments of Senator Eldridge," the page said. "He wants you back in the hearing room." The boy coughed nervously. "He says I'm to ask you what the hell you're doing."

What the hell am I doing? I'm about to throw everything away.

"Tell the Senator I am unable to come."

"Sir?"

"Go! Tell him."

John turned away and shook hands with Senator Bourne. "Well, Senator, I think we're finished here."

"I think *you're* finished," Bourne said. "If he comes asking, what shall I tell Eldridge?"

"Tell him nothing," John said. "Let him find out for himself."

CHAPTER NINETEEN

Alfie Blackwell
Somewhere in Washington D.C.
Well, at least he wasn't dead. If he was dead, he wouldn't be in such pain. Blimey, there was nothing on him that didn't hurt. Them men in the black coats had known what they was doing but he hadn't given in. He hadn't told them nothing – not a dicky bird.

He forced his eyes open. He was in an alley, but not a real dark one. There was light coming from overhead. A house maybe. He was outside a house and light was coming from the windows.

He pulled himself into a seated position, leaning against a brick wall that was still warm with the heat of the day. No sun now, but the air was still blooming hot, and wet – not raining wet but wet to breathe. He'd breathed air like that off the coast of West Africa. Hoomid they called it. Horrid was what he called it.

Was he alone? He listened but the only sound carried on the clammy air was the sound of frogs, some shrilling, some croaking. Only frogs, not people.

He was alone.

Right, Alfie Blackwell, let's see what they done to you.

Arms bruised but still working. Knuckles not bruised. *He didn't fight back. He should have fought back.* Eyes swollen into slits, won't open properly – nothing in focus. Good thing really 'cause if he ever got to see a mirror again, he knew he was not going to like his face. He moved his tongue and explored his teeth. Nothing broken and nothing loose. Well, that was something. Split lip? Yes, definitely. Not the first time for that, there'd been a fight in Rio – no point in thinking about that. He wasn't in Rio now. He was in bloody Washington and he was well and truly banged up.

This wasn't your normal beating – the kind you'd get in any port. These geezers had gone for his kidneys. He'd be pissing blood for weeks. He took a deep breath and let out a long curse at the sudden sharp pain. Cor bloody blimey, they'd cracked a couple of ribs.

He slumped back against the wall, waiting for the pain to release him. *All right, Alfie, breathe. You gotta breathe. Come on. Try again.* He took a shallow breath. Not so bad. What now? Now stand up. Ain't no one gonna stand you up, you gotta stand yourself up.

His legs wobbled and he sucked on his teeth to suppress a scream. Cor strewth, that hurt. They'd done something to his knees. Well, they ain't broken, so just stand. He staggered upright and leaned against the wall.

What now?

He'd let his governor down good and proper. He wouldn't never see him again. They'd taken the paper with Miss Sophie's address. He shouldn't have let them. He should have torn it up – no, he should have ... yeah, he should have swallowed it. He'd been daft – writing his name like he was some bleeding hero out of a book. Still, he didn't tell them who she was. He never said her name, not even when they had him down on the ground.

Blimey, they was really good with their boots but he hadn't said nothing – not in the end – not even when the red mist was blinding his eyes. He never said that he'd been following Captain Lord and he's seen Lord and Gill and Evans go inside that fancy guest house.

He leaned unsteadily against the wall and tried to work it all out. The trilling of tree frogs was so close and so loud it felt like the damned things were penetrating his brain. This was worse than that night they had anchored in the Orinoco.

Ignore them.

Think!

How come he weren't dead and how come the men in overcoats didn't care about the boarding house – didn't go inside? Well...another shallow breath, just on the edge of pain, and suddenly he had his answer. They wasn't after Lord, they was after the governor. That's the only thing what makes sense. They was after Sam White on account of some other story he was writing. Alfie had followed the tall sheriff, and the men in black coats had followed him, but not because of Lord. No, this was something else.

What to do now? He needed to find the governor but how could he do that? They'd taken the paper with the address. They'd even taken his dollar. He took another breath, deeper than he intended and his ribs reminded him that they were broken. His head was beginning to feel fuzzy but the sharp pain focused him. He was outside the guest house, he had to be. His attackers hadn't carried him away so they had to have left him where they had found him - in an alley behind the guest house looking for a way in.

So, here's the thing, Alfie boy, this is where they've put Gill and Evans and Gill and Evans is your shipmates. Shipmates stand together. Well, not always, but in a foreign port, that's the rule. So, find a way inside. Find Evans, he's a good bloke, he ain't never done you no harm, and Gill – he's all right.

He took a tentative step and then another, inching his way along the wall. He came to stone steps leading into a garden. No way to walk up them. Have to crawl.

Oh, God, that hurt! His knees weren't good at the best of times, not after Valparaiso, but now they was bloody, blooming screaming bad. He thought vaguely that he needed new curse words. His grandmother had forbidden cursing in her house and some of her lingered in his mind even after she sent him away to sea and told him not to come back. He had blocked his ears when his shipmates got to really cursing but now he wished he'd ignored the ghostly voice of his Nana, and listened to the rich vocabulary of his shipmates. He didn't know any words strong enough for the way he felt now.

He finally rolled from the top step onto the soft surface of a lawn. He turned onto his back, unable to move, barely able to even stare up into the sky. His broken nose was still working. He smelled cigarette smoke, strong and foul, but familiar. Gill! Ernie Gill had picked up them French cigarettes in Marseilles on their last trip. They was the worst smelling gaspers ever. Gauloise they called them. Someone was out in this garden smoking French cigarettes. It had to be Gill.

He would have to do it. He couldn't lie here all night. His voice was only a little louder than the tree frogs. "Gill! Hey Gill, over here!"

John Alder
Paxton Townhouse, April 26

John didn't leave. It was well past the hour for a visitor to linger in the drawing room but how could he leave? Sophie was distraught. Someone should comfort and reassure her, and Sam White was obviously not the man for that job. If anything, he seemed more upset than Sophie. There was something else about him – an air of guilt. John didn't want to think that way. Sam had obviously been good to Alfie, but he couldn't shake the feeling that Sam knew more than he was telling.

One thing was certain, none of them knew whether Alfie Blackwell was alive, or dead - just another body in the river. John thought dourly of Lord Lucan Sempter and the way that the Hudson River had carried his corpse out into the current. Sempter was found because his killers wanted him found. Would Alfie's killers play the same game – launching the boy into the Potomac as a warning?

Warning of what? Was this whole ghastly situation really about Captain Lord and the *Californian* or was it about something else known only to Sam White? If only Sophie would not look at Sam with such admiration. Couldn't she see that he was the kind of man who would break her heart?

Aidan Paxton, his face shadowed by the wings of the armchair, was fully engaged, and showing no signs of retiring to his bed. He wanted to know about Alfie.

"Who is this boy? Where did you find him?"

"He was cook's helper on the *Californian* and he was the one who brought me my meals."

"So, he's nothing to you?" Paxton asked.

"I owe him my life," Sam said. "Without his help, I believe Captain Lord would have had me put overboard long before we reached Boston."

Paxton raised his snowy eyebrows. "You really believe that?"

"I believe that I had seen too much on the night the *Titanic* sank. Alfie listened to the crew making plans and he risked everything to tell me."

"Fair enough," Paxton said. "Ye canna ignore a good deed. So, you took him with you off the ship. Did you think to take care of him forever?"

"I didn't think that far ahead," Sam admitted. "This has been ... sudden."

"This has been a failure," Paxton said. "One day in Washington and the boy you promised to care for has already been taken by Pinkertons. I wouldn't say that you looked after him at all."

"You don't understand," Sam said.

John wished he could see Paxton's face so carefully hidden in the wings of the chair. He suspected that the old man was reacting from personal experience. He had come alone from Scotland. He was secure now in the fortune he'd made, but once upon a time he had been a frightened boy, just as alone as Alfie was now.

"Does the boy have a mother?" Paxton asked.

Sam shook his head. "I think not."

"A father?"

"His father died at sea."

"So he has no one."

"Apparently he has a grandmother who sent him to sea when he was eight years old, rather than spending the money to feed him."

"And what will you do with him," Paxton asked, "if you find him alive?"

John studied Sam's face and saw the reluctant internal struggle. What *would* he do with Alfie? He'd acted on instinct taking the boy off the ship, but now he was responsible for him and that responsibility had already turned out to be a dangerous problem.

John could not guess at Sam's life except for knowing that Sam was a reporter, driven to find news. He had not even mentioned having a home city, or a permanent residence.

"Well?" Paxton asked.

"Maybe an apprenticeship," Sam said dubiously.

"Hah," Paxton barked. "So ye'd abandon him?"

"We could keep him," Sophie said. "He's a good boy."

"A good boy!" Paxton growled. "He's nae a puppy."

Sophie glared at her grandfather, hidden as he was in the shadows of the chair. "You are just being unpleasant for no reason at all. Mr. White has been very generous to Alfie and I'm sure he won't let him down."

"Hah!" Paxton repeated. "I'm not sure he won't let us all down. There's something he's not telling us. Pinkerton men work for pay. Someone is behind this and he's not telling us who it is."

When Sam failed to respond, Paxton turned his attention to John.

"What does your senator know about any of this."

"My senator?"

"Eldridge. That's who you work for, don't ye? What does Eldridge know? He's on the committee, he must know something."

"Eldridge didn't do this," John said confidently. He'd already made up his mind to turn his back on his employer, but he couldn't let him take the blame for this. "If you're asking me who hired Pinkerton men, I can tell you that it was not Senator Smith or Sheriff Bayliss, or Senator Eldridge. They wanted Captain Lord and the crewmen kept in a safe place —"

"Kept where they could be watched and made to lie," Sophie interrupted.

John acknowledged her with a slight bow. "You are undoubtedly correct Miss Paxton, but in order to watch Lord and his crewmen, they had no need to employ Pinkerton men. Bayliss set his own men on watch. I think that there is no connection between these two events. The Pinkerton men took Alfie for another reason although I cannot imagine what that reason could be." He looked at Sam. "Any suggestions, Mr. White?"

Sam turned away and before John could press him for an answer, the cowbell sound of the telephone broke the tension in the room. They all turned to look at the offending instrument, but it was Sophie who snatched up the receiver.

"Yes," she said breathlessly, clutching the phone with white knuckles. "Yes, who is this? Speak up, I can't hear you."

The three men gathered around her and John strained his ears to decipher the voice that crackled along the wire.

Sophie was flustered but she was not about to hand the instrument to anyone else. She persisted in her questioning. "Who is this? What do you want? Yes, this is the Paxton residence, but ..."

The crackling increased in volume and John could finally decipher words. "Evans. Cyril Evans."

Sam obviously heard at the same time as John and he wrenched the phone from Sophie's grasp. He ignored her shocked face and the warning growl from Aidan Paxton.

"It's me, Evans. Sam White."

Now Sam listened, interrupting only once. "Speak up, man. I can't hear you!"

Then another pause followed. "All right. Good. Okay. I'll come."

Sam replaced the receiver and looked around at the querying faces. "Cyril Evans," he said, "the Marconi man on the *Californian*. They've found Alfie."

"Alive or dead?" Aidan Paxton asked.

"Alive," Sam said. "He's badly beaten but he's a strong boy. Evans is doing what he can for him. I don't know the whole story. Evans is used to sending Morse code, not speaking on the phone and it's obvious he didn't want to wake up the whole house."

"So where is he?"

"There's a guest house across from the Capitol. It's actually called Capital View Guest House. I'll go over there now."

"We'll go together," John said.

Sam shook his head. "No need. Alfie's my responsibility. I'll take care of it."

Sam was already at the living room door when John stopped him. He kept his voice low. "Mr. White, I am coming with you. We can do this quietly or we can come to blows right here and now, but you are not going alone."

John was not sure what would have happened if Sophie had not chosen that moment to snatch up her shawl and lurch toward them, her gait leaving her on the edge of collapsing with each step. Both men turned to help her and the moment was over – the tension dissipated.

"I'm coming with you," Sophie declared.

"Miss Sophie," John protested, "you cannot. It's midnight. It's not proper."

"Howell girls don't have to be proper," Sophie said.

"Go with them, lass," Aidan Paxton said. "Ye've a good head on your shoulders. I'm for my bed now. You can tell me everything in the morning." He rose stiffly from his armchair. "We've an automobile and a chauffeur. Call for Saunders, he'll take you."

"No need to wake the chauffeur," John said, "I know how to drive."

"Then let us go." Sophie said. She reached for Sam's arm. "You may have to hold me upright. Walking is not easy."

Sam grunted impatiently but extended his arm to her. John saw the way Sophie clutched the extended arm, and the way she looked up at Sam while he did not look at her. So, John thought, Sam White does not yet know he is my rival. In fact, he doesn't even know there is a contest, but there is and Sophie has a mind of her own.

The automobile was a Cadillac bright blue with white wheels and a black roof and it even possessed an electric starter. It was the most luxurious and up-to-date vehicle John had even seen, let alone driven. He climbed in and approached the unfamiliar dashboard with extreme caution.

The garage of the townhouse possessed electric lights, and Sam opened the wide doors, flooding the street outside with light and giving John enough light to study an intimidating array of knobs, dials and gauges.

Fuel. He tapped the fuel gauge. It appeared that the tank was full. Good. What else? Choke. It would need a touch of choke. He located a lever, probably the choke, and tugged lightly. Now for the electric starter.

Sophie suddenly appeared and settled herself in the seat beside him. "Hurry up. Someone's bound to see the light and then we'll have the whole street awake and asking questions."

"I'm just making sure —"

"That one," Sophie interrupted pointing to a prominently displayed green button. "That's the one the chauffeur presses to get it started. Just push it. We don't have time to waste."

The car rocked as Sam scrambled into the back seat and needlessly repeated Sophie's command. "Just press the green button."

John pressed. Somewhere under the massive hood, a motor whined...and whined ... and whined. The engine did not so much as cough.

John frantically surveyed the instrument panel. What was he missing? Ignition. There should be an ignition button, but where? And something else – fuel. What was the matter with his brain? The Cadillac with its electric start was the latest thing in engineering, but the electric starter couldn't start an engine without fuel. There was a fuel switch ... somewhere.

He could feel Sophie moving restlessly. He was making a fool of himself.

Rescue came in the form of the Paxton chauffeur dressed in jodhpurs, undershirt and suspenders striding purposefully across the garage, carrying a tire iron and ready to do damage to whoever was attempting to make off with Aidan Paxton's automobile.

"It's all right, Saunders," Sophie called, as the chauffeur approached with murder on his face. "It's me. Miss Sophie."

For a moment Saunders seemed unwilling to release the tire iron, but then his face relaxed from murder to puzzlement. "Miss Sophie, what on earth ..."

"Just get in and drive us," Sophie said. She poked John's arm. "You get in the back with Mr. White. Hurry up."

Mortified into obedience, John scrambled into the back of the car beside Sam and watched as the chauffeur set about starting the engine.

Fuel! The fuel switch was under the back seat. Ignition. There it was just to the right of the steering wheel. Saunders pressed the starter button, the starter motor whined, the engine coughed. Saunders adjusted the choke. The engine purred. They were ready to go.

"Capitol View Guest House," Sophie said. "I assume it's close to the Capitol."

"I know where it is," Saunders said. He released the clutch and the car glided out through the open garage doors.

"We should close the doors," Saunders said. "Perhaps one of the gentlemen..."

"No time," Sophie insisted. "Leave them open."

Saunders drove obediently away, leaving Logan Circle flooded with light.

John and Sam were alone together in the back seat. The Cadillac had been designed on the assumption it would be driven by a chauffeur and the passengers' conversations would not be overheard by the man behind the wheel.

Deep under the sheltering canvas roof, Sam's face was hidden from John, but John did not need to see his face to know his tension.

Sam's voice was on the edge of anger. "There was no need for you all to come. Alfie is my responsibility."

"And the *Titanic* hearings are my responsibility," John replied, unashamedly stretching the truth. He hadn't resigned – not yet – so he could still claim to be an aide to Senator Eldridge, and, therefore, involved.

"This," said Sam, "is not about the *Titanic*. The men who beat up Alfie were sending me a message about something else."

"What else?"

"It's a story I've been following."

"What kind of story requires a crippled boy to take a beating from Pinkertons?" Sam's voice was tinged with regret. "I sent Alfie after Captain Lord because I was following two stories at once. By the time I realized he was being followed it was too late. He was already gone. I never expected this. Just take my word for it, that this has nothing to do with the *Titanic*."

"And yet the boy is in a house with the crew of the *Californian*," John said. "I'm afraid I have trouble taking your word on anything."

"Those are fighting words," Sam said. "Fortunately for you I am not interested in fighting, not over the boy and not over Miss Sophie Paxton."

"Miss Sophie," John said, all thoughts of the boy driven from his mind. "What are you talking about?"

"You wear your heart on your sleeve," Sam replied.

"I don't believe that Miss Paxton is an appropriate topic of conversation," John said stiffly.

"Relax," Sam said. "It will be a very short conversation. I am not interested in her. There, now you know the truth. She is lovely, energetic, and obviously very self-reliant. She is, I suppose, a new kind of woman."

"I really don't think —"

John could not even complete his rebuke. Sam leaned toward him, keeping his voice low. "I am not your rival, Mr. Alder."

"Rival?"

"You know what I'm talking about. You have no need to worry. As soon as I have Alfie, I'll be gone."

"Gone where?"

"Wherever the story takes me."

Although John would be greatly relieved to see the back of Sam, he could not encourage him to leave while he was still needed.

"But the story is here," John said. "Your piece on Captain Lord gave you a byline in the New York Times, surely you want to follow it up. I believe that Captain Lord and his crew are about to speak to the Senate. This is still a story."

"It's not my story," Sam said, "and it won't last. Those of you who were on the *Titanic* will always remember, but the world will move on and so will I."

Saunders brought the car to a halt. They were on a quiet side street without street lights, but a sliver of moon revealed a tall house separated from the road by a stone wall and a wide lawn. As the car halted, a figure separated from the shadows.

"Move along. No stopping here."

"Bayliss's man," John said.

"We'll stop here if we want to," Sophie declared. She tried to descend from the car to confront the man, but, unable to put both feet on the ground, she made a dramatic exit ending in a fall. Startled, Bayliss's man reached for his gun.

John vaulted from the back seat to stand over Sophie as she struggled to her feet. "Official business," he said.

The guard was silent for a long moment. His hand remained on his gun and he took in the scene. What would he make of what he saw - a brand new Cadillac, a half-dressed chauffeur, and a woman lying on the sidewalk?

"Official business," John repeated. "Sheriff Bayliss knows who I am."

"Well, I don't."

"Now you do," John said presenting his Senate identity documents for scrutiny. "We're going inside. There's an injured man in there."

"No one has been injured on my watch," the guard said.

"You weren't watching carefully enough," John replied. "Someone has been injured quite seriously. You may follow if you wish but you'd be better employed sending for a doctor."

Sophie was back on her feet now. Although she was disheveled and dusty, when she faced the guard, there was no doubting that she was also a lady.

"I'm going inside," she declared. She held out an imperious hand. "Someone will have to help me."

Sam stepped back and John escorted Sophie up the steps to the front door.

"He's in here," Sophie said as she dragged herself up the steps clinging to his arm.

"Who do you mean?"

"Captain Lord - the man who destroyed my life."

CHAPTER TWENTY

Sophie Paxton
Inside the Capitol View Guest House
Just to look at Alfie made Sophie ache in sympathy. The beating was written on his face, in his swollen eyelids and his split lip. It lived in the pain in his eyes as he drew in short, cautious breaths, and in the fact that he could not rise from the sofa in the common room.

Sam touched Alfie's forehead, briefly smoothing his shaggy hair in a moment of obvious affection. "The doctor's coming. You're going to be all right."

"I didn't tell no one nothing," Alfie said looking up at the faces around the sofa.

Sophie studied Alfie's former ship mates. They seemed genuinely concerned about him. These were some of the men that Sam White suspected of plotting to kill him but it seemed such an unlikely plot. Cyril Evans, the Marconi man, was well-spoken, educated, and obviously intelligent. In comparison, Ernest Gill was dull and somewhat oafish, but his eyes were kind. Neither of them looked like killers.

Gill stood beside the sofa tugging at his forelock as he spoke to Sam.

"We didn't know he was here. Evans went outside for a cigarette and found him. What the hell happened to him? Is this because..."

Sophie waited for Gill to finish what he was saying but he let his words fade away.

"Because what?" Sam asked.

"Did he say something about ... you know?"

"No, Gill, I don't know. Something about what?"

"We've been told to be careful, you know, when we go in front of the inquiry," Gill said. "Captain says to be quiet and deny everything, but I don't know if I can do that, Mr. White."

"I think you're past the point of keeping quiet," Sam said. "You sold your story to the newspapers."

"That don't count," Gill said. "I just have to say that I made it all up so I could get paid, and that will be the end of it. If I go along, I keep my ticket and my berth."

Sam turned to Evans. "What about you, Evans?"

"They're not going to ask me about what I saw," Evans said, "because I didn't see anything. Mr. Marconi has told me what to say. I don't work for Leyland Line, I work for Mr. Marconi. The committee wants to know why I wasn't listening in on the radio. It's simple really. My shift ends at midnight and I go to bed. That's what I'm to tell them. I'm to say that ships need to hire more radio operators and that would solve the problem."

He looked at Sam doubtfully. "I'm going to be all right, aren't I? I didn't tell any lies."

"Neither did I," Gill said forcefully. "I told the truth, but now the captain wants me to lie."

"Where is Captain Lord?" Sam asked.

Gill jerked his head toward the ceiling. "Upstairs. Top floor. Asleep I suppose, just as he was asleep when the *Titanic* was going down."

"Are you going to say that to the inquiry?" Sam asked.

"Not if he values his life and his position," Evans said.

Sophie didn't wait to hear anything else. *Asleep upstairs – not for long if she had anything to do with it.* She could not believe her good fortune. Captain Lord was upstairs and the only thing that stood between her and the man she most wanted to meet was societal propriety. Society would say she could not go upstairs, open his bedroom door and walk right in.

She turned away from the boy on the sofa. He was also a victim of the man upstairs. They were all victims. *Miss Pattison waited for her at the foot of the stairs.* "Carpe diem," she said.

"I intend to, Miss Pattison."

The stair case was steep and wound up through two floors. To Sophie it seemed the stairs represented a towering mountain, but she would have scaled Mount Everest to reach the man on the top floor – Captain Stanley Lord.

Fueled by remembered rage, she dragged herself up to the top of the stairs. She was now in a dark and narrow, hallway. She had not brought a candle and she could not find a light switch or the pilot flame of a gas light. What was she to do? Should she knock on every door? She was perfectly willing if that was what it would take.

The doorbell chimed downstairs, followed by a flurry of activity and noise. While Gill and Evans had been furtive in their phone call, there was nothing furtive about the arrival of the doctor. She heard the front door open and soon heard a deep, growl of another voice demanding to know what the hell was going on.

It seemed that Sheriff Bayliss was now awake and taking charge. The sheriff was not the only one awakened by the flurry of activity. A door opened along the hallway in front of Sophie and light spread across the hall, backlighting the silhouette of a man. Was this Captain Lord? If not, she was about to accost a total stranger, but she would do it. She would do anything.

"Captain Lord?" She could not keep the slight quaver of uncertainty from her voice. She would have to do better than that if she intended to get the truth from him.

"Who are you? What the blazes is going on?"

"Are you Captain Lord?"

"I am. And who are you?"

Sophie took a couple of faltering steps toward him, moving into the light that spilled from the doorway.

"What do you want?" Lord demanded.

"I have business with you," Sophie said.

"Business?" Lord took a step backward. "I have no business with you. I didn't send for a woman and I certainly didn't send for a cripple."

"You made me a cripple," Sophie said fiercely.

She didn't care that she lurched and dipped as she pushed past him into his room, where a bright electric light was burning. She saw the rumpled bed, no doubt still warm from the heat of his body. She had done many unusual things under the tutelage of Miss Pattison and the Howell School, but she had never entered a man's bedroom.

Well, she was in the bedroom now, and she had no choice but to sit on the bed before she fell down.

She sat and Lord stomped back into the room to tower over her. He wore a long night shirt, and as far as she could tell, very little else. He was a middle-aged man with a long weatherbeaten face. His black hair, rumpled and standing on end, was peppered with gray and his beard stubble was almost white.

He glowered at her from beneath fierce eyebrows. "Get off my bed! I didn't send for you. Are you one of the maids? What's going on downstairs?"

"One of your crewmen is receiving medical treatment."

"Who? Why? Is it Gill or Evans?"

"It's Alfie Blackwell."

"Don't know him."

"He was your cook's boy."

"Oh him. He jumped ship in Boston. What's he doing here?"

"He's with Mr. White, the man you tried to throw overboard."

"That's enough," Lord thundered. "I don't know who you are or what you want but I know who Sam White is. The man's a damned liar! Is he here, because if he is —"

"He's here."

"Well, fetch him."

"Captain Lord, I am not a maid sent to fetch and carry for you. I am Sophie Paxton, first-class survivor of the *Titanic*, and I am here to show you what you, in your cowardice, did to me."

Sophie leaned forward and lifted her skirt.

"Stop it," Lord shouted. "What do you think you're doing? I'm not interested in you. I've never heard of you."

"Sophie Paxton," Sophie repeated, "passenger on the *Titanic*. I rowed all night in an attempt to reach your ship."

"My ship?"

"Yes, sir, your ship."

Sophie began to unwrap the bandage on her left foot. Although she was well aware of Lord standing over her, she did not look up. "I was going to be a tennis champion," she said, concentrating on unwrapping the bandages. "I was going to take part in the Olympics in Berlin, but I spent a night on the open sea, and this is what happened."

She removed the last strip of bandage and revealed her truncated foot. Lord gasped.

"Frostbite," Sophie said. "If rescue had come sooner, this would not have happened to me."

Lord's voice was softened by sympathy. "I'm sorry that you have been disfigured, Miss Paxton. I've read accounts in the newspapers but you are the first victim I have spoken with. I had not thought of frostbite. Will you seek compensation from the White Star Line?"

"No," Sophie said. "I want compensation from you."

"Me? How am I responsible for this?"

"You could have come. You were so close."

"I was not close. I was twenty miles away, surrounded by ice. The *Californian* was stopped. My crew were asleep. My boilers were down. I knew nothing of what was happening. You have been drawn into believing a scurrilous liar. Sam White's story in the New York Times was pure fabrication. It's all lies."

"Really?"

"Of course."

"Ernest Gill tells a similar story."

"Ernest Gill will tell no such story to the Senate Committee," Lord said. "He was paid to lie but now he has come to his senses."

Lord pointed down at Sophie's naked foot. "Please, Miss Paxton, cover your foot. I am sorry for your trouble, but you must leave my room. I don't know what possessed you to come up here."

"Anger," said Sophie. "Anger drove me up those stairs. Every step was painful but I came because I had to confront you. I had to see the coward who did not move his ship."

"I am no coward."

"Then why didn't you come?"

"I was not there. I was miles away, stopped and surrounded by ice. I at least had the sense not to run the ice-field in the dark, unlike Captain Smith. If you're looking for someone to blame – blame him."

"You were there," Sophie said obstinately, ignoring a niggling worm of doubt that squirmed in a corner of her angry brain. "I saw your light."

"If you saw a light, it was not mine."

"Captain Smith said it was a ship."

"Did he say it was my ship?"

"No, he just said that a ship was nearby and we should row toward the light."

Captain Lord surprised Sophie by suddenly hooking the desk chair with his foot and dragging it up close to her. He tugged at his nightshirt as he sat down. With his bare feet and rumpled hair, he seemed remarkably vulnerable.

He leaned forward as if to take her into his confidence "Miss Paxton..." he hesitated and gave her a ghost of a smile. "As you are sitting on my bed, perhaps we could be informal. May I call you Sophie?"

Miss Pattison was on alert. "Cave ne decipiaris, Sophie."

"I'm being careful."

"He's going to bamboozle you."

"I won't let him."

Lord took Sophie's silence as assent. "Sophie," he said, " what I am about to tell you has not been told to anyone else. I am aware that I have been called here to Washington to be a scapegoat. Bruce Ismay has already been disgraced just for saving his own life. Smith will try to disgrace me, but the truth will come out. I already have agents investigating —"

"Pinkertons," Sophie said feeding the dying flame of her anger.

"No, not Pinkertons. I don't employ thugs. I have been in contact with maritime authorities in various ports, and they will soon give me the evidence I need. I will prove to everyone that I was not the ship you saw. The *Californian* was not alone on the ice that night. There were other ships but they were not large cargo ships or passenger ships, they were fishing boats out of Newfoundland and sealers out of Norway.

"The lights you all saw were the lights of an illegal craft. I hear that Mr. John Collins gave evidence of seeing a green light. I can assure you that my ship displayed only a white light as is required for a ship at anchor. The green light belongs to an illegal ship, a small working light perhaps. I believe that ship to be the *Samson,* a Norwegian sealer. I have personally opened an investigation into this.

"You must realize that these illegal ships don't have radios. They don't want to be known. The captain of the *Samson* would not have heard the *Titanic's* distress calls. Perhaps he saw your rockets but I doubt he knew that they came from the *Titanic* and that they were distress rockets. He may not know, even now, that the *Titanic* went down. These small boats stay at sea for many weeks but when he does make port, and when he hears of the *Titanic*, he won't come forward. He won't admit he was there."

"You're making this up to protect yourself," Sophie said.

"I'm telling the truth, but I doubt it will protect me," Lord said. "I am as much a scapegoat as Bruce Ismay. Lies are told about him and lies are told about me."

"But Sam White saw the *Titanic* from your deck."

"Sam White is a journalist who is intent on making a name for himself. His story in the Times was all a lie."

Miss Pattison screamed in frustration. "No! Don't listen to him. Don't believe him."

But what if he's right? What if Sam White is lying?

"Why would he do that?" Miss Pattison asked. "Keep your wits about you Sophie. You've been waiting for this."

"I want to end this," Sophie said. "I want Captain Lord to be right and Sam to be a liar."

"Why?"

"I'm tired of being angry."

"Tiredness is no excuse. Find the truth."

"It all makes sense – we saw the light of a Norwegian fishing boat."
"No," said Miss Pattison. "Think, girl. Think!"
Captain Lord had risen. "Sophie, I really must ask you to leave."
"No, not yet. There's something..."
"Sophie, please."
The light. The light... white and flashing. Norwegian? No, the Norwegians
wouldn't signal. Wouldn't send Morse code. Only one ship could have signalled.
One ship had a lamp powerful enough to send a questioning message across the ice.
"Captain Lord," Sophie said, "are you familiar with Morse code?"
"Of course."
"QRZ," Sophie said. "Identify Yourself. That was your signal from your ship."
Lord put his hand to his mouth and lowered his head. Sophie realized that she was witnessing the breaking of a once honorable man. When he lifted his head and looked into her eyes, she saw nothing but sorrow. His voice was little more than a whisper. "Why didn't you answer?"

Sophie thought of the chaos that had reigned on the deck of the *Titanic*. In all that activity, why had no one thought to answer the signal light? Everything changed. Suddenly she saw the world from Lord's perspective. He had signalled and no one replied.

There would be other stories. Other ships would be named. Careers would, no doubt, be ruined. Anger had been her weapon and now it was lost to doubt.

A voice came from somewhere behind her. "Sophie, it's time to leave."

She turned and found John Alder standing in the doorway.

"You heard him?" she asked.

John said nothing as he held out his hands to help her from the bed. She felt weak and empty, drained of anger and not knowing what emotion would now sustain her.

"We're going downstairs now," John said.

She buried her head in his shoulder. Tears had arrived to replace the anger, and she thought she might drown in their flood.

Lord spoke again. He was angry now and defiant. "Why didn't you answer?" he said. "Why not say we are the *Titanic* – we're sinking. Come at once."

His voice followed them as John carried Sophie down the stairs. "I would have come."

Sophie found the common parlor filled with activity with Sheriff Bayliss in charge and Alfie being bandaged by a doctor.

He looked up as Sophie entered. "You all right, miss?"

"I'm fine, Alfie," Sophie said, finding to her amazement that she was, indeed, fine. She was sure that her face was smudged with tears but they were the last of her tears. She had her answer now. She had achieved her purpose. Stanley Lord was a broken man, who for just one moment, had revealed his brokenness. He would never show it again. She alone knew the truth. It was a truth that no longer mattered because nothing Lord, or Ismay or anyone else could say or do would change the tragedy of that night. Nothing would bring back the dead.

Sophie expected Miss Pattison to give her some wise advice and a couple of Latin phrases, but Miss Pattison was silent – in fact she had vanished. She no longer haunted the corners of Sophie's mind.

Sophie looked around the room. "Where is Mr. White?"

"Gone," said John. "He asked me to say goodbye."

"But Alfie," Sophie whispered. "What about Alfie? Has he just abandoned him?"

"He says he will send for him," John said, "but I don't think he will."

"And what will happen to Alfie?"

"I am a man of my word," John said. "I said I will look after Alfie and that is what I will do. You may recall that on the *Titanic,* I said I would look after you and I did."

"Yes," Sophie agreed, "you did."

She knew he had more to say but she could not hear it – not yet.

CHAPTER TWENTY-ONE

Sophie Paxton
Senate Office Building, April 26
Sophie entered the crowded caucus room and heads turned. This was it, her grand return to society. Everything had been carefully planned to avoid revealing Sophie's unique way of walking. She didn't want to draw attention to herself. All attention must be on Stanley Lord. Tomorrow's newspapers should be filled with reports of today's hearing. They should not be filled with reports of Sophie Paxton, the poor little heiress who could hardly walk.

It was Aidan Paxton who had come up with a solution. "I'll come. We'll bring the wheelchair."

"I'm not going in a wheelchair," Sophie insisted.

"The wheelchair is for me," Paxton said. "I sit, and you push, and we'll add a couple of orderlies to provide distraction. Holding onto the chair will help you balance. You might get away with it."

"Would you really do that for me?" Sophie asked. "You never go out in public."

"I'm doing this for me," Paxton said, waving away Sophie's gratitude. "I want to hear what Lord has to say for himself. It's a strange story and we've only heard the one side. That Sam White fellow tells a good story and he says it's true. Now I want to see the man who says it's not."

"I've met him," Sophie said. "He knows what he's done."

"You met a man taken by surprise in his nightshirt," Paxton said. "Let's see if he's the same man today."

Aidan Paxton made his entrance into the caucus room. The fact that the old man was there at all drew attention away from his granddaughter and any difficulty she may have had in walking. John had reserved seats for them in the front row, just below the platform where the senators sat to ask questions. A lower table and chair were provided for the witnesses. Sophie was frustrated to realize that their privileged front-row seating would give them an excellent view of the senators and only a very limited view of the witness who would be standing with his back to them. She would not be able to see his face, and he would not be able to see her.

The senators arrived and took their assigned seats, Senator Smith in the center, of course. Sophie caught sight of John Alder seated beside the platform but not on it. She wondered how he felt about being so close to the seats of power, but having no power himself. Elections were coming up in November. If John wanted to run for office ...

She pulled her mind back to the room. What was it to her whether John Alder ran for office?

He's your white knight.

Can't I have two white knights?

No. You have to make up your mind.

Stanley Lord walked in. He was not the man Sophie had seen the night before, distraught in his nightclothes. Now he wore his uniform and carried his cap beneath his arm. He set the cap on the table and beside it he placed a leather-bound book – the log of the *Californian*. He stood to face the senators, and Sophie, as expected, could see nothing but his back. She could, however, see the faces of the senators, and they were not happy. An air of weariness hung over the room.

Senator Smith led the questioning. Although his clothes were neat, and his shirt collar stiff with starch, his haggard face betrayed him but his eyes, red with exhaustion, still projected a gleam of obsession. William Smith was a driven man. He was just the man, Sophie thought, to get the truth out of Stanley Lord. *Smith won't give up until he has his answer.* She sat in the chair provided for her and waited for whatever would come.

Senator Smith's initial approach was to ask a few perfunctory questions.

"What is your full name and where do you reside?"

"Stanley Lord, Liverpool, England."

"What is your business?"

"Master Mariner."

"How long have you been a mariner?"

"Twenty years."

Smith pulled a notebook toward him and consulted it briefly. When he looked up his face was grim. He stared at Lord for a long moment and then looked down at his notebook. He did not look at Lord as he spoke. "Where were you and your ship on the 14th day of April last?"

Lord opened the log book. "Forty-two north and forty-seven west."

Smith continued to stare down at his notebook. Lord waited. He left the logbook open and clasped his hands behind his back.

"Captain Lord, do you know the *Titanic's* position on the sea when she sank?"

"I know the position given to me by the *Virginian* as the position where she struck an iceberg 41.56 and 50.14."

Smith looked up and asked his next question. "Captain Lord, figuring from the *Titanic's* position at the time she went down, and your position at the time you sent her an ice warning, how far apart were your vessels?

Sophie watched Lord's hands. They had been loosely clasped behind his back. Now he tightened his clasp.

"Nineteen and a half miles."

Smith nodded. "And you were stopped and surrounded by ice?"

"We were."

Smith leaned forward. "Captain, do you know anything regarding the *Titanic* disaster, of your own knowledge? Did you see the ship on Sunday?" He paused. "Or any signals from her?"

"No," Lord said vehemently.

His knuckles were white as he continued to clasp his hands. Sophie knew what would happen now. Stanley Lord would deny everything. – even the *Titanic*.

Sophie barely had the patience to sit through the rest of Lord's testimony. It was going to be lies from beginning to end. What was the point of even being here to listen to him?

Senator Smith questioned Lord relentlessly. He had obviously read Sam's story in the New York Times, and also the story that Ernest Gill had peddled to a newspaper in Boston.

Faced with the words spoken by his crew members and his passenger, Lord persisted in his story. No one on his ship had seen the *Titanic*. It was impossible. The *Californian* was stopped many miles away. They were surrounded by ice. From that safe, snug position they had been aware of other ships also waiting for daylight. All captains with any sense, would have waited out the night and moved in the morning. There was, for example, a steamer with a yellow funnel. It had been seen sailing away at first light. Did anyone know the name of this ship?

Smith fought against Lord's unemotional listing of all possible reasons for his crew's erroneous reports. "Captain Lord, how do you explain your crew's sighting of rockets?"

"They reported them to me and assured me they were company rockets. They were not distress rockets. Some ship on the ice was entertaining its passengers. There was no need to do anything about that. I told the watch to continue signaling and then I retired to rest on the settee in the chart room."

"You went to sleep?"

"Yes, senator, I went to sleep."

It seemed that Senator Smith might be finished with his questioning. Lord's hands relaxed. A hum of conversation broke out among the spectators. Smith gaveled for silence and Senator Eldridge leaned forward with questions of his own.

"Captain Lord, was there objection made by anyone as to you coming here today?"

"Not to me. No."

"Did your company object?"

"No, I spoke to Mr. Thomas. There were no objections. I was given permission to go with the marshal."

Eldridge looked at Smith and then back at Lord. "The *Californian* of which you are commander, belongs to what line? ".

"The Leyland Line"

"The Leyland Line is a member or part of the International Mercantile Marine Co., is it not?"

Lord nodded. "I believe it is, yes."

"And is represented in this country by Mr. Franklin."

Lord's fingers were relaxed. This line of questioning meant nothing to him and required no lies. "Yes, he said, "Mr. Franklin."

Smith interrupted his colleague's questioning. "And in England by Mr. Ismay," he said with a note of triumph."

Lord nodded.

"And all owned by the House of Morgan," Eldridge said.

'Sophie was aware of movement beside Senator Eldridge. She craned her neck to see what was happening and realized that John Alder was on his feet and gathering up his papers.

Smith turned his head as if to rebuke the disturbance coming just at the moment when he had achieved the triumph he was looking for. With the aid of Senator Eldridge, Smith had managed to link Stanley Lord and Bruce Ismay together, and then to tie them both to J. P, Morgan. Now Smith had what he wanted - a conspiracy.

Sophie was astonished to see that John Alder was moving onto the front of the platform. His face was grim. Smith stopped his questions and turned to look at him. John stood alone looking out at the spectators, his eyes searching until he found Sophie His gaze rested there for a long silent moment, and then turned to Senator Eldridge who had also edged his way to the front. The senator was pulling on John's arm. John resisted him, turning to speak words that Sophie could not hear.

Eldrige responded by shouting angrily for a security guard. Sophie saw Sheriff Bayliss coming from the back of the room. John had only a few seconds to say what he wanted to say, but he succeeded.

"The idea of a conspiracy is all a lie," he shouted. "There's no conspiracy. I was on the *Titanic*, I know what happened. We hit an iceberg, and she sank. My name is John Alder. A vote for John Alder is a vote for truth."

Sophie watched until Bayliss had hustled John away. John appeared to have achieved something with his sudden outburst. Smith gaveled on the table but he was losing control of the room. If everything was a lie, why should anyone listen? John Alder was a *Titanic* survivor. He must know something.

Senator Smith resumed his questioning, raising his voice to be heard above the low murmur of whispered conversation, asking questions that invited lies.

Sophie Paxton
Six months later - October 31, 1912
The Washington campaign office of John Alder
In the past six months, Sophie had acquired prosthetic boots in various fashionable colors. Because she had money, she could have the boots hand-made by the best bootmaker in Washington. The prosthetic toe, snugged inside the boot made all the difference. The boots detracted from her fashionable appearance, but that no longer mattered. What mattered was the fact that she could walk now, and her gait was almost smooth.

Today she wore boots of fine brown suede to match a light tweed walking skirt and a fitted brown velvet jacket, but no hat. She had been tempted to wear a wide-brimmed hat that would shadow her face and hide her nervousness, but she was coming to John's office to be honest with him. She would not hide anything and she would not allow him to hide.

She had forced herself to wait six months without contacting him at all. If he knew she was coming today, she feared he would find a reason not to see her. She intended to ambush him and together they would find the truth.

Two weeks ago, when she decided time was up for John Alder, she hired an investigator to follow him. All she wanted to know was where she would be able to find John alone. She would not go to his apartment - that would give him the wrong message. The investigator gave her the answer - on Thursdays John worked in his campaign office, and he had no secretary. He would be alone.

So here she was waiting nervously in the rear seat of the Cadillac. John was well-known in Washington these days. His run for the senate – challenging his former employer - had put his campaign on the front page of every newspaper, but she had not spoken to him since he walked out of the Titanic inquiry. Of course, he would know that she had not forgotten him. Nanny Bess had advised her to give him space and that was what she'd done, but he'd been unable to prevent her attending his rallies. She always sat in the back wearing plain clothes and speaking to no one, but his eyes always found her. He would allow himself one long look and then it was as though she did not exist.

Saunders came around to open the door of the Cadillac and Sophie thought that she did a good job of descending gracefully. If he – John – happened to be looking out of his window, he would see an elegant young lady – one he had tried to dismiss from his life. Well, she was back - six months older and very much wiser. She had now passed her twentieth birthday. She was no longer a schoolgirl. She was a woman who knew what she wanted.

She found John sitting behind a desk in a small untidy office. The office door was already open - no need to knock. She gathered her confidence, in herself and in her prosthetic toe, and walked confidently into the office. He looked up. His face told her everything. She was no expert in love but she knew that what she read in his eyes was the reflected light of something that burned inside him – burned for her! Nothing had changed, and now it was up to her.

John was on his feet, the fire gone from his eyes. His face was set in a worried frown. "What's the matter? Why have you come?"

"I could ask myself the same question," Sophie said. "Why would I bother to come here, when you can't bring yourself to come to me?"

"I can't," he said, "not until after the election."

"Oh, so that's the problem," she taunted. "You don't want to be seen escorting a cripple. Would that be bad for your image?"

She could see the hurt in his eyes but she would not withdraw the remark. They had to reach an understanding of the truth.

"Would you like to sit?" John asked.

"No," Sophie snapped. "I'll stand. I'm quite good at standing and I'm getting better at walking. Maybe you wouldn't be ashamed of me."

"I'm not ashamed of you, Sophie. "

"Then what is it? What is keeping you away from me? What happened, John?" She gestured to the heaped pamphlets, and posters. "What is this all about? You owe me an explanation. I thought that..."

"That what?"

She wished she had worn a hat to shadow her face. Her cheeks were burning. She had intended to be bold, but now that they were face to face, it was difficult. She couldn't just throw herself at him, although that had been Nanny Bess's advice.

She couldn't say the words she wanted to say, so she asked the only other question left for her to ask. "Why did you do it, John? Why did you throw your hat in the ring, and your chances out of the window."

"Because they are my chances and my choices," John said. "Mine, Sophie. I hadn't planned to speak out like that at Lord's appearance. It was suddenly too much – so many lies. I could not write down another word that I knew was not true."

When Sophie tried to speak, he silenced her with a lifted finger. "My first thought was just to quit – walk off the stage and never come back. Then I looked at all these people in that room and they were looking at me because I was on the platform. I couldn't pass up the opportunity. It was something I had been thinking about for a while. I had hoped to run for senator some day in the future, but I realized the day had already come. The people, listening gape-mouthed to lies and insinuations and wild conspiracy rumors, had to be protected. I had no more time to waste. I knew I would have to run against Eldridge."

"But why did you walk right out without a word to me? I would have helped. You know I would. I've heard the liars. I want them to stop."

John gestured to the chair in front of his desk. "Sit down, please."

"No, just answer my question. Why did you shut me out."

He looked down and shuffled his feet in the dust on the floor. "Because I'm a man," he said.

"That's not an excuse. I don't know what that means."

He looked up again. "Where is Sam White?"

"I don't know."

"Did he come back for Alfie?"

"No... and neither did you?"

"I made inquiries," John said. "I found out that he was with you and happy."

"So, you cared about him but not me?"

"I care about you."

"Then what," Sophie asked, "has kept you away for six months?"

"My pride and your money."

Sophie sat down abruptly. "Money," she said. "Why does everything come back to money."

"Because you have so much of it, and most of us have very little. But even without money, we still have pride," John rose and reached out for her hand. "I don't want to come to you empty-handed. I don't want you to buy me a senate seat. I want to do this myself, and so I have stayed away. I couldn't have you involved. If I win this election on Tuesday, I will have won it myself and then I will come to you."

"Tuesday?" Sophie said.

"Maybe not until Wednesday. The votes have to be counted."

"And if you don't win?"

"Then I won't come," he said.

PART FIVE - EPILOGUE

Walter Lord
Titanic historian, and author
I still think about the 'might have beens' about the Titanic, that's what stirs me more than anything else. Things that happened that wouldn't have happened if only one thing had gone better for her. If only, so many if only's. If only she had enough lifeboats. If only the watertight compartments had been higher. If only she had paid attention to the ice that night. If only the Californian did come. The 'if only' kept coming up again and again and that makes the ship more than the experience of studying a disaster. It becomes a haunting experience to me, it's the haunting experience of 'if only'.

EPILOGUE

Sophie Paxton Alder
Paxton Manor, Virginia.
April 15, 1962

They had come at her command – she was still the matriarch and she wanted them all to be here today, April 15. Fifty years now since that night on the North Atlantic.

Fifty years since Sophie had first set eyes on John Alder. Forty-nine years since the wedding. There would have to be a golden wedding party next year. People would talk. Even fifty years later someone would start counting on their fingers and realize John "Jack" Alder, Jr. had been born only seven months after his parents' wedding. They would say nothing aloud out of respect for the family's loss. Jack Alder, flying for the U.S. Air Force, was shot down over France in 1944. Eighteen years and missing him was still an ache in Sophie's heart and proof that no one, however rich, emerged from war unscathed.

The world had been spinning very fast for the past fifty years producing airplanes, radios, televisions and computers. Empires had risen and fallen under the onslaught of two world wars but, despite the spinning of the world, one thing had remained constant - the loss of the *Titanic*.

Why do people still care, Sophie wondered. The tragedy had a life of its own well beyond the lives of those who were involved. Senator John Alder and his wife, Sophie, were famous now – two people who sailed on the *Titanic* and lived to tell the tale. A romantic cloud still followed them all these years later – they had met on board the *Titanic* just as the ship was going down. They had triumphed over fate.

Sophie took inventory of her guests. Her children, of course, and her grandchildren. Dick Williams was here- a medical miracle. He had survived the *Titanic*, survived the trenches of the First World War, and gone on to achieve his dream

- an Olympic gold medal. Sophie forced herself to enjoy his success without any jealousy for what might have been. That part of her life, the part where she could play tennis, was over.

Well, at least she could walk. She remembered what Alfie had said "*You'll walk funny.*" Alfie was here tonight, with his sons, all of them employed by her family.

Maxine had just arrived. She never let anyone forget that she was a *Titanic* survivor. She had been a wife for a few months and a widow for the rest of her life but she had all that she had ever wanted. She had her son, Lord Arthur Sempter, and her grandchildren, one of whom would continue the title. The title itself was not worth the paper it was written on with no lands or money attached. Maxine's family existed on investments made for them by the late Mr. Ponsonby.

Sophie had tried to find the ladies of Lifeboat #8 to be sure they knew of the event, but mostly she found death certificates. Even Sam's aunt, Ella White, was gone.

It's fading, Sophie thought. There will be nothing left that is tangible. The *Titanic* is slowly expanding to the realms of legend and myth. The companion ships were already gone completely, the *Californian* sunk by a U-boat in 1915 and the *Carpathia* torpedoed off the coast of Ireland in 1918.

Sophie looked around the room that had once been Aidan Paxton's study. It made an excellent television room. She had purchased the largest television available, just for this event. It was not large, only twenty-five inches, but it would be enough. Even those who could not see, would be able to hear.

It was almost time. She nodded to Aidan Blackwell, Alfie's oldest son and lover of all things electric or electronic.

The television hummed to itself as it warmed up. The test screen glowed into life with stripes of color. Then an announcer in a dinner jacket. This was going to be a special occasion.

"CBS presents an interview with Captain Stanley Lord." The music that followed was, Sophie supposed, just about appropriate – stirring and sentimental.

The announcer looked directly into the camera "We have invited Samuel White, noted war correspondent, to conduct tonight's interview. In the fifty years since the *Titanic* sank, many questions have been asked about what happened that night. One area of interest has always been the *S.S. Californian*. Some have called it *"the ship that did not move."*

Tonight, we bring you perhaps the only two men who can give a first-hand account. Fifty years ago, Captain Lord spoke during the American Senate Hearings of 1912. He was questioned then about an account written by Sam White who happened to be a passenger on the *Californian*. These two men have not spoken together in fifty years but they have agreed to speak today. We will begin with a series of questions from Mr. White. Over to you, Mr. White.

Sam's face came into focus. Sophie examined her feelings on seeing that face again. Fifty years had given Sam a head of snowy white hair, but he was still handsome. He was, in fact, still raffish. She couldn't hate him. She'd tried, but it wasn't possible. Leaving Alfie behind had been an act of cruelty, or so she had thought at the time. Now she knew better. Alfie needed the home that Sophie and John had offered him. He did not need to follow Sam as he wandered around the world. He had found safety with Sophie.

And what about Sophie herself? Had there been something between her and Sam? Possibly. Had that also been cruel, just to leave her without a word? No, it had been necessary and she never ... well ... almost never... thought of him again or of what might have been.

Sam White and Stanley Lord faced each other across a desk. Their stage set was decorated with *Titanic* memorabilia. Not enough to be distracting but enough to evoke memories in Sophie.

Sam questioned Lord in a professionally neutral tone.

"Captain Lord, you were in command of the Leyland liner *Californian* nearly fifty years ago, when she stopped because of ice in mid-Atlantic, apparently somewhere near where the *Titanic* sank. The part that the Californian is supposed to have played in the Titanic disaster has become something of a legend in the past fifty years, that is, that you were supposed to be lying five or ten miles away the whole time. So, what are your own views on that?"

At eighty-five, Lord had not aged well. He still had the face of a mariner with far-seeing eyes and cheeks scoured by sand and sea, but his shirt collar was loose, revealing a scrawny neck and his head moved jerkily and obviously of its own volition. His voice was firm.

"Well, my views are that we were where we gave at the inquiry, at least twenty miles from the position, from the Titanic."

Sam nodded and moved on.

"Let's talk about the various inquiries that have been made into the loss of the *Titanic*. We'll begin with Lord Mersey at the British Inquiry. You stated that there was a ship near you until about two-thirty in the morning, and at the subsequent inquiry, Lord Mersey said this in his findings, and this is from the report..."

Sam hardly glanced at his notes. Obviously, he had memorized what he intended to say as he quoted Lord Mersey.

These circumstances convince me that the ship seen by the Californian was the Titanic, and if so, according to Captain Lord, the two vessels were about five miles apart at the time of the disaster. The evidence from the Titanic corroborates this estimate. The night was clear and the sea was smooth. When she first saw the rockets, the Californian could have pushed through the ice to the open water without any serious risk and so have come to the assistance of the Titanic. Had she done so, she might have saved many, if not all, of the lives that were lost.'

Sam leaned back a little in his chair. "So, Captain Lord, these were Lord Mersey's findings. Have you ever accepted them as being correct?"

Lord shook his head. "No, not by any means. The fact that the *Californian* stopped, and the *Titanic* never saw anything when she stopped, proves it could not have been the *Californian*."

"And what effect did Lord Mersey's finding have on your career?"

"It meant that I lost my position in the Leyland Line."

"Well," said Sam showing no reaction to the captain's confession. "Let us move onto the American Inquiry. How was that? Was it like the British Inquiry?"

"No," Captain Lord said vehemently "They all sat around and Senator Smith was there. He asked me what we'd seen. Something like that. I rather forget. He wasn't a nautical man; he didn't know much about nautical affairs."

Sophie let her mind wander. She had been looking forward to this moment. Two great wars had swept through Europe and changed the world forever. Fortunes had been made and lost. Surely now, fifty years later, Stanley Lord would no longer be beholden to the old Leyland Line or any other shipping line. Now he could tell the truth. She turned her mind back to the television. The camera held a close-up on Lord's face. Sam was just a voice.

"Captain Lord, for fifty years, you have had this appalling burden of being publicly branded as the man who left over a thousand people to drown before your eyes. How have you managed to live with that really awful charge?"

Lord's face remained expressionless. "Well, I knew it wasn't true." His tone changed as he looked at Sam. "You also knew it wasn't true."

"I know what I saw," Sam said.

The gloves were off now. The polite interchange was over.

Now the interview had Sophie's complete attention. Could Sam do it? Could he reveal the man Sophie had seen. She had sat on Captain Lord's bed and seen him crumble. She had seen the moment when he realized what he had done. She thought it had broken him, but now she saw that it had not. Lord was admitting nothing.

Sam was needling him now. "Is it something you've thought over a lot, or have you re-read the papers very much?"

"No, I haven't re-read the papers at all."

"Did you read any of the many books that have been published about it?"

"Not one. Not one book, nor any evidence, did I read."

"And the films that were made. Have you ever been a filmgoer?"

"No. Never seen them. Never seen anything."

Sophie had thought she could watch the interview with a detached mind, but she realized that she could not. Stanley Lord's lies felt as fresh as they had fifty years ago. She felt a return of something she thought she had banished. When Dr. Lengyel had removed her toe, Sophie had called him a butcher. She had burned with hate for him and anyone else involved in the loss of her toe and the loss of her career. That hate had very nearly killed her, she couldn't allow it to return.

She struggled to her feet, waving away offers of assistance and quietly left the room. She walked through the dining room and out onto the terrace where twilight had fallen across the tranquil Virginia countryside. She was not surprised to hear familiar footsteps behind her. John was following her and making sure she was all right. He came to stand beside her.

"That was a mistake," she said.

"Seeing Sam?" he asked.

She turned on him. "No, you big jealous booby, I don't care about Sam."

John was laughing. "Big jealous booby. That's nursery talk. I know you've got stronger words."

"I'm saving them for Lord. He's lying and he's never going to do anything else but lie"

"But what about Sam, the famous journalist?" John asked. "Could he be lying? His story about the *Californian* is what made him world famous. He owes all his success to that story - but was it the truth?"

Sophie was shocked and hardly able to contain the thought. "He was definitely on the *Californian*," she said. "Alfie was on there with him."

"But what did Sam see?"

"Light, rockets, crewmen being told to keep quiet, escaping being thrown overboard."

"That's his story," John said. "Do we have to believe it?"

Sophie made her way to a stone bench and sat down abruptly. "Are you saying that you don't believe him?"

"I have to *not* believe someone," John said, "and I've had fifty years to think about it."

"Fifty years of being a big jealous booby," Sophie teased.

John took her hand and kissed it. "That too," he agreed. "I was so afraid you would run off with Sam White."

"Never in a thousand years," Sophie said. It was a white lie. She would have gone with Sam if he'd asked her and it would have been a dreadful mistake.

"So, you've decided not to believe Sam?" she said.

John sat down on the bench and reclaimed Sophie's hand. "I've decided not to decide. It doesn't matter. It was a lifetime ago."

He put his arm around her shoulder and pulled her toward him. Sophie leaned against his familiar strength. Night was approaching and with it would come nightmares.

"I had a nightmare last night," John said.

"I know," Sophie said. "I held your hand."

Deep in the woods, an owl hooted. Bats flitted overhead. The stars draped themselves in wisps of cloud and looked down at the two people on the bench. They were the same stars that had looked down on the proud *Titanic,* on the sleeping *Californian,* and on the iceberg with a scraping of red paint.

Inside the house the television blared with the sound of two men arguing. No one was watching. The two people who had cared most had stopped caring. They were sitting in the starlight, holding hands, keeping the nightmares away.

THE END

WHO IS REAL AND WHO IS NOT

FICTIONAL CHARACTERS
John Alder
Alfie Blackwell
Senator Eldridge
Miss Pattison
Aidan Paxton
Sophie Paxton
Agatha Paxton
Lawyer Ponsonby
Regis the chauffeur
Saunders the chauffeur
Lord Lucan Sempter
Maxine Sempter
Sam White
Nanny Bess
REAL PEOPLE
On the Titanic
Bruce Ismay
Milton Long
Sante Ringhini
Captain Smith
Ida and Isidor Straus
Jack Thayer
Charles Williams
Dick Williams

In Lifeboat #8
Nellie Bessette
Alfred Crawford
John Hart
Thomas Jones
Dr. Alice Leader
Charles Pascoe
Eloise Smith
Mrs. Ella Holmes White
Marie Young
Countess of Rothes
On the Carpathia
Harold Cottam
Captain Arthur Rostron
Dr. Arpad Lengyel
Dr. Frank McGee
Charles Romaine
Kid Homer
In New York
Sheriff Joe Bayliss
Senator William Alden Smith
Senator Burton
Senator Newlands
Congressman James Hughes
On the Californian
Captain Stanley Lord
Ernest Gill
James McGregor
Cyril Evans
In Washington DC
John Collins
Banker Henry Davidson
Banker Frank Vanderlip

THE QUESTION OF
STANLEY LORD

Entire books have been written about Captain Lord and the *Californian*. He is part of the *Titanic* enigma – one of the many questions that may never have an answer. He gave confusing evidence at the U.S. and British Inquiries and denied seeing rockets or the light of another ship. He was of the opinion that his crew had been bribed by newspaper reporters. Ernest Gill received $500. For a man normally paid the equivalent of $7.00 per month, five hundred dollars was a fortune.

At both the U.S. and British Inquiries, no formal charges were brought against Lord or Ismay. Two additional inquiries were held at Captain Lord's request, but neither inquiry cleared him entirely of popular suspicion. In February and again August of 1961, just months before his death, Stanley Lord agreed to a radio interview with Leslie Harrison.

I have used this radio conversation to create the television interview between Lord and Sam White. A full transcript of the Harrison interview is available at
https://www.encyclopedia-titanica.org/stanley-lord-in-conversation-with-leslie-harrison.html

SAM WHITE AND THE
DUCK HUNTERS

Sam White is a fictional character, but the story he was chasing was not fictional.

In November 1910 six men gathered at the Jekyll Island Club off the coast of Georgia to write a plan to reform the nation's banking system. Attendees were chosen for their expertise but, if they were seen together, their ties to Wall Street would arouse suspicion about their motives. They chose to keep the meeting secret by adopting the ruse of a duck hunting trip. They arrived only one at a time at the train terminal in New Jersey where they boarded a private train. Once aboard, the men used only first names to prevent the staff from learning their identities. For decades after, the group referred to themselves as the "First Name Club."

The six men were Nelson Aldrich, A. Piatt Andrew, Henry Davison, Arthur Shelton, Frank Vanderlip and Paul Warburg. The meeting and its purpose were closely guarded secrets, and participants did not admit that the meeting occurred until the 1930s. The plan written on Jekyll Island laid a foundation for what would eventually be the Federal Reserve System.

ALSO BY THIS AUTHOR

The Girl on the Carpathia – A novel of the Titanic
The Girl in the Lifeboat – A novel of the Titanic
The Girl in the Barrel – A novel of Niagara Falls
Air Raid – A Toby Whitby Murder Mystery
Imposter – A Toby Whitby Murder Mystery
Nameless – A Toby Whitby Murder Mystery
Alibi – A Toby Whitby Murder Mystery
Excalibur Rising – First Chronicle
Excalibur Rising – Second Chronicle

Printed in Great Britain
by Amazon

47928635R00152